PRAISE FOR
St. James Park

"Over the course of this intricate tale of politics, corruption, and shifting alliances, Doll delivers a fast-paced work of historical fiction that takes full advantage of its Prohibition-era California setting. The farming community is effectively shown to be beset by unrest, greed, and scandal, and the shifting plot will keep readers on their toes. Overall, the work has a cinematic quality, but it's always firmly grounded in elements of real-life history: As such, it serves as a cautionary tale on how social disparities and anti-immigrant bias can be manipulated to fuel the evil plans of powerful people. A sweeping tale that offers lessons from the not-so-distant past. Our verdict: Get it."

— *KIRKUS REVIEWS*

"*St. James Park* is a fun read for both those who are familiar with California history and those who love a gripping yarn. Besides the woes of the Great Depression which shattered all communities in the early 1930s, the city of San Jose had its own particular troubles. This unrest boiled to the surface, culminating in the historic kidnapping and murder of the wealthiest 'son of San Jose,' young Brookie Hart. Author John Doll immerses the reader in these momentous dynamics to ponder the fantastical 'why and how' of it all. He takes us on a fictional adventure that joins the precious smell of plum blossoms with the pungent odor of bloody sin. Doll masterfully reveals what lies just below the surface of every human soul."

—JUDGE PAUL BERNAL,
official historian of the City of San Jose

"Based on an actual 1933 San Jose kidnapping that fueled a media blitz propagated by sleazy politicians, complacent cops, and manipulative gangsters, a vengeful mob is formed in *St. James* Park bent on unspeakable violence. Written in the noir style of Dashiell Hammett and James Ellroy, [John Doll's novel] brings to life a tale that foreshadows the politics of twenty-first-century America. Cinematic in its scope, *St. James Park* is a movie waiting to be made."

—JOE TALBOT, director of
The Last Black Man in San Francisco (2019)

"From the opening lines of *St. James Park*, I was hooked. It's a genre-bending cinematic novel—evocative of a 1930s black-and-white mystery movie yet draped in twenty-first-century living color—starring unforgettable characters within a palpable sense of place: an agricultural valley unaware of the tech mecca it would become."

—CLINT WILKINS, former Encore Fellow,
Mayor's Office in San Jose

"There's a lot to learn in this imagined version of true events from the dark past of San Jose and the University of Santa Clara. John Doll's recreation is compelling and captures the era. In the end, one of the big questions about the mystery isn't fully answered. That was a brave decision for a novelist to make, but a good one that is authentic to the history."

—JAMES M. GLASER,
provost, Santa Clara University

"In *St. James Park*, John Doll paints a word picture of San Jose at a time of great upheaval—where a farming community is transformed by greed and corruption and where scandal, hate, fear, and shame move his characters to do their worst. He lovingly (and damningly) describes the region in such intimate terms that it's obvious he's connected to that history as he invites you to imagine and experience San Jose as a place with a richly layered past. The plot is unpredictable, the characters colorful and unforgettable.

"Whether you approach *St. James Park* in search of the escapism of a classic noir thriller or you're in search of perspective on the challenges of our own time, you'll find this book impossible to put down."

—BARBARA KIBBE, artist and Citizen Joy leader

"The best historical fiction thrusts the past upward and irrefutably into the present, as a force to be reckoned with. That's what John Doll has done in *St. James Park*, his breakthrough first novel, spinning a tale ripped from San Jose's history that will forever change our tech-tinted image of Silicon Valley. Revolving around events that took place in what today may seem like an innocuous park, Doll's page-turner introduces us to unforgettable characters acting out at the intersection of race, class, and the Depression-era economy—all coming together into a story that needs to be told. That he does, in a narrative voice that is at once everywhere and noir. I can't wait for the next book in the trilogy."

—JOEL BEN IZZY, storyteller and author of *The Beggar King and the Secret of Happiness*

"*St. James Park* puts Prohibition-era San Jose on the map—with crooked politicians, mystery, mobsters, and murder—in this meticulously researched and gripping historical fiction novel."

—KAMALA TULLY,
executive director, the Mesa Refuge

"*St. James Park* is an immersive roller coaster that draws you into the chaos, the greed, and the politics of living through the Great Depression. Beautifully written. John Doll shows us that . . . anywhere there is money and power, there is corruption. Disappointingly, this story of grime and crime is still relevant today."

—MICHAEL MILLER, author of *High Bridge: Matilda and Grover Battle Learned Ignorance*

St. James Park

St. James Park

by John Doll

© Copyright 2025 John Doll

ISBN 979-8-88824-807-2

All rights reserved. No part of this publication may be reproduced, stored in a retrieval system, or transmitted in any form or by any means—electronic, mechanical, photocopy, recording, or any other—except for brief quotations in printed reviews, without the prior written permission of the author.

This is a work of fiction. All the characters in this book are fictitious, and any resemblance to actual persons, living or dead, is purely coincidental. The names, incidents, dialogue, and opinions expressed are products of the author's imagination and are not to be construed as real.

Cover design by Lauren Sheldon

Published by

3705 Shore Drive
Virginia Beach, VA 23455
800-435-4811
www.koehlerbooks.com

ST. JAMES PARK

A NOVEL

JOHN DOLL

VIRGINIA BEACH
CAPE CHARLES

Author's Note

My mother grew up a few blocks from St. James Park. She attended a nearby public elementary school, an all-girls Catholic high school, and, for some time, San Jose Teachers College. She told me stories of her experiences growing up in San Jose: how the valley had changed, how the town grew to be a city. She loved her hometown.

But every so often, my mother would recount the events that unfolded one shameful night in St. James Park in the fall of 1933. She was seventeen at the time, one of many witnesses to crimes that made national headlines and ultimately went unpunished. Her persistent but jagged memories of St. James Park were the inspiration for this novel.

Prologue

San Jose existed long before there was a phenomenon called Silicon Valley. The valley had always been desirable for its sunny climate, agricultural bounty, available timber, and constant source of fresh water. After the Spaniards arrived, San Jose was established in 1777 as the first pueblo in what was known as Alta California. When Americans invaded less than a century later, the town was celebrated as the state's first capital until the newly formed California legislature decided to move it elsewhere.

San Jose had promise, but other cities swiftly gained prominence. The furor for gold created wealth and fame for San Francisco, fifty miles to the north, and Sacramento was eventually chosen as the state capital in recognition of its proximity to the mines. San Jose remained on the periphery, concentrating on its fruit-bearing orchards as well as its vineyards—until most of the latter succumbed to the phylloxera epidemic in the 1890s. After the 1906 earthquake, San Francisco gained new celebrity as "the City that Knows How," becoming the mercantile hub of the West, while San Jose was doomed to a less elegant sobriquet: "the Prune Capital of the World."

San Jose continued to capitalize on its orchards, eventually becoming the largest canning and dried-fruit packing center in the world. By the early twentieth century, thirty-eight canneries and thirteen packing plants were the economic engine that enabled the town to bloom again. With a population swelling to 57,000, San Jose was too big to be called rural but too spread out to be urban. The city built up its compact downtown to create civic pride and promoted a new identity as "the Garden City."

During the Prohibition era, San Jose gained yet another moniker: "the Wettest Town in California." While savvy businessmen exploited the wealth to be made in controlling liquor and other illicit pursuits, tensions rose between the Drys and the Wets, between ethnicities and religions, between the lawful and the unlawful. The economic depression of the 1930s exacerbated the general unrest. Jobs disappeared, and for those who found employment in the fruit orchards and canneries, wages were at rock bottom. Beleaguered workers in San Jose began to fight back.

1

NOVEMBER 1933

A dozen or so activists attended the local Monday-night meeting, mostly men, some wearing overalls, some in floppy suits. They sat in a loose circle on wooden secondhand chairs scattered around the third-floor union hall in downtown San Jose. The windows were pushed partway open, but not enough air penetrated the musty, grimy room. The talk was about how to proceed after the local chapter's downtown demonstration earlier in the week. As usual, not everyone agreed on what to do next. Tempers flared as the sun began to set.

"If they want to fight, we fight," someone said.

"You don't understand. That's exactly what they want," said another.

"The bosses are itching to shut us down!"

"Make us wage slaves."

"The cannery workers are ready to strike this time. We need to shut them all down," cried Sara Chambers, a slender blond woman in her early thirties wrapped in a cranberry crepe dress. She spoke calmly and deliberately in a high-pitched Southern lilt. The imposing and impeccably dressed woman was a familiar face at these meetings. She was the only other woman in the room besides Victoria Trinchero, who had become involved with the labor group after her first whiff of cannery work.

"We should negotiate," said Guy Upton in his rumpled gray suit. He was the local business manager. Narrow-faced, he had a goatee and possessed intense eyes behind thick-rimmed glasses. "Make known our demands. Win over the people's support. Continue to get their support and deal hard at the table."

"Negotiation is over. You had your chance. How many more pamphlets and petitions can you pass around? We know the mayor won't budge. None of them will."

Victoria looked at the young man who had just spoken. He possessed an appealingly handsome face with curly dark hair, eyes that danced, a cleft chin, and a crooked smile. What was his name? . . . Schiavo? John Schiavo. He had only recently joined the group. He sat with his legs crossed at the ankles in his dungarees, arms crossed over a white shirt, a torn fedora resting on one of his knees.

"Look what they did last month. Tried to smoke us out," someone else said.

"That ain't gonna work. We're not going away. The cannery workers will prevail," said Bruguera. This fellow was brash, a dilettante, straight out of the university at Berkeley and very much aware of his good looks and charm. Had an opinion on everything. The week before, he'd asked Victoria to go out for a drink. She considered the offer, thought better of herself, and refused.

"We won the pear strike in the valley," someone in the back said. Victoria didn't recognize him. "How about that?"

"That was an isolated case," Bruguera replied. "They want to come in for the kill."

"Who are *they*, exactly?"

Bruguera held up his hand, counting off on his fingers as he recited: "The bosses. Their lackeys. The mayor. Ripley."

There were murmurs of agreement. "We need to take more direct action," another said.

Victoria rubbed her temples, growing more annoyed at the rhetoric being flung back and forth. Everyone knew that the mayor was a flunky who succumbed to those who held the power—and that was Ripley. Thomas Ripley dealt in real estate and was influential enough to manage those holding the reins of politics. A scumbag in a spiffy suit. He got what he desired without needing to hold an elected office. Or be held accountable.

Bruguera leaned to his left, toward Victoria. "How about one of you ladies go out in back and fetch me a cup of coffee?"

Without hesitation, Victoria flung her fountain pen at his face. He ducked, and ink splattered on the window behind him.

"Nice try, Vic darling. You want to take another shot?"

"Next time, I'll aim lower to make sure you get my full impact." She pointed at his crotch. "My mama taught me never to miss."

Meanwhile, Sara folded her arms and let her gaze travel around the room. "Clearly, we have more issues to solve."

Upton waved his hands. "Time to settle down. Let's get back to business."

The discussion continued until the church bells from nearby St. Joseph's began to clang. It was six o'clock. A calling to the faithful or quitting time. For Victoria, it was the latter. She'd had enough of Bruguera—all of them, for that matter. After two hours of debate, they'd managed to agree to circulate a new demonstration pamphlet. They had not reached a consensus on its wording.

She was expected to dine with Amelia Gumina, her best friend, and did not wish to be late, again. Victoria hurried as well as she could down the steps, hampered by the dark stairwell. The one lobby bulb had burned out, and no one had bothered to replace it. Victoria emerged on Santa Clara Street and looked up at the deepening blue sky. The streetlights glistened with the first drops of rain. People scurried along the sidewalks, some leaving work to catch the trolley home, others arriving to grab a double feature at the California Fox. A pair of teenagers laughed as they precariously dangled their ice cream cones bought at O'Neill's, a shop around the corner.

Victoria walked toward Rosen's Department Store, where Santa Clara and Market Streets intersected in the heart of downtown. The lights from within the store still glowed brightly, but one of the clerks had just turned the sign, signaling Rosen's was now closed. Another clerk had come out to help an elderly lady with her purchases into a waiting sedan. Victoria hurried by them and toward Lightston Alley, an odd afterthought of a street that served as a one-lane exit from Rosen's parking lot, which was tucked behind another building and reserved for esteemed customers. The dim alley also provided a shortcut to the trolley she needed to take to get to the Gumina residence.

There was one car in the lot. Someone was walking toward the driver's side of the vehicle. His outline was unmistakable: The scion of San Jose—Michael Rosen, heir apparent to Rosen's Department Store. The owner was an immigrant of Jewish descent who through decades had transformed his dry goods and clothing store into an extensive emporium filled with everything a workingman might require and a fawning capitalist might want. The father, Alexander, was decent. His son was something else. Raised in luxury. Rejected by Stanford University because he was deemed insufficiently Anglo-Saxon. Rejoiced by the Jesuits at the all-male University of Santa Clara. Michael had graduated months earlier and was now employed at his father's department store, learning the ropes of his eventual destiny.

When Michael was young, there was a rumor that he had been selected to pose as one of the cherubs that now adorned St. Joseph's ceiling, painted by an Italian artist. Every time Victoria attended Sunday mass, she would look up, trying to figure out which one was Michael.

The former cherub was still blond and curly-haired but had a decidedly secular flair for the cards and the booze and the women who enjoyed those pursuits. He was a regular on the society pages of the *San Jose Mercury-Herald*. In short, Michael Rosen represented the privileged. Nobody should be that spoiled.

The younger Rosen was about to climb into his Studebaker roadster as Victoria approached. She was ten yards away and despite the shadowy light could not help but notice his patented smile. The smirk that would melt the hearts of most females aged thirteen to eighty in this town, though Victoria was not swayed.

He noticed her and only slowed slightly. "Victoria, it's been a while. Good to see you this evening. I'm sorry, but I must be off. I must pick up my father."

"Really? I thought you'd be going elsewhere," she said.

"What do you mean?"

"Are you going to your dance?"

Michael laughed. "The dance will have to wait." He gave her a quick nod. "Unless you're interested in joining me later for a quick one?"

He didn't wait for her response but quickly climbed into his sedan, closing the door behind him.

Victoria spared him an annoyed glance before continuing her quick march to the trolley, where she joined the throng of boarding passengers. That was the last time she ever saw Michael Rosen.

2

San Jose's fruit and vegetable food processing industry was the largest in the world by the early twentieth century. Demand for canned fruits and vegetables had skyrocketed, partially as a result of the Panama Canal opening and eventually World War I. The volume of such shipments was second only to petroleum in terms of its economic importance to California. Such profits and growth prompted rapid consolidation of the industry and necessitated the need to keep labor cheap. While men held full-time positions as mechanics and warehousemen, the vast majority of workers were women who worked seasonally along cannery lines. Cannery owners preferred women, believing they were nimbler with the tasks of sorting, peeling, and slicing, since that reflected what women did in their own kitchens. By 1930, the canneries were the largest employers of women in the state.

Three months before she encountered Michael Rosen in the parking lot near his father's store, the raven-haired, chestnut-eyed Victoria struck gold. Her third year at the University of California would soon commence, but she had always scraped along financially. Although awarded a partial scholarship, she still had to manage her living expenses. The last two summers, she cut fruit in the apricot orchards, and although not much, her wages got her by. Better money could be made in the canneries, but there had been a hiring freeze, and when they needed workers, only those with connections got the jobs. Victoria hadn't known the right people until she became friends with Amelia Gumina. Amelia was not well connected herself, but her father seemed to know everyone in downtown San Jose, and his connections were priceless.

Amelia made a deal with her father. She had spent two years at San Jose Teachers College but decided prior to the fall semester that she would drop out. Amelia was tired of being lectured to—and besides, she had no intention of ever teaching in a classroom. She wanted to learn more about her father's business. That was a real education in how to get things done. Most of the young women enrolled in the college were just there to find a husband anyway. Amelia had much higher aspirations.

Of course, her father objected to her leaving college, but they compromised that she would instead get a steady job. And that job was working on the cannery assembly line. Amelia wanted the independence and the money. She assumed that her father thought she would soon tire of the relentless boredom and hard work and return to school. Part of the bargain with her father was that he would secure a position for Victoria as well. Victoria was independent minded and feisty. So was Amelia, although her parents were not yet convinced.

That evening in September, Angelo placed glasses of cold celebratory sparkling wine in front of each of them at dinner. With a broad smile beneath his aquiline nose, he announced that Victoria and Amelia would be hired by CalPak, one of the largest canneries in the valley. He then imparted his philosophy, a version of a Piedmontese proverb: "Don't hitch a ride on a cart that is led by a mule." Victoria nodded as if she knew what it meant, content to be working with her friend and covering her living expenses for the academic year. Within a week's time, the two women were notified by CalPak to begin work the following week.

That first Monday morning, in the cold darkness of her room, Amelia's mother, Rosalia, unsympathetically shook her awake at five thirty. Rosalia prepared scrambled eggs with a pinch of garlic, parsley, and salt, ordered her daughter to eat, stood by the door to make sure she did. Then helped her get dressed and out the front door. When Amelia lagged on the porch, Rosalia guided her daughter down the steps to the sidewalk and steered her in the direction of CalPak. Her parting words to Amelia were: *"Salute per cent'anni."* Amelia hoped for just one decent day.

When Amelia approached the corner of St. James and Thirteenth Streets, Victoria was there waiting. Together they shivered as the pale-yellow sun peered over the eastern foothills. They walked hand in hand past the solitary neighborhood rooster, the only sign of life.

The CalPak No. 39 operation was located at Jackson and North Seventh Streets. There the friends witnessed a flurry of activity as people streamed in from surrounding neighborhoods. Automobiles and lines of trolleys stuffed with workers rolled in. The two women stood watching for a few moments, bracing for what lay in wait. When they found the main entrance, the indistinct chatter of workers and the clanging sounds of the trolleys followed them inside, where harsh yellow lights cast shadows on the concrete floor.

After checking in with a security guard, they were ushered to a lonesome window booth where a middle-aged Anglo woman sat, looked up, and shoved a stack of forms at them. The woman told them to read everything before signing the forms, though her toneless recital indicated they should sign without hesitation. They inked their approvals with the pen Victoria had brought, returned the forms, and were told to proceed to gate no. 5. A guard pointed the way. The gate was clogged with workers. The shift was about to begin.

The two newcomers dodged past other assembly workers, the vast majority women: mostly Italian, some Portuguese, a few Mexican. Not a blue-eyed gal anywhere, Victoria noticed without surprise.

When it was their turn to pass through the gate, they were stopped by another security guard. They needed badges before entering the production floor. He pointed them in the direction from which they had just come. Back they went to the same Anglo woman in the window, exclaiming that they did not want to be late on their first day. The woman methodically handed them their badges. If they had listened the first time, they would not be in this situation, she told them.

They returned to the gate, their badges were checked, and this time they were told to move to one side and their foreman would come and show them the ropes. They did as they were told, waiting as hundreds of women hurried by them. Finally, a snickering man with a strawberry for a nose appeared and casually examined them head to toe. Then, without even a greeting, he said, "You will do nicely." He handed them each a white paper bonnet, a long, slightly stained apron, a sharp knife, and a pair of rubber gloves. Then walked away.

They put on the gloves and stood holding their knives as the whistle signaled the commencement of the morning shift.

"What do we do?" Amelia whispered.

"Wait some more, I guess," said Victoria.

A full five minutes passed before a stout woman in her thirties with a world-weary grin arrived. Her hair was dark brown with silver strands poking beneath her cloth cap. They saw her name, Sofia Vieira, emblazoned on her badge. A Portuguese name. Before Victoria managed to introduce herself, Sofia told them to follow her. Sofia's take-no-prisoners manner led them briskly through a vast hall of fruit-processing machinery and to the assembly lines. Along the way, Sofia rattled off what to do, how to do it, impressed upon them that since the fresh fruit was delivered when it was still dark, everything had to be canned within twenty-four hours. They would be paid based on the amount of fruit that was canned each day.

Victoria objected. "That isn't fair. Workers should be paid by the hour."

Sofia stopped and put her hands on her hips. "You make the

rules?" She pointed to where they would stand during their nine-hour shift. "You good with a knife?"

"Absolutely," replied Victoria.

"I've always known my way with knives," chimed in Amelia.

Sofia gave Amelia a look. "The whistles will tell you when you get your two fifteen-minute breaks and your half hour for lunch. Hope you brought something along."

Without waiting for an answer, Sofia picked up a knife and showed them how the fruit was put through a steam bath to remove the skin. Next, the fruit would be pitted and sliced lengthways as it moved down the conveyor belt. "That's your job," she told them. Bad fruit had to be plucked from the conveyor belt; that also was their job.

"Good fruit goes into the cans." Sofia used her knife to point. "The gals down there add the sugared water. Then the cans get taken off the line and weighed. We check each one to confirm the correct weight, and then they go back on the belt. Then they go into the cook room to preserve the fruit and make sure there's no contamination. Got it?"

Victoria nodded. Amelia answered, "Yes, ma'am. We pit the fruit and pick out the bad ones."

Sofia eyed her new recruits. "You two will be cutting because that is basic, and you probably already know how to do that. Any child knows that."

Amelia made a face.

"More experienced ladies handle the actual canning process. You are expected to stay alert. The machines only stop after the whistle blows. You stop, though, when the foreman says so. Don't mess up."

"We won't," said Victoria.

"Good. Because if you do, the machines can chew up your fingers. And those knives you are holding could slit a lamb's throat. The company frowns on nine-fingered employees."

Sofia pivoted away as another whistle blew. The machinery rumbled and whirred to life, releasing scores of apricots onto the conveyor belt for the new cannery workers to begin sorting and slicing.

3

St. James Park had always been that place in San Jose where anyone could speak their mind—where a crate could be used as a podium and spectators could listen to ramblings, musings, rants, threats, arguments, or sermons. There was the preacher who warned against the impending repeal of Prohibition, how the rush of alcohol would intoxicate the flock once again. The businessman who railed against the creeping encroachment of New Deal socialism and how it would stifle the entrepreneurial spirit. A mechanic cautioned about the rise of immigrants who threatened to take jobs away from the native-born. Now Victoria had come, along with hundreds of other cannery workers, mostly women, to listen to the union organizers speak.

From her spot on a park bench at the edge of the crowd, Victoria contemplated the autumnal haze hovering above trees already losing their leaves. Out of the corner of her eye, she saw Amelia approaching, late as always. The rally had already begun.

"Sorry. My mother packed us lunch and kept asking questions—where I was going, who I'd be with, what time I'd be home. Really, she does not know when to quit."

"I'm glad you're here. You've missed some. There's more to come."

"Have I missed Sara?"

"Sara will be up soon. It's all gone according to the script."

They elbowed their way closer to the platform, where one of

the speakers was addressing the crowd. A smallish man with a big bow tie and whose white hair was plastered on the side of his head began to speak: "Wages have been cut by fifteen percent. They say: Costs have risen. We say: Those are starvation wages. They say: Trust management. They're looking out for everyone's interest. We say: They just want a return for their investors. They say we're outside agitators. Damn straight we'll agitate—"

A blue-uniformed police officer stepped up to the platform, took hold of the speaker's shoulder, and escorted the man away. Victoria watched them haul the man to a nearby police wagon.

Victoria recognized the second speaker, Guy Upton, who stepped up to take his place. "We need to fight together against the bosses. Let's fight for unionization!"

Another police officer appeared. This time there was a scuffle, and two more men in blue came up to help arrest the speaker. They put handcuffs on him and crammed him into the wagon. That wagon took off. Another took its place.

"This is America. Land of free speech," began the next speaker. Victoria was surprised to see it was Bruguera. "Our First Amendment rights ensure—"

Police officers interrupted him; handcuffs appeared. Bruguera raised his shackled arms above his head and shouted, "This is not the America that we want! We must fight the good fight. Fight for better wages. Fight to organize. Fight for what is right!" He too was taken away, kicking and scratching at the cops.

Bruguera's successor held out his arms, wrists touching. "Take me. Your actions will be resisted." The cops grabbed him as well. Victoria nudged Amelia. "I think that man was John Schiavo."

The now-familiar scene repeated. Additional speakers took the stage, only to be taken away as they began to speak. The only change to the choreography was that the fifth speaker waved an American flag. The cops took it from him when they arrested him.

Then, Sara Chambers leaped up to the platform. The small army of policemen hesitated. Up until now, the speakers had been men. The Southern woman recognized her moment and shouted, "It's time to march to city hall and give the city fathers hell!"

She rushed off the platform, moved into the crowd before she could be accosted, and reemerged at the head of a quickly forming column that intended to do as she directed. With Sara in the lead, a long parade of women, some with children in tow, marched past the perplexed police officers, who held aloft their nightsticks and blackjacks, unsure whether to stop or strike the women. The crowd swelled as hundreds of men waiting at the perimeter of the park joined the march, a tactic carefully orchestrated by the organizers.

Victoria joined in. Amelia walked beside her, and soon they were joined by Sofia Vieira, who was accompanied by her unemployed husband and eight-year-old son. Above the chanting, Sofia shouted: "It's about time Martin knew what was right. We have to fight for what is right."

Victoria didn't know whether the Martin she was referring to was her husband or her son. The boy carried a sign that read: SUPPORT CANNERY WORKER RIGHTS. DON'T LEAVE US WITH THE PITS.

By the time the marchers approached the intersection of San Fernando and Market Streets, on the verge of City Hall Plaza, police officers and sheriff's deputies had cordoned off the route. The officers stood in the middle of Market Street, twirling their nightsticks. Beyond them, on the steps of city hall, stood the mayor, the police chief, and the sheriff. Off to the side, in the plaza, stood members of the American Legion, obvious by their garrison caps. Some of them carried baseball bats. Victoria thought they must have been tipped off for this confrontation.

The marchers stopped. A few began to taunt the officers. As more joined in, the mayor could be seen motioning to the police chief, who in turn signaled his garrison. The police unholstered their pistols and fired shots into the air. Amid the sounds of gunshots and puffs of smoke, a canister of tear gas was launched into the crowd. Collectively, the marchers shuddered. Mothers grabbed the hands of their children and began to retreat and scatter in fear. Others remained resolute, moving forward into the plaza where the uniformed officers raised their nightsticks and the small mob of legionnaires held their baseball bats aloft.

Though they were toward the back of the crowd, Victoria and Amelia were propelled forward in the crush of people. Then, more bangs and pops, and responding cries from the crowd. Victoria saw smoke and glimpsed one of the canisters as it was lofted skyward in a wide arc before descending into the group of protestors. Shielding her face with her handkerchief, she grabbed hold of Amelia's hand, managing to pull her away from the worst of the melee as people around them began to scream. They reached the edge of the plaza, and Victoria glanced around for Sofia and her family.

"Do you see them?" she asked Amelia, but any answer was drowned out by a new wave of screams as another canister landed on the ground where the two women had been moments ago. It spun around like some crazy Fourth of July firework, casting tear gas on both marchers and legionnaires. One marcher, clutching a handkerchief to his face, tentatively approached the canister, then used the handkerchief to pick it up and throw it in the direction of the American Legion troops. The man cried out something indistinguishable as he let go of the hot canister. Some marchers fled but plenty remained, screaming vengeance at the police.

A man stood on top of a billboard that rose above a three-story building overlooking the plaza. He was saying something and pointing in the direction of the police. Victoria couldn't tell whether he was a protestor or an observer. Other men perched on a low rooftop started to throw fruits and vegetables at the police. Tomatoes. Prunes. Even heads of lettuce.

An overripe tomato smacked and splattered on the shoulder of the startled mayor. A cheer went up.

The mayor didn't move other than to resolutely raise his arm to signal the police chief, who gave an answering signal. With that, police commenced to shoot more canisters into the crowd. Full chaos ensued. People tripped over each other as they tried to escape the police and the legionnaires, who swung their nightsticks and bats and bashed torsos, sometimes aiming for heads, pausing only to see where the canisters would fall. Someone was throwing rocks from a building roof.

"Get down!" Victoria screamed as rocks rained onto the pavement. She crouched and pulled Amelia down beside her. They covered their heads with their hands. Amelia swore under her breath. This was not part of the intended choreography.

Someone on a megaphone was ordering the crowd to disperse. The noise was too dense and dissonant to make out exactly what was being said.

"We've got to run for it," Victoria decided, getting to her feet.

She looked back toward the center of the plaza, where a contingent of firefighters had assembled behind the legionnaires. The firefighters were wielding heavy fire hoses now pointed into the crowd. A signal must have been given, because a torrent of water shot from the hoses, spraying the ragged front line of demonstrators. Several marchers collapsed under the torrent. The legionnaires moved in, bats swinging, followed by police intent on making more arrests.

Victoria caught sight of Sofia. Her son was crouched beside her. Her husband was not with them, likely somewhere amid the street fight. When Victoria motioned, Sofia picked up her son and ran toward them. Together they ran back down the block, away from city hall, dodging demonstrators going this way and that and the police chasing everyone in and around the block, the plaza, and the street, all slipping and sliding. It seemed like some dark parody of a Keystone Cop flicker as they eluded police and more firefighters with unruly hoses and zigzagged back in the direction of St. James Park.

As soon as it felt safe, Victoria slowed to a walk, curbing her instinct for a quick getaway. Sofia put down her son, and they all strolled, carefully, nonchalantly, down the block back toward Santa Clara Street.

Amelia tugged on Victoria's sleeve. Dozens of police officers waited along the perimeter of St. James Park. Sofia too saw the threat, and they stopped.

"We need to go shopping," declared Sofia.

"What?" Amelia said, but Victoria immediately understood.

They were near First and Santa Clara Streets. Near Rosen's Department Store. They resumed their pretense of a slow walk and meandered to the store entrance. Shoppers had barricaded themselves inside and were crowding against the windows, peering out at the calamity and confusion on the street. The women pushed hard on the front double doors, where more shoppers were huddled, pushing from the other side. Those inside finally yielded, and Victoria and her friends were allowed inside.

They brushed themselves off in the lobby. Sofia adjusted her hat, then her skirt, and marched up to the nearest clerk. "My son needs some shoes."

The clerk, whose badge identified him as Mr. Harold Cord, momentarily looked stunned, then composed himself, mindful of the store's dictum: Customers came first. "Upstairs. Second floor. Kindly follow me," a fussy Mr. Cord managed to say.

The three women and the boy trailed behind the clerk as they ascended the grand staircase to the children's shoes section on the second floor. At the top of the stairs, Mr. Cord motioned to another clerk that this new party needed specialized assistance for their collective child. A slender wisp of a woman sized them up, blinked, and said, "What style did your son have in mind? For dress or for sport?"

"Something that will last," replied Sofia.

"I'm sure we can accommodate your son," said the clerk.

Victoria sensed that Sofia was enjoying the theatricality of the situation. She rifled through different shoe styles for her son, saying, "Nah, that's not right. My son has better taste than that," or "What do you mean, this style does not come in brown? My son always wears brown to match his eyes," or "Who in God's name is able to pay that price for a pair of shoes?"

The clerk looked more and more harried as she tried to oblige the discerning mother.

Victoria left Sofia to her endless indecision and crept down the stairway to see whether any of the uniforms might have entered the store to search for demonstrators. It seemed unlikely the police would barge in and disrupt an important shopping day; nonetheless, she kept her distance from the side window, shielded behind a throng of shoppers gazing at the battle outside. They stood eye-to-eye with the police officers on the other side of the window, who appeared ready to enter should a dissenter be recognized.

Victoria pretended to appraise hats and scarves on a nearby table as she stole looks out the window. A man had followed her down the staircase. She looked sideways at him as he slid smoothly to her side. He was about her age, wearing a fashionable suit, a silk handkerchief tucked securely in his front pocket. The young man had curly blond hair. She recognized him.

"May I interest you in any of our quality pitchforks?"

Victoria was holding a black suede cloche hat with a velvet band. She kept hold of it as she regarded the curly-headed gentleman. "Ah, yes. But I think I'm more in the market for something that projects. I don't know, something more dramatic. What kind of selection might you have by way of water cannons?"

He smiled. "I can see that you are a woman with a refined taste. A European model, French or Russian, perhaps?"

"The make is secondary to its function. I need a model that can withstand the vicissitudes of the seasons."

"A college woman? I'm impressed. Would it be unwise to suggest that in exchange for your welfare, you might promise me something by way of libations?"

"Kind sir, your reputation precedes you. I am a lady, and that will not be considered."

He tugged at Victoria's sleeve and drew closer to her face. "Consider your options. Promise me an engagement in an establishment that meets your station in life. Or shall I engage with those who uphold the laws of our land?"

"What do you have in mind?"

"Will you accompany me to the dance?"

"What is this dance that you speak of, Mr. Rosen?"

He laughed. "Where your dreams come true. Where adventure lies. With the company impeccable. In a location exclusive. Or I can simply call my head manager to personally accompany you to the door and throw you to the wolves prowling outside."

Victoria placed the hat on the table and spoke evenly. "My friends and I are customers in your establishment. Would it not be unsuitable if I were to raise my voice and cry in horror, in a manner that would attract one of your patrons to rise in my defense and the rest to recoil from your loathsomeness?"

He openly smirked, clearly enjoying the repartee.

"You are a toad," Victoria added softly.

"Please, out of my sight. Thou dost infect my eyes."

"Any more conversation would infect my brain," said Victoria coolly as she walked away and pretended to shop.

4

Beneath a brilliant chandelier in the ornate Sainte Claire Club flush with white marble, Hindu filigree on the wainscoting, and elephant heads adorning wall sconces, one Thomas Ripley sat across from the county sheriff. Elmore Ewing's ample belly had long fed well from the public trough. His red-rimmed, rheumy eyes resembled those of a pig. Ripley waggled his bony finger, and a waiter rushed up. "We need some chardonnay."

"Sir, we're not able to fulfill your request. The law remains in force. I'm very sorry," answered the waiter, glancing sidelong at the sheriff, who was comfortably stuffed into his chair.

"Elmore, please inform this poor man," said Ripley, a wiry man in his sixties whose scarlet tie blossomed over his starched white shirt. His dark vicuña suit was the finest available. His voice resonant and his eyes pleasantly sapphire, a broad grin could not disguise contempt.

"Don't make me get a search warrant. Find a bottle. Get it on this table. Pronto," ordered Ewing. His manner was intentionally gruff.

"Very good, sir," the waiter dumbly answered. He rushed off to the cellar.

Ripley raised his eyebrows. "The man is in such a state that he may bring us some altar wine."

"Don't be surprised. The Jesuits can produce a nice white."

"Still church wine."

"It's available and positively legal. Their black muscat is renowned."

The waiter soon returned with the maître d' in tow. The maître d' nearly whispered, "We humbly apologize. We have been able to locate a special bottle that we've kept in storage for quite some time."

He offered a bottle of chardonnay. Ripley inspected the Novitiate label that assured it was indeed an old vintage. He nodded. "I hope it is still good."

"We think so. Compliments of the house. Enjoy your meal."

The waiter opened the bottle and poured. Ripley sipped the wine. It was good. The waiter silently departed.

Raising his glass, the sheriff toasted, "To business."

"Yes. To our business. Despite his manners, our good waiter was absolutely correct. The law is the law, and that will change. Business will have to follow suit."

"Your business. Ours remains the same," replied the sheriff.

"Indeed. The repeal of Prohibition will open new markets and doom others. The initial impulse will be competitive irrationality, but overall, it will be a period of consolidation that will allow for stability. Would you not agree?"

"Sure. All I know is that any growth requires order, and that's my business."

"We see eye to eye, don't we?"

"Damn straight."

"And this new political landscape? How do you think this will affect operations?"

Ewing raised an eyebrow. He looked out the window toward the park, then spoke in a measured manner. "Roosevelt is a traitor to those who made this country. Look at this valley. The orchards. The vineyards. The factories. The valley was nothing before we got here. We made the land prosper. We earned it, fair and square. All we get is outsiders telling us how we should act. How we should do things. I don't like the interference."

Ripley smiled thinly. "If you want things to stay the same, things will have to change. The trick is to change the story. These New Dealers say they want social justice. This populism for the working man has been picked up like a tidal wave. But beneath their rhetoric, they prop up forces, like the Warburgs, who are behind the scenes manipulating the capital markets. We must expose this hypocrisy and reinforce the principle of private property. A fundamental American principle. And we need to ensure we control it for the public good."

"We've got to keep America safe for Americans. It's these immigrants who are destroying what we have achieved. I only wish we could make them go away," insisted Ewing.

"Vanish?"

"Why not? Go back to where they came from."

Ripley sipped his chardonnay, then gestured toward the wall sconces. "Look around you. Elephants."

The sheriff looked at the decor as if noticing it for the first time.

"Did I ever tell you about a marvelous magic trick I once witnessed as a young man?" asked Ripley. "I've never really forgotten it."

"I don't like magic."

"It took place in the Hippodrome in New York in, I think, nineteen fifteen. The magician called it the Disappearing Elephant. I was stunned at how he performed it. So effortlessly."

"Houdini was a hustler."

"A master artist, really."

"A Jew."

"He led an elephant onto the stage. There was a large cabinet, decorated like a circus wagon. I'd say it was eight feet on one end and fifteen feet long. It was mounted on huge casters, and his assistants rolled it around and around to allow the audience to see all the way inside. It was completely empty. There was no possible manipulation. At first, he told the audience he would make the elephant do a little magic by making a piece of sugar disappear. He offered the beast some sugar, and the elephant ate it, waving its trunk. The audience was amused. The elephant was then carefully led up a ramp into this large wagon. The doors were closed behind, and the assistants rotated the wagon a quarter turn so that one end faced the audience. This end was covered with a curtain. Houdini said a few words, which I do not remember, then theatrically opened the curtains, which allowed the audience to peer in. It was totally black and empty. No elephant. No escape. The elephant had vanished."

"Tricks are for children."

"The trick worked because it created a realized illusion."

"What happened to the elephant?"

"That is not the point."

"What's the point?"

Ripley sat back in his chair, brought the glass to his lips, and took another sip. "This is indeed a very good wine."

Ewing stared at Ripley for a few seconds, then nodded slowly. "I think you're right," he said. "It's a very good wine."

5

At nine thirty on an October evening, Angelo Gumina told his wife that there was business that needed attention. He gave Rosalia a kiss on the cheek and a warm hug to his daughter, then slipped out the front door.

The air was cool and damp. He had just enough time to enjoy his walk through the darkened neighborhood. All seemed well. The evening was serene as always. He glanced sidelong at the houses as he strolled by. Chatty neighbors who had been sitting on their stoops at this hour a few weeks ago had by now retreated to the security of their front rooms, perhaps listening to an evening radio show. Probably Rudy Vallée's *Fleischmann's Yeast Hour*. Angelo didn't care for Vallée. A crooner who couldn't sing. A cheapskate to boot.

A few slow-moving cars passed him as he continued down St. James Street in the glow of the flickering streetlights. He crossed the street and kept walking by the rows of houses. The one he liked was at the corner. The one with the big tree in front that he could barely make out at this hour. When Amelia was young, she used to shy away from this block because she was scared of the tree, its long leaves like monkey tails. "If you get too close," Angelo would whisper, "the tails will swoop down and get you!" Amelia would shriek with laughter and clutch his sleeve.

He reached Third Street, where the prestigious Sainte Claire

Club fronted St. James Park. Though quiet now, the downtown park was the center of activity for citizens in San Jose. Angelo turned left, crossed the street, and walked down Third. On his left was the Scottish Rite Temple, styled in Beaux-Arts with a dash of Egyptian ornamentation. Alongside was the First Unitarian Church, unusual with its four domes, two towers, and an arched stained-glass window above the entry. His wife once mused that it resembled something from Transylvania. Finally, he approached the Eagles Hall. Greek revival with its massive Doric columns. He stopped, smiled and saluted the eclectic collection, then proceeded toward the unadorned cement stairway down along the far side. His underground place of employment was marked only by a simple black awning. There was no signage. No flashing neon light in brilliant yellows and reds. From the outside, the place looked like it might be deserted, but anyone wanting to wet their whistle knew the unassuming spot as the entrance to a place known simply as Spades.

Angelo greeted Oliver Jones, a barrel-chested, ebony-colored man in a stylish dark suit who presided over the entryway. Oliver's job was to ensure a visitor was legit. If so, he would press a button that unlocked the door at the bottom of the steps. Not that all of this would be necessary much longer. By the end of the year, no one would need to give a password to gain entry.

When Angelo entered the club, illumination was faint. The bar was backlit with a pale-green light showing off bottles advertising various wily charms and exotic locales. Tables were scattered throughout the place. Along the walls were a half dozen booths lit by solitary white lamps on the tables. This made the patrons appear like flickering specters. During the day, when patronage was sparse, the nudie paintings adorning the walls were more visible, providing some solace for lonely stiffs. The original artwork was courtesy of an Italian painter on his break from church restoration work.

As his eyes adjusted, Angelo detected the familiar outline of a figure stooped over the bar, his face splashed with the green light. It was the bartender, Eddie Savio, a fellow Piedmontese who was wiping the bar with his towel, waiting to be relieved. The usual proles were plopped up along the bar, for the most part staring morosely into their drinks. Otherwise, the place was quiet except for a murmur of conversation from some patrons tucked away in the darker recesses.

Angelo strolled by and gave Eddie a pat on the back, earning a shrug in return. "I need you to stick around until the boss comes in. 'Bout ten." Eddie nodded.

Angelo went directly into the back room. Closing the door behind him, he flicked on the light and checked for any instructions that Gaetano Ferrone, their boss, might have left: Who to be on the lookout for. When to meet. When to order new supplies. How and when or even if those supplies would arrive, in metal cans marked BATTERY ACID—brewed in British Columbia and taken aboard a mother ship, then retrieved by small boats at isolated spots along the California coast, put on trucks making midnight runs, and delivered to appointed destinations. Sometimes they'd be caught, but most sailed through with a crew soon flush with Franklins. The intricate operation was going to change soon. Prohibition was coming to an end.

And with that end, Ferrone's string of establishments would emerge from the shadows into full view. His overall operation had been tailored like a fitted three-piece suit. If Ferrone didn't play his cards right, everything would be a mismatch—a disappointing sag here, an off-putting shade of brown there. There was bound to be more competition, big-shot outsiders armed with wads of bills. Ferrone would have to figure a way to balance the newly legitimate alcohol business with his other establishments remaining illegal. City Hall would still require its slice of the revenue, the beat cops their honorariums, the preachers their sinners. Times were tough, and there wasn't as much green being spread around. Something was going to give.

Angelo read Ferrone's instructions and clicked off the light. As he reemerged into the bar, he felt the whoosh of the cool night breeze that signaled the entry of another patron. He scanned the row of Monday-night customers at the bar, most of whom he knew by name, and asked each if they needed anything more to wet their whistle.

"Handcrafted from Kentucky," Angelo told one of the regulars, who wanted to know the source of his drink. "You know we get the best suppliers."

"This stuff is smooth, but"—the man leaned in close to Angelo and lowered his voice—"you guys gonna last?"

Angelo smiled and placed his hand lightly on the man's sleeve. "You got to roll with the punches."

The man reared back and jabbed the air. "Yeah, just like Carnera, right?"

Angelo nodded, smiled, and moved on to the next man. In time, more patrons, all men, came and went with various excuses. It got so busy that Angelo donned a half apron and joined Eddie behind the bar. They listened to ceaseless conversations about the state of the world, the lack of opportunity, the corrupt politicians, unfair bosses, bossy wives, boozy dames.

A guy Angelo didn't recognize ordered a glass of "dago red."

Angelo winced, signaled to Oliver, who now stood by the entry. The bouncer approached from behind and placed his hands firmly on the guy's shoulders.

"I believe you're done for the night," said Oliver. "Pay up."

The man looked around and started to protest. Oliver's grip tightened. "One more word, and you're yesterday's bacon," the bouncer said quietly. The guy weaseled a buck from his wallet and placed it on the bar. He didn't resist as Oliver escorted him to the door.

The evening was well underway when, at close to ten, the man himself, Gaetano Ferrone, paraded in with three of his associates in tow: Frank Lagatutta, Nick Caputo, and Sal Booksin. Oliver had come down the steps and quietly cleared out the place for the meeting. "We apologize for the inconvenience, but we're closed," he said. Most of the patrons knew enough to readily comply, but a lone straggler at the bar resisted the call to move. Oliver jabbed him in the shoulder and delivered advice basso profundo: "Hey, it'll be Thanksgiving in no time. And it'd be a shame if your shirt was all messed up with turkey stuffing. Let's move." The man slunk out without further fuss as the new arrivals shuffled in and crowded around the table closest to the bar. Someone, it might have been Caputo, bellowed, "Let's get some light here, will ya?"

Eddie turned on the houselights, illuminating the room in sudden whiteness. The men in suits collectively winced as they sat. A couple of them shielded their eyes by pulling down the soft brims of their fedoras.

"Jesus, Angelo, do something," said Lagatutta, a middle-aged, well-fed Calabrian immigrant with a scar on his neck. Eddie switched off the houselights while Angelo turned up the table lamp.

"Thank you, Angelo. That's much better," said Ferrone, speaking for the first time since arriving. Booksin grunted in assent.

"Anybody need anything before we begin?" asked Ferrone.

"You can go now, Eddie," Angelo said. "Regards to the missus."

Eddie grabbed his coat and cap and took off. Oliver remained by the front doorway. Angelo stationed himself near Ferrone's group, close enough to be on hand without intruding.

"We got a problem. Tell me what you know," said Ferrone. The boss had a prominent nose. Slicked-back gray hair, parted in the middle. Born in Rome. He had emigrated, worked as an orchard laborer, became adept at organizing what was in demand, and at long last was considered a constituent of the Sainte Claire Club, a meeting place for prominent businessmen.

"The quarterly cash flow shows that we are in the red," Sal Booksin reported.

Booksin was the newest associate. Ferrone had only recently brought him in. Smart kid in his twenties. Streetwise. Mother was from Genoa; long-gone father was American. Grew up somewhere in LA. Favored new threads and Cadena cigars. Hook for a nose.

"Sales have been steady. Costs have risen," Booksin continued.

"What costs? Supplies are steady. Our transportation costs should not have gone up. What's different? I haven't heard anything that would require further support for our local governments. In fact, that pressure should be less than it has been. So, what's the deal?" asked Ferrone.

"Bad loans."

"Which ones?"

"We extended a number of loans to patrons. There has been a difficulty in getting these loans paid up," answered Booksin.

"What are we charging?"

"Nineteen percent on an annualized basis."

"And they cannot pay the interest?"

"Most manage. But there are many who cannot. One in particular."

"What can we do?" Ferrone looked irritated.

"What we usually do. Talk to them. See what kind of collateral they have. We take possession until payments come through," replied Booksin. "And if they don't, we either renegotiate the loan or sell the collateral. Depends. Depends on the circumstances."

"The majority of these loans are?"

"Mostly racked up on our operations. The usual."

"What are we doing to correct our business outlook?" Ferrone looked to his right. "Nick, can you answer that?"

Angelo followed his gaze, mentally clicking off details. Nick Caputo was mid-thirties. Smooth dresser. Sicilian born. Bronx bred. Escaped to the West Coast after the war. Good egg.

Caputo straightened his tie before answering. "We approach the customers on an individual basis to ascertain the individual problem and then devise an individual solution."

"This is old news. This is what happens all the time. Sure, the business climate is not ideal, but we all know that. What's the 'one in particular' item?" asked Ferrone.

Caputo looked squarely at his boss and said: "Rosen."

"Rosen? Alexander Rosen?" asked Ferrone.

"No. His son, Michael," answered Caputo. He yet again adjusted his tie.

"And? What's the problem? What's the amount outstanding?"

This was Booksin's purview. "The son racked up a number of debts over time," he explained. "The precise amount outstanding is"—he checked his logbook—"$37,393.42. That includes accumulated interest."

"That's quite high. Where is he with the repayment?"

"None to date," said Booksin.

Ferrone turned to Caputo. "What efforts have you made to approach this customer?"

"What we typically do. After three months of nonpayment, we arrange a meeting. We had the meeting. He told us a cashier's check would be submitted within a week's time. We thanked him," answered Caputo.

"And the check?" asked Ferrone.

"It bounced."

"What were your further efforts to retrieve our money?" inquired Ferrone.

"We arranged a follow-up meeting."

Ferrone took a sip of water. "And?"

"And so, we met again and impressed upon him that this was a serious matter and that we required collateral to cover the loan. He said he didn't have anything of value, but his father and mother had assets. We told him that we did not care how he paid, but a loan repayment must be made on a timely basis. And we agreed on a deadline for the interest on the loan to be paid," replied Caputo.

"I take it he didn't pay," said Ferrone.

"Another delay. Said he needed more time," responded Caputo. "We told him we would need to take ownership of his roadster. He refused to give us the papers. We threatened to go to his father. He said that he would get us the money, and around and around we go."

"Perhaps we need a stronger tactic," said Ferrone.

"Maybe we ought to give Rosen a smack that he does not forget," suggested Lagatutta.

"Young Rosen poses a problem that should not be solved with force," offered Angelo.

Ferrone folded his hands together and tucked them under his chin. "Whatever we do must be solved quickly and quietly."

"Something to show we mean business," said Lagatutta.

Ferrone considered that. "What would you recommend?"

Lagatutta shrugged. "Simple and quick."

"The point is to press the fact that repayment must be made. We make it clear that this will not go away," said Ferrone. He glanced around the table. No one offered any objections. "When do you suggest this occur?"

Lagatutta looked down at a small notepad. "November 6. He parks his car in the lot next to Lightston Alley."

Ferrone put his hands on the table. "Don't use anyone directly connected to us."

"We've got two guys lined up. They're hungry for work. One guy has been an unemployed piano player and housepainter. Take your pick. The other one used to be a salesman," reported Caputo.

"I don't want to know any more. Are they any good?"

"They'll do what they're told." Lagatutta was adamant.

6

Within the silent, dark, cramped confines of the Mission chapel confessional, a young man named Winston Richter, gray eyes wide and lips barely noticeable, knelt and waited for someone to slide open the lattice panel.

Winston had graduated earlier that year and stayed on as an administrative assistant for the University of Santa Clara. His work consisted of checking attendance, running errands, sorting out receipts, scheduling guest lecturers, that sort of thing. It barely paid his food and lodging. Given the weak job prospects after graduating with a bachelor's degree in philosophy, his father had wanted him to return home. Yet Winston refused to slave once again in his father's bakery. His idea was to apply to Santa Clara's law school. If he could get a law degree, Winston thought he would be in fat city. No longer would he be humiliated by always having flour embedded in his fingernails and be forced to wake up at three in the morning to start work at four, ringing up identical loaves of bread day in, day out. Becoming a lawyer meant something. It was respectable. People looked up to lawyers. Lawyers made money.

There was only one problem: He was placed on the school's waiting list. They said he could reapply next year. Or the year after. There was a lot of competition to be admitted to the law program. Many were qualified. Few selected. They even cautioned that not everyone was suited to be a lawyer. In fact, half the students would not graduate. They were forced to drop out.

Sitting in limbo over the last several months became unbearable. He would do anything to get into law school. Anything.

He fumbled with the crumpled note in his pants pocket. The day before, he had returned to his desk to find a crisp white envelope placed inside his attendance book. His name was typed on the envelope. The note inside instructed him to arrive at the assigned confessional at precisely four o'clock the next afternoon. He didn't know who sent the note. He didn't know whether anyone knew his predicament. But the note was signed: THE COMMITTEE FOR PUBLIC SAFETY.

There had been murmurs about the Committee, but no one spoke of it openly. At one point, the administration had issued a queer statement disavowing the participation in and actions of any unapproved student or university organizations, but they did not explicitly mention any organization. Perhaps the statement was only a warning, as there were no further actions, no subsequent crackdowns.

Winston thought he understood why the administration might act the way it did. Generally speaking, the university demanded strict adherence to Catholic morality, which included rejection of certain politics that it felt was soft on godless philosophies. The rumors swirling around the Committee indicated something altogether different. Winston assumed it was a secret club that organized against New Deal politics. But that was just a rumor. He hadn't believed the Committee even existed until he received the note. The word was that despite the administration's dictum, the Committee was a subterranean organization that possessed sizable influence within the university. And that was what Winston desired. Someone to pull some levers to get him into law school.

The panel slowly slid back, revealing the yellow sheen of the translucent scrim draped between the two sides of the booth. Winston waited. Silence. He didn't quite know what to do, since in these circumstances there was the usual recitation. He tried it anyway. "Bless me, Father, for I have sinned." There was no response.

Winston squirmed. He didn't know whether he should say something else.

Finally, he heard a low, guttural sound from the other side of the scrim. A man whispered some type of instruction in a disguised voice. Winston coughed. "I cannot hear what you're saying."

The voice then commenced in a staccato fashion. "You are here of your own volition. If you fulfill our instructions, then you will be considered for induction. Your actions will dictate whether or not you will be admitted. Are there any questions?"

"If it is not presumptuous, I would ask, subject to fulfilling your requirements, whether my own aspirations might be considered."

"Your aspirations are noted." A hesitation. Then the voice continued. "You need to decide now whether you intend to follow all the instructions. If you do not want to proceed, leave immediately. If you remain, you must say 'aye' and carry out the instructions as they are given. There is to be no deviation. There are no further questions. We require your silence and obedience in carrying out our instructions. Do you wish to remain?"

"Aye," answered Winston.

More silence. Then he heard the rustle of paper, as if the speaker were reading from a script.

"At eight o'clock on the evening of November 6, you will be at Letcher's Automotive Showroom at First and St. James. Mr. Green will be there. An automobile will be available for your use. There will be written instructions in the glove compartment. These must be precisely carried out." Another pause. "That is all the information I can give you at this juncture."

Winston nodded at the unseen speaker. Seemingly done with the script, the voice continued, "You must do everything in complete secrecy or there will be severe repercussions. Do you understand?"

"Yes, I do."

"Remain here for the next fifteen minutes. Then leave the chapel.

Return to work. Do not breathe a word of this to anyone."

Winston continued to kneel in place.

"The Committee appreciates your participation. Full initiation is dependent upon how well you perform."

The lattice panel was pulled shut, and it was pitch black again. After what he thought was long enough, Winston left the confessional. He saw no one. The chapel's nave had become appreciably darker.

7

Standing alone in St. James Park, across from Letcher's showroom, Winston hugged his shoulders and shuffled his feet, waiting. The single park light above him cast a pale arc of light, like a mime at a vaudeville show. It was a cold evening. There was a slight breeze from the north. The longer he stood, the darker the sky became and the more he shivered. He should have brought a warmer coat.

He watched cars rumble back and forth past the dark, deserted business and wondered whether he should go through with it. With a final glance at his watch, he knew it was time to make a decision. He crossed the street, saw the CLOSED sign, looked for signs of life, tried the roll-up door. Nothing budged. He walked around the side of the showroom.

He came upon another door, a regular one. He banged on it with his fist, then tried the doorknob. It was not locked. He walked in. A single naked bulb dangled from the ceiling and sprayed a grim light on automobiles in various states of disrepair. A muffler lay on the cement floor; a tire leaned against one of the cars; tools were scattered around. Winston placed his hand on the hood of a car. It was slick with grease and grime and dust. He took out his handkerchief and wiped his fingers. Then he waited, perspiration dampening his forehead. There was no movement inside the dusty garage. He wondered if there had been a mistake. A sick gag. Maybe this was part of the initiation. A university colleague had once told him that he was the gullible type.

He heard a faint noise. Maybe a rodent scurrying through the workshop. A click. One of the garage doors was pulled upward. Winston took a step toward the door. A voice barked: "Stay there."

"Mr. Green? Is that you?"

"The key is in the ignition. Take the Plymouth there. Don't look around," came the gruff reply. The speaker did not show himself.

Winston stood there for a long minute. He thought there would be something else. Only silence.

A Plymouth roadster sat just to his left. He walked around to the driver's side, careful to look only at the roadster, opened the door, got in. The key was in the ignition. He turned it. The engine sputtered and died. He tried again and the roadster roared to life.

Someone opened the roll-up door. Winston peered through the windshield at the night traffic flicking by, turned on the headlights, let out the clutch, and eased tentatively out of the garage. As he nosed the car onto First Street, he risked a glance in the rearview mirror and caught sight of an older man in overalls closing the garage door. He heard it clang shut.

He drove the Plymouth north for two blocks, pulled over beneath a streetlamp, and pushed the gear into neutral. Looked around to see if anyone was following him. A few cars passed him from behind, the headlight beams reflecting in his rearview mirror. He told himself to calm down, then leaned over to the glove compartment and fumbled to open it. Inside were two envelopes. One was white, letter-sized. A note scrawled on the outside made it clear this was the one he should open first. The typed instructions inside were brief and to the point:

Drive to Hotel Whittier on Market Street, San Francisco. Use hotel lobby telephone, second booth from check-in, at precisely 10:30 p.m. Ask for the San Jose exchange. Cypress. 4098. Read the script to the party that answers. Hang up. Leave the hotel. Do not deviate.

The second was a sealed brown manila envelope. On its outside, someone hand-printed: Do not open unless the first task has been completed. We are monitoring you.

Below that was a warning: Without compliance, there will be no reward.

Taking a deep breath, Winston put the car in gear and began his journey northward, more than fifty miles. It would take him over an hour to reach San Francisco. He knew the route that would take him past Santa Clara, straight up El Camino Real, past a series of small towns until he reached the city. Having never spent much time in San Francisco, though, he had only a vague sense of where Hotel Whittier might be on Market Street.

Grasping the steering wheel more tightly than necessary, Winston kept steady through a variety of dark, closed downtowns, then through an umbrella of shadowy trees holding hands over the roadway. To his right sprawled the shadowy patch of San Francisco Bay. He compulsively checked his rearview mirror for anyone who might be following. The road remained serene but for the oncoming headlight beams that blinded him for a few seconds before the drivers sped past. Slowing at a stop sign somewhere, it might have been Redwood City, he glanced up at the white full moon. It seemed to squat just ahead, taunting him.

Was this all a fool's errand?

He continued up the road past Burlingame until he saw the murky outline of San Bruno Mountain straight ahead. The traffic along this stretch was sparse until, seemingly out of nowhere, the glare of fast-approaching headlights flashed in his rearview mirror. The car tailgated him for longer than a moment, then zoomed past, leaving him staring after two red taillights that disappeared into the night.

When the gaudy lights of a roadhouse shone ahead, Winston

slowed the Plymouth and turned into the parking lot. He required a stop-and-piss break. Seven Mile House blinked in red neon. There were a half dozen vehicles in the lot, but he didn't think he recognized the car that had sped by him minutes ago. He killed the engine.

Seven Mile House advertised that it served "chops and mashed," but Winston guessed it was better equipped to satisfy one's thirst and perhaps accommodate something more substantive upstairs. He stuck the smaller envelope in his lapel and left the larger one in the glove compartment, walked into the joint, asked where the john was. The bartender, a swarthy type with an overgrown 'stash, gestured with his thumb: *That way, outside.* The stall smelled like it hadn't been cleaned since the Crash. Winston pissed into a stack of cigarette butts. When he returned, there were a few men scattered on separate stools, interested only in what stirred in their glasses.

Winston sidled up to the counter and asked for a gin. The bartender answered: "Straight up or on the rocks?"

"Fizz." Winston fumbled through his pants pocket for change and placed it on the counter.

"That'll cost you seventy-five cents." Winston sank his hand deep into the pocket and came up with the rest. The bartender swept up the money and soon smacked down a filthy tumbler of three-fingered gin. Winston took the glass and retreated to one of the red leather booths. The seat had been stabbed in the middle; its guts were showing. A single sconce above provided questionable illumination. He sat down, took out the envelope, reread its contents, wiped his brow, then stuffed it back into his coat.

He glanced up and caught the bartender giving him the eye. Winston looked away, then back toward the bar. The man was drying glasses, holding them up to inspect each glass for spots. Winston reminded himself to quit thinking everyone was after him. He downed his gin, returned to the bar, and the bartender asked if he needed a refresher. Winston said no but asked whether sticking on Bayshore would get him to Market Street.

"Yeah, keep going. Eventually."

"Hotel Whittier?"

"Near the Fox. Can't miss it."

The *Fox*? The word threw him. He felt cloudy. The alcohol seemed to rush through his veins, and he stumbled as he hurried back to the Plymouth. The cold, fresh night air partially cut through the descending fog. When he opened the door to the car, it was obvious that someone had gone through it. The glove compartment was open. The manila envelope gone. He glanced around; no one else was in the parking lot. Cursing, he ran back to the bar.

When he pushed through the door, everything was as before. Feeling his gut clench, Winston went up to the counter. The bartender turned and looked at him as if he were a stranger. "What'll ya have?"

Winston blinked, glanced around nervously. "I've been robbed."

The bartender feigned surprise. A middle-aged guy near the bar, bolo tie askew, was smiling crookedly in Winston's direction. He held up the manila envelope, waved it with his right hand.

"You missing this?"

"Yes. That's mine."

"It's mine now." The man chuckled. "You lost it, fair and square."

"Can I please have it back?" Winston looked at the bartender, whose answering glance said: *Not my problem.*

"It'll cost you, son." Peeking out from a week's worth of gray stubble, the man in the bolo tie grinned, then got off his stool and approached. He smelled like yesterday's fish special.

Assessing his options, Winston resigned to dig out one of his remaining bills. "Here's a five."

"Hamilton might have been a more generous president."

The bartender remained stone-faced. Winston gave the man a ten. The man smiled his crooked smile again—"Thank you, sir, for your donation to the cause"—and stuffed it into his pants pocket. The bartender cracked a slight smile.

Winston cleared out of the Seven Mile, but not before sneaking another look around the parking lot. Saw no one. Grabbed the key, turned the ignition, thanking the Lord that no one had tampered with it, and whisked out of the lot northbound toward San Francisco. He glanced in the rearview mirror to see if anyone was in pursuit. In the clear, he rolled down his side window, hoping the rush of moist air would clear his head. He still felt funny, lightheaded, as if the alcohol had shot straight to his brain. Had it been spiked?

He continued up the Bayshore. A pair of headlights closed in behind him. Twice the headlights flashed. Winston ignored them, clutched the steering wheel as light flooded the cab. He abruptly swung onto the next turnoff, heading west. The tailgater shot by. Honked once but then was gone.

Not knowing exactly where he was, Winston rumbled by dark farmhouses and empty fields, but after some twenty minutes a neighborhood started to sprout. That led to an intersection with a wide street and a cluster of shuttered shops and such, so Winston took a chance and swung right. He was rewarded when he looked up at the street sign: MISSION STREET. Pure luck. If he stayed north on Mission, he would end up downtown, although the direction was not obvious because the road refused to stay straight.

The city grew denser, with large buildings on either side of the street. Winston saw a lone man walking a Labrador. He slowed, rolled down the window, and called, "How do I get to Market Street?"

The old guy pointed the direction. Winston took the advice. Making a left turn, he came to the intersection of Market. Like a carnival, San Francisco was all lit up. He turned right and soon found he was closing in on the Ferry Building and running out of road. He made an unseemly U-turn over the trolley tracks, before the oncoming cars approached, and headed back. He might have asked that lone man where the Whittier stood. The roadhouse bartender had told him the hotel was near the Fox. Had he been misled?

This direction seemed promising as this section of Market Street was alive with crowds jostling along the sidewalks. Though, on closer observation, many storefronts were boarded up. Those that remained open featured a spectrum of entertainments, some legit, others illicit. The latter were packed. Ahead Winston saw the bright, shimmering marquee of the Fox Theater. FOOTLIGHT PARADE in smashing colors. Aha! The film must have ended. A crowd swamped the sidewalk. On the opposite side of the street was a vertical neon sign and, as advertised, the Hotel Whittier.

He glanced at his watch. It was closing in on 10:30 p.m. He was cutting it close. He parked the Plymouth on a side street, hopped out, avoided the incoming trolley that clanged down the middle of the street, and, dodging the crowd on the sidewalk, headed for the revolving door of the brightly lit hotel lobby. Guests were coming and going. Swaying silver skirts, snickering gents in tails, yellow taxis hugging the curb, and doormen waving in their elaborate red-and-black outfits, looking as if they'd just come from some colonial war.

Clutching both envelopes to his breast, Winston hurried in and spied a row of telephone booths adjacent to the front desk. The second booth—the one he was supposed to use—was occupied. He sat on one of the plush sofas along the wall, looked at his ticking watch. Almost half past. A woeful-looking panhandler had taken up residence in the lobby and was begging passersby for some relief. As Winston watched, the house detective appeared and laid into the unshaven miscreant. The dick was having none of that in his hotel. Winston chewed his lower lip. Two minutes to go. And he didn't know what he should do. Try another booth or just wait?

The detective forcibly dragged the poor soul out to the street; the beggar did not go quietly. Winston looked back at the row of booths. This time, the second booth was vacant. He ran over and cut off a man in an expensive suit who had expected to use the booth himself. The man loudly complained and raised his hand to the house detective, who was still preoccupied. Winston slipped into the booth and shut the door. The man glared at him through the glass. But only for a moment. Another booth must have become available, and the stranger vanished.

One minute to go. Winston exhaled, hoping no one else had noticed him. He opened the white envelope. Reread the script. Wiped his brow. It was too late to turn back now. He grabbed the phone receiver off the hook. The operator sweetly sang: "Number please." He recited the number and heard the dull clinking of each letter and each numeral being dialed.

Nothing happened. Winston waited, uncertain. Finally, a young female voice answered: "Hello?"

Startled, Winston examined the script once again, foggily remembering the lessons from his old college debating coach: "Breathe deep. Speak slowly and enunciate."

The result was toneless and dull: "We have your son. We want forty thousand dollars. Don't go to the police or you'll never see your son alive again. We will phone instructions tomorrow."

8

While the patrons at Spades were alive and well, its back room was quite dead. Angelo waited for the others to arrive, and then at ten o'clock, all of his associates filed in one by one. When all were present and accounted for, the meeting commenced. Gaetano Ferrone greeted everyone, then turned to Booksin. "What happened?"

"Like we planned, I was posted across the street at First and Santa Clara. Saw him walk out and get in his car. Tierney and Hansen were there in position. That part was no problem."

"Anybody see anything?" Ferrone asked.

"No. It went good. No cops," answered Booksin.

"What about the woman? Anyone seen her before?"

"She's a nobody."

Ferrone nodded, then looked at Lagatutta. "Frank, what do you got?"

"I was in my car near the hospital at Fourteenth," Lagatutta reported. "The Studebaker and our tail never came through. Thought something went wrong. Went to check. Drove back toward downtown. Our lookout was there in the alley. Said they took off in my direction. Met up with Sal. Same thing. Should have seen them. Should have passed by me. Sal and I drove back down Santa Clara, checked all the side streets, but no go. That's when I called you at the club."

Ferrone looked at Caputo, who told a similar story. "The

instructions were clear. They were to go to the house on Alum Rock. We were waiting. Should have been there at fifteen past six, at the latest. Never showed. I stuck around until you called."

Ferrone slammed his palms flat on the table. "And that's why we're here, isn't it?"

He stared in turn at each man seated around the table.

"Somebody got to them. Tierney and Hansen both checked out. This should have been routine," said Lagatutta.

Ferrone produced a cigar from his inner suit pocket. "Find them." He looked at Angelo. "I want you to stick around," As the others readied to leave, Angelo sat in the chair Lagatutta had just vacated. The door opened as the trio left, and a momentary chill spread through the room. Oliver was there to lock the door and then joined Ferrone and Angelo at the table.

"Should I be concerned about any of my men?" Ferrone asked.

"They're good. Loyal," said Oliver.

"You sure?"

This time the question was directed at Angelo, who replied without hesitation. "We're sure. Our guys aren't the problem."

Ferrone looked frustrated, nervous. It wasn't often that he looked so unsure. Maybe he was losing his grip on the changes that were to come. Things that were not firmly in his control.

"We don't know who is behind this, and that remains a problem. If we can't fix it, we'll be done." Ferrone's face was flushed. He looked at his unlit cigar. "You know, Angelo, this isn't right. I stood right there by the front window of the club, watching for the kid's Studebaker to drive by."

Angelo said nothing. Ferrone had a lot to lose.

"I had one eye out for the Studebaker, the other on old Rosen." Ferrone waved his cigar. "He expected his son to be there to pick him up. I bet at first he thought his son forgot about him. Wouldn't have been the first time. There he was, looking at his watch. Waiting. Then he talked to one of his people there. So, what in hell happened?

We've done this before how many times? A deal should have been worked out by now. Quietly. Firmly. Without fuss. Order restored. Debt paid up. Like before."

"Something happened."

"You bet something happened. Somebody got in the way."

Ferrone finally lit his cigar. "I want you to make a few discreet inquiries." He took a puff. "Shake the tree. Let's see what the street has to say."

9

It was nearly midnight by the time they met at the mayor's house. Sheriff Ewing and his city counterpart, a white-haired, pug-nosed Police Chief Blackmun, sat in the parlor while the mayor, in the next room, asked the operator to place a long-distance telephone call to the governor. The mayor's wife, a matronly figure dressed in an Edwardian robe that was once popular, had offered the lawmen a glass of sherry. The police chief declined—he didn't like to drink—but Ewing took up the offer, remarking that even in these sour times it was nice to get a decent glass of sherry. The mayor's wife raised her glass, smiled. Replied: "If people could just stop and look around, the best of times is always around the corner."

Ewing saluted her with his glass. "Gertrude, I appreciate your positive nature and the quality of your booze." He knocked back the drink and inquired whether he could have another.

"Most certainly," came the response. She waddled back to the kitchen to fetch another bottle.

"'Bout all she's good for," Ewing said under his breath, earning a blank look from Blackmun, who sat fingering the antimacassar along the arm of his chair. He pulled one of the pins out of the fabric and then pressed it back more firmly, nodding to himself.

The mayor's wife returned with the second bottle and was just about to open it when her husband abruptly opened the door from his office, crashed in, and plopped down on his favorite chair. "Put that away," he said, looking at the bottle she held. "Leave us in peace." She looked disappointed but retreated to the back of the house.

Blackmun looked at the mayor, a hapless man in his early seventies who had hung around long enough in politics to hoodwink the public into electing him mayor. He should have stayed a tailor. Ewing looked at his unfilled glass.

"We're calling in the Bureau of Investigation," said the mayor.

Blackmun didn't hide his dismay. "Mr. Mayor, I don't like Washington bureaucrats mussing our hair."

The mayor nodded but said they didn't have much of a choice. "The governor is adamant," he told them. "He wants Hoover in on this. The governor needs cover. So do we. It's the only way."

"What does Ripley say?" asked Ewing.

The mayor frowned. "I don't give a rat's ass, pardon my French, about Thomas Ripley."

Ewing squinted and laughed to himself. He thought the mayor was a moron and wanted to tell him so, but he knew better. Most of the sheriff's life was spent prodding, smiling, nodding at the politicians, waiting for the precise moment when he could succeed. For now, he feigned agreement, knowing that Ripley would have a say. "What's our next step, boss?"

The mayor looked at Ewing and then at Blackmun. "What's our exposure?"

"Somebody grabbed Alex Rosen's kid. One of his daughters got the call. Alex then called us," recited Blackmun. "They want forty thousand. The caller said there'd be further instructions tomorrow. Meanwhile, we've set up checkpoints. We're set up for tracing any more calls coming into the residence."

The mayor chewed his lower lip, glanced at Ewing.

"Our boys are already making inquiries," Ewing said, admiring his fingernails. "They've rousted everyone in the vicinity and are checking on leads."

"Where was Alex when this happened?"

"Alex Rosen had been waiting at the Sainte Claire Club. His son was supposed to pick him up there, and together they were supposed to attend a dinner at the country club. Didn't show," Ewing recited.

"Why did the father need a ride?"

"The old guy can't drive. We checked out Rosen's store. One of the clerks saw the son leave and watched him get into his car, but no sign of the car now. It wasn't in the parking lot."

"Who saw him?"

"Name's Cord. He saw Rosen talking to a woman in the parking lot. We'll find her," replied Ewing.

"Did Cord say if he was alone?"

"He thought so."

"Anything else?"

There was a hard knock at the front door. The mayor opened the door, and there stood three policemen, squirming beneath the porch light. One of the men introduced himself as Officer Nolan, a lanky cop whose only notable trait was his sad blue eyes.

Blackmun stood, crossed the room, and barked, "You got anything?"

Nolan remained at the door, peering around at the men in the front room.

"Are you just going to stand there with your dick in your hand?" asked Ewing.

"No, sir."

"Well?"

Nolan entered the parlor. "Well, we found Michael Rosen's car," he said, addressing Blackmun.

"Where?" asked the mayor.

"Out toward Milpitas. 'Bout seven or so miles from here. Abandoned. Lights were left on."

"Witnesses?"

"We're searching."

"Find 'em."

The mayor gestured to Blackmun. "See if anybody saw the Studebaker."

"Right," said Blackmun, blank-faced as ever.

"The Bureau's guy will be coming in on the train tomorrow evening. Pick him up and put him up somewhere. Hotel Sainte Claire. He'll need to be here for a while. You got that? Can you arrange that?" asked the mayor.

The mayor and Blackmun looked at Nolan, who appeared surprised and murmured. "Yes, sir."

"Aren't you gonna ask who you're picking up?" asked the mayor.

"Who am I—?"

The mayor interrupted, "Name's Louis Cooper, The seven o'clock from the city. That's p.m. You got that?"

"Yes." Nolan smiled obligingly.

Blackmun dismissed his men. Ewing ventured, "Well, how in the hell can we turn this whole event to our advantage?"

"I'm not sure we can. We're just trying to keep a lid on all of this," replied Blackmun as they settled again in the front room.

"And that's precisely why the Bureau is coming and helping out," said the mayor. "I don't like it any more than you, having some federal agent poking around in our affairs. Things are tough enough with these outside agitators. But why did Rosen have to get himself kidnapped?"

"We know that Rosen gambled, whored, got into things he should not have gotten into," said Blackmun.

"We don't want to crucify Rosen. We need him," said Ewing.

The mayor nodded in agreement. "We need to guide this thing along. The last thing we need is another Lindbergh situation. We need to get ahead of this."

"We've got all our men assigned to this. We're looking under every rock, into each cesspool, even behind all the pulpits to bring in these kidnappers," Blackmun assured him.

The mayor did not look convinced.

Ewing smiled thinly. The wheels were in motion, and where it might stop, who knew? He followed Blackmun out the front door. Several patrolmen were still in the dark yard, standing around, waiting for orders.

"Get moving," Ewing snapped. "Don't stomp on the missus's begonias."

By the time he and Blackmun reached the sidewalk, they were greeted by a familiar pair of newspapermen, one from the *Mercury-Herald*, the other from the *Examiner*.

"Hear there's been a kidnapping? What's the story?" asked one.

"No story. Just a friendly chat with the mayor," said Blackmun.

"At midnight? Usually, the mayor's fast asleep by ten," said the other reporter.

"Go on home, fellas," continued Blackmun. "If there is something, we'll let you all know in good time. You know, we'll hold a nice powwow with all you heathens."

"There's a rumor that Michael Rosen was captured at gunpoint. Can you confirm or deny?"

"Fellas, you'll know when you know," replied Ewing.

"Also heard that you've found his car."

"Keep those rumors to yourselves," said Blackmun as they sauntered away into the black night.

10

His hands were violently shaking. Winston could not place the phone receiver back on the hook. By the third attempt he was successful but remained sitting in the booth, numb to the outside chatter of people parading by him. He could hardly breathe or move aside from blinking. He jerked when an old coot banged with his cane against the glass door. The man pressed his face against the glass. The face appeared misshapen. Bulging eyes that were too brightly blue, a nose damaged pink. Winston opened the door. "Are you done yet?"

Winston was done. Clutching the two envelopes, he stepped out of the booth as the man squeezed by him, saying something about the "folly of misbegotten youth."

Winston walked stiffly out through the revolving door, praying he hadn't roused the curiosity of the house dick, who was back at his post, calmly surveying the lobby. Outside, the pavement seemed alive with gesticulating passersby and animated babble. He plodded up Market, turned left on a street he did not know, and continued to walk. One block. Then another. By then, the street was quieter and darker. He looked up and saw that a streetlamp had been busted. Something so bright and promising had been reduced to a crumpled stump.

He heard a scraping sound. A figure shrouded by a blanket that covered most of its head stumbled in front of him. "Brother, can you spare two bits? I'm no bum."

"No change. Nothing," replied Winston.

"I was an honest man. I used to work up there." The man pointed to a tall building in the distance.

"I haven't a thing. I'm sorry."

"What's in the envelope? I bet you've got something to spare." The man approached and Winston pushed him away. He half ran back to Market Street. When he reached the Plymouth, he got out the key, slumped into the driver's seat, locked the doors around him, put his hands at ten and twelve on the steering wheel. And watched. Stared at humanity making its way up and down the spine of San Francisco.

He had followed instructions. It was part of his initiation. It did not give him solace. He gathered himself and opened the seal of the final envelope. It was marked Pier. Inside were more instructions and, curiously, a wallet.

> Go to Pier 32 where the Lurline is berthed. Make sure the wallet is on that ship. Leave car there.

Winston drove the Plymouth around the block and then headed down Market. When he reached the Ferry Building, he turned south on the Embarcadero. All along the waterfront, the bulkhead buildings appeared as brooding fortresses. He had guessed his direction correctly, and the pier numbers on the bulkheads increased in even numbers until he saw Pier 32 emblazoned on one of them. He parked the car beneath a stub of a hill to be used as a bridge footing for a span that would cross the bay.

Emerging from the Plymouth, Winston felt the rush of moisture in the cold wind and heard the swoop of flapping gulls overhead. Across the street, he spotted the dark silhouette of the top of a passenger ship he guessed was the SS *Lurline*, bound south to Los Angeles or across the Pacific to Singapore or Shanghai.

The Pier 32 gate was open. Moving stealthily, he entered the cavernous pier shed, surprised to find it devoid of guards and longshoremen. The smell of grease and salt hung in the air. It was mostly quiet, except for the sound of the tide smacking against the *Lurline*. Squinting in the darkened shed, he looked for a way onto the pier apron. It all appeared closed off, secure from intruders. He crept farther in, hugging the wall, until he made out a dim opening on his right. A roll-up door that would lead to the wooden pier apron. When he got onto the open apron, he stared up at the mighty bulk of the *Lurline*. The hull was so high he could not see the ship's railing. A good twenty feet of water separated him from the ship. No gangway in sight. At the far end of the apron, off to his left, maybe fifty yards, maybe a hundred, he saw the flicker of handheld lanterns. Then, there were shouts.

Winston moved back toward the side of the shed, trying to hide in the shadows. He counted five or six men, indistinct figures behind the swaying glow of the lanterns. They were coming his way. Winston took the wallet from his coat pocket and considered throwing it hard in hopes it could reach the deck. More likely the wallet would miss its mark, bounce off the ship's hull, and end up in the bay. He tucked the wallet back in his pocket and ran. His foot caught on a mooring bollard, and he went down in a heap. Pain rocketed through his left leg. The shouts grew louder. He got his bearings and slipped beneath the roll-up door. No one was inside the pier shed, though he still heard shouting from outside. He half limped, half ran out the front gate of Pier 32 and back onto the Embarcadero. Alone on the street, breathing hard, he searched for the Plymouth. The car was no longer there. He stared at where it should have been. He remembered exactly where he had parked, but it was gone. Vanished. Was this part of the initiation?

He still had the wallet and thus had failed. He hesitated on the pavement, deciding what his next move might be. The Ferry Building glimmered in the distance. If he made it there, he could try to blend in among the locals and perhaps escape on a late-night ferry.

It was a ten-minute hike. His pursuers seemed to have given up. His leg was throbbing by the time he managed to enter the terminal.

He dodged people in a hurry to buy last-minute tickets and found the waiting room, half full of passengers. Wiped his brow, caught his breath. Sat on one of the empty benches and rubbed his sore leg. An inordinate number of port security guards as well as police officers were stationed at the gates, asking questions, apparently searching for someone. Winston stayed put. If he could appear relaxed, he might remain undetected. The bells in the clock tower atop the Ferry Building tolled midnight. The terminal was about to close. Soon, he would be forced to move again.

On the bench in the waiting room was a discarded evening edition of the *San Francisco Call*. He grabbed the stray paper. Pretended to be casually reading it until calls for the last ferry to Oakland were announced on a loudspeaker. He wondered whether there was even a ferry to Alviso anymore. Not at this hour. Maybe not even in this decade. Since they'd taken his car, how would he ever return to San Jose? Who had proposed such a preposterous scheme?

He took out the wallet from his pocket and, from behind the newspaper, examined its contents: a California Automobile Association card. A Standard Oil card. The name embossed on each of them identified the cardholder: MICHAEL ROSEN. This was a cruel initiation joke. He had gone to Santa Clara with Rosen. He knew the name. Hell, everyone knew the name. Why would he have Rosen's wallet? Was it really his wallet?

The lights in the waiting area began to flicker. The last of the passengers started to queue up for the final ferry, scheduled to embark at quarter past. A cleanup crew had already assembled within the terminal and started to pick up the daily litter, mop down the floors so they could be done with it. Having surveilled the last of the outbound passengers, the cops had moved from the gates to the terminal doors, where they stood watching anyone leaving.

Ditching Rosen's wallet seemed like his only solution. He jammed it into the wooden slats of the bench in such a way that it would not be easily detected by the cleanup crew or the bums who would later do their level best to find discarded items for resale on the street. He folded the newspaper and placed it on his lap, again wondering how he might return home. Would the trains still be running at this hour? He tried to remember where the station was.

An older man in a gray suit and bowler hat approached and sat next to him. Winston squirmed.

"Nice evening for a ferry, don't you think?" asked the man.

"Yeah. Beautiful night."

"Yes. A nice night, all right. You look like a young man who might need some help."

"No. No, thanks."

The man had nestled in close. The place began to clear out. The cleanup crew was drawing near. The ticket windows were noisily shut. The last call rang out for the final ferry of the night.

"A man in need is a man who needs help. See those men over there?" Winston's unwanted companion gestured toward port security, who were still checking the tickets of each of the queued passengers. "Eventually, those guys will begin to investigate those who remain here in the building." He used his thumb to point to the police officers huddled near the main entrance.

"I've nothing to hide."

"I'm sure you don't."

Winston said nothing.

"On the other hand, you can never be so sure, can you?"

"Mister, what are you trying to sell?"

"Nothing, son. Just offering some assistance."

"I was just leaving."

"Not so fast." As Winston began to rise, the man grabbed his arm and whispered, "What we are offering is safe passage."

"What?"

"The name is Mr. White. We've come to rescue you from your predicament."

"We?"

"Oh, yes, I forgot to mention my colleagues over there." White gestured again, and across the waiting room, two men tipped the brims of their fedoras. "It's time to go."

Still holding Winston's arm, Mr. White stood, insisting that Winston follow suit. The two men in fedoras approached. One of the men took him by the other arm while the other reached down to the bench, removed the wallet, and stuck it into his pocket.

"Let's not make a fuss," said White, showing Winston the way out. White's companions joined in behind. They strode by the cops, who looked the other way.

"Where are you taking me?" asked Winston as they exited to the street.

"None other than the Hotel Whittier. You will be most comfortable there."

A car drove up. Winston saw no choice but to climb in. Mr. White took out a handkerchief and placed it over his face. The smell was pungent and sweet. That was all he remembered.

The next morning Winston awoke in an unfamiliar room, his legs dangling over the edge of a bed. The window shade was partway down, but a strip of gauze over the sill allowed in sunlight. He sat up cautiously, dizzy and nauseous.

The room was furnished like any other bedroom. It was only when he pulled the single shade open and glanced outside that he realized he must be in a hotel. There was nothing out of the ordinary in the room except for a train ticket on the bureau. The unused stub read SAN FRANCISCO TO SAN JOSE—he was still in the city. He stuffed the ticket in his pants pocket, found his coat on the floor, and stumbled out the door, into the hall, and down the staircase, gripping the rail. When he got to the lobby, he figured he must have gone down four floors. He could not recall any lobby. In fact, the night before was a blur. He glanced at his watch; it was almost 11 a.m.

He managed to reach the front desk, waited his turn until a bald clerk with a thin mustache and beady eyes motioned him over.

"Should I pay you?" asked Winston.

"What room?"

"I don't know. Fourth floor."

"Name?"

"Richter. Winston."

The clerk examined his hotel register. "You are all paid up."

11

My mother was sometimes tearful when she spoke of an earlier San Jose, before the orchards receded and the tract housing paved over old memories. A simpler, gentler, more pastoral era. Reviewing the archives of San Jose from the early twentieth century, however, revealed a more complex view. A 1902 pamphlet was circulated describing San Jose as the "Sodom of the Pacific Coast." The pamphlet declared there was rampant corruption "from the justice court and police department to the mayor's chair through all the city departments." That is something one might have expected to read about scandal-ridden San Francisco to the north, a city that at one time convinced itself vice was a necessary price to pay for economic growth. San Francisco reputedly managed its own vice operations to such an extent that Chicago crime boss Al Capone was known to lament: "Outsiders couldn't break into San Francisco." At the center of the San Francisco operation was a boss who wormed his way into the system by way of the bail bonds racket. He became so ingrained and powerful that no one could conduct vice or graft without his approval.

By the year 1933, the city of San Jose also had such a boss.

※

It was nearly two o'clock in the morning when the telephone rang and rang and the man in his pajamas switched on his bedside lamp, put on his striped cotton robe, and padded down the hall, past where his wife lay asleep in her separate room, to the front room where the house phone resided. He flicked on a light, then picked up the phone.

"Ripley here. Yeah?"

"Boss, just checking in."

"Everyone follow the script?" He settled into his chestnut leather club chair.

"We made sure. They did the business."

Ripley ripped open a box of Parodi cigars. "Good. What about the bootlegger?"

"He don't know up from down."

"Passalacqua will like that. What else?" He picked up a cigar and stuck it in his mouth.

His wife poked her head into his room as she cinched the belt of her robe. "Can I get you something?"

"Not now, Zedmere." He motioned to her that he did not want to be disturbed.

"Tea?"

He glared at her, raised his arm as if to sweep her away with the cigar. His wife retreated back to her room. "What was that again?" he said into the phone.

"We checked that the call went through."

"Good. The wallet?" He searched for a match on the side table.

"The *Lurline* sets sail at noon today. He said someone will find it."

No matches. "Hang on."

Ripley got up, went to his desk, searched through his drawers, and at last found a match and lit the Parodi. Satisfied, he drew the smoke into his mouth like he was sucking on a straw. Then returned, nestled back into his chair. "Where is our impressionable little soldier now?"

"Hotel Whittier."

"And the others?" He rotated the cigar, and a spiral of smoke rose to the ceiling.

"Same."

"They're all clammed up?" He let the smoke linger in his mouth and enjoyed the rich blend of tobacco flavors.

"We'll make sure they're good."

"Are we all clear tonight?"

"Yes, sir."

"I suppose that's all we can ask for."

He hung up, turned off the light, and took another puff in the darkness.

Later, when he walked by his wife's bedroom, he saw her light on. She was sitting up in bed, working on a crossword puzzle.

12

The morning sunshine uncompromisingly imposed itself through the window of the Hotel Sainte Claire. Bureau Agent Louis Cooper sat at the small room desk with his hat pushed down over his forehead so the wide brim shaded his eyes. His train to San Jose, by way of San Francisco, had arrived late the night before. A police car was there to meet him. A pale-skinned cop with sad blue eyes introduced himself as Officer Nolan. Cooper asked him the distance to the hotel. "Mile. Maybe a bit more."

Wanting to stretch his legs, he declined the ride and asked Officer Nolan to point him the right direction. Nolan shrugged as Cooper started to hoof it to the Sainte Claire. "You can't miss it" had been the parting words. Now the Bureau agent rubbed his eyes and squinted out the window. The sunshine was at least more welcoming than the rain in Kansas City, his last temporary home before the California assignment.

A messenger had shoved a packet through the narrow gap beneath his door. Cooper used a penknife to open the thick envelope and leafed through the file it contained. The kidnapping victim was Michael Rosen, age twenty-two, a recent graduate of the University of Santa Clara, currently employed as the executive vice president at his father's store, Rosen's Department Store in downtown San Jose. On November 6, at approximately 6 p.m., subject departed the store, walked alone to Lightston Alley, directly west of the store, to the lot where his green Studebaker roadster was parked.

According to his father, Alexander Rosen, subject was to pick him up by 6:20 p.m. at the Sainte Claire Club, a few blocks away, where the father had a business meeting. Together they should have driven to a chamber of commerce event at the San Jose Country Club in the eastern foothills. Subject never arrived. At approximately 6:40 p.m., the father telephoned the department store and was told subject had left. When Alexander called his home, his eldest daughter reported that subject was not there, either. The father placed his next call back to his store and asked that an employee pick him up. Within ten minutes, an employee delivered him to the country club. The father reported that he was annoyed rather than alarmed.

The sun had warmed the room considerably. Cooper went over to the chest of drawers to pour a glass of water from a pitcher left earlier. Before taking a sip, he took off his fedora and made an appraisal of the face staring back at him in the mirror. The lines that creased his forehead. Puffy skin that was predominantly pink. Purple smudges beneath bloodshot eyes. A fading hairline, combed straight back, making his forehead seem extended. While the top was still dark, the sides had already turned gray. All of which made him appear older than his forty-two years. The cause was not alcohol. More likely his duty, his fate. This was what happened to a civil servant. He sighed, drank the water, put on his hat, and went back to his file.

At approximately 7:45 p.m., the club's maître d' informed the father that he had a call. The call was not from his son but from James O'Neill, his son's friend. Subject was to have picked him up as well, as both were due at a 7:30 p.m. public speaking class at the Hotel De Anza, also downtown. Subject never arrived.

At about 8 p.m., the father placed a call home and spoke again to the eldest daughter, who stated that subject was still missing. He then placed a number of other calls and received no information regarding the whereabouts of his son. At that point, the father decided to call the police and spoke with the police chief. Blackmun received the call at 8:12 p.m.

The father then called O'Neill, who drove him home. The family was concerned, but Rosen's daughter stated it was not unusual for her brother to forget appointments.

At 10:37 p.m., Rosen's daughter answered the phone to a voice indicating subject had been kidnapped and a ransom demanded. The father again called Blackmun. The police chief was not immediately available, so the father contacted the county sheriff, Elmore Ewing. Ewing immediately asked the telephone company to trace all calls and put a description of subject's automobile on the state teletype. All squad cars within an hour's radius of downtown San Jose were alerted. Once informed, Blackmun and the San Jose Police soon followed suit. Within an hour, roadblocks and ferry stops were established throughout Santa Clara County and the Bay Area.

At 11:14 p.m., police received a call from the country club manager. Having finished his evening shift, the manager drove home toward Niles, a small town northeast of San Jose. He had been made aware by the father that subject had missed their appointment and reported that along a stretch of orchards on Oakland Road, he saw a familiar vehicle that seemed abandoned. The headlights were on. The manager believed the vehicle to be the same green Studebaker owned by subject. At a nearby roadhouse, he called the sheriff's department.

A squad car was dispatched and confirmed that license plate was that of subject's vehicle. There was no trace of subject in the vicinity nor any evidence of foul play. When asked how the manager knew of Rosen's car, the answer was that everyone in the county recognized that Studebaker roadster.

Cooper put the file down, took off his hat, and swirled his pen around, watching the shadows it made on the desk. His instructions were explicit: Investigate the crime in spite of local incompetence.

He had already lost valuable time getting to San Jose. He rose from the desk and scanned the city's geometry from the fifth-story window. Nice-looking middle-class town, but every place had its flabby underbelly. Room service had earlier brought up a morning cup of coffee. That cup didn't do the deed. At least, not yet. Eschewing the elevator, he took the stairs to the lobby, picked up a newspaper from the front desk, and headed into the hotel restaurant. He was greeted by a maître d who said, "Sit anywhere you want."

The place was nearly devoid of patrons. Cooper found a booth along the window that overlooked City Hall Park. Not much happening on the street. A couple of cars fluttered by. Nothing in the park. Except for some old crows.

"Coffee?" The waitress ambled up to the table. She had bleached-blond hair, rose lips, skinny eyebrows, and a stained white uniform.

"Why not?"

She poured. He took a gulp. Tepid.

"What can I get you?" she said, unenthusiastically.

"Steak and eggs."

"How about a burger?"

Cooper eyed this woman who probably wished she were in San Francisco, but the train fare only got her this far. "Is that all you got?"

She looked at him, blankly. He nodded.

"How do you want your eggs?"

"Poached."

She walked away and called back toward the kitchen, "One cow pie and a pair of dead eyes."

Cooper scanned the morning news. The Rosen kidnapping splashed the headlines. There was already a series of eyewitness accounts. One person interviewed claimed to have seen Rosen driving alone up in the Los Gatos foothills. Another found him gambling in the bayside enclave of Alviso. Someone saw him boarding the *Lurline* up in San Francisco. Everyone wanted to crack the case and see their handprints made famous in concrete.

His breakfast was unceremoniously delivered to his table.

"Enjoy."

"I will." With his fork, Cooper poked the whites just enough so that the yellow oozed out, creating a moat around the burger. He dug in.

Between bites, he flipped through the paper and read letters written to the editor. One screamed that the police had not done nearly enough, had not shaken all the leaves from the trees, and were sitting on their hands. Another claimed the abduction was the work of the communists, the same ones who had caused the workers' riot downtown some months back. Communists would no doubt stoop to kidnap a local businessman to incite a revolution. A third pointed the finger at those shiftless drifters who had lately been scrounging for jobs, hanging around in St. James Park, staying in those boardinghouses. They'd do anything for a quick buck. Another rant blamed the Mexicans, who could never be trusted. They would be itching to slash the throat of any White citizen. Yet another opined against the bootleggers who wanted another shot at infamy now that Prohibition was coming to an end.

Cooper looked up and waved his hand. The waitress skillfully avoided his gesture. Just as he started to get up, she sauntered over.

"Could I get another cup?" he asked.

She turned, retrieved a coffee pot, and returned. Cooper estimated that it took her two and a half minutes to achieve this.

"Thanks."

"Don't mention it."

"Can I ask you something?"

"Sure, sweetheart." There wasn't an ounce of sincerity.

"What do you make of this kidnapping?"

She put the tap on the pot and stood holding it loosely, her free arm planted on her hip as she stared down at him. "You know what I think? There are too many big noses who have insinuated themselves in this town."

Cooper knew exactly what she meant. "Have you ever met any of the Rosens?"

"Sure. I've been to their store."

"Ever run into Michael Rosen?"

"Who hasn't?" A smile was pasted across her face.

"And?"

"And what?" The smile instantly dissolved. "I ain't saying, mister." She sashayed back toward the double doors that led to the kitchen. As she disappeared, Cooper remained staring fixedly at the swinging doors.

13

The man with the aquiline nose leaned back in the rocking chair on his stoop as he perused the morning edition of the *Mercury-Herald*. He read enough, folded the paper, and flung it unintentionally in the direction of his orange tabby. The cat opened its eyes and looked nonplussed at the newspaper, then went back to enjoying its snooze. Angelo Gumina thought that was a splendid response.

He closed his eyes as well, inhaled slowly. Relaxed and organized his thoughts. Harold Tierney was supposed to have gotten into Michael Rosen's Studebaker. Tierney was to have been the driver. Earle Hansen was to have been following in his own car. They had been instructed to drive to the designated house along Alum Rock Avenue. At that point, Hansen was to have placed a call to the elder Rosen at the country club. An agreement would have been made. An arrangement settled on for the promised debt repayment. Tierney would then deliver young Rosen to the country club. That was how it should have played out. That was business. No more. No less.

And yet, Michael Rosen remained missing. As were Tierney and Hansen. Through his contact at the police department, Angelo had learned that the Studebaker was found abandoned. That was also not part of the script.

There was a honk from a car horn. Angelo opened his eyes and rose from the rocking chair, bent down and patted the tabby for good luck. Walking down the steps to the sidewalk, he climbed in the open passenger door.

"Where to?" asked his driver.

"Campbell. We're paying a visit to a family friend."

His driver knew what that meant. Campbell was a small town nearly seven miles to the south, past the canneries, through a string of orchards. The town did not have much to boast of. It was a smudge of disheveled buildings scattered among rows and rows of prune and cherry trees.

When they arrived, Angelo leaped out and strode past the open gate and up the stairs to the Tierney residence. He rapped on the door. A man in his seventies with short white hair wearing suspenders opened the front door, keeping the screen door closed.

"Yes, what can I do for you?" muttered the man.

"Good morning. I'm with the Salesian Brothers. Your son, Harold, played piano for our celebration last Easter. I didn't have his telephone number, but luckily he gave me his home address. I would like to check on his availability. We'd love to have him once again for our Christmas festivities coming up."

"I'm sorry, but my son is away. He's in Stockton." The old man looked nervous, perhaps because he didn't get too many visitors out here in the sticks.

"Stockton?"

Wiping his hand across his cheek, the man said, "He's been filling in for his sister. She's the organist there at the Methodist church. And you are?"

"Robert Bello." Angelo bowed and backed away. "Thank you. We'll track him down there."

"Do you want her address?" The old man stuck his hands in his trouser pockets.

"No, that is not necessary."

The man started to close the door. Angelo abruptly asked, "How did your son get to Stockton? Does he have his own car?"

"His own . . . oh, my, no. He does not have a car."

"Would he have borrowed one, or did someone give him a ride?"

The man hesitated, then said, "He took the bus from San Jose."

"How did he get to San Jose?"

The man responded too quickly. "I drove him in the family car."

"And when was that?"

"I don't know. A couple of days ago."

"I appreciate your time," said Angelo. "The Lord will provide."

"He will indeed."

Angelo heard the thump of the front door closing as he turned and headed back down the steps. The man was covering up the disappearance of his son, but he likely didn't know much. It would not take much effort to check up on the Methodist church in Stockton. He already knew that Harold's sister worked there as an organist. That would not matter. When Tierney agreed to the job, the plan was for Sal Booksin to pick him up on Central Avenue in Campbell and get him to San Jose by the appointed afternoon. Booksin, though, had received a message from Tierney saying he was already in town. Angelo paused, one hand on the open door of his car. That message should have set off an alarm.

He got in and told the driver to return to San Jose and drop by the house that Earle Hansen rented on Bird Avenue, south of downtown.

The house on Bird was modest, with weedy shrubs in front and a tall, thin palm tree that seemed to hang in the air. Once again, while the driver waited in the car, Angelo knocked on the front door. He knew Hansen had been living with his lady friend, Belinda West. No one answered. He pounded again, harder this time.

He tried peeking through the front window, but the shade was drawn tightly. When he motioned to his driver, the man reached in the back seat and retrieved an iron crowbar, got out, and walked with Angelo around to the back of the house. Once at the back door, Angelo looked around for any neighbor who might be snooping and then gave a nod. The driver pried open the door, and with a rip and a shrug, the house was available for Angelo's inspection.

Angelo entered Hansen's house; the driver stood guard. The place was not only empty, but there was also no appearance of recent activity. In the kitchen, the refrigerator was nearly empty. A half loaf of stale bread. Some beer. Angelo picked up a milk bottle and smelled it. It had not turned yet. There wasn't much in the pantries. Glasses and plates had been put away. Nothing looked awry. On the dining room table, he found unopened letters postmarked some days ago. A folded newspaper on the couch in the front room was dated the day of the pickup. He had not seen any recent papers on the front porch. Someone must have snatched them.

He checked the bedroom, which held a faint scent of perfume. Dressers were half filled. No trunk or suitcases in the closet. He checked the wastebasket in that room. Daily detritus, except beneath a used tissue he found a stray business card that read LETCHER'S AUTOMOTIVE SHOWROOM. He knew the place. There were pen marks on the card, but he could not make out what was written. He slipped the card into his vest pocket.

Back outside, no one was about, but Angelo noticed a neighbor's window shade that had been half open was now closed all the way.

"Where to, boss?"

Angelo gave the driver the business card.

Within ten minutes, Angelo's driver stopped the car at Letcher's across from St. James Park. They both climbed out, crossed the street, and, seeing that the roll-up doors to the showroom were closed, circled around the side and came up to the garage in back. The driver took out his crowbar from beneath his jacket and pried open the roll-up door. A juvenile delinquent could have done it in his sleep.

"Who's there?" said a voice as they stepped inside. "Mike, is that you?"

"Mike was called away," replied Angelo.

With his driver positioned behind him, Angelo slowly entered the garage office. A middle-aged man in a baggy suit sat amid a stack of papers. He glared at the intruders and snarled, "Who the hell are you?"

"Paying a visit."

The man folded his arms. "We're closed."

"On a Tuesday afternoon?"

"Yeah, what of it?"

"That's not good for business."

"What do you want?" asked the man.

"Information."

"So, read a newspaper."

Angelo gestured slightly to his driver, who came around him and approached the desk. The man's eyes widened as the crowbar came down fast. He stared at the crushed bones in his wrist. When the pain reached his brain, the man screamed and toppled from his chair, holding his injured wrist.

"Where is Hansen?"

"Who?" whimpered the man as he sprawled on the cement floor.

"Who do you work for?" asked Angelo.

The man hesitated. Angelo's driver knelt beside the man, grabbed his crippled wrist, and twisted. The man screamed. "No, please, no!"

The driver looked up at Angelo, who patiently drew a knife from his pocket and in the dim light twirled it around before methodically asking, "Who do you work for?"

The man wept. His pants darkened. Angelo ignored the stench of urine. At a nod, the driver grabbed both of the man's hands. Angelo placed his stiletto on the man's throat and kept it steady. The man's eyes widened. He squirmed. The knife nicked the jugular, drawing blood.

"Look what you have done to yourself," said Angelo.

The man looked pleadingly at him.

"What happened that night?"

"Don't know what you're talking about."

"I'll ask you one more time." Angelo applied more pressure with the sharp edge of his blade.

"A Plymouth. Taken on Seventh Street. That's all I did, I swear."

"And where did it go?"

"San Francisco."

"For what purpose?"

"Don't know."

"Who took it?"

"Didn't tell me."

"Who do you work for?"

No answer.

Angelo looked meaningfully at his driver. He held up the knife as the driver raised the crowbar and slammed it down on the man's other wrist. That wrist turned to jelly. The scream echoed through the garage.

"Passa . . ." It came out as a whisper.

"Who?" Angelo pointed the stiletto at the man's neck.

"Passalacqua" was the slow response.

Angelo knew the name. Paul Passalacqua. Big-league San Francisco racketeer.

"Passalacqua owns this place?"

"Nooooo."

"Who is behind this operation?"

The man on the floor squeezed his eyes shut and whimpered as if trying to make Angelo and his driver disappear by refusing to look at them.

Angelo placed his foot on the man's right wrist and pressed. A sickening, unintelligible sound came out of the man's mouth. Blood leaked out between his teeth.

"Where is Hansen? Tierney?" asked Angelo. He had to lean close to the man to hear the feeble response: "Whittier. Hotel Whittier."

14

Elbows on his desk, chin on knuckles, Police Chief Blackmun didn't change expressions as Agent Cooper strode into his office. The sheriff was there as well. Cooper kept his face equally neutral as he regarded them. Ewing finally glanced up and said, "What do you want?"

"You know who I am, why I'm here, and top of the morning to you," said Cooper. "Let's get down to it. What's the word on Michael Rosen?"

"Gone. Missing. Vanished," said Blackmun.

"Tell me something I don't know. What can you tell about him?"

"The heir apparent worked at his father's store. Went to the finest schools. Graduated from Santa Clara. Everyone seems to think he is, and I quote, 'gentle, affable, and considerate,'" replied Blackmun.

"Yeah, he's a regular Dick Powell," said Ewing.

"What else do you have?"

"I got loads. In fact, too much. The papers are screaming like it's Lindbergh's kid all over again."

"Let's hope it's not," said Blackmun. He sighed and creaked back in his swivel chair.

"When Rosen got himself kidnapped, every worm decided to get into the game to make a buck. And they've got to sell newspapers. And every son of a bitch thinks they've got a story to tell," said Ewing.

"What are the facts?"

Blackmun lowered his gaze and shrugged. Cooper knew what he was going to say before the police chief answered: "Everyone has a lead. I have a dozen leads already. Some half crocked, some halfway reasonable. But none of them are real until we check them out."

The police chief banged his fists on his desk, then got up and paced the length of the room.

"And so, which leads are promising?"

"Well, here are the top three. Number one: There's this Ruth Hillsdale who was sitting on her stoop waiting for her husband to return from work. Lives at the corner of Seventeenth and Berryessa. She swore that she spotted Rosen's Studebaker making a left up Berryessa. Without stopping. Said it happened at about six fifteen. The timing is right, and I've known Ruth for years. She's a good egg. It corroborates what the country club manager told us, except Rosen's car was found on Oakland Road. That's an extension of Thirteenth Street."

"Was Rosen alone?" asked Cooper.

"The car zipped right by her. She couldn't tell," said Blackmun.

"All right, whoever was driving could have easily doubled back. What else?"

"Number two: There's this Ernest Corral. He was driving his car up Thirteenth, by then the road to Oakland. He swears he saw¾"

"What time was this?" Cooper asked.

"About six twenty or so."

"What did Corral see?"

"A roadster, a Studebaker, he thinks, stopped along an orchard. The hood was raised. He thought someone was pretending to tinker with the engine."

"Alone? Why 'pretending'?"

"Alone, but not sure. 'Pretending' because Corral works as a foreman at CalPak, one of the canneries. He knows about machines and thought it didn't look quite right."

"Do we have a description of the man he saw?"

"No. He just thought it was odd."

"That's it? Didn't think to help the guy?"

"It was dark. He was late. Said the old lady wanted him home."

"And?"

"It might provide a clue. Or it might not. When we found the car, the gas tank was full, and the car was in good working order. But the car was found farther out on the road."

"Could it have been a rendezvous spot?"

"Maybe."

Cooper nodded, and the police chief continued with the third promising lead. "Fred Dore claims he saw Rosen parked alongside a bar with some little number on Alum Rock Avenue near King Road."

"Where's that?"

"Alum Rock is the extension of Santa Clara. It goes east up into the foothills."

"What time was that?"

"Dore said it was about nine fifteen."

"How can he be sure?"

"Because Dore had just listened to *Calling All Cars* on the radio," the chief told them. "The show ended at nine. He took his dog for a walk and says he saw Rosen across the street. Swears it was him. And a blond. In front of Winter's Café. The place is a dump. Attracts a drinking crowd."

"Aren't you supposed to enforce the law of the land?" Cooper asked.

"When you're the chief here, you can make that call. And yes, Winter's is also known for its gambling," replied Blackmun.

"Did Dore recognize the woman?"

"Not really."

"What do you mean?"

"Who can keep track?"

Ewing spat out a chuckle. "Rosen got around."

"All right. Did he gamble?" asked Cooper.

"Not more than most," said the police chief.

"In over his limit?"

Blackmun scratched his neck. "Can't find a soul who would corroborate that."

"Does he frequent the speakeasies much?"

"Who doesn't?" piped Ewing, who rubbed his belly.

"Drink too much?" asked Cooper.

"Witnesses say some, but not a lot. He can hold his own. Doesn't get sloppy," said Blackmun, clearly bored with the conversation.

"Did Rosen have any enemies?" Cooper persisted. "Did he lose his temper over debts or a woman?"

"Well, he's rich. He's got a fancy car. He's a Jew," said Ewing.

"Times are tough. People ought to behave better," said the chief.

"You really don't have much, do you?"

Ewing smiled.

After a pause, Blackmun surmised, "I'd wager this is local talent. The kidnappers knew Rosen's habits."

"How do you know that?"

"In these times, a rich kid attracts a lot of dollar signs. Flaunting it doesn't help. Neither does his last name. I'd wager it's probably some Okie or an Italian gang or Mexicans who did the deed," said Ewing.

"Could have been any one of them," agreed Blackmun.

"I'm guessing Okie. They'd do anything to make a buck. We should have kept them out of the valley. Or maybe the Mexicans. But they don't have the means to pull off a kidnapping. If they did, they'd be crucified," said Ewing.

Cooper gave Ewing a disgusted look. "What about the bootleggers? Up in the city, there are a lot of those businessmen. Parente. Passalacqua. Nichols. O'Malley. You got them here?"

"We've got it under control. Those guys don't venture much down here," said Blackmun.

"Amen to that," added Ewing, snapping his suspenders.

"I heard that you recently had some labor unrest," asked Cooper.

"What of it?" responded Ewing.

"Well, they raised a ruckus, but I think we showed them. Like I said, we're managing our own pretty well here. We don't have a Red problem," said Blackmun.

A police officer poked his head into the office. Blackmun gestured him in. The officer handed the chief a note. Blackmun read it and announced: "The San Francisco police found something. On the waterfront. Pier 32. A merchant marine went topside from his tanker this morning and noticed something on the railing."

"On the railing?" asked Cooper.

"A wallet. No cash, or so he said. But he did find something. According to the SFPD, he walked it over to the editor's desk of the *Examiner* and dumped a driver's license, a Standard Oil credit card, library card, membership to the California State Automobile Association, and business cards all in the name of..."

"Michael Rosen?"

"You got it."

15

The wind swept in sharply and blew leaves off the elms in St. James Park. They swirled about before reaching the ground already blanketed with red and yellow leaves. Thick, heavy gray clouds hovered above, scattering light throughout the park, waiting to pour. Clutching the lapels of her red-and-black checkered coat, Amelia hurried along to find Victoria pacing beneath the McKinley statue. Her friend's dark hair was disheveled, strands poking out from a lopsided floral headband. Her hands were on her hips, and she was leaning forward as if talking to herself.

"Sorry to interrupt."

"I'm so mad I could kick this old dead president." Victoria looked up and made a fist at McKinley. "A mediocre imperialist president controlled by robber barons. It's no wonder an anarchist plugged you."

Amelia offered a hug.

"A hug is what I need. Those rich cronies did it again."

"What did they do?"

After the hug, Victoria wiped a tear from her eye. "I've been suspended."

"For whatever reason?"

Victoria's voice became harsh, her cheeks reddened. "The dean of students charged that I behaved, and I quote, 'in a manner unbecoming of a young lady.' My 'extracurricular activities have proved to be incongruous with the standards required by this educational institution."' She raised her voice and used her hands to punctuate her outrage. "I was so mad sitting there listening, I could have grabbed his scrawny tie and shoved it down his throat."

"You didn't, I hope."

A sly smile emerged. "He reacted as if I did."

"Because of the demonstration? The union activities? Extracurricular can mean anything."

"He wouldn't say. He dismissed me." Victoria paused, then murmured, "I don't think I should have thrown that ashtray though."

Amelia's eyes widened. "What ashtray?"

"The one I grabbed from his office and nearly decked his secretary with as I stomped out."

"Nearly?"

"She was quick."

Amelia took hold of Victoria's hands. "You've got to catch your breath."

"Right." Victoria leaned against the brass cannon erected as part of the McKinley memorial. She took several deep breaths.

"Did you apologize to her?" Amelia asked.

"The secretary? I probably should have. I was too mad."

Amelia waited, knowing there was no use in rushing Victoria to say what else had happened.

"It may have been the organizing," Victoria said, calmer now. "It may have been because I was called in."

Amelia was stunned. "Called in? What?"

"By the cops. Aren't you listening?"

"I'm trying to keep pace with you," Amelia replied diplomatically.

"They came to my place. Asked questions."

"What kind of questions?"

"What was said."

"I'm lost."

"A cop knocked on my door. He said that I had to come with

him. He took me to the Hall of Justice. I met the sheriff. *Ew*-wing. He wanted to know what was said."

"Still lost."

"What was said between me and Michael Rosen."

"Oh, wow," said Amelia.

"I told the sheriff what Michael said. Which wasn't much."

"Wow," Amelia said again.

"I know. Then he asked all sorts of questions about the cannery union, as if there were a connection. I have no idea what that might be. How does his disappearance have anything to do with that? Then he pointed his finger at me and said that I must behave. Like I was a little girl."

"Lucky you didn't have an ashtray."

"I wish I had something. Next time." Victoria squinted. "But the point was that he thought there was a connection."

Amelia turned her back to the wind. A few raindrops fell. "Someone must have been watching the union office," she guessed. "They saw you cross the street. Saw you and Michael Rosen."

"Exactly. But who were they watching? Me or him?"

"Why were they watching at all?"

A heavier gust disturbed a flock of blackbirds roosting in the elms. Amelia watched them flutter away. "What we know is that the sheriff didn't like what he heard," she said slowly.

Victoria nodded. "I got the riot act speech from the sheriff. Next day, the school suspends me. They're in cahoots."

"A suspension is a warning." Even Amelia didn't believe those words.

Victoria clasped her hands together briefly and then glared up at the statue. She spat, "I swear there is a conspiracy of these entitled McKinleys. They must gather in some luxurious room somewhere, suck on their cheroots, and spiel out what is gloriously right and how they will right what they think is wrong. They're wretched, limp old coots."

Tired of pacing, Victoria took a seat next to Amelia on the cement memorial steps. They stared out at the trees swaying in the wind. There were few people in the park. The civil servants were back in their offices by now. An older couple quickened their pace past a few drifters who were lounging, smoking butts, playing cards on the brown grass, but even they knew the rain was coming. A pair of blues stood by the nearby water fountain that had been turned off, unsure whether to harass the drifters or flee the inevitable.

Victoria raised her fist. "I want to go right back in there and give that sheriff some business."

Amelia looked up. "It's really going to rain."

The older couple left the park. The drifters moved on. The cops decided to seek shelter.

"Could someone in the union be an informer?" asked Amelia.

"It's hard to imagine, but there's always a couple of turncoats."

Amelia folded her arms. "Maybe my father can help. He has a knack for finding things out. He hears things all the time. That's his job."

16

A couple of mornings after his meeting with the local law, Cooper again sat in the hotel's restaurant, ready to plunge into a stack of flapjacks. He had barely raised his fork when he received a message delivered from the front desk, informing him to come immediately to city hall. He looked longingly at his plate of food, took a quick swig of coffee, then got up and strode quickly through the park to police headquarters.

As he ascended the stairs to the police offices, the day guard motioned that the meeting was already in progress. Indeed, when Cooper opened the door to the main conference room, an entire team of investigators was assembled, and he caught Blackmun mid-sentence.

"... may come in handy," Blackmun was saying. He glanced at the late arrival, exasperated. "About time you showed up, Agent Cooper."

Cooper did not apologize.

"For your edification, there's this Amaral family," said Blackmun. "They own an orchard near where Rosen's Studebaker was found on Oakland Road outside of the city."

"They just found out about the disappearance?" asked one of the men. Officer Delaney. Delaney stood a little too straight, much too attentive, eager to please. Cooper immediately judged him to be one of those get-along types that would be guaranteed eventual promotion. Doubted that Delaney could even spell "obsequious" let alone knew what it meant.

"They don't have a telephone, radio. They don't get the newspaper. Don't ask me. They're Portuguese," said Sheriff Ewing, purposely mispronouncing so it came out "Portogees."

"Didn't your men canvass the entire area days ago? How did you miss them?" asked Cooper.

Ewing looked blankly at Cooper, then gestured to Blackmun.

"Ned, answer the man's question," Blackmun ordered.

Delaney acted surprised, blinked up at Cooper, who hadn't yet taken a seat at the conference table. "The Amarals must have been out somewhere. Maybe in the orchards. Maybe, I don't know," he sputtered.

"Maybe boozing, maybe sleeping it off," declared Ewing. "The point is they were unavailable until now."

"And what information did you receive from this family?" asked Cooper.

"When one of my patrolmen met them, the man of the house said he had been out. But Louie Amaral said his wife had seen cars coming and going about six thirty that evening," answered Blackmun.

"Does this wife have a name?" asked Cooper.

"Answer the man," directed the police chief.

"Madeline Amaral," said Delaney.

Blackmun waved his hand. "Proceed."

Delaney took out a notebook from his vest pocket. "Madeline Amaral said each evening she gathers firewood from behind their barn. That night when she had an armload of wood, she heard a car approaching. Then saw a flashing of lights. Then, again. Like it was a signal. Mrs. Amaral watched the car park about thirty yards away. The headlights were then turned off. She thought a man got out of the vehicle and just waited there. He was smoking a pipe or a cigarette. The wind was blowing in her direction, and she smelled it."

"One man?" asked Cooper. "Could there have been someone else inside?

"She couldn't tell," said Delaney. "She thought it odd and stayed put. Then, minutes later, she saw another set of headlights coming down their road, going slowly. This second car comes up, flashing its headlights, then stops near the first car. Both cars' headlights were then turned off, and she couldn't see much."

"What did she hear?"

"Someone telling someone to get out. One of them said something to the effect of 'Come on, big boy, get in here.' Another voice said, 'Are you sure we're on the right road?'"

"Two voices," said Blackmun.

"Possibly Rosen inside one of the cars," said Cooper.

"There's more," Delaney continued. "They made an exchange. The second car put on its headlights. Right away, one of them said, 'Kill the lights.' But before that's done, Mrs. Amaral thought she could make out three men now in the first car."

"Okay, after the transfer, there are three in one car. Maybe one guy remaining in the other," said Cooper. "Did she see anybody else in that second car?"

"It was dark."

"Then what happened?" asked Blackmun.

"Well, sir, the first car took off. But then the second car left as well."

"Let me see if I got this straight. Two cars. Only two people speak, but three men switch cars. The first car departs with those three, leaving at least a single driver in the remaining car," determined Blackmun.

"We're talking at least three perpetrators," said Cooper.

"Plus, the victim," added Blackmun.

"Could Mrs. Amaral identify whether either of the cars was a Studebaker?" asked Cooper.

"She thought one of them might have been a Studebaker. But then she said she didn't know the different makes."

"She's a big help," sighed Ewing.

"She said it was dark," said Delaney.

"How could she even tell?" asked Ewing. "Rosen's Studebaker was not found on the Amaral property but in another location at least three miles south. That was where the club manager found it."

"Remember that club manager told us the headlights were still on," said Blackmun.

"Likely meant to be found," concluded Cooper.

"It's a wonder that the battery held out so long," said Butler, a deputy sheriff who up to this point had remained silent. Butler had the type of face that never would be picked out in a lineup. Unremarkable.

"Then we can surmise there were at least three people involved in the abduction. Two perpetrators in a car of unknown make, plus their victim, took off from Amaral's place. Another man took the second car, probably Rosen's Studebaker that was ditched three miles south along an orchard. But there might be one more," said Cooper.

"More than three kidnappers?" asked Delaney.

"The Studebaker is abandoned. Its driver walks away? Not likely. The driver would have been picked up by someone in yet another car." Cooper looked at Delaney, then Blackmun. "Quite a convention you got here. Are there any other reports?"

"Did she give any description of the men she did manage to see?" Ewing interjected.

"Couldn't see much," replied Delaney.

"But she heard something. When she heard the men speak, what did they sound like?" asked Cooper.

"Not sure what you mean," said Delaney.

"They spoke English, right? Did she detect any accents?" asked Blackmun.

"Mrs. Amaral said they spoke like, uh, regular Americans," responded Delaney.

"They spoke like Americans?" Cooper repeated. "What does that actually mean?"

"Consider the source," grunted Ewing.

Cooper sighed inwardly. He was hungry. He needed more coffee. And it was going to be a long day. He glanced at Ewing with barely concealed disdain. "Yes, indeed, consider the source," he said. He was not referring to Mrs. Amaral.

17

Winston Richter sat peering out the open passenger window as Billy Snyder piloted a brand-new DeSoto Airstream around the narrow mountain curves above Los Gatos, about fifteen miles south of San Jose. Surrounded by a lush canopy of pines and redwoods, Winston could only wonder whether the Committee would ever get him a space in the law school. There had been no news, no nothing. Winston remained in limbo.

Everyone else was searching for clues about the fate of Michael Rosen. The university campus had been in high panic in the days after the kidnapping. Because Michael was a recent graduate and well acquainted with the community, the school's president, Father Seebach, halted all instruction and directed students and select administrative staff to conduct a thorough search throughout the valley and beyond. Fr. Seebach had his assistant, Wilford Kishi, organize the manhunt.

At seven thirty that morning, Kishi had addressed the student body gathered in the school's auditorium. Listed on a large blackboard, pairs of students were assigned to investigate different remote routes. Some vehicles used in the search were owned by the students. Others were donated for use by local auto dealers. Winston had been paired up with Snyder, a college senior and the entitled son of the man who controlled the largest fleet of new cars in the valley.

The Snyder family had the means of getting whatever they wanted. It was cruel that Billy, without much effort, would inherit an executive position at one of the Snyder dealerships, while Winston dreamed of never rolling dough in his father's bakery again.

Now here he was, sitting next to a red-haired, pasty-faced Snyder, who constantly wore a scarlet-and-white letterman varsity school jacket even though he never played on any of the college teams. Throughout the morning Snyder pontificated about how good he looked in that jacket and about the DeSoto's sleek look, how expensive it was, and its new automotive technology. According to Snyder, the DeSoto was "destined to revolutionize what customers would expect from a purchase." The DeSoto—this one a test model from his father's lot—was "the first full-size, streamlined automobile that is completely encased in a steel frame. The hood, waterfall grille, bifurcated windshields, headlamps, and fenders are all molded into one continuous sculptural flow . . ."

Winston stuck his head out the window, inhaling the perfume of the forest and trying to hear as little as possible about Snyder's daddy's fancy car, something he would never be able to afford unless the Committee granted him his law school wish, an entrée for success, for services already rendered.

The search that morning had been fruitless until Snyder decided on a whim to drive up Dougherty Road and then past an iron gate to a narrow paved lane lined with tall ferns. "This looks to be a back entrance of some sort. I bet you a dollar that this will lead to some estate where they might be hiding Rosen," said Snyder, interrupting himself after declaring what a "magnificent machine" the DeSoto Airstream was. Winston mumbled that indeed the lane seemed to lead to one of those fancy enclaves. Snyder crept along until they spotted the black pitched roof of a large structure. He killed the engine, pointed at the roof, and said, "Well, partner, let's take a closer look."

They climbed out of the DeSoto, careful not to make noise, and slowly walked up the lane. Winston did not hear anything except a squirrel whisking up the side of a tree. Snyder was in the lead. He stopped. Turned. Looked at Winston and whispered, "I think I've heard of this place. This is probably what remains of the old Tevis estate. Ever hear of it?"

Winston shook his head.

"The redwood baron." Snyder was dumbfounded. "You've never heard of Lloyd Tevis?"

"Nope."

"He was a builder. Made a ton of dough during the gold rush. Railroads. That sort of thing."

When they came across a large, slime-covered pond, they hid behind a redwood. To the right of the pond, just beyond a small clearing, stood a series of buildings. Snyder guessed the largest one was likely the back of the old redbrick Tevis mansion.

"We could go straight there, but I don't know," said Snyder in a low voice. "If there is something going on . . . we gotta be careful."

Winston nodded, then softly said, "Let's try that." He pointed toward a narrow dirt trail lined by high, unkempt bushes that led around the far side of the pond. "Should provide us with cover if anyone looks out."

Snyder gave him a thumbs-up. They scampered along the trail, hidden by the row of dried rosebushes.

"I distinctly remember my father saying there was a plan of some sort to use this property. But I'm pretty sure it's empty now. It's a perfect place to stow someone. Am I right?" whispered Snyder.

Winston did not have an answer.

The wind gently whistled through the pine needles amid sporadic noise from a far-off buzz saw. The sound of the saw grew more distant as they made their way around the pond, up toward the structure, both of them hunched over to remain shielded by the foliage. They heard a car door slam. The sound seemed to come from the far side of the building, no doubt the mansion's entrance. Then there were distant voices. Snyder stopped, and Winston nearly bumped into him. "Let's keep going," said Snyder. Winston nodded. They skulked along the path, then veered into the underbrush emerging alongside the mansion.

The voices grew louder but were still indistinct. Snyder pointed, and they inched forward to a spot at the mansion's corner. They each took a turn to peer around. They saw four black automobiles parked on the gravel at the entrance of the estate.

Snyder turned to Winston. "There must be a turnoff from the main road. That's a more direct route from Los Gatos." Snyder looked satisfied at his deduction. "That's how they got here."

Winston took another look. A man dressed in all black, trousers and shirt, stood on the porch of the place as if serving as a guard. When the man glanced around at the surrounding forest, Winston ducked out of sight.

"Do you think this is the place where they stashed him?" whispered Snyder.

Winston shrugged.

"This all looks really shady to me," Snyder decided.

"You might be right. If you are, we should go, uh, get help."

"But since we're here, why not poke around some? Right? There's got to be a back entrance."

"I don't think we ought to take any chances. If they are up to no good, they're not going to look fondly on us," Winston said.

Snyder peeked out again. "Look, the guy looks like a gangster."

"How do you know what a gangster is supposed to look like?"

"All in black. What else would they be?"

"Shouldn't we go for help?" Winston insisted. "After all, the authorities would know what's going on and whether these people are supposed to be here. The cops will know what to do."

Snyder thought about it for a moment. He glanced at Winston, then smiled slyly. "No, we got to do this. We're here to help find Michael Rosen. We need to find out whether they are holding him here or not. That's why we're here."

Winston nodded reluctantly.

They snuck back along the side of the building until they saw something that might be the rear service door. "Yeah, this is where the help goes in and out. I know that for a fact," said Snyder.

"Do you think someone might be guarding the door?"

Snyder glanced around. "You never know. But that's a chance we're gonna take." And with that, Snyder hauled off toward the service door. He reached the door without incident and signaled to Winston that he was going to see if the door was unlocked. Winston raised his thumb in affirmation. Snyder tried the knob, registered a smile, and disappeared into the building.

Winston waited for a moment. Nothing. Then a hand, shakily waving from behind the door, beckoned him to follow. Winston waved back, but Snyder had pulled his hand inside. Winston glanced up at the mansion's facade to make sure no guard was peering through the windows. Taking a deep breath, exhaling, he scurried to the door. He reached for the knob and carefully twisted it, gaining entry to what indeed appeared to be a service corridor. To his left was a wide entrance to a large kitchen that appeared devoid of recent activity, but there was a large range, oven, and grill. On the counter he saw a deep fryer and all manner of saucepans, stockpots, baking sheets, mixing bowls, and, dangling above on large metal hooks, tongs, spatulas, and ladles. Along the back wall of the kitchen was a wide door, he guessed to a walk-in cooler, and on the near side a giant refrigerator that was burping. He opened the refrigerator; there were cold vegetables, cheeses, and meats. When he opened one of the cupboards above, he found a healthy stock of canned food. He figured that all this equipment was ready for immediate use.

Winston left the kitchen and returned to the corridor. Snyder reappeared briefly, signaling him to remove his shoes to maintain silence on the creaky wooden floors. As soon as he did, Snyder motioned him to investigate upstairs, while, presumably, Snyder would remain on the ground floor.

In his white socks, Winston found the stairway at the rear of the corridor and slowly ascended the wooden stairs, attempting to remain silent. As he reached the second floor, he noted the long hallway and several rooms on either side and assumed the door at the far end must be the lavatory. He stopped to listen for sounds, murmurs, any potential pleas for help. Hearing nothing, he silently stepped out into the hallway and tried to open the first door on his right. It was locked. He put his ear to the door and then knocked gently. No response. He went on to the second door. Again, locked. His tentative knock was answered with more silence.

His heart pounding, he moved on to the third, fourth, and fifth doors along the right side of the corridor. Nothing. He tried the door to the lavatory. That door was unlocked. The bathroom had black-and-white hexagonal floor tiling and a no-nonsense layout of urinals, sinks, and stalls. The fixtures were old and worn. As he passed through, Winston saw himself reflected in each of the six mirrors: a befuddled shape with dark bags under the eyes. He wasn't sure whether he was seeking exoneration or simply to cover his own tracks as he helped with the search for Rosen. He sighed and looked beneath each of the stall doors for visible feet. The lavatory was empty, though by one of the sinks, someone had laid a wooden toothbrush. He squeezed the bristles: still damp.

He jumped when he heard a cavalcade of car engines turning over somewhere close by. Car doors slammed, and engines throttled in departure. And then it was eerily quiet once more.

Winston left the lavatory and headed back the way he'd come, on edge as he tried each of the doors on the other side of the long hallway. Again, all locked until he turned the knob to the second-to-last room. This one opened. He cautiously peered in. No one was inside. The bed was made. There was nothing on the dressing table, nothing to indicate the room had been occupied recently. Perhaps someone had simply forgotten to lock this door. He crossed the room and opened the dresser. Inside the top drawer was an old Bible, its black leather cover rubbed raw. The second drawer was empty. The third drawer had something that disturbed him: a short rope coiled around like a snake. Or a noose. He picked it up and puzzled over the use of such a thing. The cord-like whip was more like an instrument of torture. Could it have been used on Rosen? Maybe the gangsters had just made off with him?

A wet toothbrush and a rope weren't much to go on, but it didn't seem far-fetched to suppose this secluded estate could have been hiding something, possibly someone, possibly Rosen. Winston took the rope and stealthily left the room. He didn't bother with the very last door. As quickly as he could muster, while remaining as quiet as he possibly could, he descended the stairway, holding the potential evidence and his own exoneration in his right hand. He could show the rope to the authorities.

When he got downstairs, Snyder was nowhere to be found.

Winston scanned the hallway, returned to the kitchen. No sign of Snyder, though he could not have gone far since his shoes were still in the corridor. Which meant either he was still roaming the mansion or he'd been so rattled he just left—or he had been discovered and taken by the gangsters.

As Winston stood debating whether to leave himself, a door along the corridor opened, and Snyder's head peeked out. He gave a worrisome nod and pointed toward the back door.

"We got to get out of here," whispered Snyder.

They grabbed their shoes and ran, not stopping until they were kneeling securely beneath the bushes at the edge of the property.

"What did you find upstairs?" asked Snyder.

Winston held up the rope.

Snyder's eyes widened. "Did they use that on Rosen?"

"I don't know. Maybe."

"Anything else?"

"No Rosen. No evidence of use except for one room where that thing was in a drawer. And a toothbrush. Oh, and lots of food in the kitchen."

"I saw something, and I'm not sure what it meant," Snyder said. "There's a small anteroom next to the main foyer. I could see through the keyhole into the dining room—or maybe it was a ballroom. It doesn't matter."

"What did you see? Any evidence of Rosen?"

"There was some type of meeting happening. I couldn't tell exactly what they were saying, but at one point, there were raised voices. Someone was disagreeing with someone else. They were haggling. There was a ruckus. Then it sounded like the meeting was breaking up."

"Did they come out your way?"

"Some of them left. They went out through a set of doors leading to the front."

"I heard them leave," Winston said. "Who were they?"

"Some of them were Jesuits."

"I thought you said you didn't see them."

"I opened the door a crack when they were leaving. They were wearing black, all right. Some were wearing cassocks. Some in suits. Hey, they all wear black. Who can tell one from another, am I right?"

"Did you recognize anyone?"

"I only got a quick glimpse, but yeah. Father Seebach. Kennedy and Matthews, too. Don't you work under him?"

"Matthews? Yeah. They gave us time off so we could search for Rosen," Winston said cautiously. What was going on? Why did the Jesuits send the students in all directions while they were huddling here in the mountains? Were they in cahoots with gangsters? What about that rope? Was it used to tie up Rosen? Or was it some kind of priestly self-flagellation? Winston was confused. His head hurt.

"The Jesuits sure left in a huff," Snyder said. "I didn't hear much else, but there was some grumbling. Someone said, 'Mr. Ripley.'"

"Who's Ripley?"

"I've heard the name, but I'm not sure where."

"Are the gangsters still around?"

"That's why we gotta scram."

18

My grandmother used to say you could tell who the bootleggers were in San Jose. They were the ones who had raised flower beds in their front yards. This was because they had dug out their basements to accommodate their distilleries. She said that with an air of nonchalance, since everybody seemed to have been in on it.

I've read that a state official at the time complained there were more illegal distilleries in operation in Santa Clara County than in any other county in the state. The Jesuits in the Los Gatos hills were legally allowed to produce wine, albeit for sacramental purposes, but there were rumors of other endeavors. Speakeasies were hidden in plain sight, both downtown and in out-of-way locales. They were subject to the hypocrisy of enforcement. Bootlegging revenue was too good. Civil servant salaries too low. Temptation too high. At times, police enforced the rules; other times they looked away. There was little doubt that some enforcers would engage in a drink and on occasion notify a proprietor when they were due for an upcoming raid. Fines were issued, but bars rarely closed.

My grandmother avoided the subject of brothels and gambling, perhaps because she considered these to be more disturbing vices. Perhaps she was just modest. The state's Red Light Abatement Act of 1914 restricted bordellos, but the trade nonetheless thrived. Gambling took off on the heels of Prohibition's demise on December 5, 1933, and *soon became the county's main law enforcement problem. Like the speakeasies, illegal gambling dens were equipped with hidden false fronts, barricade doors, and secret passwords. Blackjack, dice, slot machines, and chuck-a-luck tables attracted big money. Trying to restrain gambling was about as effective as trying to outlaw liquor.*

The next evening, Thomas Ripley slammed the sedan door behind him and strutted across the sidewalk to the entrance of San Francisco's War Memorial Opera House. The sandwich board showed that tonight's performance was *Tosca*. Not his tumbler of tonic. He would have preferred to toss down a Tullamore Dew Irish at the Techau Tavern than endure hours of histrionic dago mishmash. Nevertheless, there was business at hand, so he skirted past the obliging ticket-taker with a wry wink, whisked through the grand entrance hall with its high vaulted ceiling, and sprightly ran up the elegant staircase to the appointed box.

The box door was ajar. He entered and found the elegantly dressed Paul Passalacqua sitting in a plush crimson chair, reading the evening's program. "You're alone?"

Ripley gestured that he was in fact alone.

"Good, sit. The family's downstairs chowing down. I don't expect them back until a few minutes before curtain. We've got some time."

Ripley sat. Passalacqua offered a cigarette from the slim silver box he carried in his lapel. Ripley considered the gesture but said, "Have you anything to drink?"

"I'm afraid not. The missus wants me to stick to *solo vino*. She says it's for my health."

Ripley took the cigarette. "Let's get down to business. Your boys took care of things? Tierney and Hansen are secure?"

Passalacqua placed the program on a small table and squinted at Ripley. "In one of our hotels, yes. Supremely secure."

"Keeping out of sight, I trust?"

"Until, of course, we require their services once more," replied Passalacqua, confidently.

"And that boy who made the call?"

"Picked him up. Brought him in. Sent him on his way."

"Will he remain a liability?"

Passalacqua gently waved his arm. "We will monitor him. If he plays the game, he will be rewarded. If not, poof." He leaned toward Ripley. "I want to make sure my end of the bargain remains in place. That may be jeopardized by all these investigators poking around. I don't like the idea of the Bureau getting involved."

"We'll steer Cooper in circles. That was the deal we made with the governor, who maintains a legitimacy that we require."

"How are you going to handle him?"

"We've got a local man to provide him with certain leads, to take part in the investigation, but . . ." Ripley ended his comment by taking out a match and lighting the cigarette Passalacqua had given him. He inhaled deeply.

"It's like throwing a stick to a dog. You've just got to throw it in a certain direction and expect the hound to retrieve it and offer it to his master. That's how it's done, am I right?" chuckled Passalacqua.

Ripley blew a smoke ring. "We'll keep him busy. I don't suspect there will be a problem. You'll be rewarded for what you need to do. I assure you that."

Passalacqua kept his expression neutral. "I heard you haven't resolved our land deal yet," he said, changing the subject.

"The Jesuits are tough customers. They have an expiring lease of the Tevis estate and use it as a retreat center. They want to buy out the lease and turn the whole place into a full-time seminary, but they're cash poor. We've got the title," answered Ripley, flicking ash onto the carpet.

"In turn, you want the Mission property that the Jesuits control. I want to control the downtown. Can this all be resolved?"

"It should work for both of us. With patience and maneuvering, I think we'll get there. A little misdirection, a bit of Catholic self-righteousness, a dab of Jesuit superiority. All of this will play into our hands."

"It will only work if your boys can stir things up."

"We're working on it."

The theater lights blinked twice. There was a stir in the auditorium. The opera would commence shortly.

"My wife and her mother will be back shortly. We have an extra seat. Care to hear the opera?"

"Frankly, no."

Passalacqua grinned. "I'm with you. My wife is Milanese. She's a snob. Marriage is a compromise. What can I say?"

Ripley rose from his seat. "Enjoy your show. I'm due at Valentino's on Broadway later on."

"I see. We all have our unfortunate vices." Looking at his waist watch, Passalacqua shrugged, smiled. "What we do for family."

19

On the fourth floor of the Hotel Whittier, Angelo pounded on a bright-yellow door, harder than he had intended, then stood back. He glanced along the hallway, then nodded at Sal Booksin, who tried to peer through the peephole. That, naturally, revealed nothing. Booksin produced a tool from his suit pocket and started to pry the lock.

They heard footsteps, then a woman's voice from down the hall. "Now, don't be messing around with that door."

Startled, both men looked at the hotel housekeeper stomping toward them. She stopped a few paces away and put her hands on her hips, frowning. "I'm responsible if you break that lock. It's my job on the line. Not yours."

Angelo smiled broadly at the middle-aged woman wearing a starched uniform. She looked like she knew how to throw a hook and was clearly not afraid to try.

"Look, you've got to do what you've got to do, but I'm here to see that you don't ruin my lock. I don't want to be on the wrong side of Mr. Pass Water."

"Pass Water?" asked Booksin, perplexed.

The housekeeper shrugged. "Sometimes I call him Mr. Pee."

"Ah, Mr. Passalacqua," said Angelo. "The owner of this establishment."

"That's the man."

"I understand." Angelo bowed slightly. "What do you suggest, madam?"

"I'll open the door with my key. Just keep me out of whatever you do to my guest. And don't mess up my room."

"We wouldn't think of it," Angelo promised.

The housekeeper methodically went through her pockets, found the appropriate key, fiddled with the lock, and let Booksin open the door. He and Angelo went in. The housekeeper remained in the hall and whispered, "Lock the door when you're all finished."

And then she disappeared.

Nobody was in the room, though it had been occupied. There were men's undergarments tossed over a chair. Women's clothes had been left on the unmade bed and on the still-wet bathroom floor. Toiletries were scattered around.

They opened the desk drawers and found nothing unusual. Rummaged through the luggage. Two large suitcases. No handbags. The front desk had registered the couple in room 412 as Mr. and Mrs. Frank Plummer. The two visitors knew otherwise.

Sitting on the rumpled bed, Angelo and Booksin discussed what their next move ought to be. As Angelo stared out the window, pondering the view, his peripheral vision caught a slight movement at the partially open door. Someone peered in for a moment. A man. They heard him scamper away down the hall. Angelo swore softly as it registered who he had seen. It wasn't a nosy guest, room service, or any of that. The man was thin-faced, with ears too large for his head. Those ears. Tierney.

"Get him!" Angelo said.

Booksin ran toward the door, but Tierney had evaporated.

"I'll take the stairs," said Booksin.

Angelo moved toward the elevator. "Make sure he doesn't double back," he called after Booksin, who had already disappeared through the door to the stairwell.

They had a lookout posted near the elevator. As Angelo walked briskly toward him, his guy punched the elevator door. Angelo reminded him, "Lock the room door before you leave."

When the elevator doors opened at the ground-floor lobby, Angelo politely greeted a pair of older matrons debating the merits of that morning's croissants. He tipped his fedora, but they paid no attention to the man with the aquiline nose who was in stealth pursuit of the man who had jeopardized the entire Ferrone operation. Past the ladies, Angelo delicately strolled through the lobby, raised his index finger to his driver, who appeared to be casually reading the hotel's restaurant menu. His man responded quickly and met Angelo without drawing undue notice from the house dick.

"Did you see Tierney?" Angelo said quietly.

His driver shook his head. He patted his lapel and slowly walked to the door marked STAIRS, opened it, and slipped inside.

Angelo remained in the lobby, choosing a seat that put his back to one of the huge marble pillars adorning the spacious foyer. He picked up a disused *San Francisco Call-Bulletin* from a lobby bench, pretending to scan the headlines while he monitored where the hotel dick might be, the staircase door, the elevators, and the ebb and flow of hotel guests parading through the lobby, in and out from the revolving front glass door, cozying up to the front desk, wandering into the ballroom or the dining room.

He didn't have to wait very long.

His driver opened the staircase door a crack and signaled Angelo with a slight flick of his hand. Angelo rose from his seat, folded the newspaper, placed it on a side table, and proceeded unhurriedly across the lobby. Booksin opened the same door from the stairwell, signaling that he had not seen Tierney on the upper floors. Angelo scratched his ear with his left hand and pointed his index finger downward. Booksin nodded and disappeared.

By the time Angelo reached the stairway door, Booksin and the driver had already gone into the basement. Somehow Tierney had slipped by the driver, probably while he was talking to Angelo, and made his way to the service exit below. Angelo followed and, once downstairs, strode toward a scenario he fully expected: While Booksin looked on, the driver had grabbed Tierney from behind and was holding a pistol to the man's chin.

There was a delivery truck parked in the service entry. The truck driver looked startled but reasonably got out of the cab when Booksin pointed a pistol at him.

"Take a hike around the block," ordered Booksin. The truck driver obliged.

Angelo's driver pushed Tierney into the back of the truck and closed its flaps. Angelo and Booksin got in behind them.

"Why did you double-cross us?" snapped Angelo.

Booksin took out a nylon rope, a type of double-loop garrote, placed it around Tierney's neck, and then pulled it taut. Tierney wheezed.

"If you pull on one of the cords, or if you don't answer clearly and concisely, the result, my friend, is that the rope will only tighten around your neck. Take a deep breath. And answer my questions," said Angelo, not hiding his impatience.

"Yeah" was all Tierney could gasp. Angelo had already tightened the cord.

"Yes, you double-crossed us? Or yes, you understand the consequences?"

"Answer questions," rasped Tierney.

"Tell us what happened," ordered Angelo.

When Tierney hesitated, Booksin slapped him in the face.

Angelo loosened up on the cord, allowing Tierney to breathe more freely, though the wheezing man's eyes widened as he vainly tried to keep his arms and torso from shaking.

Booksin smacked him again. This time more violently.

"I didn't want to double-cross anyone," cried Tierney.

Booksin took out his pistol, cocked it, and placed it squarely on Tierney's bulging right temple.

"You had a job to perform. You were paid for your services. Tell us before we inform your family that you've had an unfortunate industrial accident," said Booksin. "We'll deliver your remains to your family's porch," he added.

"Yes, sir," gurgled Tierney.

"Well?"

"There was a job to be done. We knew that. My role was simple."

"Your assignment was to bring Rosen to us," insisted Angelo.

Booksin lowered his gun as Tierney began to speak.

"Took the bus to downtown. Waited for Earle in the park. When I saw him, he told me the plans had changed."

"Who said the plans were changed?"

"I thought it came from you guys."

Angelo again tightened the cord around Tierney's neck. His face blanched. He was sweating. His eyes darted wildly.

"Earle said the plan was that he would do the stickup. That was the plan. That's what he said."

"And you?"

"He told me to take his car."

"The make?"

"Chevy. Never saw it before. Borrowed, maybe."

Angelo glanced over at Booksin, who nodded.

"Why did you not make it to the rendezvous point?" asked Angelo.

"Like I said, he said the plan changed," gasped Tierney. He struggled for a breath, then continued. "Hansen was outside the department store. I was in the car. Rosen walked out. Earle followed behind him. Rosen got into his car. Earle opened the side door and stepped in. I followed in Earle's Chevy."

"Tell us the route," demanded Booksin.

"East on Santa Clara. Turned left on Thirteenth Street. Toward Milpitas. Kept going. Then later on, the Studebaker stopped. I stopped."

"Where was this?" asked Angelo.

"Middle of nowhere. Middle of some orchard. Nobody was out there."

"And then?" asked Booksin.

"Then, they get out of the car."

"Just Hansen and Rosen?" asked Angelo.

Tierney started to weep, his breathing labored. His neck had begun to swell. Angelo let up on the cord. "Tell us," he said, moving as if to tighten the cord again.

"Okay, okay. There was another couple guys . . . three guys . . . in their own car."

"Three more men in another car?"

Tierney nodded.

"Where were they?"

"Parked down the road. Lights off."

"Who were they?"

"Don't know who. Never saw them before."

"There were three of them? Are you sure?" asked Angelo.

"Yeah," wheezed Tierney. He looked frantically at his captors. "Hansen and Rosen got out of Rosen's car," he said, any resistance gone from his voice. "One of these other guys comes over to me but says nothing at first. Never saw the guy before. I don't know the plan, so I wait. He tells me to get out. So, I get out. Earle and Rosen get into this other car. The other guy gets behind the wheel. The three of them leave."

"What did this guy look like? The one who drove off with them?"

"They were all wearing masks. It was too dark anyway. I couldn't see."

"What about the other two?"

"No idea."

"What happened to Rosen's Studebaker?" asked Angelo.

"One of them got in and drove away," muttered Tierney.

"What was the make of that other car?"

"I don't know," Tierney said, his voice now a whisper. "Might have been a DeSoto. Yeah, a DeSoto. New one, I'd guess."

"Are you sure?"

"Yeah," gasped Tierney.

He told them the rest as they continued to prod. He remembered that the man who got into the DeSoto with Hansen and Rosen had been older with a gruff-sounding voice. The second man, with a younger voice, had blindfolded Tierney and instructed him to get into Hansen's Chevy. They both sounded "American." The man who took the Studebaker never spoke.

"Why were you blindfolded?" asked Booksin.

Tierney insisted he didn't know. Hansen never told him the plan. The man had driven him to the Montgomery Hotel in San Jose. "He left me at the hotel," said Tierney.

"Why didn't you run?" asked Booksin.

"Said they'd kill me and my sister. Told me to stay put in the room. Next morning, there's a note under the door. Take the train and meet up here with Earle, it said. And you know the rest."

"Where's Rosen?" demanded Angelo.

"No idea. They took him away."

"You don't read the newspapers?" asked Booksin.

"The radio said he was kidnapped. Ransom, sure. But I had nothing to do with that." Tierney started to cry again. "I just do as I am told," he whimpered.

"Where's Hansen?" demanded Booksin.

"I don't know. He should have been in that room. Something went wrong."

"Have you been paid?" asked Angelo.

"No."

"Why didn't you report back to us?"

Tierney blubbered something unintelligible.

"Why don't we just do him up right here and now? Let Passalacqua take the rap," suggested Booksin.

Staring at the sack of a man beneath him, Angelo said, "Let him go."

Booksin released the garrote.

"We know where your family lives. We know about your sister. If anything you have said is a lie, you or they will pay. Do you hear me? Someone will pay. You will die," said Booksin as he stabbed his finger at Tierney's forehead.

Tierney stood bent over, breathing raggedly. He rubbed at his neck. "Am I free to go?"

"You'll never be free," replied Angelo.

Tierney crawled unsteadily out the back of the truck and limped down the alley without looking back.

Angelo went to the truck driver, who had returned from his hike, gave the man a twenty, and thanked him for his time and patience and discretion.

Having trespassed into Passalacqua territory, they didn't have much time.

No point in starting a war.

20

Ewing leaned back in a worn swivel chair and gazed at the bluish-gray spiral of cigar smoke eddying toward the ceiling of the conference room in police headquarters. Blackmun folded his arms and stared out the darkened window. At the far end of the long table, Cooper sat reviewing the series of reports that had come from various jurisdictions throughout the state. For days they had sat in this room—searching for fresh clues, eating worn-out deli sandwiches, arguing stale theories. Michael Rosen was thought to have been spotted at various points within California. Each time, the sheriff grunted that he simply did not have enough manpower to follow up on all these leads.

Officer Nolan poked his head in. "James O'Neill. It sounds like the kidnappers contacted him some minutes ago. He's right outside now."

"Bring him in," roared Blackmun.

Ewing brushed the tip of his cigar ash onto the floor.

O'Neill came in looking both shaken and excited. With little prompting, he laid out what he knew.

"At five o'clock, I had just finished my shift at the store."

"His father's ice cream place around the corner," Blackmun filled in for Cooper's benefit.

"And so I left by the back door and cut across the alley to Montgomery Street to a lot where my car was. Just as I was going to leave, some guy came up the sidewalk, a stranger—"

"How would you describe him?" interjected Blackmun.

"I don't know. Thin. Kinda big ears. He came up on the passenger side and reached for the door handle. Then he changed his mind and turned away," said O'Neill. "It was just strange, with everything right now, but then I thought maybe he—"

"Had you ever seen him before?" asked Blackmun.

"No. Never."

"Would you recognize him again?"

"Sure," replied O'Neill.

"Then what happened?" asked Cooper.

"I drove home. Got there about half past. At quarter to, the phone rang. The man sounded so casual, at first I thought it was a customer."

"Did you know the voice?" asked Cooper.

"No. I thought it sounded familiar, but no, I did not recognize his voice."

"How would you describe his voice?"

"Young. Monotone. As if reading something prepared." O'Neill thought for a moment. "Nasally," he added.

"And?" prodded Blackmun.

"He says, 'Is this James?' I say, 'Yes.' He says, 'I got a message for Old Man Rosen. Tell him to get a satchel, round up forty grand, take the ten thirty train tomorrow morning for LA. Have the money in a satchel. Place the satchel beneath seat 32-G. First class. There will be a call tonight.'"

"Anything else?" asked Ewing from across the room.

"Rosen has to be alone. No one else. No police."

"That's all?" said Ewing.

"If I contact the police, his life will be in danger."

Ewing stared at O'Neill. "Sounds like you just jeopardized the well-being of your friend."

Ignoring the sheriff, Blackmun said to O'Neill, "You did the right thing, son, contacting us."

O'Neill was escorted out the door. Cooper looked at Blackmun and Ewing in turn and asked, "Where does O'Neill fall into this?"

"The father's all right, but I hate the kid's smirk," said Ewing.

"Why contact O'Neill at all?" asked Cooper.

"He's a family friend. More likely, they know we've got a trace on the Rosen residence," replied Blackmun.

"Who leaked that we're tracing calls?" asked Cooper. "Do you have a leak?"

"Not in my shop," responded Ewing, brusquely.

"Is the man who approached O'Neill's vehicle the same man who later called him?" asked Cooper.

"It's not much to go on." Blackmun scratched the back of his neck. "Let's see if anyone can identify this big-eared guy." Turning to Officer Nolan, he ordered, "Get it done."

Later that evening, Cooper and Blackmun arrived at the Rosen residence on the Alameda, a two-story colonial revival structure with a gambrel roof. The entire family sat together as if posing for a photo, taciturn and morose. Alexander Rosen's head was crowned by a close cut of white hair and framed by tiny ears plastered to the sides of his skull. His eyes were amber and watery. Ewing conveyed the conversation they had with O'Neill. The pale old man said he could gather the money and would perform any task to get his son back.

At nearly midnight, the phone rang ominously in the front room. Everyone hurried to be in place. Ewing, Cooper, Nolan, and Rosen's oldest daughter were upstairs listening on the extension while Alexander Rosen cautiously answered the ring and held the receiver out so that both he and Blackmun could listen.

Rosen had been counseled to keep the caller on the line as long as possible so the phone could be traced and the police could locate the caller.

A voice whispered, "Is this Alexander Rosen?"

"Yes, this is he," the elder Rosen said, purposefully speaking slowly.

"Did you get the message?"

"Yes, I did."

"Will you be on that train?"

"It's difficult to get the money in such a short time. The bank doesn't open until ten. I'll have to make the proper arrangements, but I need proof that my son is alive," pleaded Rosen.

"Will you be on the train?"

"Yes, yes."

There was a long pause.

"I don't know who you are," Rosen said quickly. He looked desperately at Blackmun, who gestured for him to keep talking. "How do I know you've got my boy? What proof do I have?"

"You're stalling, and time is not on your side. Make sure that money is on board."

There was a click on the line. The caller had hung up.

Blackmun immediately called the telephone company operator and was told the call had come from a pay station on South Second Street. The address belonged to Mooney's, a downtown parking garage. Blackmun called headquarters and dispatched a squad car to the garage.

Cooper asked Rosen's eldest daughter if the caller's voice was the same or different from the one she had heard earlier.

"I'm not sure," she said at first. She thought for a moment. "The other one sounded higher pitched, scared. I'm pretty sure he was reading a script. The voice just now was gruffer, more confident. Definitely a different person," replied the daughter.

"Two different callers. Basically the same message," said Nolan.

"Why call again knowing there was a possibility it was being traced?" asked Cooper.

They waited.

Deputy Butler phoned back within minutes to report that a carload of officers had descended upon Mooney's. Nothing. The caller was gone. The parking attendant had seen a man about thirty-five years old, six feet tall, husky, blond hair, square jaw. "Nordic," the attendant had said. The man had inquired about a rental car and then asked for a pay phone. The phone was on the wall in the back. The attendant had seen the man talking but didn't hear the conversation. When the man hung up, he walked away. The attendant didn't know which way he left.

Blackmun told Butler to prepare to bring the parking attendant to the train station the next morning to see if the "Nordic" man turned up to meet Rosen Sr., and also to bring O'Neill to possibly verify the existence of the "big-eared" man who had approached his car. In the meantime, the chief alerted all railroad station agents from San Jose to Los Angeles with descriptions of the two unknown men.

Police fanned out into the downtown area in search of the suspects.

Nothing turned up.

At nine o'clock the next morning, Blackmun and two of his officers waited in an unmarked police car in the depot parking lot. A uniformed deputy was stationed near the ticket booth while plainclothesmen strolled through the swarm of passengers in the terminal. Shielded from general view by a few strategically positioned plainclothesmen, neither O'Neill nor the parking lot attendant spotted either of the two men in question. And no one matching the descriptions boarded the LA-bound train.

Alexander Rosen was on that 10:30 a.m. train to Los Angeles in a private coach in the front car. Agent Cooper sat in an aisle seat in the next car and observed all those who came and went from the front car. Deputy Butler, in plainclothes, sat at the back of the train.

At the scheduled time, the train shuddered and burst forward along the tracks through valleys, around hills, on its way down the spine to LA. Somewhere in the Salinas Valley, Cooper rose from his seat, walked down the aisle to Rosen's first-class compartment. Knocked on the door. Opened it. Rosen winced.

"Beautiful country, huh?" remarked Cooper.

"I don't get out that much."

"How are you holding up?" They both sat and watched the scenery tumbling by.

"I'm not sure whether this will do any good," Rosen said. "I feel my son is far away."

"There is hope that the kidnappers just want money. No reason why they would need to harm your son."

"Logically, yes. But something else is going on. Why are they dragging this all out, making us wait for the phone call? They could have just said from the beginning to get on the train. Are they so incompetent they did not know any call to my house might be traced?"

"Have there been threats before?"

The old man sighed. "In a way, every day is a threat. Being Jewish in a sea of Gentiles causes one to be cautious. Having a successful business, especially these days, creates tensions. Not overt threats, at least not until now, but you perceive subtle threats in their manners, the resentments of those who think: 'Why does Alexander Rosen have all this money and I am still struggling to make ends meet?' It just takes a spark. Unlike my son, I see shadows."

"What about your son?"

"Michael was raised as if he were a Catholic. The Jesuits embraced him. He thinks he's one of them. Michael sees the morning rays of sunshine. He thinks life is there for the taking. He radiates that. People like him for that. Age and maturity will mold him into a fuller person soon enough."

"Did your son ever encounter any problems?"

"No, I don't think so. Some people say he spends too much time living the gay life, but that's just a function of youth."

"And money."

"Yes, and money. That is a source of resentment, I grant you that. What do you think? Do you think all this will work?"

"We have to play the score that is given us. We'll see."

"Is it all for naught?"

Cooper was honest. "If it were a straight business transaction, this would be over by now."

Five hours later, they arrived at Central Station in Los Angeles. Forty thousand dollars remained securely in the satchel beneath seat 32-G.

And there it sat until retrieved by federal agents.

21

Days after meeting Amelia in the park, Victoria ran up the steps of her friend's house and knocked on the door. She heard the strains of an aria coming from the Victrola inside. "E lucevan le stelle" from *Tosca*.

Angelo opened the front door, the music bursting outward. Surprised, Victoria dropped her bag of sourdough and a jar of olives. The loaf flopped on the wooden porch, safely, but the jar rolled down over the edge of the porch, fell, survived miraculously as it landed, and kept going on the sloping lawn, headed for doom, gaining speed as it rolled toward the street. At a pivotal moment, a passerby, a young man wearing a gray suit and a bright, gaudy yellow tie and carrying a briefcase, stopped, stooped low, and deftly scooped up the jar with his left hand. The man examined the jar and turned toward Victoria, who had descended the stairs. Smiling, the man announced, "Still intact."

"You're a lifesaver."

"Olivista? Is it any good?" The man looked up at Angelo. Winked at him. Angelo stood watching, deciding his next move.

"Better than most. No worse than others," said Victoria as she took back her jar.

"Now, that's a recommendation," said the man.

Amelia slipped by Angelo and stood on the porch next to her father.

"Now that God and fate have brought us together, are you one of us?" asked the man, taking a step closer to Victoria. "Are you familiar with the Bible? Do you know Luke, second chapter, forty-ninth verse: 'And Jesus said unto them, how is it that you sought me? Wist ye not that I must be about my Father's business?'"

Victoria frowned.

"Bless you, my child. Do you know our Father's business?"

"I'm not buying what you are selling," pronounced Victoria.

"Do you know the story of the Prodigal Son? Luke, fifteen, verses eleven through thirty-two?"

Angelo went back inside and placed a phone call.

"It's the story of a son, richly endowed, who left his country and squandered his father's wealth in wild living . . ."

Amelia disappeared back into the house and returned with a broom.

The man smiled broadly at Victoria and then glanced up at Amelia.

"It's for your own good, my children. We are called to struggle and strive, and make our way through life, and lay down our lives for Christ. Am I right? I believe I am. 'Wist ye not I must be about my Father's business.' This is my task."

Amelia ran down the stairs, broom in hand. Gripping it with both hands, she reared back and, without hesitation, swung and walloped his right hip.

The man dropped his briefcase, his smile replaced with a look of surprise.

"This is my task!" said Amelia. She swatted him once again, this time aiming higher, hitting him square in the back.

The startled man jumped, then stumbled backward and with widened eyes ogled Amelia, who was gearing up for a third swing, this time going for the fences: the head.

The man put his hands up and muttered, "My task. My task is to spread God's word to this town, around this world . . . to rid the filthy sin that is all around us."

Amelia swung again. This time the man caught the broom and tossed it aside. "You need to be careful," he said, a hint of a warning in his tone as he regarded the two women. He retrieved his briefcase and treated his audience to a sharp heel turn, continuing on his way. Amelia and Victoria watched as the would-be preacher disappeared down the block and around the corner.

Angelo reemerged onto the porch. A roadster swerved from the traffic and stopped in front of the house. Sal Booksin rolled down his window. Angelo pointed in the direction where the man had disappeared. Booksin nodded, put the car into gear, and gave chase. Angelo retreated into the house.

Victoria lingered on the sidewalk, trying to decipher what had just occurred. It had all happened so quickly.

"Come sit," called Amelia, who had returned to the porch. Victoria followed her to the Adirondack chairs and sat down, still puzzled as she watched the traffic flow back and forth.

"Don't ask anything about that," whispered Amelia.

Soon enough, Rosalia poked her head out the front door and said, "Supper is ready. I heard a man's voice. Who was that?"

"We were being accosted by some petty two-bit preacher peddling his religion," said Amelia in a singsong voice. She swung her legs as she spoke.

"Oh, them. They're making the rounds these days. They want everyone to swallow their guilt like air," Rosalia said.

"We sent him on his way. Your daughter has a healthy swing," said Victoria.

"What's bred in the bone." Rosalia put one hand on her hip. "Both of you must come in for supper. You must be cold out here. Amelia, are you wearing a sweater?"

"No sweater. It's not that cold. Don't worry."

"I brought you a modest offering." Victoria sat up and handed Rosalia the sourdough and the rescued olive jar.

"Come on inside," declared Rosalia.

In the dining room, Rosalia had set the table with deep-blue everyday plates and a wooden salad bowl coupled with tiny glass cruets, one with olive oil, the other balsamic vinegar, and, as the centerpiece, a steaming heap of linguine with lemon garlic sauce. Rosalia placed the loaf of sourdough on a cutting board. Amelia tore off the heel and gave it to her mother for good luck. Angelo appeared from the kitchen carrying a small wooden tray of glasses. Two were filled with dark-red wine. The other two were paler, rose in color.

"I have to apologize, Victoria," announced Angelo. "Rosalia always has me water down the wine for you young people. I don't think God ever intended it this way, but"—he looked at his wife—"we all know who makes the rules around here."

Rosalia gave him a satisfied nod.

Picking up a glass carefully, Angelo said, "You must realize that for His first miracle, Jesus changed water into wine. Not the other way around. I think he'd be shocked to see this travesty."

"I think Jesus's teaching would be rather than insist on looking at everything half empty, it is best to appreciate what's half full in life," laughed Rosalia.

Amelia made a face, took a loud gulp, then put down her glass. "I think it was in the Gospel of John. Mother Mary was disappointed there was no wine for that wedding, a half-empty situation. In response, her dutiful son transformed the stone pots of plain water into delicious wine because full glasses of wine were needed for the happiest of occasions. And what's a wedding without wine?" said Amelia, gesturing for another glass.

"You want a full glass of wine? Fine. You want a wedding? Hah. Angelo, pour her red wine and fill it to the brim. And, for your insufferable insolence, you'll have to wash the dishes."

Angelo poured the red wine. "And you, Victoria, do you condone such disrespect for one's elders?"

"Absolutely," came the answer. Victoria drank her watered-down wine and stuck out her glass for more.

"Such youth," said Rosalia, cracking a smile. "So now you'll have to do the dishes too."

"Cheerfully," responded Victoria.

"To our youth. May they remain exuberant and passionate and beautiful as the Madonna. For us elders, may we suffer for the consequences of their sins," toasted Angelo with a raised glass and a smile.

"Amen," uttered Rosalia. "Now eat."

The room grew quiet as the linguine was finished. Breaded veal cutlets were then passed around the table. Angelo surveyed the scene, and somewhere between his first and second helping, he said, "I noticed there was a cannery workers' demonstration last month."

Victoria and Amelia exchanged glances.

"The workers needed to stand up for themselves," Victoria said. "Wages have fallen. Eight dollars a week is criminal. So, yes, there was a march. You know what happened. We all do. The marchers didn't even get to city hall. The cannery workers just wanted their voices to be heard."

"And who tossed the first stone?" asked Angelo.

"They started it," said Amelia.

"They might have started it, but wasn't it the intent of the organizers to get noticed? Or was it the intent of city hall to demonstrate there is no tolerance for unionization in this town?"

"But who is telling the police to crush the union?" asked Victoria. "Mrs. Gumina, may I have another glass?"

"Certainly," responded Rosalia. She took Victoria's glass and this time filled it.

Looking at her father, Amelia replied, "You know the answer."

"The cannery owners," Victoria quickly declared. She paused. "Who are they, exactly?"

Angelo put down his fork and regarded Victoria as if realizing something about her for the first time. An air of confidence that had until now escaped his notice. "It's not only the cannery owners, like

Ripley, who owns CalPak and Libby," he said. "It's a larger alliance that includes Southern Pacific, the banks, and other big businesses."

"They are using the police to prevent workers from organizing," declared Victoria.

Rosalia turned her attention to her daughter. "I hope you are not getting mixed up in any of this."

"Mama, you know me better than that," said Amelia, uncomfortably.

Angelo took his fork and knife and tore into another piece of veal. He glanced at Victoria, who met his gaze.

"Workers who participated in the demonstrations have been fired," declared Victoria. "They've made arrests."

"You'd think the police would have better things to do. Bigger fish to fry." Rosalia then tried to change the subject. "I'm fearful of what has become of that poor boy, Rosen. Everyone is saying how upset they are. The police have come up with nothing." She dabbed her lips with her napkin, placed it back on her lap.

"They've brought in the Bureau of Investigation," Angelo remarked, then stuffed another forkful of pork into his mouth.

"I know that, but what have either of them done?" Rosalia wanted to know.

"The police have detained a union organizer," said Victoria, shifting the conversation once again.

"Is that a fact?" responded Angelo.

"John Schiavo. Ever heard of him?" asked Victoria. "The rest were arrested but then let go. Schiavo didn't make bail."

Slowly, Angelo said, "Should I have?"

"He's sitting in the county jail right now."

Rosalia got up and started to clear the plates.

After a pause, Amelia pondered out loud, "Why would anyone pick on Michael Rosen? Why him in particular? Why not his father? He's the one with the money."

"Was it just money or was it because he represents something else?" asked Victoria.

"The papers won't admit to anything," said Rosalia, returning from the kitchen. "His family, though, represents a certain glue, stability for this community. These days have become so uncertain, demonstrators in the streets, people kidnapped . . ."

"Yes, someone has upset things," said Angelo.

"Who would want to stir things up?" asked Victoria.

"When they find out who did it, they'll pay. I hope to God it wasn't an Italian. We'd be back to the anarchists throwing bombs again. I hope this Schiavo fellow in jail has nothing to do with any of this. It would be a mark on all of us," lamented Rosalia.

"The papers say that Baby Face Nelson's men have been spotted in the North Bay," Angelo said.

"The papers are always filled with conspiracies. They sell fear on a daily basis. That's how they make money," said Rosalia.

"And keep us all on edge. Ultimately, though, they will pin it on someone," said Amelia.

"They'll find someone to take the rap," agreed Victoria.

"They'd better find Michael Rosen first," said Rosalia. "I worry about him. It's always the mother who worries."

As the meal went on, the conversation wound back and forth, and at points along the way there were arguments, to which Rosalia finally proclaimed, "*Basta.*"

Amelia playfully threw her napkin at her father and missed. It landed instead in her mother's glass, spilling red wine on the white tablecloth. Rosalia looked momentarily annoyed, but she persisted that peace be upheld.

Angelo sat back, cracked open walnuts, and enjoyed himself until he noticed the time.

"I must be off to work," he said, rising from his throne at the head of the table. He apologized to his wife, daughter, and their guest. Retreating to the bedroom, he picked out which overcoat would be appropriate, patted it down, grabbed his fedora, and came back into the dining room just as it erupted into an argument about the forgotten man in the musical movie that had come out earlier in the year, *Gold Diggers of 1933*.

Angelo stood there, fedora in hand, and looked at Victoria. When there was a brief lull, he simply announced, "I'm glad you came this evening. I hope you come back soon."

"Thank you for inviting me," responded Victoria with a smile.

"Thank you for allowing us to be part of your family," said Rosalia.

Angelo hesitated for a moment, as if he had not quite decided to add anything. Noting his hesitation, Rosalia stood, hands on her hips. "Angelo and I know full well about your suspension. You don't have to pretend. This is something we'll look into. We will find a solution."

Victoria sent a surprised glance at Amelia, then smiled and accepted a warm hug from Rosalia.

Angelo shrugged. "Never underestimate she who conducts a symphony." He looked directly at Victoria. "You mentioned a man in jail. Schiavo? Was that the name? Seems to me, I may have heard of him. My advice to you is that you might want to stay clear of him."

"Angelo, you better go. You'll be late," ordered Rosalia.

In offering his hand to Victoria, Angelo said, "We are always here." Victoria grasped his hand warmly. Rosalia gave her husband a kiss on the cheek. Angelo passed by the table, put his hands on Amelia's shoulders as she remained seated. "Be good. I'll be back after midnight. Don't wait up."

He headed out the front door. They listened to his footsteps fade away, then resumed their discussion. Amelia asked about the merits of *She Done Him Wrong*, and that created another round of loud arguments.

22

That evening at Spades, Ferrone sat in his customary booth toward the back, bathed in darkness. The only illumination was the faint refraction of the mirrored green light behind the bar. When Angelo entered, Ferrone stood, silently greeted him with a hug. Both sat. There were a few regulars hunched over the bar. Otherwise, the place was quiet. No need to use the back room. Ferrone drummed his knuckles on the table. "I appreciate your efforts to locate these guys."

"We only talked to Tierney."

"I know that. We must proceed cautiously," murmured Ferrone. Angelo nodded.

"What did you get out of Tierney?"

Angelo recounted what Tierney and his police contact had supplied. "Hansen had young Rosen in his car, the Studebaker. Tierney followed in Hansen's car. Said they changed the route on him. Met up with men in a DeSoto at some out-of-the-way orchard. One guy takes Rosen and Hansen into the DeSoto. They drive away. The second man takes the Studebaker away. Another takes Tierney back to town."

"Where did they take Rosen?" asked Ferrone.

"Tierney said he didn't know."

"Who has young Rosen?"

"Everything points to Passalacqua."

Ferrone nodded. "Why would they do that? Where do you think they have him? What happened to Hansen?"

Angelo shook his head. "Who knows? Why send the elder Rosen to LA for a drop-off that didn't happen? What's their game?"

"Maybe to throw the investigators off? Maybe to gain some time? Who can tell?" asked the faint outline of Ferrone. It might have revealed a shrug. It was too dark for Angelo to ascertain.

"Their moves might suggest they want to implicate us," Ferrone continued. "After all, Passalacqua allowed you to talk to Tierney. I don't think that was random." He took another drink.

"We're watching Passalacqua's movements."

"And he is watching us," concluded Ferrone.

"To what end?"

"To what end indeed?"

"It would seem at some point soon, someone will sacrifice a pawn."

"That would be logical, but there's a problem."

"Which is?"

"Chess has its limitations. It's only a two-person game." In the shadows, Ferrone folded his hands together, then abruptly rose from the booth and headed for the door. Angelo followed and waved toward the bartender, who pressed a button, alerting Ferrone's driver and bodyguard by the exit. When the door opened from the stairwell, yellow light splashed across the bodyguard's face. Angelo was still behind Ferrone, who did not turn around. "I have another appointment," Ferrone said. "We need to consider our next moves. We are in a compromised position."

Ferrone started up the stairs, then turned as if remembering something. "A conversation with that federal agent should be arranged." He gave Angelo a nod, then left the building.

Angelo retreated to the back room and did his paperwork for the evening. He stayed there until the St. Joseph bells melodically clanged twelve times. Time to go home.

Angelo grabbed his overcoat, climbed the steps to the street, and walked the lonely path homeward. He could have asked his driver to give him a ride, but he liked to walk, especially at night. He did his best thinking then.

At that hour, few cars were on the street, and even fewer people. When he passed by, St. James Park was dead but for the lingering perfume of sweet magnolia. Angelo continued along the park's edge, then turned right at St. James. Somewhere down the block, he noticed a slow-moving automobile creeping up the street. The car sped up as it passed him, then braked abruptly in mid-block. Angelo stopped, instinctively. He reached into the pocket of his overcoat. His pistol was gone.

He flinched.

The car was some thirty feet away. Someone rolled down the window. A revolver poked out.

Angelo thought of his wife and daughter waiting for him at home.

The automobile accelerated and zoomed away into the silvery night. Angelo stared after its disappearing rear lights.

23

The mood on the return train ride from LA was somber. Both the elder Rosen and Cooper were exhausted. Rosen asked why the ransom had not been picked up or even acknowledged.

"Frankly, I don't have a clue." Cooper glanced at the old man. He looked small, tucked into his wool overcoat.

"I've heard of similar kidnappings," Rosen said as he lifted his index finger, which looked more like a twig to Cooper. "It's something we all have to deal with, but what it comes down to is this should have been a business transaction. I don't understand why it wasn't."

Cooper could only respond that times were tough, men were desperate, the stakes higher than initially imagined. "A solution might be more difficult to reach."

Rosen put his hands on his lap. "I'm not sure how the stakes are any different. In my business, I've had my setbacks, but things got resolved. Back then, can you imagine being an immigrant, creating a business in a town where everyone distrusted you as an outsider? Now I operate the largest department store between Los Angeles and San Francisco."

He fell silent, staring out the window as the train sped past rolling hills and the occasional stand of oak trees. After a lull in the conversation, Cooper offered, "San Jose must have come a long way."

"With each step of progress, someone else wants in. The banks. Southern Pacific. Those gentlemen on Market Street require their share."

"The world has gotten more complicated."

"And everyone must pay."

Cooper let it go at that. Rosen closed his eyes, attempting to make peace with what might come next.

Back in San Jose, Cooper interviewed potential leads and reviewed reports about the disappearance of Michael Rosen. There was little solid evidence. Ransom notes had started to pile up: nine from within San Jose, but at least thirty more were mailed from San Francisco, Oakland, Sacramento, and Los Angeles, as well as from small towns throughout California. Sorting through them was a laborious process. Many were easy to dismiss. A few were deemed credible. It took time for local investigators to sift fact from conjecture and follow up on viable leads.

Alongside the ransom notes, there was only the presumably credible eyewitness testimony of Madeline Amaral, who stuck to her story about multiple abductors. But other witnesses reported on the whereabouts of the telltale green Studebaker the night Rosen disappeared. Some claimed to have seen the car all over county roads; one insisted the car had been climbing the eastern foothills. Still others said downtown Oakland, and a smattering of sightings were called in from various San Francisco neighborhoods, the Central Valley, Salinas Valley, one even as far as San Juan Bautista. Upon further investigation, these did not appear promising. Cooper judged that some so-called witnesses wanted to muddy the waters, while others just wanted a bit of attention.

Cooper interviewed a longshoreman who confirmed Rosen's wallet had been found on the railing near where the SS *Lurline* was docked at Pier 32. It was puzzling that Rosen's wallet was discovered at all. Cooper ordered it tested for fingerprints. The prints were smudged and therefore useless, but the discovery of the wallet did suggest that Rosen, after the Amaral ranch episode, might have been taken to San Francisco.

No other confirmed evidence had emerged.

Cooper wired Bureau headquarters to report that little progress had been made in the case and assessed that local authorities were neither sufficiently motivated nor competent enough to achieve a substantial break in the case. Chief Blackmun, Sheriff Ewing, and the mayor were willfully sitting on their respective haunches. They seemed to prefer to wait for clues to appear. The Bureau responded that Cooper's role was to assist in the investigation, not lead it, and reiterated the governor's office directive that he remain steady in a subordinate investigatory role.

One morning, eight days after the abduction, a ransom note postmarked in San Jose was delivered to Rosen's Department Store. A young employee in the mailroom opened the envelope, his eyes widened, and he promptly rushed over to the head clerk, Harold Cord, who read the missive and telephoned Alexander Rosen, who then ordered that the envelope be immediately delivered to police headquarters.

Ewing announced that he thought this note was a clue possessing substantial merit. Blackmun agreed. Cooper demurred. Rosen was optimistic.

Later that morning when the squad room had been assembled, Blackmun read aloud the handwritten note:

You have permitted this case to receive too much publicity. Killing him is the easy way with little risk to us. We will give you a final chance. If you want your son alive, you will comply with our demands. At 7 this evening, you must drive south on Monterey Highway toward Los Angeles. Bring $40,000. Drive your son's roadster. You will see a man in a white mask by the side of the road. Stop. Pay the man. No police. Post the number 1 on the department store front window this afternoon to acknowledge this message and agree to pay for your son's safe return.

Rosen blanched at the ultimatum. "I've got to do this. But there is a problem . . . I can't drive."

Cooper immediately responded, "I'll drive. I'll go in your place and deliver the ransom."

"That's not going to work. The note said Rosen was to drive," declared Blackmun.

"All right then, we'll tell the kidnappers that. We'll make an appeal on the store sign."

The police chief was not convinced. However, Rosen agreed it was the only plausible solution, so Blackmun ordered a sign made to hang on the storefront: the number 1 in big bold letters, and then, below, an appeal: I CANNOT DRIVE.

By 2 p.m., the sign was on display in the store's prominent northern window. Police lookouts were stationed on building roofs across the street while undercover cops combed the streets. The afternoon edition of the *Mercury-Herald* published a front-page appeal written by Alexander Rosen, stating that his family wished to cooperate with the kidnappers and that the family was acting in good faith, reiterating that the senior Rosen was unable to drive and the family requested proof of custody before payment could be made.

"Do you think they'll take the bait?" asked Cooper, again sequestered in Blackmun's conference room along with Ewing.

Ewing tapped his finger on his chin. "Hell, I don't know. They might just mail another letter. Or they might risk another telephone call. Depends on how hungry they are."

Later that afternoon, Cooper, Blackmun, Ewing, and the core investigative team returned to the Rosen residence. Blackmun had instructed the telephone company to remain vigilant with dedicated switchboard operators who stood ready to track any incoming calls. At 7:20 p.m., the chief operator alerted the police chief on the separate line to the Rosen kitchen.

"Two calls have been placed to the Rosen home in the past eight minutes. Each time, the calling party hung up," said the chief operator.

"When were the calls?" asked Blackmun.

"The first at 7:12 from a pay station, Ballard 4593, at the southeast corner of First and San Antonio streets."

One of Blackmun's officers flipped rapidly through the city directory. The phone booth was located in the Montgomery Hotel, a couple of blocks south of Rosen's Department Store.

The second call had come in at 7:19 p.m. "Ballard 7591," the operator informed the police.

An officer skimmed through the directory and announced, "That's a public phone in Owl's Drug Store. Tenth and Santa Clara."

"Our man has a car. He's using his nickels at one pay phone at a time. The guy is torn between fear and greed," deduced Cooper.

They waited.

Blackmun could not sit still. He chomped on his cigar on the back porch, half watching the squirrels climbing up and down the trees, but he remained in proximity to the kitchen's phone. Cooper sat in the front room, reviewing his notes. He briefly inspected the condition of his nails. They were in rotten shape. Ewing sat in an easy chair. He read the sports section over and over again. Both sisters nervously perched by the phone near where Ewing sat. Alexander Rosen paced clumsily around his house. His wife sat at their kitchen table, attempting to chop vegetables, mincing them into oblivion.

The minutes slipped by. Then they stretched out to nearly an hour. At 8:30 p.m., the phone rang, jolting everyone from their stupor. Alexander Rosen was ready to answer the phone, but Cooper signaled him to let Rosen's eldest daughter answer first. Nervously, she picked up, and with Cooper listening in, she voiced a tentative "Hello?"

"Is Mr. Rosen there?" a male voice whispered.

The daughter took a breath and managed to utter, "One moment, please."

Ewing headed to the kitchen, where Blackmun was set up on a separate line. "Anything?" Ewing whispered. Blackmun held out the receiver so the sheriff could listen in. "Waiting," came the response from the operator manning the phone.

At a signal from Ewing, Cooper nodded to Rosen.

"Did you post the sign?" the voice asked when Rosen got on the line.

"Yes, it's there. You see, I can't drive. I wish I could, but I never learned how. I'm sorry."

A hesitation.

"Okay, you get O'Neill to drive you. Leave immediately."

"I want to make sure my son is fine. Let me talk to him. Let me hear Michael's voice."

"No. I need your answer. Yes or no, will you go?"

"Yes, sir, I am willing to go through with this. I'll do anything to get my boy back. I just don't know whether I can get James O'Neill to go immediately. I think he would go if I asked him."

"You need to do this right now."

"Yes, yes. Let me call James first. Then, if I can't, I'll get someone here to drive me. Maybe my daughter can. She is not an accomplished driver. Should I try James first? Wouldn't that make more sense?" said Rosen, trying to extend the conversation.

The line went dead.

Cooper hurried to the kitchen, where Blackmun and his team anxiously awaited word from the chief operator.

"Ballard 4923," said the operator.

Blackmun's officers again raced through copies of the city directory. It took a solid minute to discover the pay phone location: 222 South Second Street.

"The Plaza Garage," Blackmun and Ewing said together.

Blackmun put a call through to police headquarters and barked an order at Deputy Sheriff Butler: "Get your hide over to the Plaza Garage."

As Blackmun hung up the phone, Rosen's sad eyes looked hopeful.

Deputy Butler, along with officers Nolan and Delaney, all wearing civilian clothes, jumped in their vehicle and flew toward the garage on South Second Street. They raced by the Rosen's Department Store and the parking lot where Michael Rosen had been abducted, and within three minutes reached the entrance of the Plaza Garage. To their surprise, they were met by four deputy sheriffs.

The garage office was near the entrance. The seven men ran up and identified themselves to a frightened attendant.

"Did anyone use your phone in the last few minutes?" asked Delaney.

"No one, but there's the pay phone in back," came the answer.

The cops immediately spread out and proceeded toward the back of the garage.

At the far end, in the shadow of a weak overhead light, a man stood hunched over the phone mounted on the wall. The officers silently approached. He must have heard or anticipated their arrival because he slowly turned around while speaking into the phone. They peered at the heavy-browed, ruddy-skinned man with large ears and wavy brown hair. There was a nervous smile on his face as he looked back at them.

"What's your name, mister?" Butler asked.

Rather than answering, the man asked, "What's this all about?"

"Raise your arms," said Butler. A quick frisk revealed no weapon.

"No problem. I don't have anything. I was talking to my sister," said the suspect, still smiling awkwardly.

"You were speaking to Alexander Rosen," declared Butler.

The man's face melted into a pale shade of ghost. He let go of the phone receiver, and it dangled loosely on its cord.

"Mister, you are under arrest."

24

The notoriety of gangsters started with Prohibition. Mobsters had been just small-time operators dealing in various forms of vice, but the Volstead Act was the seed that spawned the creation of widespread organized crime, initially in larger cities, but over time such activities permeated smaller towns throughout the country. People either saw these gangsters as those who thumbed their noses at an unpopular law or feared them as dangerous outsiders who shook up the status quo. Celebrity gangsters were romanticized by the media and given monikers like Al "Scarface" Capone, Pretty Boy Floyd, and Machine Gun Kelly. Their pictures appeared on most-wanted posters. Stories of their exploits were splashed across the headlines.

One such incident was the infamous ambush at Kansas City's Union Station. On June 17, 1933, Frank "Jelly" Nash, a repeated bank robber, was being taken back to jail when three gangsters, attempting to free him, opened fire with machine guns. Nash was killed, along with four police officers. One of the gangsters was reputed to be Pretty Boy Floyd. An intensive manhunt was organized, and Floyd fled. On November 13 of the same year, local San Jose papers got a hot tip from an informant who would not give his name for fear of reprisal. Pretty Boy Floyd had been spotted with another man and two women at the abandoned New Almaden quicksilver mine south of San Jose. The implication was that he might have been connected to the kidnapping of a department store heir. Police searched the mine shafts and tunnels but found no trace of Floyd. While this was likely a red herring, another gangster was indeed hiding out in nearby Sausalito: Baby Face Nelson.

In late 1933, Nelson was tending a bar at the Walhalla and living quietly next door to an unsuspecting town constable. Nelson was also reputed to be employed by Joe Parente, a notorious San Francisco bootlegger known as the "king of the Pacific coast rumrunners." And it was at this time that Nelson met John Paul Chase. The story goes that Chase was the wheelman in a contract murder Nelson carried out in Reno, Nevada. Soon thereafter, both began robbing banks with John Dillinger. Despite his presence and proclivity for violence, there was no evidence that Nelson was involved in the San Jose kidnapping.

That night, police hauled in the kidnapping suspect to the Hall of Justice. The young Irishman with the large ears was taken in handcuffs to an interrogation room on the second floor. The suspect sat in the small room with a nicked-up desk, gooseneck lamp, peeling linoleum floor, smudged gray walls, and not much else. His sunken brown eyes skirted back and forth. He looked guilty as hell.

By the time Cooper had a chance to interrogate him, Blackmun and Butler had been at it for nearly half an hour. The guy was slumped so that his torso spilled over to one side of the curved-back wooden chair when Cooper entered.

"He ain't budging," determined Butler. He and Blackmun remained in their seats. Ewing walked in and said nothing.

"It's your turn to take a swing," said Blackmun, nodding at Cooper.

Cooper took a seat across from the suspect.

"What's your name, son?" he asked.

The suspect said nothing. He absently scratched at the edge of the desktop with his fingernails.

Cooper slammed his fist down hard so that it shook the desk.

The guy flinched. "Harold."

"Harold what?"

"Tierney."

"Why do you think you are here?"

Tierney looked up at Cooper, then stared at the scratches he'd made on the desk. "I told them over and over again." His voice had a vexed tone.

Cooper said nothing. Waited for an answer to his question.

"I was in the parking garage using the pay phone," Tierney muttered. "Talking to my sister." He glanced sideways at Butler. "He brought me in for nothing."

Cooper waited.

"They said I had something to do with a kidnapping, but that's a lie. I was just talking to my sister." Tierney folded his hands together, as if in prayer, before giving Cooper a pleading look. "Why won't you help me?"

"Why were you in a parking garage? Why not call from your home?" said Cooper.

"Because it was . . . private. My sister didn't want my parents to know." Tierney glanced at Butler, then stared beyond Cooper at a spot on the far wall. "She's in Stockton," he added miserably.

"What was so private?"

"I'd rather not say." Tierney looked down at his hands once again.

"Where were you the evening of November 6?"

Tierney put his elbows on the desk, resting his chin on his hands. He couldn't seem to sit still or look Cooper in the eye.

"I stayed home that evening. I was with my parents. They can vouch for me."

"Where are you working these days?"

"It's slow right now, but I've got feelers out for some work," said Tierney. He rubbed his forehead with both hands. "Sometimes I paint houses."

"Is that all?"

His sunken eyes took a further plunge. "I play the piano sometimes."

Cooper looked at the unemployed piano player and occasional housepainter and part-time crook: The man was sufficiently nervous and irritated.

"Where did you meet Michael Rosen?"

"Don't know him."

Cooper was not convinced. "You never heard of him?"

"Never met him. Never been to the store where he worked. Not my kind of place."

"But you've heard or read about the kidnapping?"

Tierney's voice quivered. "I don't know a thing about that."

"What do you know about Michael Rosen?"

"Nothing." Tierney sounded like an adolescent insisting innocence after being caught shoplifting a Charlestown Chew chocolate bar.

"How did you know he worked at his father's store?"

Tierney's brown eyes begged mercy. "I just assumed he worked there."

"Why would you assume that?"

Tierney looked everywhere except at Cooper. "You're confusing me." There was no empathy to be found in the faces of the other lawmen. He again fixed his gaze on a stain on the wall behind Cooper.

"When did you first hear about the kidnapping?"

"My father mentioned it."

"What did he say?"

"He said Michael Rosen got abducted."

"When was that?"

"I don't remember." Tierney broke down in tears. "Might have been after Sunday church."

"What does your sister do in Oakland?"

"She is an organist. For the Methodists."

"You said she was in Stockton."

"I . . . you're confusing me." Tierney deflated. He rubbed his fingers across his forehead.

"Where is Rosen now?"

Tierney began to whimper. "I tell you, I don't know."

"Are you afraid of someone?"

No answer.

Cooper waited. Finally, Tierney meekly whispered, "No."

"Have you ever been to the Hotel Whittier?"

"Yes. No. Never been there."

"You've never been there, yet you know the place. What if I told you we have witnesses who say you made a call there on the evening of November 6?"

"It wasn't me. Never been there," gasped Tierney. "That is a goddamned lie. Never been there is what I said."

"Have you been to the waterfront in San Francisco?"

"Once or twice, sure," managed Tierney, wiping his eyes.

"Do you know the *Lurline*?"

"Who?"

"We have another witness who places you at Pier 32 on the evening of the kidnapping. Were you there?"

"No, that wasn't me. They're mistaken."

"Who are you afraid of?"

"Nobody."

"Who are you covering up for?"

"Nobody."

"We know you were not alone. Who was with you?"

"Nobody."

"Where were you that night?"

"At the movies. The California Fox."

"What played?"

"Double feature."

"Name them."

"Can't remember."

"Name one of the actresses."

"Jean Harlow. Yeah, Jean Harlow," Tierney said, hopefully.

"You said earlier that you spent the night with your parents."

Tierney glanced over at Ewing, who stared back, his rheumy eyes expressionless.

"The boy is lying," said Blackmun.

The interrogation went on into the night. Tierney stuck to his story. He admitted no guilt, professed shock at his arrest, and denied any knowledge of Rosen's abduction. Closing in on 12:30 a.m., Blackmun threw up his hands and suggested they call it a night. Cooper objected. Tierney should be questioned until they obtained useful answers.

"That may well be, but this isn't your case," responded Blackmun. "We'll be better off in the morning. Let him think about the uselessness of his answers."

Cooper withdrew and took the lonely walk back to his room at the Sainte Claire, frustrated but knowing full well his role was to assist rather than assume responsibility for the interrogation.

The hotel night manager opened the door for him. The lobby was dead and about as cheerful as a mausoleum. He climbed the stairway, fumbled for his key, stepped into his room, and loosened his tie and collar. Looked at the water jug on the dresser, wished it were something better. He sank into the only chair and kicked off his Oxfords, then lit a Lucky Strike and ditched it before surrendering to sleep.

At 5:37 a.m., Cooper awoke and pulled off his sweat-soaked clothes from the night before, took a shower. The hot water felt fine. So fine he could have stayed there for twenty minutes, but after a two-minute rinse, he turned the knob to cold, braced himself, then got out to shave and get dressed. He headed for the restaurant, intent on grabbing a bite. When he got there, the place was not yet open, despite the sign outside indicating it should be.

Cooper pounded on the door. Soon enough one of the kitchen staff, a skinny Mexican busboy, opened the door and let him in. The busboy retreated into the kitchen and quickly returned to Cooper's booth with the morning menu and a pot of freshly brewed coffee. "Black?" asked the busboy.

"Please."

"Keep the pot?"

"Yes. Flapjacks?"

"It'll take a few minutes. Bacon or ham? Eggs?"

"Where's your waitress?" Cooper asked.

The busboy shrugged. "That would be Blond Betty. Betty gets here when she feels like it."

Cooper ordered bacon, ham, and eggs but focused on his steaming cup of java. He dared a sip, and it burned his lips.

He put down the cup and stared out the window at the sun slowly rising over the buildings along San Carlos Street.

Betty the bleached blond slunk through the door in the neighborhood of 6:40 a.m. She headed directly into the back room. Looked like she'd had a late night.

She brought a tray that held one dish bearing a stack of flapjacks and another with two eggs over easy, two strips of bacon, a slice of ham. Cooper grunted his approval and asked for toast.

Closing in on 7 a.m., a newspaper boy who could not have been more than ten years old tapped on the windowpane near Cooper's booth. The boy carried a stack of the morning edition. Cooper gestured for the newsie to come in. The boy ran through the lobby to where Cooper sat, handed him a folded-up copy, and then stuck out his hand. Cooper reached for a coin and gave the boy more than what was needed.

He opened up the newspaper to a screaming headline: CAPTURED! TWO SUSPECTS IN ROSEN KIDNAPPING.

Cooper carefully read the newspaper account, gathering that while he slept, the police chief or the sheriff, or the two of them, must have continued to interrogate Tierney. At some juncture, Tierney had admitted to the crime of abducting Michael Rosen. He further implicated an accomplice whose name was Earle Hansen.

About that time, the toast appeared. Burnt.

Police had stormed into a room of the California Hotel, not far from the Sainte Claire, where they arrested Hansen. Given when the morning edition was likely printed, Cooper deduced it wasn't long after he left that Tierney broke down and implicated the second man. It was mighty fast work. That or Blackmun and Ewing might have known all along.

Cooper bit into his toast. One bite was enough.

The police held Hansen, but they still had no idea where Michael Rosen was. The paper repeated the options. Lots of them. Recycled from earlier editions. Rosen had been seen on the deck of the *Lurline*. Disembarked from a train at LA's Central Station. Spotted entering the back room at the Cal Neva casino. Lost money at roulette in a boomtown called Las Vegas.

Cooper waved his hand and called for the bill. The waitress was nearby, diligently looking the other way. By this time, other customers had started to fill the booths.

Cooper laid a couple of bills on the table, marched to the hotel's telephone booth, and placed a call to the Bureau's field office in San Francisco. At that hour, he was able to talk only with Benson, the office's Eagle Scout, a young man eager to please. The syrupy flapjacks and charred toast sank in Cooper's stomach when he heard the man's unctuous voice. Nursing his impending bellyache, he left Benson with a terse message. Cooper next sent a telegram straight to Hoover, J. Edgar, letting the Bureau director know what was fact, what was unverified in the Rosen case, and the apparent duplicity of local authorities in combination with the complicity of the local press. In light of the suspects being captured, Cooper's missive asked, was his presence still required in San Jose?

Cooper stepped out onto the sidewalk to inhale a Lucky Strike while he waited for a response. The morning air was chilly. He wished he had brought along his overcoat.

After stubbing out his cigarette, Cooper returned to the hotel lobby. The place was now very much alive. Guests were snapping up newspapers. The newsboy was making a killing. People read aloud to others, providing their own opinions of what had definitively happened. In the space of two minutes, the two suspects held in the Hall of Justice were summarily judged. "String them up. That's what should be done!" bellowed one big-bellied man.

The front desk clerk motioned to Cooper that a response had come. It simply read: STAY WITH THIS ONE UNTIL FURTHER NOTICE. Cooper crumpled the telegram from the Bureau and headed toward the Hall of Justice. If he was still on the case, then he wanted another crack at Harold Tierney. And an opportunity to break his newly discovered accomplice, Earle Hansen.

25

Perhaps it was fortuitous that the university had resumed classes the same morning the newspaper announced the apprehension of Michael Rosen's captors. Normalcy had resumed in the valley, at least on the surface. So had Winston's daily work routine, though he held his breath every time someone walked by his desk. There had been no further messages or instructions to execute covert errands or make anonymous telephone calls. Perhaps the Committee had deemed his work complete. In that event, he wanted some type of reward, as was promised. On the other hand, if the Committee somehow thought the kidnapping had been a failure, Winston hoped he was off the hook, at least as far as the authorities were concerned. He'd gone over and over the events in his mind, trying to be sure there was nothing that could link him to the two men the police had arrested.

At noon, he heard something: a low rumble throughout the campus, then shouts and cries that grew louder. Football season was over, but there was another type of rally in the courtyard below. Winston rose from his desk, looked around to see if anyone else noticed. The department secretary looked determined to continue her typing. The office manager continued to stare at the memo he was supposed to compose. Someone outside began pounding a drum. At that, everyone in the office stopped what they were doing and went to stare out the windows.

Winston pried open a second-story window and leaned out. A crowd of mostly students had formed in the courtyard, and more were emerging from nearby buildings and various campus portals. Soon enough he saw Jeremy Rollins, a one-time child actor in the silent flicks, hanging over the balcony of the Montgomery Laboratories building on the other side of the courtyard. Rollins went to work on his audience, beginning in a hushed whisper and building to a theatrical soliloquy: "The time has come for Santa Clara to come together as a student body. All of us as one. One of our recent graduates has fallen. To the criminal element of our society. This element does not belong. In our valley. In our community. They have taken him away. For ransom . . ."

The courtyard was fully packed. Rollins gave a courtly gesture and picked up the tempo.

"They do not belong. We must preserve our Judeo-Christian values. We cannot sit back and watch. We must defend these values. We must be vigilant. We must seek vengeance. We must act to right the wrongs."

Rollins paused for effect. His audience maintained their rapt attention.

"For thirty pieces of silver, they have taken him! We can only become saved if we understand. Understand the nature of this crime. And with this crime we cannot sit back. And watch him suffer. We must act to right the wrongs. We must seek vengeance on those who threaten these values and seek to profit. Because they do not share our values. They will never reach the Kingdom of God Almighty, because they have come to take away our brother."

The cheerleader's voice began to rise again in staccato fashion.

"This institution, this Santa Clara, has selflessly embraced Michael Rosen as if he were a Roman Catholic. This act of cowardice threatens the fabric of our interdenominational spirit. It is a work of evil. Evil that lurks. Within the cracks of our society. This evil must be stamped out. This evil must be eliminated. We seek Christian justice. We want justice!"

"We want justice!" echoed the students.

Several of the Bronco football players, distinguished by their scarlet-and-white letterman jackets, screamed the loudest. They stomped and raised their fists. "We want justice! Tierney and Hansen! We want justice!"

The crowd picked up the cry. Over and over again until Rollins finally waved his hands to quiet them. When the noise died down, Rollins launched into a variation of the Bronco fight song.

Justice, justice, for the Broncos have the ball.
Have no fear, we will not let Michael fall.
And when we get Tierney and Hansen, that'll be all.
There'll be a hot time in the old town tonight.

The crowd picked up the verse and sang wildly. Shouts of "Hail, Santa Clara!" and "Justice, justice!" rang out amid the raucous singing.

And when we get Tierney and Hansen, that'll be all.
There'll be a hot time in the old town tonight.

As the crowd launched into a third repetition of the improvised song, Winston remained leaning out the window, scanning the faces in the crowd. Some of the Jesuits stood beneath the columns, arms folded, faces betraying nothing. Wilford Kishi was there among the priests, though the university president's assistant was half hidden in an archway. Winston had always kept notice of the young Japanese man who managed to work under Fr. Seebach, but he didn't know much about him.

Rollins raised his hands once again, trying to shush the crowd. The students would not have it. The chanting had reached a crescendo. Rollins climbed on top of the balustrade and waved his arms until they at last calmed down.

"Just a moment, just a moment," said Rollins. "I beseech you. I have a special colleague who wants to speak. You know him. Michael knows him. We all know him."

Rosen's best friend, James O'Neill, emerged onto the balcony, looking weary.

"I love this school. Michael loved this school. Santa Clara," said O'Neill in a slow, measured manner. "He had high hopes, having graduated earlier this year, to continue his service in commerce in San Jose. He wanted to spread what was right and what was just in these difficult times. I beg you to never forget Michael Rosen, what he has done for our school, for our community . . . We'll get Michael back!"

O'Neill could not go on. He stepped back out of view as the players in their letterman jackets took his place, raised clenched fists, and demanded, "Justice, justice, justice!"

The noise was nonstop until the chapel bell clanged, signaling that the rally was over. The crowd dutifully lined up and marched once around the courtyard. Then, solemnly, the students and various priests split off and filed into the surrounding buildings. Winston shut the window. Soon enough, the office returned to its former sedate state. Typewriters began to click and tap again. Back at his desk, he managed a semblance of composure as he resumed filling out his daily forms. But his thoughts remained on Fr. Seebach. What was he doing at the Trevis estate with a bunch of gangsters? Who was this Ripley character? Who represented the Committee? And when would he be rewarded for the things he had done? He devised a plan to find out.

26

Cooper saw the pack of them: newspaper reporters huddled outside the Hall of Justice, scribbling in their notebooks, and photographers adjusting their bulbs, ready to aim and flash their cameras. In a matter of hours, the kidnapping had flourished into national news. He turned up his collar, slipped to his left, and came around to the building's side entry. Deputies posted there escorted him through the lobby and up the steps to a corridor leading to the rooms where Tierney and Hansen were held.

"Where's Blackmun?" said Cooper when he saw Butler.

"Not here. He's back at city hall. The sheriff is leading the interrogations."

"Tell him I want answers."

Butler nodded and tapped on the door. It was opened from within. The door snapped shut before Cooper could follow Butler inside. Thirty seconds later, Butler stuck out his head and motioned Cooper to enter. Cooper kept his clenched fists in his pockets, resisting rage.

They were all there. Around the table sat a rotund Ewing and his deputies. There was one face he didn't recognize. This man was in his sixties, wore an impeccably tailored dark suit, and sat at the head of the table. He had an air of confidence, but his youthful smile belied a sagging chin and pasty face. His thinning, short white hair looked pasted on his pate. "Name's Ripley," said the man, remaining in his chair. He did not bother to offer his hand. "You must be one of those Hoover men."

"He's been assisting in the interrogation," said Ewing.

On the far side of the table sat a sullen, drained, and cornered Tierney with his ludicrous ears. One side of his face was bruised. His right eye was bloodshot. His greasy hair stood on end.

Ripley grinned at Cooper. "While you slept, the sheriff's department further questioned Mr. Tierney, and like most criminals he soon became entangled in his story. He finally confessed and has named Earle Hansen as his accomplice."

"So I gathered," Cooper said evenly. "It was fortunate that Hansen was captured just in time for the morning edition."

Ripley merely smiled.

"Glad you finally made it over," said Ewing to Cooper. Tierney sat with his arms wrapped around his body and looked down at the table. He resembled a crumpled autumn leaf.

"Do you mind if I talk to him?" asked Cooper.

"It's all right. I'm done here," said Ripley, confidently. He stood and started toward the door.

"Why don't you stick around?" asked Cooper.

"No, no. I've business to take care of."

"By all means. He's yours," Ewing said to Cooper. "We'll be outside. Let me know when you are done. Then we can talk." Ewing closed his binder of papers and got up.

"Yes. We'll talk."

"Glad you can be of service," Ripley said, giving Cooper a wink. Picking up his briefcase, Ripley made a beeline out the door. Ewing followed.

Cooper sat at the table. He looked at the three deputies one by one. The first had to be fresh on the force. Cooper asked him his name. Kane was the answer. The second was more seasoned, a chunky, broad-shouldered, blond-maned athlete named Gibson. They only gave their last names.

"That leaves you." Cooper looked at the third deputy, probably in his early forties—hunched, hooded gray eyes, long nose. There for the long haul, seeking that horizon, a pension after thirty years.

"Ben Miller."

"Glad you have a first name." Cooper smiled thinly. "What happened?" He had the sense that he already knew how Miller would answer.

"They managed to get answers out of him. It was tough going, but they did it."

Cooper inwardly winced at the banality of the response. Tierney remained silent, staring at the table. "The man has been beaten."

"I hadn't noticed," Miller replied.

"And you," said Cooper, staring at Tierney, a pitiful heap of flesh. "What do you have to say for yourself?"

Tierney's eyes darted back and forth as if trying to register what a correct response might entail.

"All right, son. Let's forget about last night. Never happened. Tell me how you kidnapped Michael Rosen on the evening of November 6."

Tierney found a spot on the wall to stare at. Then Gibson prompted him with a shove in the side. "It was all Earle's idea. He came up with the plan."

Cooper opened his notebook. "Tell me again how it happened."

Looking at Gibson, Tierney recited nervously: "We wanted the money. Earle planned it. We snagged him downtown outside his old man's store."

"You had a car?"

"Um, yes."

"Make?"

"Chevy sedan."

"Hansen's car."

"His father's." He glanced pitifully up at Cooper. "That's what he told me."

"You were in the alley..."

"We waited until Rosen left the store. He talked to some woman on her way somewhere. Then got into his car. Earle moved in."

"Where were you?"

"In the Chevy."

"You took Hansen's car. Why?"

"That's what he wanted."

"What happened?"

"Rosen starts up his car. Hansen opens the passenger door. He had a pistol."

"Where did you get the gun?"

"Don't know. Hansen got it. Said he bought it from a bootlegger."

"Naturally. Go on."

"They drive away. I follow. Up Santa Clara toward the hills. Then we headed out of town toward Milpitas."

"Where were you going?"

"No idea."

"No plan?"

"Hansen had the plan. I followed."

"Was this his plan or someone else's?"

"His plan. He never told me."

"Might it have been the bootlegger's plan?"

Tierney looked confused. "What bootlegger?"

"Who was the woman?"

"What woman?" Tierney seemed even more lost.

"The one who talked to Rosen."

"Don't know," mumbled Tierney.

"So, just you and Hansen. Anybody else?"

"No, definitely not."

"And then?"

Tierney could not answer.

"Where did Hansen go?"

"He goes and stops in an orchard. Middle of nowhere."

"Did you honk the horn at any point?"

"No. I flashed the headlights."

"Why?"

"Because I didn't know why he had stopped in the middle of nowhere."

"Did you see anybody?"

"No."

Cooper waited.

"So, uh, Earle gets out. Rosen gets out. They come over and get in. Sit in the back. We drive away."

"Rosen's car was left behind?"

"That's right."

Cooper made a few notes, enumerating this lie, among others.

"We were still in Earle's car. He's in back with Rosen," said Tierney when Cooper prompted him to continue.

"This is the Chevy, right?"

"Right."

"Hansen's still got the gun?"

Tierney nodded. "We drive north. I'm driving, okay? I'm the driver. Earle's in back with Rosen. At some point, there is a road sign, and Earle tells me turn west. We head to the bridge."

"Which one?" asked Cooper.

"He means the San Mateo Bridge. Hayward–San Mateo," said Kane helpfully.

"So, there was a plan?" Cooper asked, ignoring Kane.

"Earle told me we were supposed to go to Oakland."

"Change of plans?"

Tierney shrugged. "I guess. We're on the bridge, about halfway across, and Earle said to stop. I stopped."

Tierney stopped talking and squeezed his eyes shut.

"Come on," said Gibson. Cooper gave the deputy a cold stare. "Go on, son," he said to Tierney, a bit more gently.

Tierney opened his eyes, looked at Cooper and then at the wall. "I look through the rearview mirror. Earle has a pillowcase over

Rosen's head. The guy is fighting. Earle coldcocks him with the gun. He's out cold."

"Why would Earle do that?"

"He said he planned it that way."

"Which way was that?"

"Don't know."

The room was stuffy, and Cooper wanted coffee. He also wanted to coldcock a few deputies and their boss. "So, Rosen's out cold," he said to Tierney. "Then what happened? You dumped him into the bay?"

"No, on the road. On the bridge. Then, uh, we took off."

"You drove away? Why? Why would you leave him?"

"Earle said that was the plan. His plan."

"And he always told you what to do?"

"Told me I was the driver. That was all I was supposed to do."

"Did someone pay you?"

"Earle's supposed to pay me. But no, not yet."

"After you dumped Rosen, where did you go?"

"Home."

"Hansen?"

"I think Earle went home too."

"No one else?"

"No."

"Why did you kidnap Michael Rosen?"

"For the money."

"Yet you left Rosen on the San Mateo bridge?"

"That was Earle's plan."

"What happened to the gun?"

"No idea."

"There was a call to Rosen's family that evening from San Francisco. Did you make that call?"

"No."

"Where were you?"

"At home."

"Where's that?"

"Campbell."

"Had you ever met Michael Rosen before? How did you know it was him?"

"Earle took his wallet to check."

"When was that?"

"When they got into the car."

"You mean, you kidnapped him and *then* asked him for his wallet to check his identity?"

"That's about the size of it, yeah. Earle wanted to be sure."

"And what did you do with the wallet?"

"Ask Earle."

"You have stated that it was all Earle Hansen's fault, yet you were the one caught and arrested in the parking garage. On a pay phone, talking to the victim's father. You placed the call to demand a ransom. You said you dumped Rosen on the bridge, yet you wanted payment for the kidnapping? How do you reconcile that?"

Tierney looked blank.

"How do you explain all of that?" Cooper said.

"It was all Earle's idea. His plan. Not mine. I'm just the fall guy."

Cooper couldn't argue with the very last comment.

There was an insistent knock on the door. Miller got up, opened the door. It was Butler. He had orders to take Tierney.

"We've received death threats on him and the other one," Butler said. "The sheriff doesn't think it's safe to keep them here any longer."

Butler moved to put handcuffs on the prisoner.

Cooper said, "Wait a minute. I'm not done with him."

"Sorry, Agent Cooper, those are my orders.

"I'm not finished."

"Orders are orders. This one's going to be taken to Potrero Police Station in San Francisco. The other one, Hansen, is already on his way there."

Cooper figured that the man in the green tie had arranged to hustle Hansen out. Thomas Ripley had no apparent connection to the Rosen case and yet had been allowed into a police interrogation. Then, when Cooper arrived, Ripley had scurried off to deal with some unnamed business.

"You're taking Tierney to San Francisco yourself?" Cooper asked Butler.

"No. Sheriff Ewing is going to personally escort the prisoner."

Cooper's hackles went up.

27

In the opulent Liberty Hill neighborhood of San Francisco, a gaily painted Queen Anne–style manor imposed itself on the corner. The colorful structure was replete with a turret tower, steeply pitched roof, canted bay windows, and a generous wraparound porch.

Later that afternoon, while fashionable men were discreetly let in and out a side door, Ripley strode up the front stairs and pushed the door buzzer. When there was no answer, he pressed the button repeatedly. He did not appreciate the treatment. He was not a customer.

Finally, the door was opened by a heavyset man with a large mustache.

"Linforth," said Ripley, not hiding his irritation.

"Yes, sir. I'll first have to pat you down."

Ripley put his hands up in mock surrender and allowed the man to do his job.

Once satisfied, the guard indicated that someone named Ruby would show Ripley to the upstairs offices. In a moment, a blond, sad-eyed waif appeared. Her makeup resembled war paint, her eyebrows punctuated in a manner that expressed perpetual shock. She did not say anything but led Ripley up the grand staircase to the second floor where Lawrence Linforth, Esq., oversaw his legal services. As Ripley entered, Linforth rose from behind a large oak desk. He might have been the spitting image of Rutherford B. Hayes. A long, pointed gray beard attempted to compensate for his receding hairline. Close-set eyes gave him a cross-eyed, slightly inbred look. The men shook hands, and Ruby withdrew.

"How is the governor these days?" asked Ripley.

"If we can keep him sober, he'll manage."

They sat on the sofa. They talked about the health of their families and how they intended to spend the holidays.

The waif returned with refreshments. The men toasted each other's health and sipped an imported brand.

"Ah, very nice," determined Ripley.

"I understand arrangements have been carried out down south. Did those two boys spill anything?" asked Linforth.

"No one has, and no one will believe them. We've got men on the inside to make sure there are no slipups."

"Naturally," said Linforth, seeming much relieved.

"Both prisoners have been transferred," said Ripley.

"I'm sure that they remain quite cozy."

"Just so that we are in agreement."

"Assuredly so, but realize it will be necessary at an appropriate point to release some pressure so that other actions can proceed. Reports I have received indicate the Committee's position has recently improved and"—Linforth sipped his drink—"we don't want things to boil quite yet. It's best to have things simmer for a while."

Ripley nodded, reached into his pocket for a cigar.

Linforth offered a light.

"Would you care for a smoke?" asked Ripley.

"The wife doesn't want me to indulge. Thank you. I respect her wishes."

While Ripley began to puff, Linforth asked, "How is the transaction proceeding?"

"The Jesuits remain stubborn, but one way or another the good fathers will eventually sell us the Mission property."

"You know that's a crucial piece. The Jesuit land will enhance our investment. Think of it as trading apricots for dirigibles—"

"Planes instead of prunes," snickered Ripley.

"Exactly. It's a prudent investment. Something that pays handsomely. Makes the governor look awfully good," said Linforth. "The old drunk will be praised as a visionary."

They both laughed.

"Father Seebach thinks he has a strong hand. Thinks he's holding out for a better deal, but—"

"Let him pray, huh?" Linforth chuckled. "And how's your partner?"

Ripley shrugged lightly. "A two-bit hood. He serves his purpose. With your assistance, we can rein him in. Am I correct?"

"Most assuredly. And the man Hoover sent?" asked Linforth.

"Merely a bureaucrat. He just doesn't know it. Civil servants are restrained by the rules that are given to them."

"We are good then? We will soon be square on all accounts."

"I think we are good," agreed Ripley. "But we'll need to get those two back down in San Jose when the time comes."

"We're quite in agreement."

Ripley started to rise. Linforth lifted his hand.

"I appreciate the time you took to get up to the city. Is there anything else I can offer? Care to sample the treats of the house?"

"I try not to mix business with pleasure."

"The governor would disagree."

"Another time, perhaps."

The meeting concluded. Ruby had been waiting for him outside Linforth's office and accompanied Ripley downstairs.

"Are you sure you wouldn't want to spare some time with me?" she asked him.

"Thank you for your hospitality, but I'll take a rain check," Ripley told the girl, knowing full well how Linforth operated and having no wish to be ensnarled in an indiscretion that would be a liability down the road. Ruby withdrew without another word after they descended.

The mustachioed doorman opened the front door, and Ripley breezed past him and down the entry stairs.

Across the street, Sal Booksin sat in darkness. He watched Ripley cross the street to his waiting Plymouth. A door was opened, and Ripley climbed in. The Plymouth headed off. Booksin followed.

Another car farther down the block started up.

28

After watching Tierney be dragged away in handcuffs, Cooper grew more enraged by the minute. He fired off a series of telegrams to Washington and placed telephone calls to colleagues in San Francisco. His main line of inquiry and speculation: Thomas Ripley. Hours later and without much luck, he returned to the Hall of Justice and stared down the unapologetic deputies Kane, Gibson, and finally Miller, who bit his lip and turned away. No one said anything as the minutes lapsed.

At last Gibson relented and flatly announced, "There are officers now combing the bridge for evidence and dredging the bay for the body."

"Is that so?"

"We'll find something soon," assured Gibson.

"And in the meantime, we've registered more death threats against the two, uh, suspects," added the youthful Kane. Cooper wondered if he was old enough to shave and how he could manage a law enforcement position when he didn't look like he could even vote. Who rubbed whose back to get him into the sheriff's department?

"It's the radio stations," continued Gibson. "There's talk of possible mob action against the prisoners. They'd be in danger if they stayed here. The governor announced that he would not tolerate a breakdown in law and order, that it was time to take a tough stand, that action should be taken." As a deputy sheriff, Gibson looked the part—had probably played college football and acted like those concussions had had an effect.

"When did the governor make this announcement?" Cooper wanted to know.

"Before you came in," replied Kane.

"Which time?"

No one answered. Cooper waited.

A weary Miller leaned against a desk, scratching his unshaven face. "You know, we are still investigating, still interrogating. No charges have been filed yet. And, in fact, there is no body. And without a body, there is no crime." Miller was the oldest of this trio and probably didn't have a clue what to do after retirement. Cooper had seen many Millers along the way. Not one of them ended up well.

"When I spoke with Mr. Tierney last night, he continually denied any involvement in any kidnapping." Cooper glared at each of them. "And now he has admitted his role and blames everything on Earle Hansen. How do you reconcile his change of heart, aside from the condition of his face? What made him change his story?"

"I came on duty at eight this morning," offered Gibson. "So did Kane."

Cooper looked at Miller, his eyes hard. The deputy glanced toward the hallway before answering. "Sheriff Ewing has a reputation of getting results," he said evenly.

"You surmise that his forcefulness resulted in Mr. Tierney's confession? What do you suppose made the difference?"

Gibson and Kane were mute.

"Was it perhaps the inclusion of Mr. Ripley that was decisive?"

Kane put up his hands as if in surrender. "We weren't there. We don't know."

"And you?" Cooper pointed his finger at Miller.

"I was not part of the interrogation. I was outside." Miller was evading any responsibility.

Cooper exhaled. He looked at each of these men and said, "What can you tell me of Mr. Ripley?"

All three deputies seemed nervous, young Kane more so. "Ripley is an adviser to the mayor," he told Cooper. "They bring him in when things need to get resolved."

"What does he do?"

Kane glanced at the others. The others stared at the floor. "I've heard he's a real estate guy," admitted Kane.

Cooper slammed his hand on the desk. "Who is he in cahoots with? The mayor? The governor? Why did you allow a *real estate man* to sit in if not lead the kidnapping investigation?"

"Don't know." Miller stuck his hands in his pockets and stared directly at Cooper. "Why does that matter?"

"Do you think I can have a talk with Ripley?"

"You'll have to make an appointment," replied Miller. Cooper wondered why Miller was being so evasive.

With the brick wall of bureaucracy staring him in the face, Cooper, suppressing his outrage, tried another approach. "Do you think you at least could arrange for me to interview Tierney and Hansen in San Francisco?"

"I think so," said Miller. Cooper was tired of Miller's antics and Gibson's brute stupidity. When they left the room, ostensibly to make such arrangements, Kane remained, fidgeting beneath Cooper's gaze. The deputy kept glancing at the closed door, not knowing whether to leave or not.

"I'm pretty sure you'll get to interview them. They're okay. They just do what they are told," Kane said.

Cooper stared at Kane and then asked, "What would it take to get a decent drink in town?"

Kane blinked. "Well, sir, as you know, federal regulations are still in place, but we have tended to take a looser approach since the law will soon change."

"Is there a good place that you might recommend?"

"You might try a place across the way. On the other side of St. James Park. They call it Spades. There's no sign. There's just an awning. Easy to find. Say that you know me. You'll get in. You might get what you need."

Cooper nodded and then looked at his watch. "Can you boys pick me up tomorrow at eight in front of the Sainte Claire?"

⁂

Back in his hotel room, Cooper began typing his report to the Bureau. There were a host of questions that remained open:

1. Were Tierney and Hansen the only perpetrators of the kidnapping, or were there others who had been hired, and if so, who was behind the kidnapping?
2. If the kidnapping motivation was money, why had the ransom not been collected and Rosen returned?
3. Why were local law authorities jerking him around?
4. What was the relationship between public officials and the release of certain information to the media?
5. Why was this Thomas Ripley, a real estate developer, involved, and whose interests did it serve?
6. And where the fuck was Michael Rosen?

He yanked out the page and retyped it, grudgingly amending the last line to wording his bosses would tolerate. With his anger partially reined in, he spent most of the afternoon composing his report, then gave it to a hotel clerk to mail off to Washington. He hoped his missive made clear to Hoover that there was more to San Jose than this bucolic facade of a place that marketed itself as "the City of Heart's Delight."

After hours hunched over a typewriter, he busted out of the hotel, relieved to enjoy a walk-through of nearby St. James Park. The weather remained brisk and windy. Elm trees, mostly, swayed. Birds flitted from one branch to another. Some sun peeked out occasionally through rain-bloated clouds. He glanced at the bronze statue dedicated to President McKinley and mused: Who was the political hack who thought that might give this Podunk town some respectability?

The wind picked up, and Cooper turned up his collar as he swished through a carpet of dead leaves. More leaves fell as the wind swirled. The civil servants were losing the battle, Cooper thought. Nature would have its way no matter how many times they swept.

He jaywalked across Third Street, peered up and down the block, and noted the parade of associations: a Christian Science church, an Episcopal church, the Scottish Rite Temple, and the Freemason Hall. Musing over their incongruity, Cooper located the simple black awning announcing nothing and descended into the place he guessed was Spades. The bouncer gave him the once-over. Cooper mentioned Kane's name, and the bouncer buzzed him in.

The place was weakly illuminated by a low green light. Cooper squinted and headed toward the bar with its shelves of neatly arranged bottles. He sat on a stool. It wasn't long before he was approached by a distinguished-looking gentleman who appeared to have expected his arrival. The man with an aquiline nose asked Cooper what his pleasure was.

"Whiskey. Irish. Not Scotch."

"Let me see about that. Wait here for a moment."

The gentleman left, presumably in pursuit of the right bottle or at least liquid with a label that declared it to be one hundred percent genuine whiskey from the required homeland. Cooper waited. The man returned and announced he might have something of interest. "I rummaged around in back and found this bottle. A Jameson from County Cork. I hope this will do."

The bottle was dusty but looked like the real deal.

"Let's open it up, shall we?" suggested the man.

"That's the ticket..." Cooper looked questioningly at the bartender.

"Ah, my name is Angelo."

"Cooper."

"Ah, yes."

Angelo twisted the cap, expertly sized up the bottle, and poured whiskey in a tumbler. Cooper seized the glass and brought it to his lips. "Very good. Tastes like real Irish."

"It is the real thing. We don't fool around here."

"Indeed you don't," said Cooper as he indulged himself again.

"We may be a small town, but we have principles. Or at least we used to. These days, who can tell? San Jose has always managed to miss its potential."

"How so?"

Angelo refilled Cooper's glass before answering.

"This town was the first Spanish pueblo in Alta California. It had all the potential: rich agricultural bounty, timber, access to water, everything. When the Americans came, the town was the first capital of the State of California. Promising, yes? The legislators met in their first session. The only thing they accomplished was drinking. The legislators declared: 'Let's have a drink. Let's have a thousand drinks.' And that's what they became known for: 'The Legislature of a Thousand Drinks.' Those drunken scoundrels lost any progress for San Jose. They soon moved the capital elsewhere. San Jose is the capital that got away. Ironic, isn't it?"

"That they frittered it away?"

"That they'll fritter away their self-respect once again."

"The irony is that the reason those bums moved the capital was because they were all drunks. And yet here we are. You are the purveyor of alcohol, a forbidden substance. How do you square that?" Cooper asked. In the darkness, he saw Angelo's smile.

"Ah, do you find that a contradiction? There are contradictions everywhere. Look at you. You are from out of town. Obviously, here on some sort of business. Most would be in town for the cannery business, the engine that drives the valley. You do not seem the type. Your appearance would suggest a bureaucrat of some sort. The question is: Are you here to enforce the Volstead Act or to ignore it?" Angelo raised his glass. "Since you enjoy the Jameson, my bet is that you are ignoring it. Otherwise, I think Oliver, our doorman, wouldn't have let you in. Given the events of late, may I suggest that you are here for investigative purposes?"

"You didn't answer my question."

"I think it is amusing that you sit here representing the government, in an illegal bar, drinking an illegal Irish whiskey, and conversing with a possibly illegal immigrant. What are you doing about the cultural crime of the century? Nothing."

"That's right. Nothing. But you still didn't answer my question."

"Principles are a function of the circumstances over which you have no power. It's survival. I arrived from Northern Italy at the turn of the century. What did I know? Wine. I worked the vines at first, then at a winery until those sap-sucking bugs infected all the vines. There was the earthquake. I worked some in import-export, then along came Prohibition, so I adjusted what I know and what I could do. Debts have to be repaid. Principles evolve. And, you know, to continue in this profession one has to be honest. What else could I have done? What else would they have permitted me to do? I like my work. I have a nice family. I meet many interesting people."

Cooper nodded, wondering if this bartender was always so forthcoming or so elusive. Nonetheless, he played the game while his glass was generously refilled. They touched on many subjects—the grim economic news, national sports—none of which held much mutual interest, all of which studiously avoided the recent events in San Jose. He felt that Angelo was testing the conversation with verbal jabs and flinches, and then, with an audacious wink, Angelo threw a right hook and pointedly inquired about Cooper's past.

"Grew up in Salt Lake City," Cooper amiably said. "Went to law school in DC. Joined the Bureau in twenty-five. Been with them since. I travel a lot."

"Married?"

"No."

"And so, through your travels, what have you learned?"

"Not as much as I would have liked, but I've learned that all towns operate the same way."

The bartender held up the bottle. Cooper nodded. Angelo poured.

"Towns like this one are not unlike the one I recently left. Kansas City," Cooper said, softened up by the liquor.

"Do tell. I'm all ears."

Cooper downed his drink. Angelo quickly refilled his glass. "Frank Nash, arrested for robbing banks. He got a pardon, got out, robbed a mail train. That's a federal offense. He was caught again and sent to Leavenworth, escaped, got caught again. The Bureau was called in. I was in charge. Our job was to escort Nash back to Leavenworth. That meant going through Kansas City. There was a local boss, named Pendergast, who ran the town. He wasn't an elected official, but he controlled everything. Everything needed his approval."

Cooper paused, which signaled the bartender for another round. Angelo did his duty.

"Nash was escorted to Kansas City. On the morning train. With me were two Bureau agents and two city police. As well as the policeman who had caught Nash. At the train station, Nash's custody would be transferred to me. The Bureau was to take Nash back to prison. We arrived at the train station in two cars."

Cooper paused and cleared his throat. Took a few sips.

"I still remember that morning. Peaceful, quiet. A blue sedan barrels into the parking lot and stops at the far side of the station. Local cops say the occupants work for Pendergast. They have the mayor's daughter with them. She's sitting next to the driver. The train arrives. Nash is handcuffed. We lead him out of the station. We get him into the back seat of one of our cars. Just as we are about to climb in, a green

Plymouth shows up. Two men jump out holding tommy guns. The city cops have guns, but Bureau agents are not allowed weapons. One of the men shouts, 'Let 'em have it!' Bullets are flying. A bullet grazes me. I go down. I bleed a little on the pavement, but four men are shot dead. Another is untouched. They completely miss him somehow."

Cooper slammed his fist on the counter. He didn't mean to slam it so hard.

"They killed Nash, too. Shot him square in the forehead. What was the point? Maybe that was their intention all along. To make sure Nash kept silent. Maybe they just got jumpy and shot them all up? I don't know. They all disappeared." Cooper fluttered his hands in the air. They just flew away.

"The Bureau swore that Pretty Boy Floyd was in on it. The mayor's girl got a pass. Not even picked up for questioning. No one touched Pendergast, of course. It was a clean sweep for the home team."

Cooper stared at his empty glass. Angelo poured another shot.

"It's never about who pulls the trigger. It's about who is pulling the strings."

Angelo wiped the bar top with his towel. "And what does this tell you? What bothers you the most?" he said softly.

Cooper took another swig.

"The Bureau used the massacre to compel Congress to allow agents to carry guns. Don't get me wrong; I agree with that. That should happen. But Hoover wanted more. He wanted the Bureau to be its own police force. Not to be under the thumb of the Justice Department. In order to do that, certain accommodations had to be made. Pendergast was never implicated in any of this. The more I think about it, I'm inclined to think Floyd might not have ever been involved. Hoover needed mob machine-gun bullets and Floyd's notoriety to generate the needed publicity to arm his agents. Hoover has been pressuring . . ."

Cooper stopped in mid-sentence. He realized where he was and who he was speaking to, and he had enough remaining wits to know that he had drunk and said too much. It was time to shut his trap. He apologized and got up to leave.

Angelo smiled. "We must talk again."

29

Gazing at the stars in the night sky, Victoria tried to connect those discrete points of light and determine their relationships. Sometimes a pattern emerged, possibly forming a picture, a complete constellation. Amelia's father had given her a clue: John Schiavo. Admonished her to stay away. It wasn't yet a picture, but enough so that she was intrigued to learn more. She had remembered him being taken away at the demonstration and recalled his curly hair, bright-brown eyes, and lopsided smile. Schiavo had a habit of crossing his legs at the ankles as he pontificated about the exploitation of the workers in the orchards of plenty.

Still suspended from classes, Victoria was on her way to the union offices, determined to get more information. She rapped her knuckles on the third-floor door where a modest sign read: CANNERY AND AGRICULTURAL WORKERS' INDUSTRIAL UNION. Guy Upton, the union's business manager, opened the door slowly.

"It's only me," said Victoria brightly.

"Yeah, it's only you," replied Upton sourly when he let her in and double-locked the door behind them. Though Upton was in his late twenties, his intense eyes beneath the glasses that framed his face made him look older. Upton had modeled his look after the revolutionist Trotsky. The CAIWU had wisely assigned him to desk work instead of organizing in the orchards or firing up the canneries.

Nothing beyond a fountain pen and a typewriter. "You can't be too sure who's going to be at the door these days. The police. Vigilantes. The American Legion. They're out in swarms."

"When will Sara be in?" Victoria plopped down in his chair.

Upton stood with folded arms as he stared down at her. "She's out. She went to Los Gatos with the Beaumonts. Moneyed liberals, you know."

"Will she be back soon?"

Upton seemed reluctant to answer, as if trying to decipher her motivations. Victoria stared back at him until he relented. "Doubtful she will be back anytime soon. She left you a note with her telephone number."

"You read her note. Addressed to me? How dare you!"

Upton stared at her. "You don't understand. There are spies everywhere. I need to know what's going on."

"You read other people's mail?" said Victoria, incredulously.

"Someone has infiltrated our union. We suspect that there is a traitor." Upton looked Victoria up and down. "Why are you here today?"

"What do you know about John Schiavo?"

Upton kept his eyes on her. "Schiavo got arrested like the others. Beaumont money got everyone out on bail but him. He's still in jail. The judge refused the bail."

"Why would the judge do that?"

"That's a mystery. Not only that but we haven't been able to reach him. He's even had his own attorney handling his case."

"Who is his lawyer?"

"I don't know." Upton shuffled the papers scattered all over his desk.

Victoria was resolute. "How do I track him down?"

"Give Sara a call. She might know." He handed over the note. Indeed, it read that someone had infiltrated the union, to be cautious and trust no one.

Victoria grabbed the phone and rang the operator to reach Sara in Los Gatos. It took some time for Sara to be located at the Beaumont estate. Meanwhile, Upton ignored Victoria, and she ignored him.

When Sara did come on the line, she sounded uncharacteristically annoyed. Victoria was unclear whether it was Schiavo's felony charge or the phone call that had her upset.

"What do you know about this guy who is representing Schiavo?" Victoria asked her.

"A Sacramento attorney."

That seemed odd, thought Victoria. "Do you know him?" she asked.

"No. We know his name is Francis Dash," Sara said.

"Why would Schiavo want someone from out of town? And why Sacramento?"

"We're baffled. Can you check up on this Dash fellow?"

"I will," Victoria promised.

"Guy has the number. I know he's difficult, but he's one of us. Let me know what happens. If you ever run into difficulties, you can come to Los Gatos. Guy knows the address."

They ended the call, and Victoria looked at Upton. He was no longer shuffling papers and had been watching her. Harnessing her annoyance, Victoria asked, "Guy, could I get that number for Dash, please?"

Upton's answer was to open his desk drawer, search its innards, pull out a stack of notes, and look methodically through them until he found a scribbled note with Dash's contact information. This he offered to Victoria. She took the note from his extended hand and immediately placed a call to Sacramento.

"Yes?" said a woman's voice.

"May I speak to one of your attorneys? Francis Dash?"

"Let me see." Victoria waited for an uncomfortable amount of time. "He's not in right now. Could you leave me your name?"

Victoria gave her name and said, "Mr. Dash is representing a colleague of ours. John Schiavo."

Seemingly unimpressed, the woman replied, "He's a busy man and requires an appointment."

Victoria hesitated, thinking that this would require her to travel to Sacramento. "I would like to see him as soon as possible."

"Ah, well, Mr. Dash is currently in San Francisco at a conference. And will be there for the next few days."

"Is it possible to meet him in San Francisco?"

"Let me see. Please hold." Victoria heard the woman talking to someone else and, though muffled, a man's voice seemed to be giving her instructions.

"Yes, we can arrange for such a meeting," the woman said. "It appears that we can accommodate your request, but the meeting will need to take place at the Hotel Whittier. Are you available for a noon appointment tomorrow? Do you know where it is?"

"I can find it."

"It's on Market Street." Another pause. "Please arrive at the reception desk in the lobby. Give them your name and the front desk will direct you to Mr. Dash's room. Is that all right with you?"

"Yes, but isn't this all a bit . . . ?" Victoria did not like the idea of going to a man's hotel room.

"That is the best I can do. I hope you understand."

Victoria had to commit. "All right. It's a deal."

"You'll be expected. Noon." Then, a click.

Victoria felt the heat rising in her cheeks as she pondered the inappropriateness of the arrangement. Perhaps stranger still that she had agreed to travel to San Francisco when a phone conversation might have sufficed.

She sat so deeply in thought that she didn't notice Upton's departure. Alone in the office, she hunted around for the next morning's train schedule to San Francisco and a streetcar map to determine how best to get to the Whittier.

30

The next morning, Cooper made a short detour on his way to San Francisco. He asked Deputy Kane to stop off at the Amaral ranch. There he interviewed Mrs. Amaral about her prior testimony. She repeated her story of seeing a car arrive, flash its headlights, and someone getting out of the car to smoke. Minutes later another car arrived; she saw headlights flash again. Three men, maybe more, got out of the second car and into the first. The first car departed, and then the second.

"It was dark, but I'm pretty sure the first one was a Chevy," said Madeline Amaral.

Cooper wrote everything down in his pocket notebook. "When the second car arrived, how many voices did you hear?"

"Goodness, I could not tell."

"You were pretty sure the second automobile was a Studebaker roadster, correct?"

"I don't know. When the police came, they told me there had been a kidnapping and it involved a Studebaker. I just put two and two together."

Cooper put down his fountain pen and looked at her. "Could you recognize any of the occupants of either car?"

"No. I just saw the figures of three men."

"Tell me again how many people were in the first car?"

"Maybe two? Maybe more."

Cooper checked his notes. "Okay. You told police that one man got out to smoke. Could you tell what the other man was doing?"

"Like I said, I heard somebody say, 'Get in there, big boy.' I think that was the man who had been smoking. Then someone asked if they were on the right road. No answer. So, then he says, 'Where are we going from here?' Then, someone else said—"

"You heard a third voice?"

Mrs. Amaral nodded. "He said something... I couldn't hear all of it, but, oh yes, he said, 'Take him to the hills.' It sounded like whoever was talking was inside the car."

"This is all very helpful," Cooper said. "Can you tell me when the Studebaker left?"

"I don't know. They all left about the same time. One car went north. Whoever was driving the Studebaker turned around and went south."

"So, there might have been a third car?"

"I really can't say."

Cooper reread what she had told deputies. "This is what you told the police when they first arrived?"

"Yes. But..." Mrs. Amaral bit her lip. "Well, there's a bit more. Later that evening as I was making dinner, the sheriff and his deputy drove up. They wanted me to repeat what I had seen. When I told them I thought there were only two cars, the sheriff said that it was best to stick to that story. He meant to say it *casually.*"

Cooper nodded thoughtfully, grasping the implication. He thanked the woman and then continued on his way. Despite her understandable uncertainty, Cooper thought it reasonable to assume the Studebaker Mrs. Amaral had seen was Rosen's car. Michael Rosen and at least one other person had been inside. The Chevy, possibly Hansen's car, had carried at least two occupants. If the Studebaker had been left behind, then someone returned later to move Rosen's car and leave it for the police to find. Whether or not a third car had been involved that night in the orchard remained a mystery, but one thing was crystal clear: There were more people involved in Michael Rosen's kidnapping than just Harold Tierney and Earle Hansen, despite Ewing's insistence.

As Kane drove the car northward, Cooper reviewed Hansen's testimony. Hansen had admitted to the crime. He and Tierney had discussed the kidnapping for several days before it was carried out. Together, they waited outside Rosen's Department Store. But according to Hansen, it was Tierney who had approached Rosen's car and ordered the heir to drive at gunpoint. Hansen further maintained that he was the one who had followed in another car. He'd driven his Chevrolet sedan until Tierney signaled him to stop in a dark, deserted orchard. Rosen was then transferred from the Studebaker to Hansen's Chevrolet.

Hansen expressed puzzlement as to why the Studebaker had been found in another location. He had no explanation. They'd driven off in the Chevy, he said, eventually arriving on the Hayward–San Mateo Bridge. That again had been Tierney's decision. Inexplicably, Tierney stopped halfway across the bridge. And Tierney ordered Rosen to hand over his wallet. After they divided the money, Tierney placed a pillowcase over Rosen's head.

In Hansen's version, Tierney had opened the car trunk, revealing cement blocks, which they affixed to Rosen's chest and ankles using baling wire. This contradicted Tierney's testimony that never mentioned the cement blocks or the baling wire. Tierney then threatened to throw Rosen off the bridge. Hansen pleaded with Tierney that he did not want to be implicated in a murder. So, they left Rosen there on the bridge and drove back to San Jose. Hansen drove. He dropped off Tierney in Campbell and then returned briefly to his place on Bird Street.

Hansen said he then drove to San Francisco, first to place the first of the telephone calls to the Rosen family, and then to the waterfront, where he threw Rosen's wallet into the bay. In the end, he returned to San Jose late. The exact time was uncertain. He was afraid to stay at his home, so he booked a hotel room and was captured days later. While he admitted to kidnapping Rosen and then robbing him as well as making ransom calls in the hopes of more money, Hansen claimed he'd been an unwilling contributor in the kidnapping scheme.

The newspapers had only released Hansen's version of the story.

San Francisco's Potrero Police Station on Third Street had a relaxed Mediterranean feel with its tiled roof and a scalloped parapet, but it served as a fortress, located near the waterfront in a place designed to manage the wayward and unruly longshoremen and sailors. An out-of-the-way spot to store Tierney and Hansen pending an indictment.

When Kane and Cooper arrived, a score of newspaper reporters had gathered outside the station entrance. Onlookers were scattered around across the street, perhaps wishing to remain anonymous. Inside, Cooper asked the desk sergeant where Tierney and Hansen were being held. The desk sergeant pointed up with his pencil.

As Cooper ascended the stairs, he was greeted by a local police detective, who confided that Hansen was adamant he had been falsely accused.

"I want the names of everyone who has been in contact with Hansen since he left San Jose," ordered Cooper.

The detective unlocked Hansen's cell door and remained in the hall as Cooper stepped inside and beheld Earle Hansen for the first time: six feet tall, nearly the same as Cooper. Huskier though. Blond hair, square jaw, blue eyes. Nordic indeed. Hansen was sitting on the single bunk, staring at the opposite wall. He shifted his stare to Cooper for a moment, his eyes bloodshot but defiant.

Cooper reached into his pocket. "Do you want a cigarette?"

Hansen shook his head. "I never touch the stuff."

Cooper put the pack of cigarettes back in his pocket without lighting one.

"Let me get this straight," he said to Hansen. "You used a Chevrolet sedan, owned and used regularly by you, a vehicle that neighbors would probably recognize, and yet you used this vehicle to kidnap someone? Does that not sound a bit odd?"

Hansen shrugged. "Only car we had."

"Was there a third car with you at any time?"

"No. Just us rabbits."

"Your friend Tierney said you made all the decisions."

"Tierney's a moron. Literally, a moron." And Hansen was a stooge.

"Your testimony indicated that cement blocks were attached to Mr. Rosen's body."

"Yeah, so? That point was to scare the guy. Tierney tied him up long enough for us to get away. It was just baling wire. I'm sure the guy unraveled himself. Probably called his family to pick him up."

"You are suggesting the Rosen family is hiding their son?"

"I'm suggesting Old Man Rosen wants publicity. He wants sympathy. To get people to shop at his failing department store. The kid will turn up at some convenient moment. Everyone will cheer."

"After you left Rosen, you dropped off Tierney at his family home in Campbell, then drove up to San Francisco. All told, that's over a hundred miles. Is that correct?"

"Yup. That's the story." This guy was unbelievable.

"You admitted driving to the Hotel Whittier. Why there?"

"Seemed like a nice place. They're known for their fried pork chops and mashed potatoes."

"And you placed a ransom call that evening to the Rosen family?"

"That's the size of it."

"Even though he would have been able to get out of his ropes—"

"Baling wire."

"Even though you say he was able to get free, you drove all the way to Frisco and still demanded ransom." Who was he trying to fool?

Hansen half smiled. "It takes balls, I admit. Timing is everything."

"And you made repeated calls?"

"Sure. Why not? They've money enough."

"Yet you never picked up the money the first time. Why am I having a hard time believing any of this? Why drive all that way to San Francisco to place a call?"

Hansen shrugged and leaned back into the wall, this time cracking a wide-open smile and saying nothing.

"Having accomplished that, you say you then drove to the waterfront and threw Rosen's wallet into the bay. But the wallet was found on a rail, not lost in the water. Strange, wouldn't you think?"

"Stranger things could be imagined."

"After failing to accomplish the simplest of tasks of disposing of a wallet, you drove another sixty miles back to San Jose to your father's place in Willow Glen."

Hansen did not blink as he stared directly at Cooper. "Pop needed the car."

"Are you familiar with Belinda West?"

Hansen grinned. "We're the best of friends."

"But she was not with you that evening?"

"Not that night."

Cooper took out his packet of cigarettes, this time lit one. "Let's get back to what transpired in your car on the bridge," he said to Hansen. "You said you tied Rosen up with baling wire. Where did you get that?"

"It's been in the trunk for years."

"You also had concrete blocks."

"Pop grabbed those off a construction site and never quite knew what to do with them."

"You brought a pillowcase with you . . ."

"You never know where you're gonna sleep at night. Best to be prepared."

"Where did you get the pistol?"

"Interestingly enough, Tierney got it. Never told me where."

"Tierney said you struck Rosen."

"He's seen too many movies."

"So, what happened?"

"Can I get some coffee? Hot this time?" Hansen asked.

"In a bit," Cooper said. "Tell me about the bridge."

Hansen stared at him for a long moment and then resumed the story.

"When we stopped on the bridge, Tierney took his wallet, and we divided the money. There was more than I thought, but I figured, hey, there's always room for more. I grabbed the stuff from the trunk and Tierney said, 'Am I going to tie this guy up?' I said, 'Heck, use the wire.' Rosen started to squirm, so I hit him. We tossed him out onto the bridge, tied on the cement blocks. Told him if he squealed, he'd be fish food. He shut up. I hit him again so he knew I meant business. This time, he's out cold. There wasn't much reason to hang on to him, so we bailed. That's it. Can I get that coffee now?"

"I want to know what you have to say about Tierney's version of your story."

"Like I said, he's not the brightest bulb in the universe."

"Back when you rendezvoused in the orchard, who else was there in your car?"

"Just me."

"A witness saw and heard more than just you and Tierney."

Hansen looked worried for the first time. "No, no one else was there," he said stubbornly.

"You said that you abandoned Rosen's Studebaker in the middle of the orchard, but the police found it miles away. The headlights were left on," Cooper added, as if an afterthought.

"Probably some teenagers had some fun that night," said Hansen mockingly.

"Was there a third car?"

"No. Don't you listen?"

"Why did you two go west over the bridge? Wasn't the original plan to drive east into the hills?"

"You're dreaming."

"Who else was in your car?" Cooper demanded.

"Nobody," yelled Hansen.

"Where is Rosen?"

Hansen shrugged.

Cooper decided to circle back. "Why did you have cement blocks and baling wire if the plan was to stash him in the foothills?"

Hansen stared at Cooper. "I want some damn coffee."

Cooper poked his head out and asked the detective to bring Hansen a cup of coffee.

"With cream!" Hansen yelled.

"Where did you get the cement blocks?" Cooper asked again.

"Tierney borrowed 'em from a construction yard somewhere downtown and stashed them in the trunk."

"You stored cement blocks in your father's car?"

"Yeah, but he'd never notice."

"If you were supposed to stash Mr. Rosen in the foothills, why have these blocks at all?'

"Harold wanted them just in case."

"Harold thinks he was a patsy in all of this. What about you?"

Hansen laughed at the suggestion. "He's guilty as sin," he said.

The detective returned with the coffee and handed it to Cooper, who passed it to Hansen.

"You earlier said your father was the one who acquired the cement blocks. But now Tierney stole them? Which is it?"

"I'm sure you misheard." Hansen swallowed his coffee, smiled broadly. The man looked like he had not slept in two days, but his stupid grin still looked like a million bucks.

Cooper wondered how much of Hansen's demeanor was his own arrogance and how much was blind faith in whoever was pulling his strings. He crushed his cigarette beneath the heel of his shoe, looking down at Hansen as he did so. "Mr. Hansen, why are you smiling?"

"That's a good one, Louie," replied Hansen.

Funny, mused Cooper as he turned away from Hansen's smirk; not once during this entire case had he mentioned to anyone his given name.

31

Victoria jumped on the streetcar, paid the fare, and hung on to the swaying straps as the trolley pulled and tumbled toward Market Street in San Francisco. At the intersection of Third and Market Streets she got off, intending to walk the rest of the way to the Hotel Whittier. She imagined herself striding into the Whittier like a fast-talking dame in the movies, getting what she needed—answers for why John Schiavo was still being held—and getting out of there like it was nothing.

It was a longer walk than she imagined. The wind much stronger than anticipated. Swirling. Brisk. A sniff of salt in the air. By the time she found the Whittier, she already felt a mess. Her ankles were sore, and her hat would have blown all the way to the bay had she not pinned it. As it was, her hair was sticking out in all directions. Her eyes had teared up. It might have been the wind, or it might have been the exhaust from all the traffic. After standing and looking up at the Whittier, impressive to say the least, she stepped through the revolving door, whirled halfway around, and came out into a very silent, solemn lobby. She steadied herself and adjusted her hat. Dabbed at her eyes with her handkerchief. Approached the front desk.

A middle-aged, thin-lipped hotel clerk stood erect behind the desk. He dully recited a greeting, looking almost as if someone had thrust a gun into his gut and forced him to be polite.

"Good morning," said Victoria.

The clerk responded in kind. She looked at her watch. It was nearly noon.

"I'm looking for Mr. Dash. I have a noon appointment," said Victoria brightly, perhaps too much so.

"What is your name, please?"

"Victoria Trinchero." She definitely spoke too quickly.

He peered down, used his finger to scan a sheet of paper that he read from, and answered, "Please take a seat."

"How long will it be?"

"We'll call you." The clerk did not bother to look up.

Victoria did not like to wait. She had not come all this way to sit. Nothing was ever accomplished by being patient, letting things unfold, waiting to be called.

Twenty minutes passed, and there was no call for Victoria Trinchero. Doubts surfaced. Amelia's father had cautioned her. Or had he meant to encourage her? Sara had asked that she follow up on Schiavo's lawyer. Or was that a half-hearted gesture to placate her? Sitting in a hotel lobby seemed useless, and she grew impatient, endlessly glancing around at the comings and goings of visitors. It seemed the place had an inordinate number of men keeping watch at the doors to the ballroom. She got up, retrieved the morning's newspaper from the front desk, and scanned the articles chronicling the latest in the Rosen kidnapping.

Closing in on one thirty, Victoria heard a commotion outside. From where she sat, she could see out the glass entry doors where cars had started to line up outside the hotel. Taxis. Fancy cars. The police. Drivers, guards, photographers, onlookers gathered outside, waiting. The sidewalk was packed, and the noise of the growing crowd became louder. Victoria walked up to the concierge and asked what the fuss was all about. The answer was that a banquet for the chamber of commerce was taking place in the grand ballroom. Businessmen. Politicians. Important people who moved and shook the town, said the concierge. Be patient, he told her, which seemed odd. The gathering was nearly finished, and people would soon depart. In the meantime, the lobby needed to remain tightly secure, he said. No one in. No one out until the banquet was done.

More annoyed than ever, Victoria started to return to her seat. As she turned away from the desk, she noticed a young man outside, peering in. At first, he was just another face. Then she connected the dots. Days before. In San Jose. In front of Amelia's house. The odd-mannered preacher who had rescued her jar of olives. Amelia's father made a call. One of his men went to search for the preacher who had gotten away. And then Amelia all but telling her to forget the incident. Victoria didn't forget. The preacher was dangerous.

She moved quickly away and stepped behind a large column near the grand staircase. The doors to the banquet doors opened, then quickly closed. This was done only so that more hotel security men could move into position. Guards lined up outside the double doors, along the corridors and the staircase. Victoria hesitated, not sure where to move, still preferring to remain out of view of the front doors.

"Victoria Trinchero!"

Hearing the page ring out for her name heightened Victoria's unease. Not sure whether to go to the front desk to meet with this Francis Dash, Esq., or somehow make a run for it, she froze. Why was she even here? And now that unseemly mobster preacher was standing right outside, peering in, perhaps in pursuit of her. She had no way to know, but everything felt wrong. Why had she made this headlong plunge to the Whittier? Why didn't she heed the words of Angelo Gumina to stay away?

"Miss Trinchero!"

Victoria did not move.

The ballroom doors opened, releasing a throng of people, mostly men, from the large ballroom. They poured into the lobby, chattering loudly, and spilled toward the main doors. The sight of the unruly crowd jostling for their turn at the doors reminded

Victoria of a drain that was just unclogged. She moved away from the protection of the column and maneuvered through the stream of finely dressed businessmen and socialites, gesturing them out of her way. She literally pushed and shoved and pirouetted her way into the ballroom. "Excuse me, please," she murmured in quiet desperation, not daring to look back. She ran headlong into a barrel-chested man, who loudly remarked, "Young lady. Watch where you are going." To which another man responded, "Chester, you should be that lucky."

Victoria's destination was the kitchen, which might offer an escape through the service portal to the street. She rushed to the far side of the ballroom and snuck past the kitchen crew, who were beginning to clear the tables. When she entered the kitchen, more workers were cleaning plates, glasses, pots and pans. They were all dark-haired women, recent immigrants. A few of them looked at Victoria briefly and then went back to scrubbing.

There was a door on the far side. As Victoria approached it, a round-faced woman held up her hand and pointed to another door. "The way you want to go is back there. Not here. Not safe," the woman said.

Victoria quickly reversed course and opened the door the woman had indicated, which led to the kitchen manager's office. Empty. But another door inside the office opened onto a service corridor. She ran past doors indicating different back-of-house functions, avoided the door marked LOBBY, and continued down the corridor that eventually doglegged to a street exit. She used her shoulder to push open the exit and felt the cool moisture of San Francisco fog.

Outside she found herself in a parking lot surrounded by the high walls of the hotel. She had been confused by the Whittier's labyrinthine twists and turns and was relieved to hear the sounds of the city: car horn honks, whistles, pistons firing, shouts, the squeal of tires, jackhammers. She guessed the parking lot would lead her away from Market Street. She skirted several parked service trucks as she hustled through the lot toward a street she could hear but not see. At the far end was a portal to a large thoroughfare. She ran through the arch and at last emerged onto the street. The sign read: MISSION STREET.

Holding her side, she took a few deep breaths and was answered by a shout. "Hey, come back here!" yelled a man inside the lot. She fled down Mission Street, not fully sure the shout came from a pursuer, but there was no time to look back. At the corner, she saw a #30 trolley. The driver stopped momentarily, only to resume again. "Wait!" Victoria cried weakly. As if answering her plea, the trolley stopped again, though not for Victoria. An elderly woman using crutches had wished to get off. The delay enabled Victoria to hop on board.

She fumbled in her purse for the right coins. The driver shut the door as two men, ties flying as they ran, tried to stop the trolley again. They yelled at the driver. Banged on the side of the streetcar.

"I hate those types," the driver said. And pulled away.

Victoria caught her breath as the trolley accelerated west on Mission Street, but she did not know the city well enough to figure out where this streetcar was heading. An Irish matron holding a bag of groceries sat across the aisle.

"Quite in a hurry, I see," the woman said. No doubt she had watched the show put on by Victoria and her pursuers.

"Where are we going?" Victoria asked her, too harried to bother with courtesy.

"The Mission District. Where do you need to be?"

"Where is there a public phone?"

"Um, I'd try Owl's at Sixteenth. They've got everything. A nice soda fountain." She flitted her eyes at Victoria's clothing, her hair. "A place to tidy up, too."

The Irish lady directed her when to get off the trolley and pulled the cord for her. Victoria kept an eye out for anyone who might have followed as she crossed the street, located Owl's, and entered the pharmacy. The place was huge. There was nothing quite like it in San Jose. And indeed, there was a soda fountain and in the back a row of phone booths. Her hands shook as she plugged in the correct change and gave the operator the number for Amelia's residence. She needed to talk with her friend. Instead, Rosalia picked up.

"I need help," Victoria blurted.

Victoria recounted where she had been and what had happened.

"You're in danger," Rosalia told her. "Where are you now?"

"Owl's?" she answered, as if it were a question.

She should keep out of sight, Rosalia instructed. There was a movie theater on Mission Street. "Just past Nineteenth. El Capitan," she said. If Victoria just stayed put inside, Rosalia would send someone to pick her up. "Sit in the back. We'll get someone there as soon as we can. Don't go with anyone you don't recognize. Stay still."

"Is someone really after me?"

"You'll be fine, dear. Enjoy the feature." Rosalia hung up.

Secure in her telephone booth, Victoria watched the activity in Owl's. Customers streamed in and out, looking around, purchasing items, sipping soda through straws. She felt thirsty but was afraid to move. Maybe it was that shifty young man with the wide tie in the corner who stared at each young woman who walked in. Or maybe it was that old guy propped up alongside the back wall with a toothpick hanging out of his mouth as he perused the crowd. Who could tell whether they were merely regular creeps or whether they had been hired to capture her?

She waited in the phone booth for a long time. An impatient old gentleman with a quizzical look rapped on the glass door of the booth. She reluctantly opened the door. He asked whether she minded taking all the time in the world, just sitting there, doing nothing, while he had to place an important call. Rather than making a fuss, she gave way, glancing first at the guy with the toothpick, who pretended not to see her. Then, at the young man, who smiled and began to say something. She brushed right by him. He didn't make a move. Victoria headed straight out the door and walked briskly toward the theater.

As advertised, the El Capitan with its impressive Mexican baroque facade took up most of the block. Victoria bought a ten-cent ticket, sat in the rear, on the right, and watched who might be venturing in for the matinee show, which had already begun. It was awfully dark, though, and difficult to even see how many were in attendance. Victoria could not concentrate on what the story was about. She remained in her seat as the film's credits scrolled down. The house lights came up. There must have been at least a dozen who left their seats and another dozen or so who remained. She scrunched down in her seat and did not look up until the lights were turned off once again and the second feature began.

Many minutes into the second film, Victoria began to relax and make sense of what she was watching. The main actor was familiar. She had seen him before but could not place the name. The female lead was more distinctive. Positively, it was Constance Cummings. Or perhaps Ann Harding. Or Mary Astor.

Someone tapped her left shoulder. Victoria panicked, ready to bolt.

"Relax, it's me," came Amelia's voice from behind her. "C'mon, let's go. Sal's got the car running in front."

Amelia held Victoria's hand as they left the theater. Indeed, there was an automobile and a familiar figure at the wheel. It was the man she'd seen chase after the preacher outside Amelia's house days before. He leaned over and opened the side door of the car. Amelia and Victoria climbed in. Their driver got out of there in a flash, made a couple of right turns, then scooted onto the straightaway heading south.

"I'm glad you're safe," said Amelia.

Victoria told them what had happened.

"Weren't you warned to stay away from Schiavo?" barked the driver. Amelia introduced him as Sal Booksin.

"We wanted to know why he was arrested and bail was denied," Victoria told them.

"He was sent to inform on the union," replied Amelia.

"That doesn't make sense. He's been to the meetings. He was there at the demonstration. How would you know he's disloyal?"

"We've been watching the Whittier for some time. It's run by an operation we don't trust," replied Booksin. He glanced back at Amelia.

"Tell her," said Amelia.

"Paul Passalacqua. He's a dangerous man."

"Who?"

"He controls a lot of operations in San Francisco and wants to expand to San Jose."

"What does he have to do with Schiavo?"

"Schiavo is Passalacqua's snitch," answered Booksin.

Victoria looked at Amelia. "You're not as innocent as you've appeared."

"No one is."

"Your father got us cannery jobs."

"You needed the money. My father needed to know what was going on. Schiavo was feeding union contacts to Passalacqua. Didn't my father tell you to stay clear?"

Victoria did not answer.

"Passalacqua was hired to shut down the union," said Amelia.

"And wants to run us out of business," added Booksin.

"Does Dash work for this mobster?" Victoria asked bluntly.

"As far as we know, there is no Dash," replied Booksin. "They wanted to know who would ask about Dash so they could keep you quiet."

"What does that mean?"

"Keep you out of the way until they make their move. And before you ask what that means, their move is to expand business into San Jose. Now, you must be aware that Amelia's father is more than just a bartender. With saloons becoming legal soon, the entire business and various relationships will be changing," said Booksin.

"That's both an opportunity and a vulnerability," said Amelia.

"Passalacqua wants to take over our operations. Shut us down," said Booksin. "Expand into gambling, loan-sharking, that sort of thing. That's the future."

"Mama does not approve," added Amelia.

Exasperated and still somewhat frightened, Victoria turned to Amelia. "Why doesn't your father scream to the papers about this?"

"That would be complicated," said Amelia.

Victoria silently struggled to grasp the implications of what she was hearing. She stared out the window as the car continued southward.

"Why is Schiavo being detained?" she asked abruptly.

No one had an answer.

Victoria looked out the window again, hoping to let the scenery calm her. The small downtowns, the orchards, the ranches, the scattered houses looked somehow ominous. She wondered what other secrets she didn't know.

Booksin asked where they should take her. Victoria said that her boardinghouse would be fine. They shook their heads and told her that would be impossible. Passalacqua's men would look for her there.

"You should stay with my parents," Amelia said. "The house is well protected."

"I want to see Sara. She's in Los Gatos right now," said Victoria.

"Isn't she the one who sent you to San Francisco?" asked Amelia.

"She wouldn't have purposely sent me into a trap. There's no way she knows about any of this," declared Victoria, hoping she was telling the truth. After all, she had just learned how very little she knew about her own best friend.

32

The whereabouts of Michael Rosen remained unknown. The ripple of emotion over his disappearance had turned into waves of anger. Campus leaders led another rally when the kidnappers were whisked out of town. The Jesuits became alarmed when trash cans were overturned, a chair thrown out an open window, classes were disrupted by crusaders, and graffiti started to appear on the walls of the Mission chapel demanding, among other things, that "rough justice" be served.

In an attempt to bring the student community together, Fr. Seebach organized a noon vigil for Michael Rosen in the old Mission church. A mass was said. In his homily, Fr. Seebach asked that everyone pray together and preached for calm and order. He blessed the host, and communion was offered with an attempt to overlook the pervasive undercurrent of discontent. The mood in the chapel was palpable. Fr. Seebach continued the mass, but the restlessness could not be contained.

During the prayer after communion, Fr. Seebach was interrupted when James O'Neill rose from his pew and said the vigil for his dear friend was all wrong. "You've turned this into a requiem," said O'Neill. There was still hope for Rosen's return, insisted O'Neill. "Michael would have wanted action, not thoughts and prayers."

Fr. Seebach was astonished that someone would behave so

unabashedly at his mass. O'Neill stood his ground and said if there were a trial, it would be a sham. The lawyers would devise tricks to either prolong the case through a semblance of due process or settle for a plea agreement to a lesser charge. The congregation clapped. Fr. Seebach raised his hand to quiet his flock, whereupon another student, Frank Salatino, stood and argued that if there were a trial, the judge would prescribe vague direction and wide discretion to the jury, who in turn would be moved by the presumed dire circumstances of the defendants. Whereas, maintained Salatino, it was obvious to all that Hansen and Tierney had savagely kidnapped their former classmate. Salatino claimed that to do nothing was a sin. His classmates had a duty to act.

Yet another, Robert Puglia, jumped up and cried that he had heard enough. He demanded justice. The assembled students clapped once again. There were even a few cheers. Fr. Seebach raised his hands to calm his young congregation, though it looked more like he had surrendered. He could not bring himself to deliver the final blessing. The students marched out.

During that mass, Winston took the opportunity to slip away and ask the registrar for certain files he knew were kept in the archives room. When the clerk disappeared to fetch the files, Winston leaned over and opened the registrar's drawer, grabbing the ring of keys that opened every door in the administrative building. He selected the one key he needed, the one that unlocked Fr. Seebach's office.

Holding the key in his right hand, Winston slunk along the colonnade toward the administrative building, which was deserted during the chapel ceremony, then scampered up the stairway to the second floor. He ran, slid across the slick terrazzo floor to Fr. Seebach's office, and thrust the key into the lock. It jammed. He jiggled it, twisted it sideways, but the key would not open the lock.

Taking a deep breath, he tried again. The key dropped from his hand. It clattered to the floor, the sound reverberating down the hallway.

Winston took another deep breath, relaxed a bit, wiped his brow. He tried again to work the key into the lock, gently this time. Twisting it just so, he found success. He glanced around the wide hallway and then stepped inside.

He had never been in Fr. Seebach's office before. It reeked of the musty residue of incense and cigars. Stacks of documents covered the desk. Winston carefully lifted and inspected and replaced each of them to its original place and stack order; nothing appeared of significant note. The desk drawers were locked. He went to the filing cabinets against the far wall. They were locked as well. For a few moments, Winston roamed the room, deciding which drawer or cabinets to spend time on. He traced the dull blade of his penknife along his cheek. The most logical place would be the most obvious one—the center pencil drawer of the desk. This would be the place to store a daily calendar. Winston knelt on one knee and inserted the blade to pry open the drawer and felt little resistance. The drawer was jimmied open.

He hurriedly inspected the contents: pens, pencils, paper clips, handwritten notes, a black rosary, a handful of pamphlets announcing plans for the new theological seminary above Los Gatos, and a stack of business cards; he didn't recognize any of the names. Reaching into the far reaches of the drawer, he found what he was looking for: Fr. Seebach's weekly schedule. He scanned the recorded appointments, noting the times of certain meetings, who they were with, their subject matter. He found the page for the date he and Snyder had been up at the old Tevis estate in the hills. There was nothing. No mention of Ripley. Nothing about a real estate transaction.

Winston thought for a few moments and then went back through the schedule more carefully, this time noting the repetition of one word: "Alma." It was mentioned several times in recent weeks, sometimes in reference to construction plans, other times about fundraising strategies, most of the time just scrawled next to a time of day. It must be Seebach's name for the Tevis estate.

While he could not discover any mention of Ripley, he did decipher a scribble on November 26, a few days ahead, a Saturday, that mentioned an "Event." In fact, the notation was underscored twice, marking some significance. In the page margin, in small script, there was something hastily written. It looked like "HW." Winston searched through the ledger for anything potentially connected to an event or HW. He found nothing. He put the schedule back in the drawer and took another look at the pile of business cards and slips of paper containing snatches of notes. On a scrap of paper, Seebach had jotted two words: HOTEL WHITTIER.

Hotel Whittier. HW. Winston's brow began to sweat.

On that same scrap, there was a number, not a phone number. Maybe a hotel reservation number? Perhaps it was meaningless, although the more he thought about it, he knew it would be inconsistent for a university president to stay in a hotel in San Francisco. If Fr. Seebach needed lodging, he would stay at the archdiocese's residence.

Winston felt lightheaded. He put everything back and hastily left the office. As he neared the stairwell, he heard footsteps. A security guard? The campus never saw the need. A janitor? Not scheduled for today. A stray Jesuit? If so, an explanation would need to be quickly devised and defended.

"Stop right there," commanded a voice.

Winston stopped dead in his tracks as Wilford Kishi, Fr. Seebach's assistant, appeared at the top of the stairs.

"Shouldn't you be in the chapel?"

"Shouldn't you be?" countered Winston, putting his hands on his hips.

"You've got an excellent point." Kishi smiled. A ray of sunlight through the arched window peeked over his shoulder. "May I ask your purpose for being here?"

"I can ask the same of you."

"Certainly. I was asked to follow you, of course."

"By Fr. Seebach?"

"Not exactly. But I can say by the people who control this institution."

"The Committee?"

"The formal name is the Committee for Public Safety. Fr. Seebach is more a figurehead of this university. The donors and the alumni are powerful people."

"How do you know?"

"Like you, I, in a manner of speaking, provide services for them."

"I certainly don't work for this Committee," said Winston.

"Oh, don't you? You have forgotten the Hotel Whittier already?"

Winston gave up on feigning innocence. "How did you know?" he asked Kishi, who shrugged.

"I passed the notes," he told Winston.

"Why did you do this?"

"Same reason as you. To get somewhere. There was an opportunity. I took it. So did you. Now we're caught."

"What do they want from me?"

"They wanted to see if you were, in fact, worthy. Whether you'd carry out their instructions. Whether you'd keep your mouth shut. That's really why I followed you. To warn you. They can crush you."

Winston felt rooted to his spot next to the stairs, perplexed and even more troubled as he better understood his predicament. "Do you know who they are?"

"We don't need to know. We're pawns. If necessary, pawns can be sacrificed. Don't forget."

"Do they know why I am here now?"

"It doesn't matter. Consider this a friendly warning." A pause. "Now you can give me the registrar's key."

33

Seemingly overnight, Potrero Police Station became the focal point of growing demonstrations demanding retribution against Michael Rosen's kidnappers. With increasing intensity, citizens gathered daily with a common goal: harsh punishments for the two kidnapping suspects. They carried handmade signs, chanted, banged on trash cans. New discoveries in the case against the two accused men fueled the rancor of the crowds. A local fisherman found baling wire and a scrap of cloth believed to be from the victim's shirt on the eastern mudflats of San Francisco Bay. Three days later, a sand-soaked fedora, similar to the one known to be worn by Rosen, had been found by a wandering beachcomber on Alameda, an island next to Oakland.

The *San Francisco Chronicle*, followed by the *San Jose Mercury-Herald*, printed surprisingly similar opinions, arguing that the guilt of the two men was unquestionable. Their signed confessions were described as cold-blooded, the crime premeditated and sordid. Any competent juror would render a verdict of guilty. Any sentence should be swift and unrelenting, claimed the authors.

By November 24, three days after Tierney and Hansen had been deposited in San Francisco, local police determined the Potrero station was ill-equipped to handle the increasing presence of angry demonstrators. They agreed to transfer the prisoners to the Justice Department confines next to city hall, where they could be better protected. The next morning's news headlines published a statement from the California governor, who expressed his thoughts and prayers for the victim's family. To Cooper's intense chagrin, the reports also mentioned the new location where the accused were being detained. Cooper wasted no time voicing his strong opinion to Bureau headquarters about how that had happened.

By noon, an angry mob had formed around the federal building, this group much larger, more organized than the ragtag, unruly crowds seen in Potrero. The horde confronted federal workers with raised fists, printed signs, and repeated chants for unforgiving justice. When the jostling and shoving escalated to punches being thrown, a fleet of police reinforcements from San Francisco ceremoniously streamed in, first by motorcycle, then by paddy wagon. In relatively short order, the entire crowd was easily and entirely dismissed. Cooper marveled at the orchestration of this so-called demonstration. An hour later, the sidewalk in front of the federal building had nothing but its usual sidewalk traffic.

And yet through all of this, no one knew the whereabouts of Michael Rosen.

Police diligently followed up numerous tips about where Rosen might be found in the Bay Area or Los Angeles, or as far away as Portland and Seattle, various towns in the Sierras, Denver, Kansas City. Additional Bureau agents were dispatched from district offices to chase down the far-flung leads. Some information suggested Rosen might have been taken out of the country, to Vancouver, Ensenada, or Mexico City.

When a radio commentator voiced "the need to execute justice swiftly and without remorse," newspapers and the radio took up the cry, further amplifying popular sentiment. Pastors and politicians began to whip up their respective flocks. Newsboys hawked frenzied headlines. Citizens were ripe for direct action, frustrated by the slow-moving wheels of justice.

Cooper had been working with a team of federal prosecutors to pursue an indictment against Hansen and Tierney. H. H. Pope, the US attorney, assured Cooper and Bureau officials that this could be accomplished immediately and with more likely outcomes, albeit lighter sentences for the hapless pair. A federal indictment would ensure that the levers of the law could then proceed in a steadfast and methodical manner. However, when the federal grand jury reviewed the request for indictment, they rejected it on the grounds that the submitted paperwork was incomplete. Cooper urgently wired Washington to press Hoover to intercede. The federal prosecutors needed more time to resubmit the indictment. The goal was to keep the case in San Francisco but under federal jurisdiction: less risk, certain outcome.

Meanwhile, Sheriff Ewing signed a complaint that allowed the county district attorney to file a separate indictment charging Tierney and Hansen with kidnapping under the recently amended California Penal Code. This new measure allowed a death sentence order for those convicted of kidnapping done with bodily harm. Despite the possibility of a harsher sentence if the County of Santa Clara retained the case, Cooper's main concern, which he emphatically delivered to his bosses as well as Sheriff Ewing, was that the contradictory and inaccurate testimonies of the two accused, as well as some of the witnesses, might undermine their respective cases. Without evidence of bodily harm, a conviction under the California Penal Code was at best a crapshoot.

H. H. Pope officially wired Washington to confirm whether an indictment should proceed under federal statutes. The Bureau's chief counsel wired back, stating that local jurisdiction should take precedence because of the alleged nature and potential penalty of the crime. Cooper continued trying to convince the Bureau that the obvious holes in Hansen and Tierney's differing testimonies could sabotage the outcome of a local trial. The Bureau replied that any such discrepancies would come out in due course. When Cooper pressed again, he was told in no uncertain terms that the affair would be resolved locally. His role was to monitor the delivery of the prisoners back to Santa Clara County, and to remain on hand to ensure the matter was resolved.

While Cooper simmered, Sheriff Ewing held a press conference and said the prisoners would be immediately remanded back to San Jose. He requested the governor to deploy the California National Guard to help protect the accused. The governor promptly refused.

Ewing and his supporters were undeterred. Immediately after the San Jose press conference, an armada noisily set off from San Francisco to San Jose. Motorcycle cops led the parade, followed by Ewing in a siren-blaring Buick. Hansen and Tierney, handcuffed and shackled, were placed in an armored vehicle that followed Ewing's Buick coupe. Five more police vehicles brought up the rear. Cooper rode in one of the trailing vehicles with Deputies Butler, Gibson, and Kane. He'd seen Tierney and Hansen only briefly as they were hustled into the armored car. Hansen's bravado had evaporated. Tierney seemed as confused as ever.

As the motorcade got underway, the radio reported that crowds were forming in St. James Park.

"What do you make of all of this?" Cooper asked. "Where is your chief? His silence has been thunderous."

Butler exhaled wearily. They had been over this time and time again. "Chief Blackmun felt that the sheriff's office should be the focal point for the investigation since the crime took place in county jurisdiction," he told Cooper.

"The kidnapping took place in downtown San Jose," snapped Cooper. "That is the purview of the San Jose Police Department."

"The crime was what they did to him at the bridge. That took place outside of San Jose but within jurisdiction of Santa Clara County," responded Butler. "It's the sheriff's responsibility."

"You don't know whether that even occurred," retorted Cooper, barely concealing his contempt. "The lies and deceit, and I'm not just talking about Hansen and Tierney, curse this entire investigation."

"It's a matter of time before the body is found. It's fanciful that you still do not recognize the inevitable," Butler said, letting his own anger show.

They sat in silence for the next fifty-four minutes. Butler stared at the road ahead. Cooper observed the small towns passing, with their sloppy gas stations, lonesome roadside cafés, retail stores with newly blinking Christmas decorations, and then row after row of barren trees bracing for the inevitable winter.

It was getting dark when the parade of vehicles neared downtown San Jose. The noisy motorcade turned off at First Street and headed to the front of the county courthouse across from St. James Park. This was a diversion while the armored car carrying the prisoners slipped down a side street toward the back end of the courthouse, which also served as the rear entrance to the county jail.

As the radios had advertised, a hundred or so people were waiting to catch a glimpse of the two criminals. When the motorcade stopped, these people became angry at Hansen and Tierney's absence. They surrounded the motorcade, jammed their faces into each of the windows: Where were the kidnappers? They began to beat on the hoods and sides of the vehicles. The police told them to back off, the show was over, go home. And not to worry—they'd have another chance.

That evening Cooper stewed alone in his hotel room. The governor did not want federal interference. Blackmun had washed his hands of this affair. Ewing was in charge. Cooper had his orders from Hoover. Orders he did not agree with, but there it was. Eventually, a late supper of fried pork chops and mashed potatoes in the hotel restaurant helped to lift his gloom. Cooper finished eating, walked out of the place, headed toward the county courthouse through St. James Park.

It was dark by then. Aided by the cold weather drifting in, the grumbling crowd had eventually drifted away. The park was pretty much dead. Even the hoboes and drifters and bums found better corners to settle in for the night. Cooper realized he wanted to speak with that man with the aquiline nose.

Cooper was greeted by the familiar bouncer at Spades, who this time promptly buzzed him in. When he entered the dark speakeasy, all he could see was the green glow of the bar. He approached and asked the bartender whether his boss would be in tonight.

"You mean Angelo?"

That's right; his name was Angelo.

"Who should I say wants to see him?"

"Let's just say a colleague. Someone with mutual interests," replied the Bureau agent.

Cooper took a seat in a booth along the wall as his eyes adjusted to the bar's dimness. Then he watched the mostly silent movements around him. Most were men drinking alone, medicating, he deduced, the loneliness of their unfulfilling work in the shop, office, assembly line, warehouse, wherever they toiled on a daily basis. Lucky even having a job in these times, they came in one by one hoping for some social interaction. Tonight, the highballs were their only companions.

Cooper saw Angelo purposefully stroll in, greet the bartender, and when the bartender pointed in his direction, Angelo walked to Cooper's booth and simply nodded.

Cooper nodded in return. "Nice to see someone friendly again."

"Good to see you. What can I do you for? A drink perhaps?"

"Something that will lift my spirits," said Cooper, arching his eyebrow.

"The only spirit we can provide is in a bottle. What will you have? Irish, I suspect. Not Scotch. That's the best I can do."

"That would be grand," Cooper said with some bemusement.

Angelo ambled over to the bar. Eddie produced a bottle of Dunville's, opened it, and handed it to Angelo, who returned to Cooper's booth with the whiskey and two tumblers. "Go ahead. I barely touch the stuff," he told Cooper. "But, for you, I'll just take enough to wet my lips. I suspect I'll need to keep my wits about me this evening."

Cooper poured himself a shot, scooped it up and down the hatch.

"The floor is yours," Angelo said. "What's on your mind?"

"As you are no doubt aware, I've been working on the Rosen incident . . ." Cooper looked steadily at Angelo, whose expression registered this was old news.

"Throughout this investigation, I have realized there are levels of deception," Cooper said, at last earning raised eyebrows from Angelo. "As part of our respective organizations, I have done my homework and I suspect you have done yours as well, so I thought we would lay our cards on the table. Off the record."

Angelo's eyes seemed to glow. He looked down a moment, then stared back at Cooper and replied in a careful, delicate manner. "I know that you need to bring resolution to the crime committed. That's what your superiors want."

"But you know there is more going on," suggested Cooper.

"Indeed. Like Kansas City, as you might say, there is always more than meets the eye."

"Local officials are in on it," Cooper said bluntly. "So is the governor, I believe. Maybe even Hoover. To which, I conclude: to what end?"

Angelo picked up the whiskey and poured another glass for Cooper and one for himself. Both men drank, and then Cooper continued. "The testimonies of the accused kidnappers have been fabricated. There are certain similarities, but more discrepancies. These two men say they acted on their own, but that is a lie. More were involved. That I can say. They should have been kept in San Francisco for safekeeping, but they were brought back here. We wanted to prosecute them in federal court, which would have kept them in San Francisco for the trial, but that has been overruled. That's all I can say."

"What has that got to do with me?"

"We know about your proprietor, Gaetano Ferrone. The Bureau has kept tabs on him for some time. We could shut you down."

"And yet you don't."

"That's not why I'm here."

"Why are you here?"

"You already said it: to solve the crime. Or at least that is what I have been instructed to do."

"Which crime do you refer to?"

"Let me ask you, to what extent have you been involved in the Rosen kidnapping?" countered Cooper.

"From my perspective, there have been a series of crimes," answered Angelo with a slight smile. "To begin with, our business has strived to maintain integrity. Other forces, some of which you already are aware, now seek to create chaos." Angelo let that sink in for a moment. "They use disruption as a distraction for their own purposes."

"I understand. But you have not answered my question."

Angelo sat back and folded his arms. "That is something that comes up, now and then. It's not something we're particularly proud of or do on a regular basis. But there are times when things need to be corrected. The fact of the matter was that a young man got in over his head due to his lavish lifestyle. That is about as delicately as I am willing to put it. This young man refused to pay up. He thought he was too big to pay. Too arrogant. He would have been taught a lesson in how repayment is enforced. I want to insist that we stay within the boundaries of decency. We remain honest. That is how we survive. Repayment that evening was expected. We were hijacked."

Cooper rubbed his chin, glancing around the room, which inexplicably had been cleared out. Cooper looked back at his table companion. They were quite alone. Angelo offered him a cigar, lit Cooper's and then his own. The green light of the bar seemed to dance off-kilter as Angelo smiled wryly at him.

"You wanted to lay cards on the table. The cards are all face up, wouldn't you agree? It's time you show me what you have," said Angelo quietly. "Tell me why you're really here. Off the record, naturally."

Flush with Irish whiskey, the Bureau agent told the bootlegger what he knew and what he thought. The barkeeper told him what he thought he ought to hear. It was a full two hours later when they left Spades and went their separate ways.

34

Booksin drove. Amelia sat in back. Victoria rode shotgun. At sunset, they reached the hills of Los Gatos. Driving up a narrow unpaved road, Booksin danced the car around potholes until they reached a brown stucco gatehouse at the edge of a cliff. Victoria jumped out, opened the unlocked gate, and they continued up the winding road. At one point, Booksin stopped the car so they could watch the creeping shadows cross the orchards below. Mount Hamilton to the east was still visible. Another mile up, the road relaxed. It was wider and flatter. Gravel had been generously poured. Beyond the next ridge, the shadowy outline of the Beaumont estate came into view. Closer up they could see the large two-story structure was painted ocher and ocean blue. Red tiles adorned the roof. Oversize windows took full advantage of the sweeping views. As the road swooped behind the main house, they passed a manicured garden leading to a spiderweb iron gate. Sara Chambers stood at the gate waving furiously.

"Welcome!" cried Sara, her entire body moving in excitement at their arrival.

Victoria got out of the car and somewhat cautiously greeted her friend. "Look at you," she said. Sara was wearing a long pleated skirt, a rose-colored, long-sleeved shirt, and big brown boots. A far cry from her union garb.

"It's so great that you can stay with us. What a pleasure to see all of you!" Sara exclaimed. Introductions were made, and Sara offered to show them around.

"It's so nice to be out of San Jose," said Amelia.

They would meet their hosts later, Sara explained. "The colonel is taking his daily pilgrimage up one of the trails. He requires time for solitude every afternoon until sundown. Violet is up in the poet's cottage composing her verse."

Booksin asked to use the telephone. Sara guided them to the servants' quarters near the garage. She knocked on the door and asked whether the telephone might be available. Booksin stepped in while Sara returned to the others. She began telling them about the history of the estate, how the Beaumonts had traveled the world and that the place reflected many cultures.

In a minute, Booksin was back. He told Amelia that he needed to leave. She should join him. "No," whispered Amelia. "It's best that I stay here for a bit. What could be safer than this?"

"Then it's important you stay put until this blows over," Booksin cautioned.

He made his apologies to Sara and departed. The three women strolled the grounds. The place was a mishmash of architectural styles and a clash of different influences. An enormous amphitheater overlooked the valley. "Like something you'd see in the Roman Empire," said Sara. On the opposite side was a two-story-tall cement statue of a bare-breasted woman warrior whose spear, Sara explained, was either Greek or Persian or something else. Gazing up at the cement breasts, Victoria asked, "Just who are these Beaumonts, anyway?"

Sara laughed. "They say the colonel was a lawyer to the bankers up north. Disgusting as that sounds, he made his money, bought land here, and built his dream estate. He and Violet are heavy contributors to the unions. They help fund our work throughout the state."

They continued the tour, with Sara keeping up her running commentary. "They have two hounds lounging around somewhere. Brutus and Trotsky," she told them. "You'll meet them at dinner."

Victoria was not sure whether she meant the Beaumonts or the dogs.

As it was nearly dark, they ended the tour by retreating to the main structure. The exterior was brightly lit. They entered into a large room with high ceilings, a shimmering chandelier. The Chinese teak furniture included a half dozen couches with intricately decorated pillows. Large Persian rugs adorned the dark-stained hardwood floor. Full bookcases ran along the walls. Brass figurines of Indian goddesses decorated each of the side tables.

A woman with gray-flecked hair tied in back appeared from behind a door. She was introduced as the cook. She said dinner would be served next door in the dining room and would be ready when the Beaumont couple appeared, adding that there would be nothing fancy served. Indeed, when the guests sat down for the meal, the dishes came out one by one. No meat. Certainly no pasta. Cauliflower, zucchini, bell peppers, and other vegetables. Brown rice. Barely cooked. Sara explained that the Beaumonts preferred their food "wholesome, as God intended." Not even with salt and pepper. Wine, however, was celebrated. A bottle for each guest stood in front of each plate.

The Beaumonts arrived through a set of doors, followed by the two hounds. The bushy-bearded, roly-poly colonel stomped through the living room wearing a loose indigo tunic and green dungarees tucked into his boots. His frail-looking wife wore a crimson kimono, her hair held together by chopsticks. Barefoot, she glided in from the patio. Victoria gauged she was midway through her forties, while the colonel must be pushing seventy.

Somewhere between a carrot and a butternut squash, the colonel launched into a diatribe about the injustices the proletariat were enduring. Factory owners refusing to pay a fair wage. Workers discharged without warning. Oppressive property taxes. Feckless New Deal administrators acquiescing to the East Coast capitalists. California fat cats conspiring with old Army generals to create a filing system of people who might be deemed dangerous. Their secret fund to pay their own public relations specialists to write copy for local papers and scripts for radio. No one at the table attempted to interrupt. Nearing the end of the meal, the colonel burped, then dovetailed his musings to the current dictators in Europe.

To punctuate a point about Mussolini, the colonel raised a glass of red and pronounced, "At least the dagos really know how to make this stuff." Took a slug. Poured himself another.

Victoria and Amelia remained still.

"My husband means the Italians know the art of fine winemaking," murmured Violet, who had not said a word until this point.

Then, abruptly, the meal was over. The colonel and Violet rose and expressed their gratitude that Sara and her friends could "break bread" with them, but now it was late, nearly ten o'clock, and they had a very busy tomorrow ahead of them.

As the Beaumonts departed, the cook called the two hounds. She let them outside for their own supper.

As soon as they were out the door, Victoria picked up her fork and pointed it at Sara. "On your recommendation, I went to San Francisco, and . . . how could you lead me into danger?"

"I'm sorry about that. When you tried to contact Dash, they knew." Sara brushed a stray hair from her forehead. "We needed to know who our Judas was. For all we knew, it could have been you, though we had suspicions about Schiavo. He had access to our files."

"We know that already," replied Victoria.

"Of course you do." Sara glanced at Amelia, who watched silently.

"Who wanted our records?" asked Victoria. She stabbed her fork into an uneaten portion of zucchini.

Seemingly taken aback, Sara composed herself by slowly taking a sip of burgundy. When she placed the glass back on the table, she said, "In his prior life, the colonel has known a 'fixer' named Linforth. This Linforth has always served as counsel to the bourgeoisie. He has been intent on finding out who is organizing the workers. They all want to know this. They want to break the movement. They got

Schiavo to pass along that information." She dabbed at her lips with a napkin. "So, you see, we had to know." She looked at Victoria. "I'm sorry that you got yourself involved..."

Amelia spread her hands on the table as if revealing cards she had kept close. "It's much more complicated than that, Sara."

"I agree. If Schiavo provided the information, wouldn't he be rewarded? Why would he be arrested?" asked Sara.

"His arrest depends on who is calling the shots. My family knows he was connected to a San Francisco gangster and now to Linforth. They are in cahoots with the cops," said Amelia. "We don't know why or whether Schiavo still has a role to play. Did the cops arrest him to get him out of the way? Maybe it was to protect him. Maybe he was installed in the jail to make sure the kidnappers stuck to their stories..."

"Maybe to just shut him up," said Victoria.

35

That evening, Angelo received a call from Booksin, who reported that Amelia and her friend were safe. In turn, Angelo informed him that their saloon in Alviso had been held up at gunpoint. Quite a commotion. Nothing taken. Patrons and staff were shaken. The masked culprits left as quickly as they had come. Angelo had called Ferrone, who said, uncharacteristically, not to worry. Things were being handled.

The next morning, around five o'clock, Angelo woke up to a ringing telephone. His wife stuck the pillow over her head. In the dark, he found his robe and slippers and went down the hall to take the call. Nick Caputo was on the line.

"Got a call from Ferrone's driver," he told Angelo, his voice staccato. "The guy got up early. That's what he does. Walked over to the garage. The Hudson Super Six was gone. Went up to Ferrone's house. Had a key, but the door was double-bolted. Pounded on the door. Nothing doing. Broke open the door. Nothing upset inside. Except nobody's there. The boss was missing. So was the missus. Guards gone. Maid gone. Even their dog."

It wasn't like Ferrone to just leave like that. Angelo told Caputo to go over to the place and look for himself. Then meet him at Spades. Bring the driver, too.

Angelo asked the phone operator to ring Booksin. When he got on the line, Angelo told him to come, pick up Rosalia, and get her on the 7:35 southbound train. "Make sure someone accompanies her." He asked about Amelia. Booksin said that she was safe for the time being in Los Gatos. Angelo then instructed Booksin to arrange for his wife and later his daughter to stay in their safe house in Avila Beach. Angelo's next call was to Frank Lagatutta. "Get everyone to meet at Spades by eight o'clock," he told Lagatutta.

"Tonight?"

"No. This morning. Soon as you can. Sal and Nick already know."

"Got it," Lagatutta said, and hung up.

Angelo went to the kitchen and made the morning coffee. He put in twice the amount of coffee needed. When it finished brewing, he poured a healthy cup, not for himself. His mind was churning. He didn't need the brew at this point. He took the cup to his wife, who still intended to sleep, despite all the chatter that she valiantly tried not to decipher.

Angelo sat on the bed next to her. Rosalia was sleepy and irritable, but when he told her the news, she took the cup, drank, got up. Started to pack. She knew the drill. By the time Booksin arrived, she was dressed and waiting. Booksin assured her that Amelia was secure in a wealthy couple's estate high above the valley. Rosalia told Angelo not to do anything too reckless. He smiled. At his age? He helped her with the luggage. Booksin stashed it in the back seat. A parting kiss. The engine turned over. And then, Angelo was alone, his mind running through the possible scenarios.

At eight, everyone was there. Lagatutta, Caputo, and the rest. They all knew the boss had gone missing. Booksin walked in just as the others were taking their seats. He nodded at Angelo and sat next to Caputo.

"What do we know?" asked Angelo.

"We don't," said Booksin.

"Passalacqua?" asked Caputo.

"In all likelihood," replied Booksin.

"So, what do we do? Sit back and do nothing?" said Lagatutta. "We ought to go after that bunch. We know they're up to no good."

"Hold on," cautioned Angelo. "We've no proof."

"They grabbed the boss. Isn't that proof enough?"

"No proof," said Caputo, echoing Angelo's warning. "Besides, they had all the opportunity in the world to blame us for the kidnapping . . . and they didn't."

"The police haven't bothered us either."

"Not yet," asserted Lagatutta.

"Nick, get ahold of Kane," instructed Angelo.

"Already dropped by his house on the way over," said Caputo.

"And?"

"Didn't hear about Ferrone. Didn't know about Passalacqua."

"What does Kane even know?" asked Booksin.

"He knew that Blackmun backed off on the kidnapping interrogations. The police are now onto something else," replied Caputo.

"I thought Ferrone was handling Passalacqua," said Booksin.

Angelo just stared at the man. "Clearly, something upset that." He tried not to sound sarcastic.

"Passalacqua has made a move on us," said Lagatutta. "We need to attack."

"We need to be strategic. First, we need to find out what happened to the boss. Second, we need to take precautions," said Angelo.

"We need to do more than that," responded Lagatutta.

Angelo stared him down. "We remain in a defensive posture for now. We will strike when necessary."

No one argued with him.

36

A faint rose haze emerged over the windswept mudflats on the southeastern shore of San Francisco Bay. The narrow silhouette of San Mateo Bridge in the distance provided a somber backdrop to the squadron of brown pelicans fluttering across the dawn sky. Collars rolled up against the brisk air, two men slogged across the muddy stretch exposed by the early low tide. One man held a lantern, the other a rifle as they made their way toward the shoreline. On the lookout for flocks of wood ducks, the hunters noticed a dark object that seemed stuck in the muck. It was likely an old sea lion washed up on the deserted beach, or maybe some unwanted jetsam.

As they drew closer to the dark mound, they saw the muddy swath it lay on was alive with movement. The man carrying the lantern held it aloft, revealing hundreds of small crabs scurrying to and fro. The arrival of the hunters startled several gray gulls pecking at the mound. The birds flapped away and began circling overhead. Whatever it was, something was dead. The wind shifted directions. The two men got more than a mere whiff.

The first man put a handkerchief to his nose. His companion prodded the thing with his rifle. It was dead all right. Inert. Rigid. He prodded it again. "Damn," he said. He used the tip of his rifle to push away a wet strip of cloth obscuring the head. Pushing aside the sodden fabric took a while, but when he did, he visibly shuddered. In the glow of the lantern, the fishermen stared down at what remained of a human face. It was infested with crabs eagerly consuming its soft materials, the lips and eyes. Small creatures peeked out of the nose and crawled in and out of a portal that had been once a mouth.

The second man put his rifle down, covered his nose, and squatted over the corpse. He located an arm, pulled back more soaked material, and there was a hand. And on one of the fingers was a ring. They could read its inscription: UNIVERSITY OF SANTA CLARA.

Two hours later, Ewing and his swarm of deputies used a tarp to drag the body across the mudflats to where the county coroner's team waited at the edge of the frontage road. They had taken pictures of the crumpled remains on the beach; in a few more hours the tide would return to wash away all traces. Four men hoisted the corpse into the coroner's wood-paneled wagon, which immediately departed for San Jose, where the body would be formally identified and examined as to the cause of death. By the time the cavalcade reached downtown, newspaper reporters had sent off their dispatches with exclusive photographs of the two duck hunters and their discovery. Sheriff Ewing emphatically stated the "floater could in fact be anyone." They all needed to "keep their shirts on" until positive identification could be made.

Not a soul was convinced. They all knew who it was. Ewing wanted to tantalize them. Loved the publicity. It was part of the job. And they all went along for the ride.

37

Cooper had gone downstairs to the hotel restaurant. Before he could ask for breakfast, his bottle-blond waitress uncharacteristically enthused: "Have you heard the news? They found him."

Cooper showed her his empty cup.

"Coming right up."

Cooper knew that meant whenever she got around to it. "Bring the pot," he said firmly.

Betty's news wasn't surprising. Cooper had deduced that Rosen's corpse would be discovered at an appropriate moment, publicized at the dictated time for best exposure. He knew enough of this town to understand there was still much he did not know. He saw little point in dropping in on Blackmun, who had become ever more inaccessible. The police chief no longer acknowledged Cooper or seemed interested in controlling the groups of angry, vocal citizens stalking the downtown streets. Cooper hoped that Blackmun still had some shred of dignity and would enforce the law if the situation worsened.

The sheriff had never been straight with him, Cooper now knew. While Ewing's role now was to protect the two prisoners, from what Cooper saw, the man engaged most of his time with the press. He was lately too busy to even make a show of collaborating with the Bureau.

Betty at last arrived with coffee. Cooper poured it himself and downed the first cup, poured another. He fingered the crumpled letter in his coat pocket. Someone had delivered it beneath his door during the night. Its author had not revealed themselves, but it was written on University of Santa Clara stationary. The sender clearly wanted to convey a connection and professed knowing relevant facts about Cooper's investigation. The letter—not a rant or a threat—suggested that Cooper consider certain relationships of the "broader business community" that included Thomas Ripley and the university president. There was also mention of a local organization known as the Committee for Public Safety whose aims were to "employ direct action to preserve the values of the community." This sounded like a vigilante group. The letter writer implored the Bureau to look into these relationships. There was "an effort afoot to escalate activities that could snowball into something dangerous."

Before taking his breakfast, Cooper had placed a call to the university rectory and, to his surprise, reached the president's secretary, who agreed to a brief interview later that day. The secretary stipulated that it must be brief since the president needed most of the morning to prepare an announcement scheduled for that afternoon.

Cooper had plenty of time before the meeting. He nursed his third cup of coffee and glowered out the window at the newsboys screaming headlines up and down the sidewalks.

"*Michael Rosen dead! Read all about it!*"

"*Seagulls have feast by the bay!*"

"*Murderers sitting pretty in county jail!*"

"C'mon, get your copy before they're all gone," cried the newsies. They were making a mint, with people buying up newspapers like hotcakes at a church social. And that was only half of it. The radio blared in the restaurant and, Cooper surmised, throughout homes and businesses around San Jose and beyond: "*. . . murdered in cold blood. A kidnapping gone mad . . .*"

Two duck hunters had discovered Rosen's corpse, his eyes pecked out by scavenging birds, the radio announcer gushed. "*Left dead, alone on the mudflats! . . . Tierney and Hansen have confessed.*

Don't forget their names. Don't forget what they have done."

Cooper wasn't surprised to learn that Sheriff Ewing had been there to retrieve the body. According to the radiocaster, the sheriff had deemed it a "desecration." The county coroner was able to identify Rosen only by his class ring—the ring given to him by the good fathers of the University of Santa Clara. With the prisoners now back in the county jail, Ewing was quoted as saying, "And there they will be until justice is served."

A young seminarian met Cooper in the lobby of the university's administration building. As they strode down the corridor and then up the stairs, Cooper noted the place had the usual humdrum of a business; everyone was dutiful to their daily schedules. Perhaps they hadn't received the latest news about Rosen. Or were concealing what they had heard on the radio. He didn't see anyone reading a newspaper. It might have been any old day.

Who was the confederate among them? Cooper could not tell.

The seminarian knocked on the president's office door. A voice replied granting permission to enter. The voice belonged to a chubby man, smaller than Cooper had imagined, clean-shaven with a broad smile and slight dimples. The president had twinkling blue eyes behind his steel-rimmed glasses, a bowling ball–shaped head covered with wisps of whitish hair swept back with oil. He introduced himself as Fr. Seebach. "Glad to make your acquaintance," he said to Cooper, who mentally noted the man's youthful composure and vigorous handshake. The priest beckoned the federal agent to take a seat and sat across from him, declining to remain behind his desk.

"I know you have come a long way to investigate the crimes committed in the valley," Fr. Seebach said. "I'm pleased the culprits have been found and that your justice will prevail. Though I'm painfully sorry to hear about Michael who, you know, graduated from our university last year and has retained his strong ties to this community." The priest sighed and bowed his head briefly. "He will be missed. His spirit is large."

Cooper's immediate impression was that this man recalled a figure from Renaissance paintings. But which one? A father figure? No, someone else. It might have been the slight smile, the way he tilted his head. The man resembled a putto, a cherub. The messenger spirit that dwelled between the divine and the human. A cherub gone to seed.

"I am glad you are paying your respect to our brethren," Fr. Seebach was saying. "What can I do for you? I suspect your investigation . . ."

Cooper reared his head back slightly as he watched the priest.

". . . well, it must, ah, be concluding?" Fr. Seebach's voice trailed off, seemingly distracted by the bemused look on Cooper's face.

"The investigation remains open," Cooper said tautly. "There are details that need to be explored to ensure a fair shake to all."

Seebach sat back in his chair, surprise registering on his face. "How can I possibly help you?" he asked.

Cooper folded his hands. "While the accused have confessed, there is a question of motivation for these crimes."

"Isn't the motive of the kidnapping obvious?"

"Perhaps, yes, but why murder the boy if the motivation was simply money? The kidnappers would have been paid and Rosen released. If it wasn't for money, then what was the motivation?"

Fr. Seebach put his index finger to his bottom lip. "Indeed. A perplexing problem. Again, how may I be of help? It's been said that the Lord comes to us disguised as ourselves. Is this something that has greater implications? Is there a spiritual component to what you are seeking?"

"What I am seeking is information that you may possess," said Cooper somewhat wearily.

The priest nodded sagely.

Cooper took out his notebook, skimmed his notes. "I understand that today is an important day for you—"

"Most certainly it is," exclaimed Fr. Seebach, looking as if he might suddenly leap out of his seat. "This is the day that we execute an agreement that allows us to begin work on our new theological seminary in the Santa Cruz Mountains. It's a project we have been working on for a long, long time. The opportunity to build such a project will help the Jesuit community for decades to come—"

Interrupting as discreetly as possible, Cooper inquired as to how this opportunity was to be financed and with whom.

"This has always been a multifaceted deal. One of our trustees, Thomas Ripley, has provided financial assistance to the seminary project, beginning with the sale of some of our bayside property. He and his consortium of buyers have paid top dollar, which allows us to purchase the Tevis property. Ripley and his people helped to arrange a construction loan to build the entire project using the remaining portions of the sale proceeds from the land transfer. We met earlier and agreed to terms, but today the agreements will be executed so that both parties can mutually benefit. The Jesuits will gain a new seminary in the hills—"

"And what do Thomas Ripley and his investors gain?" asked Cooper.

Fr. Seebach's voice took on a professorial tone as he answered. "I suppose access to property that will become more productive and therefore more valuable. The existing use has been as orchards. And unfortunately, apricots, prunes, and cherries no longer pay the bills. A consortium purchased a series of properties and sold it to the federal government for an airfield. They told me they think it will serve as the site for the Navy's lighter-than-air dirigible fleet, a newfangled piece of technology. The land in question is the last remaining piece."

Fr. Seebach got more comfortable in his chair and fondled the rosary beads around his neck.

"The investors think there are significant opportunities in such technological developments that would justify this huge investment," he continued. "The Jesuit community understands change. It is not our prerogative to question such opportunities. Our respective goals are sizably divergent, other than we see that such investments may create an economic incentive that would result in more employment in these troubled times. And that is good, would you not agree?"

Cooper nodded at the last statement, then asked his own question. "If Mr. Ripley's role is to be the catalyst for this transaction, then why is he taking such a prominent role in the testimonies of Earle Hansen and Harold Tierney? Why has he been involved in that affair at all?"

"I was not aware of that." Fr. Seebach sat up. "Isn't that something you ought to ask Mr. Ripley? Yet I understand your problem and your resolve. Some questions are difficult and take time to fully understand. We must trust in the deliberate action of God's work."

"Will Ripley be at the signing later this afternoon? I would like to talk with him."

"It's been a long time coming. I'm sure he would not miss the opportunity of this special event."

Cooper peered down at his notes. "I understand there is a Committee for Public Safety that operates on your campus."

"If there is such a committee, then it is not sanctioned by the members of the Jesuit community," Fr. Seebach replied smoothly.

Cooper looked up. "Padre, I have heard rumors about the existence of such a committee. And I suspect that Mr. Ripley may be somehow connected to it. That concerns me."

Fr. Seebach looked up to the ceiling with the air of one considering peeling paint that might require some patchwork, then back at Cooper. "That I do not know. I hate to be redundant, but this is a question you need to pose to Mr. Ripley."

Cooper scribbled in his notebook for a moment. Then he fixed his gaze on Fr. Seebach. "Why, do you think, was it necessary to kill Michael Rosen?"

The priest's ever-so-beaming face collapsed in a frown, as a celebrant might if an altar boy missed his cue and neglected to ring the bell at the precise moment of the holy transfiguration.

"Why would it be?" he said, staring back at Cooper. "That's your job. I do not play detective."

The door opened, and the young seminarian entered and mentioned solemnly that Fr. Seebach needed to prepare for the signing ceremony. The seminarian also relayed that the San Jose Police chief had called and wanted to convey to both of them that the crowd at St. James Park had grown larger and increasingly unruly. And before he was dismissed, the seminarian said that the chief had received a telegram from the Bureau's San Francisco office. It read: Gaetano Ferrone, a San Jose businessman, was discovered dead in Lake Tahoe. Cooper crumpled the note, stuck it in his suit pocket.

Cooper asked to use a telephone, and the seminarian escorted him to an empty office. He first tried Blackmun, but he was unavailable. All he got at the Bureau office was Benson, who was next to useless, so he hung up on him.

When he strolled into O'Connor Hall, a small group of local dignitaries was already sat waiting for the proceedings to commence. Fr. Seebach greeted each of them, patted them on the back, whispered in their ear like a politician seeking support for an upcoming municipal election. Ripley was nowhere to be seen.

When the signing ceremony commenced, Fr. Seebach provided an extended homily on the hopes and desires of what would be accomplished by the impending agreement, how the disposition and development of the Tevis property nestled in the bucolic hills above Los Gatos would create a great theological center for training Jesuit seminarians. The center would be called Alma College. After a quick prayer and blessing, Fr. Seebach introduced his counterpart, a distinguished gentleman: Lawrence Linforth, Esq.

Linforth apologized for Ripley's absence; he had been called away that morning to attend to urgent business. The lawyer recited a prepared statement and spoke elegantly about how negotiations had culminated in a mutually beneficial agreement.

Cooper spun on his heel, hailed a cab, and returned to downtown

San Jose, intending to track down Ripley and see what was happening in St. James Park.

⚜

Cooper tried Ripley's office on the top floor of the First National Bank at Santa Clara and First Streets. He rode the elevator to the fourteenth floor and then walked into the foyer, where a young secretary sat admiring her nails and a man sprawled on a bench positioned against a wall. He was smoking and reading a newspaper. Both looked up as Cooper marched past them. The secretary blurted, "Say, mister, you can't go in there! It says *private*."

"Ripley in?" asked Cooper.

"Not today," replied the secretary.

Cooper made his move toward Ripley's door.

The man reading put down his newspaper. "Hey, do you understand English?" he said to Cooper.

"He's gone," insisted the secretary.

"Where'd he go?"

"I never know." She shrugged. "He never tells me. He just comes and goes."

Cooper opened the door and poked his head in. Indeed, no Ripley. As he walked away, Cooper sneered when he heard the secretary say, "Might try the university . . ."

Having struck out, Cooper headed to St. James Park. Within a block, he could discern that someone had hooked up a contraption so that everyone could hear each pronouncement coming over the airwaves. By the time he reached the edge of the park, it was nearly filled with people. The usual bums and hoboes were greatly outnumbered. One radio bulletin reported that a Rosen's Department Store employee had been asked to identify a gold signet ring that remained on the finger of the corpse. This employee recognized that the ring once belonged to Michael Rosen. The family would not corroborate, but the employee emphatically told the radio interviewer that Rosen had always worn a ring bearing the name of his alma mater.

Then, another late-breaking bulletin blared. Rosen's dentist had matched his own records to the information given to him by the sheriff. The radio announcer said there was now absolute proof that Michael Rosen's body had been positively identified, then repeated the information that the accused were sitting in the county jail next to St. James Park. The announcer kept exclaiming in his newly found Latin: "*Corpus delicti, corpus delicti!*" The phrase was like an electric jolt through the crowd. A few onlookers, then nearly everyone began to raise their fists and shout revenge against the accused. It became a chant: "We want justice! Stop protecting criminals!"

The cry rang out over and over until another radio news flash raised the ante. Someone turned up the volume. "*Alexander Rosen has forbidden his employees to take part in any demonstration, threatening dismissal if they do.*" The announcement was met with boos and hollers. A radio reporter interviewed a man who only identified himself as another of the department store's employees. "*I don't care if I'm sacked.*" Cheers. "*Michael Rosen was my colleague. All I gotta say is they'd better lay down those guns when we move in!*" Applause.

Cooper had seen and heard enough.

38

Winston found another note after the signing ceremony. He had returned to his desk and discovered the small envelope in the pocket of the jacket left hanging on the back of his chair. The missive was brief: a time, a place, a password. Signed by the Committee.

At the specified time, Winston furtively ventured to the Adobe Lodge near the Mission chapel. Inside, in the back, was a barely noticeable room once reserved as a sanctuary for silent prayer; it now served as a storage room. Winston knocked on the door, gave the password—*Ora et labora*—and was ushered in. Sitting around a large table, amid stacks of various detritus, all of them were there: Jeremy Rollins, the child actor turned cheerleader; Michael Rosen's friend James O'Neill; the quarterback, Frank Salatino; and Billy Snyder, looking fresh from his father's auto lot. Winston knew a few of the others, though not well: Puglia and Slavitch, both football players; O'Hara and Lombardi, whose fathers each ran a cannery; and some he only knew their faces. All told, there were about two dozen university men crammed into the tiny room.

Lombardi began the meeting with a prayer, a recitation to uphold Catholic values and individual liberties, and then he launched headlong into recent events. The cold-blooded murder of Michael Rosen was an affront to these values and everyone's liberties, he concluded.

Cheers and catcalls erupted.

O'Neill stood. "As you well know, the police have brought back the murderers. We are sick and tired of what's going on. We demand action. We need to get something done."

Winston watched everyone pound the table with their fists. If he had thought to bring his rosary, he might have clutched it in his pocket.

"They are guilty! They admitted it! They should be sentenced immediately!" someone cried. More pounding.

O'Hara spoke up. "I can't believe we have a legal system that bends over backwards for the guilty." Someone else echoed, "It'll take years to crucify these guys."

"Some natty lawyer will file appeals. These guys might even get off," quipped Salatino, who now stood leaning against the wall.

"Not with this governor," boasted Snyder. "He'll see that things will get done."

"Hear, hear," several responded.

Lombardi ground a fist into his other palm. "Where is the justice?"

"I say we take action," said Salatino.

Rollins rose. "We need justice now. Not later. Not after a grand jury ponders the matter. Not after a jury trial. Not after a determination of guilt. Not after sentencing. Not after the countless appeals. Not after the appeal to the governor. But now! Justice must be served now!"

O'Hara took the floor amid the clapping and nods of agreement.

"Let's not forget who is behind this whole thing," O'Hara said. "They've done it before. Causing strikes. Slowdowns. Stirring up things with their talk of unions. We know the Reds are behind this. The Reds are anti-business. Anti-prosperity. Anti-Christian. Anti-American!"

"They watched his every move from that office across the street and nabbed him when the time was ripe." O'Neill was red in the face. "Right in front of the store. To brazenly show they could."

"No, no, it's those damn Okies who have invaded this valley." It was Slavitch speaking now. "What's going on is that these migrants are dirt poor, see our garden heaven, and want some of it. We should have prevented them from taking root in the valley. They're rootless. No morals. They're not us, and they resent us. They resented Michael. They're behind his murder. They are the ones who ought to pay."

Winston swung his gaze around to see who would agree with Slavitch. A few murmured their affirmation, but the room seemed divided.

"Hansen is a Red, and I can prove it," said O'Hara. "My father says his cannery is infested with union agitators. They want to burn down all the institutions."

The debate over who deserved blame grew more intense. O'Neill pounded on the table in a vain attempt to quiet things down. "Does it really matter?" he asked. "They've got the guys in jail right now."

Rollins stood on his chair. "Order, order!"

"Will you guys shut up? We're here to talk tactics. What's the plan?" shouted Lombardi.

"Who put him in charge?" said someone near the back. Winston didn't recognize him.

The arguing died down, and it was Snyder who spoke. "They are starting to gather as expected in the park."

"I heard that the police won't interfere," interjected Puglia, standing near the door, arms crossed.

"Where'd you hear that?" sneered Salatino.

"It's true. I assure you," said Puglia.

"There needs to be a vanguard for righteous action," someone said.

Winston was unsure who had spoken; no one seemed to take responsibility. Throughout all of this, the one person he might have expected was not in the room. Where was Wilford Kishi? He was smart not to be there. Someone probably would have wanted to blame everything on the Japanese.

Slavitch, in his letterman jacket, gained everyone's attention. His voice boomed definitively. "These punks ought to get some Bronco justice!"

"Justice, yes!" screamed Rollins. "Bronco justice!"

That became the chant. Someone started scuffing their shoes on the floor, which quickly grew to collective stomping. They pounded the tabletop.

"Well, then, it's unanimous," said O'Neill, speaking above the noise. "Eleven tonight."

"Boys, let's get organized," Rollins said with exaggerated calm. "There'll be a necktie party in the old town tonight."

39

Angelo scanned the congregation of angry people that had filled up St. James Park. The evening was cool, though warmer than usual. The skies had changed, the shadows lengthened. The trees in the park looked to Angelo like enormous hands intertwined over the crowd. Just beyond the park lay the county jail, the locus of the agitation.

Angelo gripped the rail in front of Spades and examined the crowd for anyone who might pose a threat. His men were inconspicuously stationed at various points along Third Street. So far, so good.

Oliver called his name from below. Rosalia was on the line. He trotted down the steps as quickly as his old knees would allow and picked up the waiting telephone. Rosalia was safe in Avila Beach. He could exhale.

Booksin sat drumming his fingers against the underside of his chair.

"Can you place a call to Amelia?" Angelo asked him. "I need to make sure everything remains square."

"Sure enough," replied Booksin.

Angelo returned to his post. In just the few moments since he'd stepped away, the crowd seemed to have grown bigger and louder. A continuous parade of automobiles circled, their headlights becoming a nearly unbroken halo around the park as darkness descended. Mingled with the sounds of the car horns, radio bulletins encouraged citizens to come downtown in the name of civic pride. Overloaded streetcars dislodged passengers. People from the neighborhood strolled around, curious to see what the fuss was all about. Police officers drifted along the perimeter of the crowd.

Angelo remained motionless at the stairs. The streetlamps were switched on, a morose accompaniment to the headlights and the glow emanating from the many windows of the county jail. Shadowy forms moved beyond the windows; Angelo wondered how it must feel to be inside looking out at all those angry people. Soon enough, a small cadre of sheriff's deputies emerged and formed a line in front of the jail.

The crowd continued to balloon in size. People passed by Angelo as they made their way to the bar below to bolster their intent. At least revenue would be up. Angelo's men patted down each customer before allowing entry. Switchblades were confiscated. A club taken away. Even a large umbrella—no rain was expected. There were no revolvers.

Booksin followed the bouncer to say that Amelia was still secure in Los Gatos. Booksin looked haggard, and Angelo said as much. "Stay close. I may need you. It isn't safe to go home. We'll be at the Torino later tonight."

"I think it's best that I check up later on your daughter," said Booksin.

Angelo nodded his thanks, and Booksin took his leave.

St. James Park was by this time overflowing. The crush of people clogged the surrounding streets. Automobiles could no longer venture close. Drivers abandoned their vehicles and joined the milling pack. The empty cars strewn haphazardly along the roads added to the growing sense of unrest.

Angelo noticed the uniformed police officers present earlier had withdrawn. He looked at his watch. It was 10:27 p.m. when a group of maybe two dozen young men showed up at Spades. It didn't require the trained eye of a detective to figure out these men belonged to the university. Each was searched and patted down. Some attempted to resist the infringement on their entitlement; Oliver did not take any of their guff. None of the young men carried anything other than their stuffed wallets. After passing Oliver's scrutiny, one by one the new arrivals entered the confinement of the saloon.

Angelo followed them down the stairs. His glance to Oliver was met with a slight nod. The bouncer knew to keep an extra eye on them. The young men began to wave their wads, expecting immediate service, intending to get lubricated straightaway.

The barkeep glanced across the room. Angelo touched his earlobe: Let them have their drinks. Angelo remained standing discreetly to one side, listening to their chatter and soon hearing enough to glean what was on their minds: "Undesirables have taken over San Jose and need to be taught a lesson. Thirty pieces of silver is not reward enough," one of the students shouted.

Many of the other patrons had left by the time the rowdy students started to chant, "Bronco justice!" Oliver looked at Angelo, who gestured to let it pass. The message was silently conveyed to Angelo's other men. And then, as quickly as they descended, the young men departed. They had been in the bar less than an hour.

The barkeep exhaled. In less than an hour, they would close; all the excitement was in St. James Park. "Maybe we ought to shut down now," suggested Oliver. "Just to be safe."

As Angelo was considering the advice, the federal agent sauntered down the steps. "We need to talk," he said to Angelo, who showed him to the back room. They settled on one of the couches.

The barkeep, one Cooper didn't recognize, entered through the curtained opening and offered the agent a drink. Cooper accepted. "I reckon I'll need more than my wits about me this evening."

When the drink came, he downed it, wiped his brow with his handkerchief. "I am sorry to hear of your loss," he told Angelo.

Angelo kept his alarm in check. Rosalia? Amelia? As far as he knew, they were safe and secure.

"You must have heard already," Cooper said.

Angelo had heard nothing.

"Officials in Lake Tahoe attested that it was a mere accident. The information we received was that Gaetano Ferrone had walked out earlier, most likely for a smoke."

"He used to say he was walking his cigar," commented Angelo.

"When he did not return and could not be located on the grounds of their residence, stated his bodyguard, there was a search for him, initially around the adjacent properties, but eventually the lake itself."

Angelo didn't flinch, though he knew what was coming.

Ferrone had been found face down in the water. A local man running his motorboat in the dark, something he apparently did often without incident, had struck the body. The boat driver notified the sheriff's department, and it was they who did the initial assessment, to be confirmed by the coroner, that Ferrone might have slipped while taking a walk along the cliffs and had drowned. While his skull was fractured, that was most likely caused by the motorboat. "Or so they said," Cooper concluded.

Angelo closed his eyes and said a silent prayer. "That was no accident."

"No. Indeed not," replied Cooper.

Angelo excused himself for a moment while he informed Caputo, who would tell Lagatutta, and so forth.

"Was Passalacqua's gang behind this?" asked Cooper when Angelo returned.

"Ferrone had been in negotiations with them. Ripley. Linforth. For some time. They wanted more property. More access. It's really all about real estate. In a down market, that's when you buy up things," said Angelo in a measured tone. Only his hands, as he gestured to emphasize points, betrayed his emotion.

"You think it's more than the ending of the Volstead Act?" Cooper wanted to know.

"Most assuredly."

"What went wrong?"

"They exerted pressure on us. They threatened to expose our role in the kidnapping. You know, we admit our role. But recent events show that they—"

"Who are *they*?"

"Passalacqua's men . . . took over the kidnapping. You know the rest."

"To what end?"

"To keep us on our heels."

"And the murder of Ferrone?"

"Would indicate something more."

"How much more?"

"We don't know."

"And the crowd outside?"

"The mob?"

"What do they want?"

"You tell me."

"Retribution for Michael Rosen's death," said the Bureau agent.

One of Angelo's men rapped on the wall of the doorway. "Boss, you need to come."

"One moment, please, my friend," said Angelo as he rose from the couch. The club had suddenly become noisier. Raised voices. The shatter of glass.

Angelo's men had already taken action. Four patrons had started a fight, Oliver told him. "They didn't like the 'smell of the place.'" Angelo looked at his dark-skinned friend. He didn't need to be told what the miscreants might have called him.

"How are things going in the park?" Angelo asked.

"Not well."

"That's not our concern at the moment," Angelo reminded his men. "Focus on the security of this establishment. Outside is the cops' responsibility."

Angelo returned to the back room. Cooper was writing in his notebook.

"Is everything all right?" the agent asked.

"Some drunks. They had too much. They didn't like what we had to offer. It is taken care of."

"What's it like outside?"

"They seem to be getting more belligerent."

"I'll need to check for myself what is going on," said Cooper.

Frank Lagatutta entered the room, regarded the federal agent with surprise, then turned to Angelo. "Something is happening."

"I thought you resolved that."

"Here, yes. But across the park, no. At the jail. They're throwing rocks. It's turning ugly."

Cooper got up, strode past Angelo into the bar. Up the stairs and across the street.

Angelo followed him to the street and watched Cooper vanish into the raging crowd. People were running, scuffling, cursing, yelling. Several streetlamps had been broken with well-aimed rocks. The jailhouse window lights had been darkened. The only light now came from the headlights of the cars left on the streets and the glow of fires being lit around the park.

St. James Park was in pandemonium.

40

Cooper elbowed through the crowd. The throng of people grew denser as he neared the county jail, and they jostled one another trying to get closer to the jail steps, where two dozen deputies equipped with billy clubs attempted to keep the mob at bay. It was akin to a raging tide: The crowd surged up the jail steps only to retreat when pushed back by the cops. And then there was another surge and a retreat. Back and forth.

Deputies had hastily constructed barricades consisting of no more than wooden planks nailed atop sawhorses. These were positioned at the top of the steps in front of the jail's main doors. Sheriff Ewing paced behind these barricades, bantering with his deputies and at times with people in the crowd, telling them to "go home." Cooper noted that Ewing looked oddly at ease for a sheriff whose jail was nearly under siege. Perhaps the sheriff was reassured by the deputies placed on the balcony above, all wielding short-barreled shotguns loaded with tear-gas canisters.

Cooper was intent on speaking with Ewing. Why were only county deputies guarding the jail? What happened to the San Jose Police who had withdrawn from the park? Who ordered that? Why hadn't the National Guard been ordered in? When Cooper reached the stairs, deputies used their clubs to form a shield so that he could make his way through the barricades. Just as he did, someone slugged him from behind. The blow hit him in the head. The mob heaved forward again. Wincing from the blow, Cooper hunched past the line of deputies and then stood, looking back at the moving tide of brandished fists and hot, resolute faces. Radio bulletins continued to blare indistinctly over the thunder of the mob.

Ewing had disappeared. Cooper immediately gestured to a deputy that he wanted to be inside. They cracked the door for him, and Cooper was let in amid an uproar from the mob. Once inside, the deputies locked and barred the main doors. Cooper spied Ewing; the sheriff was now yelling orders at his deputies. There would be no opportunity to get the lowdown. Instead, Cooper marched upstairs and asked a jailer to open John Schiavo's cell.

The jailer dutifully let Cooper inside the cell. The prisoner, a disheveled-looking, unshaven soul in his late twenties, was standing at the window, staring at the crowd below. He turned when Cooper entered. "Who are you?"

Cooper flashed his Bureau credentials. Schiavo looked him over. "Get me out of here!"

"You need to talk." Cooper took out his notebook from his inside jacket pocket.

Schiavo folded his arms. "First, get me out."

"What were you first, a union organizer or a gang member?" Cooper asked.

Schiavo's hooded red eyes stared back. He sat on his bunk and put his hands on his knees. "Look, I was a stevedore on the waterfront. Things dried up. They offered me a chance."

"Who?"

"Not gonna say. They put me in here."

"Okay, no names," said Cooper. "But if you want to get out of here, you'll have to cooperate. Have you ever heard of the Committee for Public Safety?"

"Yeah, sure, if that's what they are calling themselves."

"What were your instructions? What did you get out of this?"

"You release me. Then we'll talk."

"Under these circumstances, your best option is to remain here. A locked jail cell may be your best protection," said Cooper.

The jailer was pacing back and forth outside the cell door, doubtless overhearing the conversation. There was gunfire. The acrid smell of smoke permeated the air.

Schiavo sniffed, then rubbed his eyes. "Is that . . . ?"

"Yes, they've fired tear gas," Cooper said evenly. He waited.

"They wanted me to give them names," Schiavo said after a moment. "Names of union members."

"That's it?"

"Names of organizers trying to unionize all the cannery and farmworkers. Get me out of here."

"And you provided lists?"

"Yeah, they got what they paid for."

Cooper scribbled a few notes, looked back at Schiavo. "And for that, they put you here?"

Schiavo shifted his weight uncomfortably. "Well, the police came and arrested me."

"The charge?"

"They said there was a warrant for my arrest and that I would have legal representation. The charge was vagrancy, but that's a laugh. Then some attorney showed up. Called himself Dash."

"Was his name Linforth?"

"No. This Dash fellow said the Committee's plans had changed. That I needed to prove my loyalty. That I would be charged as an accessory to the kidnapping if I did not cooperate."

"The Rosen kidnapping?"

"Yeah."

"What did Dash direct you to do?"

"Sit here and rot. Keep my mouth shut."

"What about Hansen and Tierney?"

"What about them?"

"Was it just the two of them?"

"They've got their guys here."

"Who else was involved?"

Schiavo looked at him incredulously. "Are you kidding me?"

The jailer entered the cell and said that Ewing wanted to speak with Cooper. "Immediately."

Cooper put away his notebook. "Don't worry," he said to Schiavo. "I'll be back."

As the door clanged shut, Schiavo gripped the bars and pleaded, "Federal man, get me out of here."

"C'mon, big boy, shut your trap. You'll get yours," said the jailer.

As he walked away, Cooper remembered those words.

41

Winston trailed a few paces behind the students as they left the basement bar and crossed the street to the park. At first, they remained on the perimeter of the chaos. It wasn't time yet. Responding to a signal from Slavitch, they skirted the crowd and headed for Letcher's Automotive Showroom at First and East St. James. At the rear of the building, O'Hara pounded on the garage's roll-up door until it was slowly opened from within. A man in blue overalls stood inside. He was wearing a white cloth mask. He gestured toward the truncheons piled on the floor. "Take the stuff. We also left a battering ram in a construction site. Next to the jail," he told them. "Take what you need. Then get out of here."

"Hide 'em under your jackets," ordered Slavitch. "We don't want to tip anyone off."

"Don't forget your masks," said the man.

Indeed, on the hood of an automobile that needed repairs lay several white cloth masks. Next to the masks were two long strands of hemp rope. Snyder took the ropes. Everyone else, including Winston, grabbed a mask and a club.

"Now get out of here. Get lost," ordered the man once more.

The time was near. They crossed the street into the park and pushed and shoved to the front of the jail. The crowd at the steps had been there for hours. Some didn't like this new group taking their space. A shoving match ensued. The students, operating as a unit, forcefully pushed the others back. Onlookers seemed either cowed or relieved that someone was finally taking charge.

Arms interlocked, the score of deputies continued to resist the surging mob. Puglia, Lombardi, and O'Hara stood their ground and screamed at the cops. The deputies did not move, even when O'Hara spat in one of their faces. Someone on a bullhorn ordered the deputies to press forward, to clear more space in front. And the deputies obeyed, holding their billy clubs chest high to push back the angry citizenry. In the midst of the spontaneous scuffle, Puglia threw a punch. A deputy blocked it with his club and, in turn, swung hard and knocked Puglia to his knees. O'Hara tried to help Puglia up. He didn't stand a chance. As O'Hara reached for his truncheon, he was slammed to the ground by the same deputy, who returned in kind: He spat on O'Hara, then stomped him with his boot.

At the front of the line, Salatino and O'Neill pressed forward into the riotous crowd, then, nearly in unison, jumbled backward as they were shoved away by the deputies. The men crowding behind the students did not appreciate being jostled; they pushed harder, hands and elbows grinding into the backs of Salatino and Slavitch. At that point, whether or not the word had been given, Salatino and Slavitch reached for their truncheons and started to swing in earnest, first at the men behind them, then at the deputies in front.

Rollins backed off a few yards and used his bullhorn. "It's time to attack, compadres!"

Puglia, O'Neill, and others wielded their truncheons and joined the fray. One student took a hit, tumbled. One of the deputies clubbed him repeatedly. But as the forward section of the Santa Clara team seemed to be crumbling, reinforcements stepped in and attacked the deputies on the right flank. The deputies had not figured on organized resistance. They were skilled in close-hand combat, but slight hesitation on their part allowed the second line of students, Winston among them, to break through.

The deputies stationed on the jail's balcony blasted tear-gas grenades into the crowd. The gas bombs exploding all around the jail steps stunned the attackers. The disoriented mob retreated, some running blindly to escape the noxious fumes. In the melee, screams of agony erupted as men fell and were trampled by the panicked mob. Winston tasted the smoke on his lips. His eyes burned. An eerie collective wail echoed from the crowd. Winston stumbled away from the jail steps, his vision obscured by the smoke that seemed to be everywhere. He could not see where the rest of the team had gone. Vainly holding a handkerchief to his eyes, he realized he was alone amid the mob. He turned in a jerky circle, searching for his companions among the cloudy, half-lit figures of men running and fighting. He tripped over someone who had fallen and didn't seem to be moving.

Indistinctly at first, then growing louder, a rhythmic chanting rang out. Winston ignored the screaming all around him and moved toward the jail. Over from the left flank, he spotted some students, heads down, vigorously pushing forward. Salatino, Slavitch, and Lombardi were in the lead. Once they got to the top of the jail steps, they brandished their truncheons and cleared a path that allowed the other students—who had found the thirty-foot cast iron beam in the adjacent construction site, sharing the weight between them like pallbearers—to reach the doors. All of them wore masks.

The sight of the battering ram had an electrifying effect on the crowd. Despite the smoke and gas, scores of embittered men rallied and again rushed up the jail steps. Some brandished tire irons from the cars abandoned in the streets. A group swung in and attacked the line of deputies at their right side. The attackers flung bricks taken from the construction site, aiming at the prisoners' windows and the tear-gas firing squad above. Some hit their marks. Momentarily, the fusillade directed at the crowd stopped. And then, from the jail balcony it commenced once again, though each time the deputies beat back the onslaught, more men swarmed in to take up the fight. A battle cry was given, and the overwhelmed deputies retreated into the jail just as the students, joined now by other men, began to use the battering ram to smash relentlessly against the doors.

Winston went sideways and escaped to the side of the building. Standing off to the right, he took in the scene. The mad crowd still jostled back and forth, dodging the occasional bursts of tear gas still firing from the jail's balcony. Those clutching the battering ram pounded rhythmically. In the park, Winston glimpsed Rollins standing at his assigned post next to an elm tree. Snyder was doing the same at another elm about twenty feet away. Both men had donned their masks. Maybe Winston had missed the signal. He was the only one of the Santa Clara team not wearing his mask. He hesitated only briefly before sliding his hand into the well of his pocket and pulling out his mask. He secured the ties behind his head and the back of his neck. It was time to act.

42

By midnight, a riot gale was in full force. Now lacking deputies, the mob turned its full attention on the building itself. They wanted entry and lobbed bricks, stones, anything they could get their hands on at the heavy doors barring their access. Only the deputies on the balcony remained visible, still defending their fortress by shooting tear gas into the mob. Now savvy how to react, some in the crowd caught up the gas grenades in their handkerchiefs and threw them back, forcing deputies to retreat from the balcony's edge. When they showed themselves again, they were met with a rain of bricks. One of the projectiles struck a cell window on the south side of the building, shattering the glass and earning cries of terror from the prisoner inside. On the roof, two deputies maneuvered a searchlight to pan light over the crowd below. That worked as a slight deterrent until a well-aimed brick broke the lens into a thousand pieces.

The press had been there all along. Their cameras flashed repeatedly, a rapid-fire stutter of blinding light. Eyes could not adjust that quickly. Someone watching at a distance might have likened it to a sped-up silent film montage. Only, nothing was silent about this scene on the jailhouse steps.

"Safety is our number one issue. We must secure the jail!" bellowed Ewing. He had gone up to the balcony and stood glaring out over the crowd below. His orders were passed on down the line.

"Where are Blackmun's men?" asked one of his deputies. "What happened to them?"

Ewing didn't bother to answer.

The masked men below him continued to ram the jailhouse doors. Everyone defending the building heard and felt the echoing thud. The marauders seemed impervious to the smoke bombs deployed from above, reminiscent of a horde of Vandals outside a castle. The heavy vibrations shook the entire structure.

Ewing came down the interior stairs and yelled at an aide to call Blackmun and demand reinforcements. The aide responded that the phone wires had been cut.

"Goddamn Blackmun," muttered Ewing. He and his men were on their own.

With the crowd cheering them on, those wielding the battering ram kept up their assault. The thudding persisted every ten seconds or so, the impact reverberating. Each time the ram hit the door, there was an answering cheer from the mob.

The last of the tear gas was launched. The wind kicked up, and smoke rose into a gray fog that swirled upward, completely enveloping the deputies on the balcony; they retreated inside. On the second floor, a deputy foolishly opened a window, allowing the gas to seep inside the jail. Seeing this, the men ramming the doors doubled their efforts as the mob cheered and chanted for retribution.

Cooper started down the stairs. He felt oddly lightheaded and had to stop midway and hold on to the railing to keep his balance. Below in the jail's lobby, Ewing was addressing his deputies. "Keep steady, men," urged Ewing. "Don't use your firearms."

Still on the stairs, Cooper saw and heard enough to realize that Ewing was ordering his deputies to place their weapons in the vault on the ground floor. The deputies seemed as shocked as Cooper.

"Sir, why should we give up our own protection?" screamed a wild-eyed Kane.

"I don't want to see anyone hurt," yelled Ewing. "Do what you are told. That's an order."

The pounding from outside became louder and more insistent. Cooper leaned hard on the railing, half unsure whether the hammering was the assault on the jail doors or the jackhammers that had taken up residence in his skull.

"But, sir, our orders are to surrender?" questioned Miller. "The men need to remain armed. To protect themselves. To protect those in jail. To restore order."

Ewing ignored him.

The deputies were alarmed, but one by one they reluctantly surrendered their weapons. The firearms were taken to the basement vault, the door locked, and the key delivered to the sheriff. No one knew how much longer the main doors could withstand the abuse.

"Get us out of here," cried a prisoner. "We're sitting ducks."

"I'm not one of them. Let me out!" shouted another.

"I know who done it. I know!" a prisoner shrieked. "For God's sake, get me out. Get me out now!"

Their pleas went unanswered. The deafening pounding continued.

Winston breathed heavily through the fabric covering his face as he shoved through the screaming crowd. He reached Slavitch and the others, found a place in the line of men, and laid hold of the battering ram. "Again!" Slavitch ordered. Winston fell in step as the team backed up a few paces and then thrust forward. The shock of contact vibrated up his forearms. The metal hinges gave slightly, but the door did not budge.

The gas in the air burned their eyes, choked their throats. The masks didn't help much. The men holding the beam all grunted as one each time they reared back and then deliriously thrust the battering ram into the doors, faster and faster with the crowd urging them on. Winston kept his head down. Tears poured down his raw cheeks, soaking his mask. Within moments, he could no longer see. His arms were aching; each time the ram slammed into the door, it jarred his battered hands. He didn't see how he could manage another round. And then, it happened. They broke through the doors.

The crowd deliriously surged forward. Winston slipped and fell under the rush of men savagely climbing over him. Boots trampled heavily across his back. Winston was briefly pinned down by the weight, but then he stumbled up and staggered forward, carried along by the sweaty, red-faced men who piled into the jail.

Cooper was still hunched over on the inside steps when the mob broke through. From what seemed like very far away, he heard Ewing say: "It's all over, men. Brace yourselves."

There was no time for reasoned words. Authority had surrendered. Countless men spilled into the jail and pushed up the stairs. Cooper's singular goal became to remain where he was, hugging the railing, trying to steady himself against the crush of bodies. He lost his grip on the railing, flailed awkwardly as he fell across the steps. And then it was black and silent.

43

The holding cells were on the second floor of the jailhouse. The maelstrom of angry men pushed aside the shocked deputies and raced up the stairs. Winston joined them. He saw the sheriff standing against the wall, looking deflated as he let the mob flow by him. Winston heard a *pop!* and saw the sheriff falling into a heap. Someone must have nailed him with a beer bottle.

"Don't do this, boys. It ain't right," pleaded one of the deputies.

"You better stand aside if you know what's good for you," ordered a young man with a white mask. That might have been O'Neill. Winston, carried along with the flow, was not quite sure. He hadn't expected this to happen the way it did. Not with so much chaos. Not with the sheriff being knocked out like this. That was not part of the plan.

Without their sheriff, lacking their weapons, most of the deputies looked as frightened and panicked as Winston now felt. Slavitch had said there would be little resistance once they got inside. No one mentioned that violence would be directed against the deputies. Winston watched despairingly as three of the deputies were slammed to the ground. Some staunchly put up a fight but, as on the outside steps, they were outnumbered and overwhelmed. They had been foolishly obedient; their weapons were locked up in the vault. There was little they could do against the mob. The sheriff lay on the floor, the key to the vault swiped from his pocket. The masked men had known where to look.

It might have been Puglia who yelled, "Stand aside! We're going to take them."

No one answered.

"Which cells are they in?" screamed Puglia.

One deputy simply pointed up the staircase. A posse of men had already overtaken the second floor, presumably going cell to cell, looking for the two accused.

Winston followed the pack. Some were masked. Others not. A man in street clothes lay unconscious on the stairs. "There goes the federal guy," snickered a man Winston did not know.

O'Neill seemed to be in charge now, not caring that his mask had slipped off. Finding the first cell in view securely locked, he demanded keys and to know which corridor the two prisoners were in. A deputy wearily pointed down the corridor of cells. The light was dim.

"Keys?" O'Neill again demanded.

"Yeah, here." The jailer, who held a ring of keys, dutifully handed the man the whole lot. "Right over there." He pointed to the cells. "We've got only six prisoners."

Slavitch took the keys, fumbled with the ring, looked pitifully at the jailer.

"That one," said the jailer, pointing to a key. "Not there," the jailer added, but Slavitch was already inserting the key in the latch of the nearest cell. Five men rushed in. A man was huddled in the corner, hands raised, his body shaking. "I'm not who you want," he pleaded. "I only ride the rails. That's all I done."

Slavitch grabbed the hobo at the collar and hauled him upright. "Is he one of them?"

The jailer shook his head no.

Slavitch tossed him back. "Goddamn Okie."

Someone slugged the hobo.

"Which one?" snarled Slavitch, looking at the jailer.

The jailer grabbed back the ring, selected a key, and gave it to Slavitch, who moved to unlock the next door. He had difficulty getting this one open.

"That one gets sticky," offered the jailer. He stepped close to the door and jiggled the key while the men hovered around him. After a moment the door sprang open, revealing the outline of a man trying to escape into a crack in the corner of his cell. Someone produced a flashlight and shined it on the prisoner's face. He looked wild with fear.

"That's him. That's one of them," said the jailer, matter-of-factly.

Hansen lunged at them.

Puglia punched him. Slavitch tackled him. Hansen landed hard on the cement cell floor.

"Where's the rope?" asked O'Neill.

No response. "Rope!" someone cried.

Rollins carried a length of rope and elbowed his way into the cell. Slavitch grabbed the rope, and he and Puglia bound Hansen tightly, wrapping the rope around his torso and then his arms so he could not swing at them. Slavitch looped more rope securely around Hansen's neck and gave a sharp tug, meant to show who was boss. Hansen struggled to breathe but managed to spit on Slavitch.

Puglia punched Hansen in the gut. Someone else followed suit. A third man threw a savage haymaker that broke Hansen's nose. From where he stood just outside the cell, Winston heard the bones snap.

"That's all," declared O'Neill. "He's pretty much done now."

Salatino and Puglia pulled Hansen back upright. Slavitch slapped him on the face. "How ya feel now?"

"Walk!" ordered Puglia. "Walk!" echoed the chorus of men.

Hansen complied, but did so twisting and turning his body, snarling like a badger caught in a trap. Blood dripped out of his nose. Slavitch jerked on the rope on Hansen's neck. Hansen lunged forward. They dragged him out of the cell and down the stairs.

"I'm not the guy," Hansen rasped, his mouth bloody. "They set me up." He repeated the words over and over again.

"Like hell," someone yelled.

"You'll pay," screamed someone.

"You'll pay for your sins," whispered Winston, perhaps to himself.

Hansen was paraded out through the jail. Men jabbed and kicked him. Some tore at his clothes. They all wanted a piece. His face was a bloody mess, his nose twisted. Near the main doors, Hansen fell to his knees. "I was set up. I had nothing to do with it. Please, God, please. Have mercy on me. Please believe me."

His reply was a roundhouse kick to the side of the head. Hansen tumbled over on his side. Slavitch yanked the rope. Someone ran up to him and used a brick to smash in Hansen's battered face. Hansen lay in a heap, no longer screaming or saying anything.

"Let's get the other guy!" someone yelled. Winston followed the men back up the stairs, where the jailer stood waiting. He knew they weren't finished and complied when Lombardi ordered him to open another cell. The prisoner inside insisted they had the wrong guy. It was Schiavo. They would have dragged him out, but the jailer intervened. "Don't do it. He isn't one of them."

"Then who the hell is he?" yelled Lombardi.

"He ain't the guy," repeated the jailer.

"What's he in for?"

"He was arrested for the union riot," replied the jailer.

"Good enough for me," said O'Hara.

"No, no. That's not true," pleaded Schiavo. "I'm with all of you. You want Tierney. Not me."

"He's a communist. Let's get rid of him," hollered a man holding a brick, ready to slam it into Schiavo's head.

Nobody moved. They were unclear what to do. Lombardi was at a loss.

"Let's clean out the Reds while we're at it. What are we waiting for?" said another man.

"That's not the business tonight," yelled Lombardi. "We have a plan. Let's stick to it."

"Tonight or tomorrow. Why not now?" asked O'Hara.

"We should just get rid of them all. They're meat," cried a man.

"No, no," repeated Lombardi. "We want Tierney. Not this man." He whirled around to the jailer, who smiled and held up a key.

"Find which cell, Winston. Do your job!" yelled O'Hara.

Winston looked at the man holding the ring of keys.

"Far end. On the right," said the jailer, and pointed the way.

Unconvinced, O'Hara gave Schiavo a hard shove. He slumped to the cell floor.

Winston and the others followed the jailer to Tierney's cell. The jailer took his time unlocking the door as Lombardi shined a flashlight past the bars. Tierney was already hysterical. He had grabbed hold of the ventilation grate and pulled himself up as high as he could. He hung in the corner like a deranged orangutan.

"Get him down," ordered Lombardi.

It took three men to dislodge Tierney, who held on until someone swung a tire iron at his kneecaps. Tierney wailed as he flopped to the hard floor. The man with the tire iron beat him like a wild beast. Others joined in, punching and stomping on Tierney until he was absolutely still.

"We don't need a rope for this one," determined Lombardi.

O'Hara grabbed Tierney by one of his heels and gestured for Winston to take the other. Everyone had a chance to kick the inert prisoner. They dragged him down the stairs, his head thudding on every step until it hit the ground floor. The man's teeth had been knocked out. His mouth was a bloody hole. His arms and legs stuck out at unnatural angles.

At the front door of the county jail, Tierney was reunited with Hansen.

"Let's do it, boys," cried O'Neill. "Let's get it done."

They hauled Tierney outside first. When they emerged with him on the front steps, a lusty howl resounded. Five masked men took the lead to drag Tierney down the steps, across the street, and onto the turf of St. James Park. The crowd hurled insults, spat, and kicked Tierney's body. They arrived at a solemn elm tree where Snyder stood waiting. They'd already slung a rope over a high tree branch. Rollins affixed the noose around Tierney's neck, then yanked on the rope to make sure the branch was sturdy enough to bear the weight. A bevy of men hoisted Tierney high above the crowd. Automobile headlights provided the spotlight, focusing on the star performer for that evening. The lights from dozens of flashlights danced up and down, around the trees, and on Tierney's body, his head, chest, groin, as if he were some dreadful vaudeville act. This was what happened to those who broke the rules.

A near guttural murmur drifted through the park. It slowly became an incomprehensible chant, a growl from a suffering beast. And then, rather than reach its crescendo, the sound abruptly stopped. Some laughed in relief. There were a few scattered cheers. Some clapping. Applause for what had been performed.

Some in the crowd recoiled and retreated into the darkness of the park. Others stepped forward to get a better look. Some tentatively approached, while some got right up next to the hanging corpse to admire their handiwork. Tierney's face by now was so badly beaten that it no longer resembled a human. A beast had been captured, slaughtered, and hanged.

Some people got close enough to touch the body. One young man took off Tierney's shoes and waved them to the crowd. Another used his penknife to cut up Tierney's clothes and passed scraps on to the crowd. Everyone seemed to want a piece of this populist exactitude, this execution of the people's justice. Tierney's carcass swayed less than thirty yards from the statue of President McKinley.

Then it was Hansen's turn.

A tree limb had been chosen about twenty feet away from where Tierney's body swung. Snyder had enlisted a teenage boy to climb the tree. It wasn't needed at all, but the boy sat on a limb, waiting for Snyder to throw the rope over. With a gleeful look, the boy guided the rope through the branches. He was having the time of his life.

Hansen was brought into the park with the rope they'd used

to tie him still around his neck, at this point serving as more of a leash. Slavitch yanked and pulled on the rope as if Hansen were an unruly barnyard mutt. Men pushed and prodded him at every step. Someone placed a crown of twisted roots and brush on his head. Someone else said that was blasphemy and ripped the bramble off his head. As he staggered toward his fate, Hansen tried to wrench his hands free, to escape the rope by pulling it up over his head. The man with the tire iron swung it hard against Hansen's back, causing him to lurch forward. They delivered him to Snyder, who grabbed the dangling noose and placed it around Hansen's neck. Snyder made sure the knot was tight. Then, as before, the signal was given to pull.

Five masked men yanked Hansen fifteen feet into the air. His arms mimicked trying to fly away, while his legs, like two slippery eels, slithered back and forth. There was no snapping of bones. Instead, Hansen's neck became extended as if loosened from the rest of his body. In the haphazard glare of headlights and flashlights, Hansen's body dangled and twisted for what seemed like an eternity.

Some close at hand could no longer watch Hansen's body struggling for evaporating life. The onlookers further back, wanting to see, pushed closer to get a glimpse, but then stopped. They couldn't witness this either. It must have been a rancher, Winston figured, because it was an old man in overalls, holding a lit torch, who stepped boldly up to the perimeter of where Hansen was trying to stay alive or willing himself to die and not succeeding in either. In that limbo, the rancher raised his torch to Hansen's pant legs. The flames soon enveloped Hansen's writhing body, at last sending him on his way.

The crowd was quiet until someone in the darkness had the audacity to marvel: "Look, a human torch."

The body was in flames until the clothing burned off. The smell of burning flesh permeated the air. Some held their breath, some grabbed their handkerchiefs, but most of those nearby had had enough and backed away. Others filled the ranks and held matches to the corpse, starting with the toes, and anything that remained to be burned. After some time, there were no longer flames, just a charred wreck of human flesh. More people came to get a good look; some had cameras with flashes. Winston saw a matron with a young son stand beneath the elm and pose for a photograph in front of the remains. More people got in line for photographs, some somber, some smiling. The photographer told them to drop by his studio the next day to retrieve their souvenirs.

Winston had touched, seen, heard, smelled, even tasted enough death. He got the hell out of St. James Park. When he crossed the street, he tossed his white mask down the gutter and shuffled away into the darkness.

44

Spades was devoid of customers. Everyone had vanished to see what the citizen mob would do, fight the uniforms, get dosed by tear gas, and pound their way into the county jail. It didn't matter much whether the cause could be blamed on foreigners, Okies, hoboes, or Reds, but it was clear it didn't take much to get a group of disgruntled men and women riled up to do what the puppeteers behind the scenes had wanted them to do. The hangings were proof. At least, that's how Angelo reasoned. Bottom line: Saturday-night patrons who usually came to the bar to swallow their collective sorrows had now lynched two human beings and desecrated their bodies on the other side of the park.

Oliver came to join Angelo at the top of the stairs. Angelo raised the collar on his coat as the night air grew chilly.

"There's a lot of madness over there," Angelo said softly.

"I'll say."

"You think we ought to close up for tonight?"

"Yes," Oliver replied. "We're secure. We'll be fine."

"Okay, we might as well."

"Frank and Nick are somewhere in the crowd," Oliver told Angelo. "Suspect they'll be back soon, though."

"I have a few calls to make. Then we'll shut the place down. Sound all right to you?"

"That's fine with me, boss."

Angelo descended into the bowels of Spades. He switched on the light in the back room and picked up the telephone. He could still hear the din outside from the park. "Number, please," asked the operator. Angelo asked for the number in Avila Beach. "Sorry to call you so late," he said when Rosalia came on the line. "I just wanted to hear your voice."

"Oh, I'm all right. I wish you were here with me," replied Rosalia. "I took a walk on the beach earlier this evening, just to hear the surf. The moon was out, and you could see silhouettes of pelicans soaring above the water. When can you come down?"

"Things have got to be resolved here. Spades was busy earlier this evening, but now it has quieted down. We are closing early."

"Good. Is Amelia okay?"

"Very secure. Away from this mess."

"That's something, anyway."

"I should tell you that deputies in Truckee have convinced themselves that Gaetano must have been walking along a rocky cliff and then somehow tripped and fell into the lake and eventually drowned."

"My God, really?"

"Yeah."

"And Chiara?" Ferrone's wife was still missing.

"It's not clear whether she even made the trip." A long pause. "Be safe, my dear."

They talked a bit more until Angelo said that she needn't worry and that he would be down when he could.

Something crashed in the bar. A bottle hit the floorboards. A scuffle of feet. Angelo listened for a moment, certain that Oliver would take care of any mess. The telephone rang. It was Booksin calling from a roadhouse near the Beaumont estate.

"Boss, I heard there was a riot downtown. What's going on?"

"I think it's best you come back after all," said Angelo.

"Want me to check on Amelia first?"

Angelo thought for a moment. "Yes. Make sure both of them are safe. Rosalia would insist. Then meet me at the Torino."

Angelo had intended to place a call to his daughter, but the hour was late, and Booksin would check on her without disturbing anyone. Everything would be fine.

Someone rattled the knob on his office door. It wasn't locked, and the door opened. It was not Oliver. Or any of his men. Or anyone else he might have expected. While he did not know the man, he did recognize the make of the pistol. Pointed straight at him. The man didn't say a word. Two other men came in. One was holding a pillowcase. The other had a length of thick twine.

45

In the extravagantly lit dining room of the Beaumont estate, Victoria and Amelia were huddled at one end of the enormous wood table, listening to the nearly constant radio reports about a deadly riot in St. James Park. The radiocasters provided dreadful, detailed accounts of how vigilantes had dragged the two kidnappers from the jail and strung them up from trees in the park, all witnessed by thousands of onlookers.

The Beaumonts had long retreated to rooms unknown within their estate. Sara had left earlier for a Salinas meeting. Amelia sat next to the telephone, making constant attempts to contact her father. At first, the operator said there was no answer, then the line was busy, perhaps dead. The operator apologized, but because of all the telephone traffic that evening, it was impossible to tell what had happened.

Interviews came and went over the radio. Some who had seen the events in the park registered shock and disgust. Others pronounced that the murderers got what they had coming and that it was about time there was some law and order in the town.

Around 1 a.m., there was a knock on the front door, then a muffled voice. Victoria leaped to her feet. Amelia was nearly out the back door. Victoria motioned to Amelia to wait and then moved down the darkened hall slowly while Amelia looked in the kitchen for something with which to defend herself.

Victoria silently looked through the door peephole. The visitor was a man. Alone. It was dark, but the man looked a lot like Sal Booksin. Nonetheless, she asked, "Who is it?"

"Booksin."

By then, Amelia had crept up behind Victoria with steak knife in hand. She nodded, and Victoria opened the door. Booksin saw the knife, held his hands up, and said, "Your father instructed me to check on your well-being."

"Well, hello to you," said Victoria.

"How's my father?" Amelia demanded. "I've tried calling him."

"I spoke to him thirty minutes ago. He wanted me to make sure you were safe, then join him downtown," Booksin said, then looked at Victoria. "And hello to you, too."

"Is my father safe?"

"As I said, I spoke to him. The place should be okay. The action is across the park at the jail."

"But if everything was fine, why did he want you to check on us?" asked Amelia.

"If it were safe, we'd all be in bed," said Victoria, giving Booksin a hard look.

Booksin sighed. "All right, I did my duty. I got to go."

"Not so fast," said Amelia.

"You're not leaving without us," added Victoria.

"I'm not sure whether it's safe yet downtown."

"The radio reports say it's all over, but we need to see for ourselves," insisted Victoria.

Booksin shrugged, weighing the consequences.

"I'm sick and tired of being stashed in places," argued Amelia. "I want to make sure my father is okay."

"Try calling him again," said Booksin.

Amelia called for the operator, gave her the number, and waited. The operator said that no one answered.

"We're wasting time," determined Amelia. She ran to retrieve their coats and purses. "Let's go," she told Booksin.

Victoria put on her coat, looked at Booksin. "What are you waiting for?"

Booksin couldn't think of a decent reply.

They climbed into his Ford sedan, and he drove into the valley and through the miles of orchards. The night remained quiet. They saw only two or three cars on the road, headed in the opposite direction, flashes of headlights that blinded them momentarily. When they reached the outskirts of downtown, there was a slow-moving line of cars in retreat, as if the county fair had just closed up for the evening and there was no place to go but home.

Booksin drove up Race Street, turned onto the Alameda until they ran into a complete traffic mess, so he turned at Autumn, and then again on San Augustine. Their immediate destination was the Torino Hotel, a quiet, secluded place nestled in a spot near the creek, near the Convent of Notre Dame. The Torino was the designated secure place downtown; it usually catered to itinerant lodgers and occasionally to Ferrone's organization. Booksin parked the Ford behind the hotel, climbed out quickly. He marched up to the side door, knocked, and an elderly woman in a veil answered. She shook her head, indicating that Angelo had not yet arrived.

Amelia and Victoria got out of the car and started to walk away toward downtown. Booksin ran after them. As the trio approached St. James Park, the area around the jail was still thick with onlookers. But indeed the main event was over, and people drifted away from the park. The rank scent of burnt human flesh still hung in the air, but the police had carted away the two bodies and were urging people out of the park.

"The cops disappeared during the assault on the jail, but now they are here for cleanup duty," Booksin observed.

"Evil descended into this place," murmured Victoria, looking around at the damage done.

Amelia remembered a line from Dante. "It goes something like

'The soul that had been changed into a beast went hissing off along the valley's floor.'"

The three of them crossed through the park and reached Third Street. Spades looked unassuming as ever. Except Oliver wasn't at his post.

"I would have expected to see him out in front," Booksin said, his voice grim. "He is always the last one. Makes sure everything is right."

Booksin took the lead going down the steps. Victoria and Amelia followed. The door to the club was shut but not locked. Booksin flicked on a light. A broken bottle lay on the floor. Open bottles had been left on the bar. A couple of glasses on the tables. "It looks like they just got up and left," Booksin muttered. "This doesn't look right."

He hurriedly checked the storage room and the back rooms. All empty. Amelia opened the cash register. There was still money in the box.

"I'd wager they came through and swept everyone out in one fell swoop," concluded Booksin.

"Who are 'they'?" Victoria wanted to know.

Rather than answer, Booksin picked up the telephone to see if it was still in order. It was. He made a series of calls to see if he could reach anyone within the organization. No such luck. "We need to get out of here," he decided. "And get back to the Torino."

Taking a circuitous route, avoiding St. James Park, they walked cautiously down Third Street to Santa Clara, where Booksin indicated they should turn right. They all knew that any stranger standing or walking or riding in a passing car might be on the lookout for them. On Santa Clara, there was still substantial activity along the sidewalk and in the street. People scurried on their way, and cars were nosing into traffic. A police van flashed its spotlight at several of the automobiles. They might have been driving too slowly, or perhaps they were just in the way, or maybe the police were searching for particular suspects. Averting their faces, the trio kept walking as the van slowly passed them, shined the light on them briefly, but the driver did not stop nor turn on the siren. The van continued on its way.

Up ahead, something was happening on Market Street. A small crowd had gathered at the cannery union office building. Victoria stopped momentarily, as did her companions, and then Booksin whispered to slowly continue walking. A half dozen or so police officers were on the street in front of the building, directing people not to stop and gawk but to continue on their way.

A policeman eyed Victoria as she quickly glanced at what the officers were doing: They were carrying out boxes of files, even the large file cabinet. The trio kept walking. Victoria peeked back to see the boxes were being loaded into a police van. She gasped. "They're ransacking our files!"

"They want names, addresses," muttered Amelia. "They want to lock 'em all up."

46

Cooper didn't know how long he had been out. He was hunched up against the jailhouse wall, his legs sprawled on the staircase. His head throbbed. The slight movement of looking down the stairs made him feel dizzy. So, he remained where he was, eye level with the legs of the men running up and down. His ears were ringing. He touched the side of his head. Moist. Saw a smear of blood on his hand. His eyes burned, the taste on his lips vaguely metallic. A civil war was raging in his stomach. The tear gas, he reasoned.

He remembered hearing shouting. Someone had been pleading: "Keep them away from me. Keep them away." Cooper closed his eyes against the fog and noise cramming his brain. He was trying to remember something else. Images and snippets of dialogue competed for the attention of his beleaguered mind. At last, he grabbed onto a single image: the visage of Fr. Seebach as a smiling cherub. Then, a painting on a chapel ceiling. A train station. A green Plymouth. Someone shouting, "Let 'em have it!"

The images blurred again in his mind, blended with the noise around him. He gave his mind the task of deciding what had happened already versus what was happening now. Someone had repeated, "Come on, big boy," in a foreign accent. A police officer, no, a sheriff's deputy, had also used that line: "C'mon, big boy." The line repeated over and over in his head until he realized he was saying it aloud. It was the same thing the jailer had said. The one who hovered by the door when Cooper was speaking with Schiavo.

Cooper didn't know the jailer's name. The man worked for the sheriff. So did Butler. The same one who had captured Tierney. Butler had been there during Cooper's initial interrogation of Tierney. Whenever Tierney was confused, he looked to Butler, then fell into line. Butler had been there for the wild goose ride to LA. And Butler had reported that Ferrone was dead. Butler kept watch on everything Cooper did.

The jailer. Butler. Who else? Kane, doubtful. Gibson, probably. Miller, likely. Stooges all of them. Had it been Ewing's deputies who took over the kidnapping? Had they taken it upon themselves to dispose of Rosen and dump him in the bay? Had Ewing orchestrated this, or were the deputies working for someone else? For what reason? Why didn't Tierney and Hansen speak up? Who had silenced them? Had a deal been worked out? Why the sudden shift of their fates? Did any of this even make sense? Why did Tierney and Hansen have to die? Cooper knew they were likely dead. So they could not say what had actually happened to Rosen.

Someone poked him. He opened his eyes and saw a gruff older man staring at him, looking annoyed. A doctor by the looks of him. Big black glasses. A stethoscope. The doctor took his vital signs brusquely, as if it were Cooper's fault he had been slugged in the back of the head and gassed. The doctor spoke to someone nearby. "Take this one to the hospital."

After Cooper was loaded onto a stretcher, they carried him downstairs. He numbly realized that the jailhouse was in shambles. There was broken glass everywhere. The night wind swept in, and it was cold. They carried him down the front steps. There didn't seem to be too many people around. It must be all over. He tried to ask what had happened, but they would not say. They put him into a hospital van. Before he passed out again, it occurred to him that

Tierney and Hansen were probably already laid out on cold slabs in the county morgue next to Michael Rosen.

47

Cooper opened his eyes to morning light that was much too bright. He kept his eyes at half-mast, shielding them with his hand. His stomach ached. His head still felt like it was swirling. His eyes could not focus. He detected someone with a long white veil hovering by his bed. As the veiled person drew closer, there was a distinct scent of incense, lavender, and Lysol soap.

"Can you please pull down those shades?" he tried to say. His words did not come out right.

"You seem to be a lot better today," said the veiled woman, and she pulled down the window shades. The light eased inside the room, but Cooper still felt the warmth of the sunshine.

"Where am I?" That sounded better.

"O'Connor's Hospital. They brought you in last night. You should rest. Indeed, take the time for reflection."

"Why am I here?"

"You need to rest. The doctor will be in shortly," the woman in the veil recited. Through blurry eyes he watched her depart.

For the next hour, Cooper focused on the ceiling panels. He tried to move his head, but then his vertigo would return.

He slept. Woke when he heard someone. A stout man dressed in white had walked in, stopped, looked at his clipboard, glanced down at Cooper, apparently a doctor who abruptly said, "Besides that hit on the side of your head, someone gave you knockout drops. My guess is chloral hydrate."

"Slipped me a Mickey Finn?"

"You see stars, then it knocks you out and leaves you with gastrointestinal distress, the kind that can last for hours. And then there is a concussion."

Cooper nodded. "That about sums it up."

"How's the head?"

"Still throbbing . . ."

"And your stomach?"

"Feels like my insides have been turned inside out."

"You'll have to roll with the punches." He put his clipboard under his arm.

Cooper smiled weakly but said nothing.

"You also suffered from inhalation of tear gas, but that was temporary. I've seen worse. You'll live."

"Has anyone been here to see me?"

"Ask Sister Mary Dolores."

"A nun?"

"Your nurse." The doctor turned away. Social calls weren't in his purview. His mind was already on his next patient as he headed out of the room.

"When can I get out of here?" Cooper called after him.

The next time Cooper woke, he was startled by someone placing a wet compress on his forehead. Sister Mary Dolores. In her full regalia. He recalled her smell.

"Thank you, Sister," he mumbled.

"You need to take it slowly. Rest heals."

He asked whether she could gather recent newspapers. Sr. Dolores said she would find something but cautioned him that the news was horrible.

"It will help me get my bearings. Bring as many different papers as you can."

"As you wish."

"Has anyone tried to see me?"

"As far as I know, there has been no one. But from your identification, we have contacted your office. They said they would send someone down to check up on you. San Jose Police were informed as well."

"Please, no visitors."

He did not offer a reason for his request, and she did not ask for one.

※

When Cooper awoke, he still felt groggy, but better. A pile of neatly stacked newspapers had been left at his bedside. He sorted through them. The news of the lynchings made not only local headlines but national ones as well. The accounts were by and large consistent. In most of the papers, the governor pronounced the lynchings as the best lesson California had ever given the country. Crimes like those committed by Tierney and Hansen should never be tolerated, and justice had been served.

Not all the reactions were uniform. A local doctor prescribed that mob action was never justified and that such actions came out of the depths of savagery and were the curse of organized government.

A pastor reflected that what the citizens did to the kidnappers was not only morally upright but should be extended to those convicted of gambling, prostitution, and liquor. These vices, he extolled, were the honey that brought in the flies: Why not make this the occasion to clean up once and for all the general lawlessness of Santa Clara County?

A Stanford law professor argued that the arrested men should have been tried by jury and a conviction would have been meted out, and that it was crucial to abide by the rules of the law.

A San Jose high school teacher directed her students to clap for one minute in honor of those who rendered due justice upon the kidnappers.

A retired judge simply opined that those who did the lynchings had done a damn fine job and further stated that lynching was a sincere demand for law enforcement. He congratulated the people for their noble example in dealing with criminals.

The mayor of San Francisco said it was not an action by a mob but a gathering of respected citizens whose feelings were outraged beyond control.

The district attorney of Alameda County reflected that the lynchings were evidence of popular distrust of legal institutions.

The former president, Herbert Hoover, condemned the lynchings, stating that these actions undermined the very foundations of a civilized society, while President Franklin D. Roosevelt deemed the mob action a "vile form of collective murder."

And so on.

As Cooper unfolded the last paper, a slip of paper fell unnoticed to the floor. This newspaper, the *Mercury-Herald*, delivered the most comprehensive account of what had happened, most of which Cooper knew. But the story included information not conveyed in the other reports, including that Sheriff Elmore Ewing had been struck and knocked unconscious during the onslaught. According to this paper, the sheriff only heard after the fact that the officers' weapons had been locked in the jail's vault.

It was evening when Cooper was awakened by his nurse bringing a tray of food. Seeing the mashed potato mush and withered peas made him hungry. Sr. Mary Dolores said that meant he was getting better. She watched silently as he ate.

A note had been picked up and left on the tray. "Where did this come from?" Cooper asked her.

"It was on the floor. Perhaps an admirer?"

"Doubt that."

When his nurse collected the tray and left, Cooper read the note:

I HAVE INFORMATION THE BUREAU SHOULD KNOW. CONFIRM AT BALLARD 7431 W. SOMEONE WILL DIRECT YOU WHEN AND WHERE.—W. K.

The next morning, the hospital released him, and Cooper sent the Bureau a telegram acknowledging his plight. In turn, he was instructed to return to the San Francisco field office when ready. Cooper interpreted that as an opportunity to further investigate the recent events in San Jose. Whether the local police had visited while he lay sleeping in a hospital bed, Cooper did not know. He was wary of local law enforcement at this point, and it was best to steer clear of them. Who had drugged him and what was their intent?

He dragged himself to the Hotel Sainte Claire and used the lobby phone. A woman answered the phone. Cooper recited a message to be given to W. K., the writer of the cryptic note. After lunch, the front desk said that he had a message. It said to be at the intersection of North Fifth Street and Jackson at three o'clock that afternoon. Cooper asked the concierge for directions. It was a bit of a walk, the man replied, and he offered to arrange for a taxi. Cooper declined. Perhaps, by stretching his legs, using his wits, he would feel better. He also wanted to see Angelo, and the bar was on the way.

He got there soon enough and found Spades to be shuttered. Nobody answered when he pounded on the door. Storekeepers nearby didn't want to say anything. Most passersby ignored him as well. The few who briefly answered his questions said they didn't have a clue whether the place was temporarily or permanently closed.

Cooper continued on his way. Crossing St. John Street, he observed mainly residential structures. It looked to be a solid working-class neighborhood. A few properties verged on unkempt, understandable with the times being what they were. As he stepped over the train tracks at Washington Street, the neighborhood grew seedier, weeds cropping up; he saw peeling paint on front stoops, clutter in the front yards. There were some empty lots, some properties looking abandoned, the windows covered with wooden slats. From the general appearance, he guessed some of these housed transients.

As he crossed Empire Street, the neighborhood changed once more. The houses were smaller, packed tightly next to each other, and neatly kept. A dark-haired child, six or so, swung on a tire hung from a tree branch. When the boy saw Cooper strolling by, his eyes grew large, and he jumped off the swing and ran up the steps into his home.

By the time Cooper reached the designated meeting spot, he had entered a small business district. The signs were in Asian script, though some had subtitles in English. Squinting, he read signs for Roy's Station Coffee and Tea on the corner and, next to that, the Gombei Restaurant and retail shops of some sort, something else beyond that. Across the street, on the corner, was a grocery store, and then a pair of warehouses, a gasoline station. It wasn't yet three o'clock. So, there he stood, obviously the stranger in this neighborhood.

At precisely three o'clock, Cooper saw a slim young man in a white shirt and starched khaki pants approaching. He must have come from one of the stores. He walked up to Cooper, who asked, "What do you call this place?"

"I call it home," replied the man. "I'm Wilford Kishi. You are Agent Cooper, I presume."

"That I am. What information do you have?"

"Follow me."

Kishi led Cooper up the street, half a block, past a doddering old man with a cane, then through a door that led down an alley to a place where the light was dim and the air was chilly and smelled of grease. It might have been a working garage, but now it was devoid of automobiles and mechanics. Except for two chairs placed in the center of the place. Kishi invited Cooper to sit and apologized that he had nothing to offer by way of refreshments. Cooper said that it didn't matter, took out his notebook and pen. "Okay, so why are we here? What information do you have that might be of interest in this investigation?"

Kishi's expression was carefully neutral. "I worked for Fr. Seebach. I served as a conduit for the Committee."

"Were you aware that this involved a kidnapping?"

"Later, I knew. Not at the time."

"Why talk now?"

No response.

Cooper wrote in his notebook. "Tell me about the Committee for Public Safety."

"They are wealthy university donors who want to keep the status quo. Fr. Seebach needed to keep the alumni satisfied. He needed their support. I later learned that their effort was to eradicate unionization in the canneries, really any line of business."

"When did you know the Committee wanted to stop unionization?"

"Earlier this year, they demanded that Fr. Seebach expel the student editor for writing about labor justice as a reflection of Catholic teaching. The Committee got their wish."

"When did you know there was more to all of this than just keeping some donors happy?"

"It changed with the kidnapping."

"How did you know there was a link?"

"The timing. That night of the kidnapping. The hotel in San Francisco."

"What was your role?"

"Through messages I received for tasks to be performed by others. I suspected that I sent notes to those who were needed to light the fuse."

"To light what fuse?"

"The reaction after they found the body of Michael Rosen. To rile the students so they would take action."

"Against Hansen and Tierney," Cooper said.

Kishi nodded.

"Tell me who was the first recipient of your notes."

"That was when the kidnapping occurred. It was Winston Richter. A recent graduate. A lowly college clerk with limited prospects. He was the perfect candidate. Richter was predisposed to perform any task to benefit his station."

"Like you?"

"Like me, yes."

"Why?"

"I graduated along with Richter and, like him, had few prospects. Take a look at me. Who would take a chance on me? Fr. Seebach took that chance when no one else would. Otherwise, I'd be back doing laundry."

Cooper said nothing, waited.

"Isn't this the land of opportunity?" Kishi said wistfully. "Until that night, I thought the information passed back and forth was harmless. Cloak-and-dagger, sure, but that's all."

"Is Fr. Seebach a member of the Committee?"

"No. I don't think so. He wanted a legacy. His new theological seminary. To do that, he needed the cooperation of his donors."

"What did Fr. Seebach promise you?"

"He hired me to be his assistant. He was very proud of that fact. Having an Asian to work for him, to serve him."

"What did the Committee promise you?"

"Enrollment in the engineering school. I would be the first Japanese to be admitted."

"How did they convey that?"

"Indirectly. Through a message I received. Each time I fulfilled one of their tasks, I would receive a reward."

"A reward?"

"Some cash. The bigger the task, the larger the reward. They promised to deliver."

"Including promising you would be accepted into the engineering program."

Kishi nodded wearily. "And scholarship funding."

"Did they deliver?"

"Not yet."

"Who else did you give notes to besides the clerk, Winston Richter?"

"Various students."

"The purpose?"

"To take action against the kidnapping."

"Did you know the Committee was behind the kidnapping?"

Kishi glanced around the garage. "I'm not sure who was responsible for that."

Cooper asked who was on the mysterious Committee. Kishi gave him the names of students who participated in actions on behalf of the Committee. Kishi then asked, "You know who William Snyder is?"

Cooper shook his head.

"William Snyder is the largest auto dealer in the county. I think he is part of it."

"Who else? Ever hear the name Thomas Ripley?"

"We all know him as a major donor to the campus. I suspect he had a very large role."

"Who conspired to carry out the lynchings?"

"That I don't know. I just passed notes about meetings, not the agendas," answered Kishi nervously.

"Why did they need to hang two men?"

Kishi stared at him blankly.

"Let's get back to who else was on this Committee. You mentioned William Snyder."

"Yes."

"Paul Passalacqua?"

"I've read about him, but that's all. He's a San Francisco gangster, right?"

"Linford?"

"Signed the agreement with Fr. Seebach, but that's all."

"Anyone else?"

"Besides Ripley, I don't know, but you'd have to guess that anyone with a major stake in any large business in the valley. I can give you some names of likely alumni."

"Where were you the night Tierney and Hansen were strung up?"

Kishi looked briefly stricken, recovered. "Home," he said firmly. "I stayed around here. Once I heard the radio reports, do you really think I would venture out on a night like that?"

"Why would the Committee want to kidnap Michael Rosen?"

"I'm not sure, but I'd venture that they didn't appreciate Alexander Rosen. Maybe because they saw him as an uppity Jew."

"Do you know why they decided to kill him?"

"No. That was a shock."

"Why would they want to kill Tierney and Hansen?"

"Honestly, I just passed the notes. I suspect that Ripley and others might be pulling the strings for others to act, but I never read the notes. You need to investigate them. They pulled the strings and manipulated the puppets. Winston Richter did some actual work for them. I'm not proud that I passed notes."

"Why have you told me all this? What do you want?"

"Isn't it obvious? I know what I did was wrong, but if they know my betrayal, I'll need protection," Kishi said, again stoic.

"What if there is an inquiry?"

"A Japanese man to testify against those powerful people? I just want to get out of here alive."

"I'll see what can be arranged."

Kishi nodded. He looked at Cooper carefully and asked, "Have you considered why they wanted the Bureau to get involved?"

48

Christmas decorations were displayed in the windows of Rosen's Department Store, but the holidays would not undo what had been done. The mood downtown had turned somber; the gray, chilly weather didn't help. Santa Clara's campus was deathly quiet. Only final examinations remained. Winston remained at his desk every workday, kept his head down and performed his tasks. He did not receive any cryptic notes. The conspirators were silent. Fr. Seebach would not even convene an invocation. No one wanted to remember the shameful events that had unfolded just three weeks prior in St. James Park.

One evening at Winston's boardinghouse, a telephone call came through. The caller was someone from the school's registrar. That was unusual. That person did not give his name and asked Winston to meet the registrar at 7:30 the next morning. Winston tried to think what he might have done wrong. Plenty. Or perhaps there would be a reward for services rendered? Either way, why would the registrar's office take the time to call him knowing he'd be at work anyway the next morning?

Winston did not eat much that evening. Nor did he sleep well. He woke up twice in the night and had difficulty getting back to sleep. The morning greeted him with sullen gray clouds that squatted over the western hills. Crossing the street to enter the campus, Winston kept his hands in his pockets, head down, bracing himself. He plodded past the chapel, across the front lawn, toward the administrative building. He looked at his watch: 7:20 a.m. Perhaps he should have attended the 6:30 mass. Why was it the registrar who wanted to see him, not the dean of students? Perhaps an enrollment slot had been freed up? Why had he been such a reckless fool, to agree to make that ransom call, wear that mask, rush in to carry out the desecration?

He tentatively ascended the cement steps. The weak yellow lights on the banister looked like floating halos. He tried the front door. Still locked. It was still too early. Winston gently rapped on the door. After several minutes, the door screeched open, revealing an ancient priest who looked at Winston but said nothing beyond waving him inside. His footsteps echoed on the tiled lobby floor, making Winston even more self-conscious. He looked back at the old priest, who watched to make sure he proceeded to the registrar's office at the far end of the main corridor. The registrar's office was not completely lifeless. He saw the silent shadows of employees behind the glazed windows facing into the hallway. As he entered the office, he glanced back again. The old priest had disappeared.

Warm, oblique light seeped through the glass door of the registrar's private office. Winston knocked twice, and the registrar grunted for him to enter. The officious, bespectacled priest sitting behind his desk wore a slight smile on his otherwise grave visage. He beckoned Winston to sit. Winston responded that he preferred to stand.

"Fine. Take it any way you want." The priest coughed.

"Yes, Father."

Patiently taking off his glasses and picking up a sheet of paper from his desk, the registrar said: "It appears that you've done it this time."

Winston wished he had taken up the offer to sit.

"There has been a change of heart"—the registrar paused to cough into a crumpled handkerchief. "The administration has been grateful for your steady work on behalf of Santa Clara. This has been noted by the most senior representatives of this university. But . . ."

Winston felt his knees buckling. He had wasted everything on the futile errands ordered by the Committee. And it was Kishi who had delivered all the orders, instructed him. He should denounce Wilford Kishi, here and now. It was not his fault that he had done... What had he actually done? All of it had been that Jap's doing.

"We will no longer require your services beginning the next semester," uttered the registrar, punctuating "semester" with an extended fit of coughing. He managed to blurt, "Nasty weather we're having..."

"If I can explain—"

"No need," said the priest, waving his hand as if he were blessing a repentant sinner.

"Please, Father."

"You had been considered for enrollment in the law school, and, I might add, given your diligent work and satisfactory grades, your application initially appeared promising."

The registrar sipped from a cup of water before continuing. "However, we have received a request from the Bureau of Investigation inquiring about your activities recently. This, as you know, does not conform to the standards we require for a prospective law student or an existing university employee. As such, your application is hereby terminated as well as your employment."

"B-but it's only an inquiry," Winston stammered, "not an indictment."

The priest smiled thinly. "You know as well as I that there has been a dark cloud over the university because of... recent events. Something that has tarnished this institution."

Winston could barely stand.

"Fr. Seebach duly recognizes your contribution to the Jesuit community and wishes you heartfelt gratitude. In recognition of this, he has authorized me to extend a gratuity for services rendered." The registrar held out an envelope. "Never confuse the sign of the cross with the sign of the dollar."

Winston took the envelope. The priest struggled to stand.

Winston knew the meeting was over. "Thank you, Father," he replied, without thinking.

By the time he was outside the administrative building, he could not even feel the enveloping coldness of the winter weather. He ripped open the envelope. Two hundred dollars in cash. No note.

Thirty minutes later, Winston waited nervously on the platform at the train depot in Santa Clara. He had returned to his boardinghouse, where the landlord said an Agent Cooper had come looking for him but departed. Cooper was probably looking for him on the campus by now. Winston intended not to be found. By the time Cooper figured out he wasn't at work or home, Winston would be on a train somewhere. Whichever train arrived first. North or south. It happened that the next train was south toward Monterey, where his father's bakery stood.

He fidgeted and scanned the other passengers holding tickets. The train was scheduled to arrive at 8:15 a.m. It was already twenty after. He went to the stationmaster, who, when asked how long before the southbound train would arrive, just shrugged. "Should be here any minute." Winston stayed inside the stationmaster's lean-to and peeked through the grease-streaked window to see if this Cooper character would appear.

"Then again, something might have held it up," said the stationmaster.

Winston debated whether to bolt. Before he decided, the train's whistle blew somewhere up the line. The tracks rumbled. Brakes squealed. Winston remained in his feeble hiding place. The train had to be around the bend; he could hear it but not see it.

The whistle screamed again. Finally, the train appeared and rattled into the station. Winston climbed aboard and endured five long minutes wherein the train just sat on the tracks. He closed his eyes, imagining federal agents storming onto the car. But no one seemed to come looking for him, and finally the train lurched and staggered and picked up speed.

Winston had taken a seat next to the window, and he looked out. The train passed an overpass or two, sickly trees, tattered telephone poles and scattered structures, and then entered a large railyard where Winston saw a settlement of wandering hoboes. The makeshift shacks would be torn down and taken away when their numbers grew too big and the police felt it was imperative to stand up for law and order.

Winston started to relax; he had gotten away. But within minutes the train began to slow down again as it crawled into downtown San Jose. A number of passengers waited to come aboard. He closely watched for anyone who might resemble a law enforcement officer. There was a pair that looked like the type, and he kept tabs on them. He couldn't help but notice an odd threesome: a Black man who looked vaguely familiar and an older man and a younger woman, both of them White. When they boarded, the Black man sat in the double seat facing his companions. Winston only saw the backs of the two but finally remembered where he might have seen the barrel-chested Black man in a tailored suit.

49

On the night Harold Tierney and Earle Hansen were dragged from the jailhouse to their deaths, Amelia, Victoria, and Sal Booksin had crept back to the Torino Hotel. The night manager let them in, locked the door, pulled down the shutters, and guided them to the rooms above. Booksin asked to use the telephone, intending to again try his luck at finding anyone left among his colleagues. With Ferrone dead and Angelo missing, the rest might have scattered. Or worse. They needed to regroup. He did not immediately call down to Avila Beach; Rosalia did not need to hear anything until there was definitive information.

Victoria and Amelia could not sleep. They sat in their dark room, listening to Booksin on the downstairs phone; he kept calling and calling and failing to reach anyone. The organization must be in tatters, thought Amelia. She was petrified for her father. At this point, Passalacqua's men were surely sweeping up anyone they had missed.

Booksin eventually ran out of numbers to call and came upstairs. He looked in on his two charges and then went to the room across the hall. Closing in on four that morning, there was a noise downstairs. In the dark, Booksin instinctively reached for his pistol, a newer Smith & Wesson .38/44 he'd hidden under his pillow. He silently opened his door. Passalacqua must have found them. The last mess that needed to be cleaned up.

Booksin remained silent and alert as he proceeded step by step down the stairs toward the barely lit foyer. He heard a click and the slight whoosh of a door opening. He stayed poised near the bottom of the stairs, hidden in the murky shadows, his weapon ready. Another noise erupted from inside the building. He swerved toward the door that led to the kitchen. A shuffling of feet. The exasperated night manager, in his socks and robe, briskly entered the foyer above him. Booksin retrained his gun on the main entry door. Waited.

The front door creaked open. A dark hand. An agitated voice. "It's about time," whispered the night manager, which evoked a low chuckle. "I was worried about you."

"You can put down that gun, Sal," said Angelo. He and another man stepped into the foyer.

Startled, the night manager looked toward the stairway. "Oh, please. Put that away, Mr. Booksin."

Booksin complied.

"Never trust a man who sleeps with his pants on," chuckled Angelo.

Booksin merely nodded.

"Never trust a man who has nothing to say," added Oliver.

"My *nona* used to warn me: '*Dagli amici mi guardi Dio; dai nemici mi guardo io,*'" added the night manager, who waggled his finger, looked at Oliver, and then said, "It means while enemies might be known to you, it's not always clear if you can completely trust the people you consider to be friends."

Booksin smiled. Angelo shrugged. Oliver gave them his time-honored belly laugh.

"Don't wake up our clientele. We've got rules here," pleaded the night manager.

❦

At morning's light, Victoria knocked on Booksin's door. No answer. She tried the door, found it unlocked, and poked her head in. No Booksin.

Meanwhile, Amelia went downstairs, her apprehension mixed with annoyance at the boisterous noises coming from the dining area. She was tired from too little sleep and too many worries. She entered the dining room and saw three men eating, talking, drinking.

"Why didn't you wake me?" she said, the anger in her voice masking the relief that flooded through her.

Angelo only smiled.

Amelia returned to the foot of the stairs and called up to her friend. "Victoria, you should come on down for breakfast."

Somewhere between stacks of flapjacks and cups of coffee and strips of bacon, they heard from Angelo what had transpired the night before. He had been in the Spades basement when two men appeared—no doubt, Angelo theorized, to do what they had done to Ferrone and presumably his wife.

"I miscalculated thinking the danger was primarily across the park. At the jail," said Angelo.

"Some of our men must have been already compromised, some might have gotten out, some must have been disposed of," added Oliver.

"Which left me all but alone downstairs when they came in. No doubt with help from someone inside. A bartender. But they never accounted for Oliver, who swiftly and graciously disarmed them. They've consistently undervalued his contribution to this organization, and because of their inbred ways, they have paid for it dearly."

Angelo took a bite of pancake.

"It took some time to decide the best location where they should spend their eternity," he said.

Victoria blanched. Amelia remained nonchalant.

Over the next days, they agreed that the best course was to remain within the confines of the Torino Hotel. Angelo was able to get through to Rosalia, who begged him to join her in Avila Beach. He told her that Passalacqua's men were likely searching for remnants of the conquered organization, and the time was not right to expose themselves to travel, but given long enough, Passalacqua might give up the hunt.

Booksin continued trying to contact trusted colleagues and ascertain who was still operational. A few responded. Frank Lagatutta had hopped on an outbound freight train and decided against joining other stowaways in an empty car. Instead, he rode the rails by squeezing underneath the train car. Outside of Salinas, the conductor stopped the train, and the railroad bulls attacked people scrambling out of the empty boxcar and beat them to a pulp. Lagatutta managed to slip out through the fields during the melee, found a farmhouse, asked for mercy. Packing a shotgun, the farmer relented and allowed him to spend the night in the barn. In the morning, he hitched a ride into Salinas, wandered around downtown until he spied the bus station. He noticed some sheriff's deputies haranguing single men who had attempted to board the buses. Lagatutta stayed away from the buses and spent a few nights in a flophouse before hitching a ride to Monterey. There he stayed in a dump near the canneries until he met a fisherman who was sailing south to San Luis Obispo. The fisherman dropped him off at the Avila Beach pier.

There was news that Nick Caputo had escaped using one of Ferrone's cars, rested along the highway, and then laid low by spending the next night in a hotel in King City. He called Rosalia at Avila Beach one evening, saying that "things seemed all right" and he was estimated to arrive later that afternoon. He never made it. Days later, his car was reported to have been found in a ditch along the highway.

In a telephone conversation Victoria had with the colonel, Beaumont sounded alarmed. Although Sara Chambers had earlier left for Salinas, sheriff's deputies arrived at the estate midday after the lynchings. The men said they wanted to interview Chambers but would not say why. The colonel told the deputies that he could not recall where she had gone and dutifully said if she contacted his household, he would certainly inform the sheriff's department. It was all obfuscation, and the deputies knew it. Three days later, the colonel received a message that Chambers had been arrested in an orchard outside of Sacramento. She, along with sixteen other union organizers, was charged with criminal syndicalism, a felony. The Sacramento newspaper heralded this as a victory over the "spreading cancer of Communism."

Angelo learned that Placer County had convened an inquisition regarding the suspicious death of Gaetano Ferrone. Based primarily on the report from the coroner and testimonies from various other local law enforcement, it was determined that his death was an accident. While that conclusion was not a surprise, there were no details whatsoever about what had happened to his wife. She was deemed missing. The family's missing three employees were also not explained or even acknowledged since the inquiry had been narrowly focused on Mr. Ferrone, whose body had been positively identified.

Several newspapers reminded their readers of the loss of Michael Rosen and the "troubling resolution" of the two accused. Sheriff Ewing was reported to have quickly recovered from his apparent wounds suffered that night when "citizens attained justice," as one newspaper called it. Stories about the lynching began to fade away. And there was hardly a mention beyond a one-liner that a fatal stabbing had also occurred that evening. It had been inflicted on another prisoner, identified as a drifter named John Schiavo.

The newspapers provided a forum for heady debates between community leaders and local government authorities on whether a grand jury should be convened to look into the matter of "swift justice" and whether there had been lapses in protecting the two accused. The governor reiterated his stance supporting the "populist actions of the citizens of San Jose," stating that recent events would serve to "deter the criminal element."

The *Mercury-Herald* was alone in reporting the "unfortunate looting by persons unknown" of the CAIWU offices in downtown San Jose. No arrests were made.

And, of course, there was no mention of the systematic dismantling of the entire Ferrone organization in San Jose. There was a letter to the editor, penned by a former speakeasy patron, lamenting the closure of Spades and railing about the absurdity of Prohibition. The letter writer praised the new era where "a man could once again get a decent drink."

A couple of days later, in a brief item tucked away in a remote section of the newspaper, Chief Blackmun was quoted as saying the Spades Club had been closed for operating in violation of the Volstead Act and would remain closed until further notice. A day later, Blackmun decided that, due to local advocacy, "a number of similar establishments would be reviewed for permit violations for an indeterminate period."

Another story that barely drew notice was in a side column on page 7 of the *Mercury-Herald*, mentioning the upcoming groundbreaking ceremony in the New Year to restore an estate in the Los Gatos hills. The restored site was intended to serve as a new Jesuit theological seminary.

As days passed and grew shorter in the winter season, San Jose residents turned their attention to other events. Christmas was coming. And 1934 should be a better year, perhaps a more prosperous year. No one wanted to relive that night in St. James Park.

◈

A plan was made to leave San Jose. In early morning, Angelo, Amelia, and Oliver took their seats on a southbound train. Oliver had arranged for them to sit in a four-seater so that he could see everyone seated in the car. Amelia sat by the window next to her father while Oliver sat across. No strangers dared to sit in the empty seat.

As Oliver surveyed the passengers, a young man at the far end of the car winced, looked away, then focused on his lap. Oliver didn't view the man as a threat, though he could not immediately place the face. Seeing as the seat next to the guy was empty, he had half a mind to go over and sit right next to him, just to register how much he could make the little guy squirm.

Angelo opened a book to read. He had seen enough of the newspapers. Amelia was content to watch the scenery roll by. Oliver kept his arms crossed and pretended to take a snooze.

The train was more or less an express to Los Angeles with few stops along the way, one of which was San Luis Obispo. Angelo anticipated trouble so just in case had asked Booksin to take his car and use a circuitous route to Avila Beach. Victoria volunteered to accompany him. The idea was that Booksin would be there when the train rolled into San Luis Obispo.

Just around noon, Oliver, who had been feigning a nap, noticed movement down the aisle. Amelia was absorbed in a game of solitaire, Angelo engaged with *The Count of Monte Cristo*. A man in a gray suit and fedora had entered from the far end of their compartment. Oliver watched to see where the man intended to go. The man moved slowly toward them, but then stopped, turned, looked at that squirming young man. Said something to him. The young man blanched and pressed up against the window.

Oliver uncrossed his arms. The man in the fedora approached and tugged slightly on his hat. His face bore a wistful, familiar smile.

Angelo had recognized Oliver's initial concern and looked up at the visitor, who immediately sat in the empty seat. Amelia also lifted her gaze, half bothered that someone had interrupted her game that had not gone as planned.

"Look what the cat brought in," remarked Angelo, smiling.

"You're the one using up your lives," said Cooper.

"Oliver, you must remember our civil servant?"

"Sure, who could forget such a face?"

"And let me introduce you to my daughter, Amelia. This is a federal agent who has been investigating the crimes committed in San Jose."

"Louis. Call me Lou," said the agent and reached out his hand.

"Charmed," said Amelia, flatly, and grasped the agent's hand, firmly.

Cooper folded his arms, waited for Angelo to ask the questions.

"What brings you specifically here?" Angelo asked with an air of unconcern.

"The investigation churns onward," replied Cooper evenly, meeting Oliver's gaze.

"They say it's all over. That justice has been served," said Angelo.

Amelia pursed her lips. "What possibly would the Bureau want at this point?"

"We lack a motive for the kidnapping, for the murder, and the collapse of due process."

"Isn't the answer to all three money?" said Amelia.

"You still haven't answered why you are here on this train," said Oliver gruffly.

Cooper smoothly deflected once more. "There are leads that remain uncovered. They need to be pursued so we can learn the truth."

"I noticed you have a friend on the train," said Oliver, inclining his head toward the nervous young man, who immediately tried to melt into his seat when everyone but Cooper glanced in his direction.

"Sad-looking toad," offered Amelia.

Cooper shrugged. "He's another lead. Someone you should not bother with. I suspect that he'll be getting off in Monterey." He looked at Angelo. "In the meantime, I'd like to hear your story."

Angelo nodded, explained what had happened, and omitted the parts that were better off unspoken.

Cooper listened. He did not ask questions, except one: "How long did you know that Ripley wanted you out of business?"

"When he realized there were greater opportunities to exploit, and when authorities appeared to go along," replied Angelo matter-of-factly, then paused and admitted, "When we were no longer needed.

We were aware of Passalacqua, of course, but clearly underestimated what he desired."

There was silence except for the rumbling of the train along its uneven tracks.

"And where will your investigation lead?" asked Amelia.

Cooper rubbed his forehead. "We continue to gather evidence, and if there is merit and cause, we present it to the US attorney, who may convene a federal grand jury and decide whether to bring charges. Or the county district attorney may decide to employ its own grand jury. Although, frankly, we don't see that ever happening."

"No. Ripley will take care of that," agreed Angelo.

The train slowed as it entered a railyard. Several passengers rose to their feet, gathered their belongings, and prepared to disembark. A final lurch of the train caused a few passengers to sway and curse. The passengers already standing clogged the aisles while others, seated, watched with impatience. Still others closed their eyes, wanting to get going again. The cab door opened, and the conductor called out: "Salinas!" A cold breeze met the stale air of the railcar. Oliver kept a close eye as passengers departed and new ones hopped on. He lightly tapped Angelo's knee and flicked a finger in the direction of two stiff, middle-aged Anglo men who entered the cab and looked nonchalantly around. They stood out in their nearly identical gray suits.

"Bureau agents," Angelo said. "They don't blend in so well."

The agents sat three seats behind the same young man that Oliver had been watching. Upon noticing the two Bureau agents, the hapless man could do nothing but look out the window, perhaps silently cursing that it was too late to have made his move.

The conductor walked down the aisle asking for tickets. The next stop was Monterey. Cooper asked when they would arrive. "Within an hour," the conductor replied. The train started to crawl again, then picked up speed.

About five minutes into the ride, Angelo noticed a man peering in through the window of the vestibule. Rather than enter the cabin, he turned away abruptly. A look passed between Angelo and Oliver, who immediately stood up, mentioning that he needed to stretch his legs. He disappeared into the next compartment.

Angelo asked Cooper more about the two agents, then about the politics of Hoover's new bureaucracy. As it turned out, Cooper liked to elaborate on his work. Angelo listened with interest, while Amelia preferred to start yet another game of solitaire. Several minutes into Cooper's soliloquy involving details of his past, Amelia stopped play, asked questions, and there was an interplay of opinions and aspirations. She was intrigued by his story of the Frank Nash ambush in Kansas City and how the Bureau subsequently issued revolvers to its agents.

The conductor came down the aisle once again, this time announcing they were approaching Monterey and would remain in the station for fifteen minutes before continuing south.

When the train slowed and stopped, passengers again jostled one another to leave. Winston gave a hopeless glance around the car when one of the two Bureau agents gently poked him on the shoulder and suggested it was time to leave. Winston seemed frozen in his seat. The agent spoke to him again. Finally, Winston got up. One agent kept a hand on his back, urging him forward, while the other tugged on his sleeve. Together they shepherded Winston down the aisle toward where Cooper sat.

Cooper rose. "Come along, Mr. Richter. We have much to talk about."

The departing passengers trickled into the station. Winston and his escorts were the last to disembark. Angelo and Amelia remained seated, both of them gazing out the window of the train.

Oliver hovered just inside the train doors, scanning the clusters of people arriving and departing from the station. His eyes found their target: The man who had been scrutinizing their cab had taken cover just beyond the end of the train. He hunkered close to the outside wall of the car, hardly noticeable in the bustle of the busy station. Oliver watched him silently.

Winston looked submissive as Cooper and his colleagues led him away from the platform. Suddenly, a blue Packard sedan careened into the parking lot and screeched to a halt, thirty feet from where Winston and his escorts were about to enter the station. One of the agents assisting Cooper unbuckled his holster.

Two men jumped out of the Packard, both wielding shotguns. The driver stayed put. Cooper took a defensive step back. The Bureau agents instantly grabbed Winston and started to pull him back toward the train.

"No, we're here for the pickup!" cried one of the new arrivals. "The sheriff sent us," said his companion. The Packard did not have any sheriff markings, and the men still held their shotguns. Everyone froze.

"Sorry. We're just late," said the first man. He lowered his gun, and his partner followed suit.

"You must have gotten lost," deadpanned Cooper.

One of the deputies smirked; the other remained stone-faced.

"Glad that you finally made it," Cooper told the latecomers, "but we could have done without the drama."

One of the Bureau agents helped Winston, who had tripped and fallen in his haste to reboard. The agent dusted him off. Winston looked as if he might fall over again.

"Our instructions were only to bring him in," said the first deputy. His partner remained mute.

"No one realized there would be more than one of us?" asked Cooper.

"Shucks, the sheriff never told us how many there'd be."

Cooper slow-blinked, then instructed that the witness be placed in the back seat of the Packard and told one of his agents to accompany him. "We'll take your car," he told the deputies. "You two will have to wait."

The first deputy, initially perplexed at the math involved, did not like the idea of being left behind. He started to object, quickly realized he would get nowhere with Cooper, and decided he would send for another car to fetch him and his silent partner.

Cooper returned to the train to say his goodbyes to Angelo and Amelia, who had come to stand beside Oliver at the train doors.

"That was quite the scene," remarked Amelia.

"These two aren't the brightest bulbs in the universe," Cooper said wearily. He nodded at his three temporary traveling companions. "I'll be leaving you at this point to have a visit with Mr. Richter. But seeing that you may have an unwelcome traveler, one of my men can accompany you to your destination. The question is whether that man is after you or Richter."

"My guess, he's one of Passalacqua's," said Oliver. "But that remains the question."

Cooper instructed the second Bureau agent to check each of the train cars to see if the mysterious man had reboarded the train. Oliver followed the agent. A quick search resulted in nothing. Angelo shrugged when Oliver reported back with the news.

The whistle blew. The conductor began his rounds.

"Need any further help?" asked Cooper.

"We'll be fine," answered Angelo. "I'm sure someone is more interested in your man."

Oliver did not agree with this assessment. Neither did Amelia.

Cooper stared at Angelo for a moment, nodded, then offered his appreciation.

"Until we meet again," said Angelo.

Cooper shook each of their hands, then headed to the waiting automobile.

Angelo and Amelia went back to their seats. Angelo continued with the adventures of the count. Amelia graduated from solitaire to the crossword puzzle of the newspaper. Oliver could not stay still. The Bureau agent sat stiffly and stared out the window.

※

The sun dipped below the western mountain range, the sky momentarily erupting in brilliant red streaks before darkness began its descent. Angelo finished with the tales of the count and was lulled into a much-appreciated nap, leaving the book closed on his lap. When the train slowed jerkily, he woke up, asked Amelia whether this was their stop. "It is," she replied. "Where's Oliver?" asked her father.

"Off on patrol."

"And Cooper's man?"

"Disembarked at King City," said Amelia.

Oliver returned to his seat just as they were coming to a halt in San Luis Obispo. The train had arrived late, and a number of people stood on the raised platform holding their bags, ready to get on board. Oliver elbowed his way down the aisle to make sure their passage to Avila Beach was waiting. The station lights were not as bright as he would have preferred. As the train doors opened, he eyed the impatient crowd. He did not recognize anyone on the platform. Booksin should have been there, but he was nowhere in sight. It felt all wrong. Too many options for disaster. Oliver was ready to say they should remain on board and push directly to Los Angeles when Lagatutta showed himself. He stepped from the shadows, accompanied by Eddie Savio, the former Spades bartender. After a brief, cordial acknowledgment, Lagatutta signaled, and a pair of cars approached. Lagatutta then boarded the train and escorted Angelo and his party quickly out to the two waiting cars. Oliver remained pacing along the platform, searching for the would-be intruder. He felt convinced the man had continued on the train with them.

"That's enough, Oliver. Let's go," Angelo insisted. Oliver finally relented, and they hit the road. As they turned onto the winding road toward their Avila Beach hideout, Oliver kept a watch for headlights in case someone tried to follow.

Perhaps thinking of it as an estate was a misnomer. The Avila Beach residence was a three-story Victorian originally built as a rest point for travelers heading up the coast, including those fortunate enough to garner an invitation to stay at Hearst Castle. After the stock market collapsed, so did Avila's business. Angelo's family positioned itself to snatch it up. The hillside property was protected by a long, twisting driveway amid a forest of sycamores and live oak. The secluded domicile was well defended and secure, and nowhere near the beach, despite its name. When her husband and daughter arrived, Rosalia greeted the group with open arms, plates of risotto, and bottles of red wine procured from a nearby vineyard that had managed to skirt the rules.

Booksin and Victoria hadn't been seen yet, though Rosalia said Sal had called to say their journey would take longer than estimated. Angelo's brow furrowed at this news.

The evening was devoted to a reunion of parties long separated. The next morning, the dozen or so of what remained of Ferrone's organization sat around in the front room and paid their solemn respects to the memories of Gaetano Ferrone, presumably his wife as well, and Nick Caputo. Oliver opted out so that he and another man could comb through the forest for footprints or hints of intrusion.

"Passalacqua has succeeded," summarized Angelo. "There's no going back."

"Shouldn't we put up a fight?" asked Lagatutta.

"We would risk our own exposure in what happened to Rosen. We would never win that battle" was Angelo's sober reply. "They have the police, most of the newspapers, the governor. Ripley outplayed us."

"They planned it so we could never get a foothold. That has left us vulnerable," agreed Lagatutta. "But we just can't sit still."

"Things will never be as they were," surmised Rosalia. "The rules have changed. We need to think of the future."

"Shouldn't we talk about just what happened?" asked Eddie.

"An excellent point," acknowledged Angelo. "Ripley's game included, among other things, real estate. That's why they made the deal with the Jesuits. Passalacqua wanted to extend their business operation. We were in the way. They neutralized us. The so-called Committee for Public Safety was hardly more than a group of brash college boys—"

"Supported by well-heeled alumni," interrupted Rosalia.

"¾who wanted labor out of the way and the focus on the lucrative cannery business," continued Angelo.

"A bright new day," remarked Amelia, sourly. "Brought to you by Ripley's police."

"Don't forget the governor, dear," said Rosalia.

"What about our new friend at the Bureau?" asked Amelia.

"He may or may not be our friend," said Rosalia, rubbing her chin. "But he is an ally. I suspect there is a curious divergence in the meaning of justice between Washington and Agent Cooper."

"So, what's our plan?" asked Lagatutta, irritated that no one had answered his question.

"We can't sit here holding our . . ." Savio caught himself, remembering the presence of the ladies.

"Coffee cups?" finished Amelia sweetly, earning some welcome laughter.

Rosalia looked sagely at Savio. "We don't have the problem to which you refer. But do I need to remind you that a delicious sauce always takes a long time to simmer?"

More laughter. Savio looked befuddled.

"What my dear wife refers to is an old Italian proverb that says to 'wait for a time and place to take one's revenge, for it is never well done in a hurry,'" said Angelo with a glint in his eyes.

The bantering stopped when gunshots were heard in the distance. Lagatutta glanced at Angelo, who nodded. Oliver must have found the interloper. At a glance from Angelo, two men promptly stood and headed out the door.

The telephone rang. Rosalia got up to answer the call.

"What's our plan?" reiterated Lagatutta to the few now remaining in the room.

50

Victoria unfolded the road map and ran a finger along different potential routes. Booksin thought he already knew the best route down the California spine. They did not agree. Instead, they argued back and forth, weighed alternatives, proposed solutions, tore at each other's proposals on ways to get to Avila Beach in one piece. They agreed the state highway system would be watched and therefore should be avoided when possible. A backroads route made sense, but which one? Neither wanted to be stuck on some isolated stretch of road that rendered them even more vulnerable. They begrudgingly settled on a route.

At daybreak, they took off in Booksin's Ford roadster. The car was stuffed with the organization's valuables: mostly financial records, some revolvers. Their agreed-upon route took them south of San Jose's orchards along a winding road past the old quicksilver mines of New Almaden, where they accessed another road that snaked through the undulating terrain. At Hecker Pass, they headed west. Traffic had been light until this stretch. As they approached civilization once again, the trucks looked local, hauling whatever they hauled, back and forth, to wherever they were going. No one seemed to notice the man and woman in a roadster. By noon, they arrived in the valley apple town of Watsonville.

Initially, Victoria had objected to going through Watsonville because of what occurred nearly four years earlier: A local newspaper published a photograph showing an embrace between a White woman and a Filipino man. Citing this as a threat to its morality, hundreds of Anglos roamed the streets, hunting and cruelly beating Filipinos.

Booksin argued they would need to stop there for gasoline. Necessity prevailed. Victoria took an immediate dislike to the place.

At Second Street near Main, they pulled in to get gas. The attendant pumped while Booksin and Victoria walked across the street to get supplies at a grocery. The place had next to nothing on its shelves. They got what they could: God-knows-how-old bread, overripe cheese, and pockmarked fruit. A sour-smelling man in a T-shirt and suspenders took their cash, in between furiously scratching his head.

They shoved on and drove on a series of farm roads that connected toward Castroville. An hour down the road, the Ford started to thump; then came knocking sounds like someone whacking a hammer wildly against the engine. Smoke billowed from the hood. The car shuddered and came to an abrupt stop. In the middle of a field of artichokes. And not much else. Booksin swore, got out, and waited for the smoke to die down. He wrapped a handkerchief around his hand and lifted the hood.

"We're done," he said grimly.

"Maybe we can hitch a ride to town," suggested Victoria.

"We just need to get out of here."

Victoria did not respond to the obvious. They had to wait a while, both of them tense, before an old Chevy pickup approached. The driver slowed down, took a long look at her, glanced at him, and stopped.

"Castroville?" asked Victoria.

"Climb on in. I'm going to the Parker Ranch ahead," said the driver. He was in his fifties. Looked local. Wore a dirty cap and smelled of diesel. Had not shaved in days.

"How far up?" asked Victoria.

"Far enough. Can drive you to the ranch, but you'd have to walk the rest of the way."

"Is there a garage in Castroville?"

The man nodded. "What else would you be looking for?"

Victoria climbed into the cab. Booksin jumped into the flatbed.

"What's the name of the garage?" Victoria asked the driver.

"Parker."

"Kind of a local thing, isn't it?"

"Pretty much." He looked pleased with himself and drove toward the ranch.

After minutes of Victoria staring out the window, Parker asked, "What brings a couple of city people down these roads? Out to enjoy the great outdoors or rob some banks?"

"We thought we'd take the scenic route to Monterey," replied Victoria. "Problem?" She looked back at Booksin, who was surveying the road ahead.

"No problem at all. Just sorry to see that your fancy car decided to go on strike."

"Is a Ford fancy?"

"You got me there," agreed the man.

A large wooden sign indicated that Parker Ranch lay ahead. Parker swerved the Chevy and halted alongside the road, leaving a cloud of rising soot in their wake. "Well, here you are."

"Thank you kindly, Mr. Parker," said Victoria brightly as she got out. Booksin was already waiting on the road.

"The garage is a mile thataway." He pointed. "My nephew will probably try to rob you. He ain't much of a farmer. The garage keeps him out of trouble. Mostly."

They watched as the pickup seemed to gather itself and enter Parker Ranch.

Booksin took off at a near jog, and Victoria ran to catch up. Fifteen minutes later they saw the garage; it wasn't the wreck Victoria had imagined. The man who might have been another Parker slowly looked her up and down, regarded Booksin at her side, then asked, "I don't reckon you came all this way on foot just to see me." Same Parker wit.

"Our car's stuck a couple of miles back," said Booksin.

"I've got a Packard needs fixing right away. When I'm done with that, I'll see to your car. What do you have?"

"Ford roadster." Booksin handed over his keys. "Where can we clean up and get something to eat?"

"Say, are you a Parker?" asked Victoria. "I think we met your uncle."

"I'm Sam. Everybody wants to be a Parker around here. Some are. Some aren't." He pointed up the road. "There's Mollie's Roadside Café up ahead. A bit of a walk. She's married to one of them. Food's not half bad. If you like Mexican."

"We'll camp there until we hear from you," said Booksin.

At Mollie's, Booksin managed to place a call to Rosalia saying that they would be delayed. How long he did not know. After a wait, the food was served. Sam was right. The enchiladas, rice, and beans were not half bad.

"Are you Mollie?" said Victoria to the raven-haired woman who was both waitress and cook.

"Nah, Maria Luisa. But, yes, I run the café. They thought it should have an American name." She laughed. "Otherwise, who'd come?"

After nearly a three-hour wait, Sam strolled in, waved to Maria Luisa. The Ford had blown a rod. Booksin had figured as much.

"It ain't pretty. Will cost you," Sam said.

"When can you get it fixed?"

"I might be able to get the part tomorrow from Salinas. Lucky that you got a Ford. Otherwise, it would be much longer. Maybe a week."

"Fine. Just get it done."

"Tomorrow or the next day," said Sam, clearly not wanting to get their hopes too high. "Where will you be staying?"

"Do the Parkers manage any accommodations around here?" asked Victoria.

"Nah. None of the Parkers have strayed into that line of business yet," replied Sam. "And nothing in Castroville that I'd even put my granny in."

"What is reasonable?"

Sam looked bewildered; then a bright light must have momentarily blazed because he grinned and said, "There's the Alexandria."

"All right," said Booksin.

"It's in Salinas."

"That'll do," determined Victoria. "I'm assuming that you will offer to drive us there."

"Yes, ma'am. I'll just put it on your tab," said Sam, sounding as if he'd just hit the jackpot.

Hotel Alexandria was on Main Street, smack in the middle of downtown. The front desk clerk asked whether they'd prefer an enclosed room or one with a view. The man didn't bother asking whether they wanted separate rooms. Victoria thought it must have been that obvious.

The next morning, Booksin rose from the bed, looked through the blinds, and saw downtown starting to perk up. He sat back down on the bed. Then, abruptly, he said, "I need to check up on the car."

He washed up, got dressed, said, "Be back in a moment" as he closed the door. Down in the lobby he asked the clerk to place a call to the garage. Sam said the part had arrived. The car would be ready at eleven o'clock. Booksin paid the clerk for the night.

Victoria was dressed and ready to leave when Booksin returned to the room.

"Wait," he told her. "I'll get the car. Fifteen minutes after I leave, you need to clear out. Go out the back way. There's a bake shop down the block. I think it's called Figueroa. Stay there. I'll be back to get you no later than noon. If I'm not there by three, call Rosalia. She'll tell you what to do next."

Before she could put up a fight, he told her it was best to be cautious. She relented and he was gone.

Victoria stood at the window to see whether he had crossed the street. He wasn't in sight. He'd probably left through the back way as well. He hadn't said how he was going to get back to the garage, about ten miles away in Castroville.

She waited as instructed, then found the downstairs service door and slipped outside, feeling the December chilliness as soon as she pushed open the door. She bought a bun and a coffee at the bake shop, then sat and watched and waited. The hours passed with no sign of Booksin. By three o'clock and several cups of coffee later, she was nervous and jittery. She crossed the street to the Rexall's drugstore and placed a call to Avila Beach. "Stay put," Rosalia told her. "We will send a car for you."

51

Winston sat in a pale-green, stifling room without any windows. The floor alternated between faded red and smudged white tiles. The wooden table was scuffed. Someone had etched a square on its top with a stab mark in the middle. He was surrounded by suits he did not know except for the one named Cooper who sat in but said nothing. The rest of them fired questions at him.

"What was the purpose of the kidnapping if the result was just to murder him?" "Who put you up to the kidnapping?" "Were you ever contacted by a man named Thomas Ripley or his associates?" "What did they offer you in return for making that phone call from the Whittier?" "When did they first contact you?" "How did you know they were going to lynch Harold Tierney and Earle Hansen?" "Why did you participate in the kidnapping of Michael Rosen?" "Were you ever contacted by anyone in the Santa Clara Sheriff's Office?" "Why did you not contact the police?" "Have you been contacted by people, specifically Italians, who operated illegal saloons and other such establishments in San Jose?"

On and on it went. Winston said as little as possible. He tried to sidestep most of the questions but ended up telling them about the notes he had received and little else. That's all he knew, he told them stubbornly. The agents taunted him, saying he would end up in prison. He gambled that they were bluffing and stuck to his tactic of answering what mostly was true, leaving out details and specific people. Eventually, they would have to let him go, he convinced himself. He was an insignificant cog in the works.

The agents left the room and left him alone for hours, or so it seemed. He could not calculate how long he sat alone in the dreary room. The day may have slid into dusk; he could not tell. The four green walls all looked the same. He put his head on the desk, closed his eyes.

At some point, he heard the click of the door opening. Agent Cooper came back into the room. He offered Winston a glass of tepid water and sat across from him. After remaining silent during the initial interrogation, Cooper now flicked through the pages of a notebook he carried with him and began to speak. The Bureau of Investigation had confirmed the fingerprints on Rosen's stolen wallet belonged to Winston. This was direct proof of his involvement in the kidnapping. Further, Cooper said, the Bureau had accumulated a series of eyewitness accounts that placed Winston in the Hotel Whittier telephone booth on the night of the kidnapping.

Telephone records verified that a call had been placed from the Whittier to the Rosen residence during the time Winston was seen in the hotel lobby. Kishi had admitted that he left notes for Winston, instructing him to take certain actions involving, initially, the kidnapping, and subsequently the mob that led to the lynching of the two kidnapping suspects. Cooper mentioned that Winston had been dismissed from his university position for his participation in these events and, in particular, for breaking into the president's office. All of which meant Winston had a lot of explaining to do, some of which might mitigate the potential of federal charges against him. Such charges would most likely result in a lengthy sentence. Winston should expect to enjoy the hospitality of San Quentin Prison for the foreseeable future.

Winston listened and wept. Then he spilled all he knew. How the Committee for Public Safety had recruited him and the roles he had performed. What he expected to gain for his participation. Who led the lynch mob.

There were questions he could not answer. Winston could not say how Rosen's wallet had moved from Rosen to Hansen to himself, although he did reveal that one of the "gangsters" at the Ferry Building had taken it, which might have explained how it ended up found on a waterfront railing, but not why that particular location. Winston also did not know how the wallet might have been transferred from the kidnappers to the envelope he had received at Letcher's garage.

Winston pleaded that he had no knowledge of who called the shots for the kidnapping and later the lynchings, or what their motivations might have been. The names Thomas Ripley, Lawrence Linforth, and some unknown Italian guy as well as local law enforcement officials were tossed around and asked about repeatedly. Winston insisted he did not know about them but suspected there might have been underworld involvement. "I was a mere pawn," he whispered, tears still running down his face.

The one question Winston routinely attempted to dodge was the inevitable one of why he had gone along with this stunt in the first place. He tried various answers until he latched on to the one Cooper seemed to reluctantly accept: "Every now and then, you get an opportunity. Sometimes it may not be right. But it's something you've got to seize. Because if you don't, then someone else will."

After a time, how long Winston could not fathom, Cooper got up and left the room. Later, one of the federal agents who was present during the initial interrogation and whose name Winston had not been told came to say that he was free to go. The agent said Winston's testimony would be presented to the federal district attorney for his decision on whether an indictment against Winston would occur. Until that time, Winston should remain in touch with the Bureau as to his whereabouts. The agent gave Winston his card with a phone number. Winston stuffed it in his front pants pocket. The agent asked whether they could drive him to his parents' house, an address they knew to be near downtown. Winston initially declined but then accepted.

Two agents drove him to his parents' address in Monterey. Winston asked that they drop him off a half block away. They let him out of the car, and he walked slowly toward the house, knowing they would not leave until he had reached his destination. Winston walked up the driveway, past the arbor, and pretended to continue up the stairs to the back porch, but instead, out of view of the agents, he crept to a walkway hidden by a hedge. The narrow walkway led to the garage behind the house. The door was not locked, and he entered the garage and sat in his father's workshop for some time. When he reemerged, the agents' car was long gone. He walked away. He would not see his parents. They had expected him to succeed. They had freed him from working in the family bakery in exchange for getting a university education. He could not return home and disappoint their expectations.

By then it was dark, and the streetlights had come on. Winston walked to the bus station, purchased a ticket to Reno, Nevada, and sat on a bench to wait. There were few people in the station. His bus would arrive in fifteen minutes and depart in twenty. He had time to kill. He bought a Mars chocolate bar and read the local newspaper.

He was relieved to no longer see stories about what had happened in St. James Park. The main headlines were something about a man who held up a grocery in Watsonville. The story included a picture of the man. He looked vaguely familiar. According to the news story, the man had been a wanted suspect. He was pursued by county deputies. Caught on the outskirts of Castroville driving a stolen car. Guns were fired. The man was shot and killed resisting arrest. The paper interviewed a local resident named Sam Parker who witnessed the shooting. The sheriff's spokesman identified the shooting victim as a mobster on the run from the San Francisco Bay Area.

⁓

In the months that followed, Winston eventually drifted southward to Los Angeles. He tried his luck at getting a job in construction, in retail, in anything where he could be employed—no luck. He finally landed in the Bunker Hill district near downtown Los Angeles. Rents were cheap. He wandered the streets in search of employment. Like other places he'd tried, jobs were scarce, until he noticed a freshly painted sign on a neighborhood doorway. Someone needed a baker. A Portuguese man was the proprietor. Winston told the man he had experience. Showed what he knew. Took the job he was offered.

He had written some letters to people he knew back at the University of Santa Clara. There had been no responses other than a RETURN TO SENDER stamp on the envelope he had addressed to Wilford Kishi.

52

The New Year did not feel very new. It seemed dreary and haggard. Though the news had moved on, the collective memory of what had transpired in November lingered like a thick fog, leaving the denizens of San Jose little room to celebrate. On the 3rd of January, Cooper left San Jose and took a hotel room in San Francisco. He had completed his findings and sent them to the federal district attorney for review. His report was based on numerous interviews that had taken place in the preceding weeks. His San Jose departure was abrupt; neither the mayor nor the police chief nor the county sheriff cared to read or hear what Cooper had written. Sheriff Ewing's parting words were "Cooper, you're finished around here."

By mid-January, a county-level grand jury convened, but the scope of their inquiry was limited to the issue of the sheriff choosing to order his deputies to store their firearms in the jail's vault during the melee. Ewing testified that because of the mob's ferocity, he felt the prudent course was to eliminate access to weapons lest those intending to enter the jailhouse use them, potentially resulting in greater violence than what had occurred. The grand jury deliberated and delivered a different conclusion: Sheriff Ewing should have equipped his deputies with firearms to restrain the mob and preserve control of the events. Ewing was reprimanded for his actions.

The grand jury did not address or dispute the predominant narrative of the politicians and newspapers: Michael Rosen was kidnapped by Harold Tierney and Earle Hansen for ransom. Something went wrong with the plan. Tierney and Hansen murdered Rosen. Because of their incompetence at covering their tracks, they were captured by local law enforcement. They confessed their crimes, and when their guilt became known, the public was emboldened to take action immediately. The lynchings were unfortunate and, given the circumstances of the two men's crimes, unavoidable. A sign of the times.

Reacting to the grand jury's conclusion, the *Mercury-Herald* published an editorial absolving the city of guilt:

> The kidnappers deserved it, but San Jose did not . . . The feeling that inspired the mob is easy to understand. The sheer atrocity of the crime justified the eventual outcome . . . There was no failure of government. There had been official lapses, acknowledged by the grand jury, but overall, the officers of the law had done their duty well. They had apprehended the perpetrators of the crime, secured their confessions, and made a perfect case to confirm those confessions.

Case closed. A chapter best forgotten.

Cooper waited in an outer office of the San Francisco federal building. At last, he would have an audience with US Attorney H. H. Pope. Sitting with his briefcase on his lap, fedora on the seat next to him, Cooper observed the only sound in the room was the steam radiator that clanked like a death rattle. He was ushered into Pope's office, and the two men shook hands. H. H. Pope looked the part with his piercing blue eyes, strands of white hair swept back over a balding pate, chiseled granite–like facade. He greeted Cooper in a low baritone voice. After the small-talk preliminaries, they got down to business.

Pope acknowledged Cooper's recommendation that the federal government pursue its own case into the conspiracy of the kidnapping and murder of Michael Rosen as well as the lynchings of the two alleged perpetrators. However, the attorney cautioned, there were jurisdictional constraints to what federal law allowed, and it was atypical to pursue a case that was at odds with what the local jurisdiction had already taken up. "A trial of the defendants would have better answered many troubling questions that you have raised, but"—Pope waved his hand theatrically—"this, alas, did not occur, and further, a grand jury was convened to look into the matter, albeit under narrow parameters, and they determined there was no evidence for which they would recommend further inquiry and action."

There was little his office could do, he said. "But, nonetheless, let's talk through your findings."

Cooper opened his briefcase, opened his notebook, and quickly reviewed his findings. He knew the matter by heart, but he intended to be precise. There was sworn testimony of more than two kidnappers and no clear explanation of how Rosen's automobile got to its final location, unless there were additional people involved.

"True, but your witness was dismissed as unreliable, first by local law enforcement and later by the Bureau in Washington."

"But Rosen's Studebaker?" Cooper pressed.

"Granted, an unresolved issue," Pope decreed with a wry smile. "The problem was the alleged kidnappers had confessed to their crimes."

"Their testimonies changed over time and contradicted one another," argued Cooper.

"Yes, but their confessions agreed that only two of them participated."

"But there was Winston Richter's confession to making the ransom call after being directed to do so. Richter's fingerprints on Rosen's wallet and his testimony about possible underworld involvement. That fact alone suggests more than the two suspects."

"Any investigation has its abnormalities," said the lawyer. "I confess, this is problematic. You mentioned that Richter had been 'directed.' By whom?"

Pope was clearly enjoying this exchange. Perhaps a little too much. Cooper pressed on. "There is the suggestion Richter's actions were prompted by an organization connected to the university."

"Yes, the so-called Committee for Public Safety. I read that with great interest," said Pope slyly. "Your Committee was hell-bent on reducing labor unrest in the valley, is this not correct?"

"Yes."

"How is that connected to kidnapping Rosen?"

"There is evidence of wider, more complex conspiracy, even a suggestion that the sheriff's office might have been involved in the kidnapping."

"All conjecture, certainly, with no firm evidence," replied Pope. "Your report also refers to rival businesses that operated illegal saloons, gambling, and other illicit activity leading to other related crimes. Again, I do not see any connection. The federal government does not recognize Black Hand gang activity any longer, and it has certainly never acknowledged this to exist here on the West Coast."

"There was the matter of the raid against CAIWU offices the same night of the lynching. Wasn't that fact curious?"

"The US Attorney's Office was conducting its own inquiry of the legality of such raids," allowed Pope. "They occurred not only in San Jose but in other agricultural counties. As you know, prosecution of individuals engaged in union organizing is ongoing. We continue to monitor the legality of such prosecution."

"But at your own admission, don't you see a link between the raid and the existence of the Committee?"

"The links you propose are tenuous and mostly without reasonable conjecture, let alone any direct testimony we could use to further an investigation. Further, I don't see a reasonable connection to be made regarding how your Committee might have influenced or directed the lynching of the two men."

"These were prominent university students!" Cooper argued, struggling to keep his anger in check. "Photographs taken that night show their direct participation. Photographs that were published in the newspapers. Only the faces of these college boys were conveniently smudged out. The press concealed their identities. Don't you find that troubling?"

"This is not the first time newspapers have done this disservice," admitted Pope. "The problem as I see it, Agent Cooper, is that you have assembled a number of pieces to a puzzle that fit, but clearly others that do not, and a lot of pieces are clearly missing. A pattern has not emerged, and yet you would have us indict an entire community, the local police, sheriff's office, maybe even the mayor for either inaction or complicity in the kidnapping and murder of Michael Rosen."

The attorney looked at his timepiece. Cooper understood his time was nearing the end.

"That is exactly why I submitted the report," he said wearily. "It offers preliminary evidence for the sake of directing a federal grand jury to undertake further investigation. Those missing and leftover pieces *will* reveal a pattern. Those troubling details *do* provide the key to proving a widespread criminal conspiracy."

Pope folded his hands, looked at Cooper. "You have never fully explained why it was necessary for Rosen to be kidnapped in the first place."

"I did. I have evidence that young Rosen did not pay his outstanding debt. The Ferrone organization took steps to recover this amount in a, let's say, 'amicable' way, but others used this for their alternative purposes."

"And the lynchings in St. James Park?"

"To suppress the actual facts of the matter."

He hadn't mentioned Ripley. It hadn't seemed strategic. Now Cooper wondered. Perhaps Pope believed him but Ripley was too powerful to indict. Perhaps Cooper doubted himself. Either way, it was over.

"I'm not saying you haven't presented tantalizing evidence," Pope said formally. "But this office must proceed only with investigations that possess . . . significant merit. Your report, and I regret this, lacks such merit.

"No one wants to investigate," said Cooper.

Pope met his gaze. "That's the size of it."

Cooper walked back to his hotel, heedless of the steady drizzle that quickly became a downpour. He waited in his hotel room. Did not go out much. Saw no one. There was no reason. His assignment had been deemed complete.

In less than a week's time, the Bureau's orders were issued. He was to join an ongoing investigation in Oklahoma, where an unseemly number of banks had been held up by a young couple. In the early morning, he boarded a ferry, stood leaning on the rail as the boat crossed the windswept bay, and embarked on a train heading away. It would start all over again.

He had come as a stranger and left as one, ultimately neither satisfied nor disappointed.

53

Angelo Gumina was a patient man. He waited as the seasons changed and changed again. The late-spring blossoms adorning the garden lent a festive air to the Avila Beach estate. A gentle aroma came from the purple heliotrope and bluish lilacs growing near the front porch, where the man with the aquiline nose spent many an afternoon in a wooden Adirondack chair, biding his time. The time to grieve was over. One by one, most of the few remaining members of the Ferrone organization slipped away, professing their esteem and loyalty alongside goodbyes. Angelo understood. The old business was gone. For many it was time to turn the page. Only Oliver and Frank Lagatutta remained. Angelo's daughter and her friend were of course staying at Avila. Amelia and Victoria looked forward to the upcoming fall, when they would attend universities back East. Angelo and Rosalia had offered to finance them—with one condition. Something they all understood had to be done before life could move forward.

※

Ewing ran again for county sheriff, and this time he lost. By June, he was out of a job, and the local support he once depended on evaporated. His campaign mistake was that he reiterated his role in the capture of the two kidnappers and promised greater community safety through more stringent law-and-order measures. That might have worked, but no one wanted to be reminded of the lynchings. Whereas his opponent kept hounding on what the grand jury had concluded: In the face of a mob bent on violence, Ewing should not have disarmed his deputies.

Ewing pulled up stakes and left for Los Angeles to start his own private investigation business. He became embroiled in one case in Laurel Canyon. One morning, he was found face down in a swimming pool. No one, certainly not the alarmed owner in whose pool Ewing had turned blue, professed any knowledge of why Ewing was even there. The county coroner declared that Ewing's high blood alcohol content would have impaired his judgment. The evening edition of the *Mercury-Herald* devoted a paragraph on page 10 to the story of his demise.

Passalacqua, who had swiftly taken over Ferrone's establishments in and around San Jose, faced a different quandary. With Prohibition ending, the opportunity was to consolidate the alcohol-related businesses, reduce liquor supply costs, coordinate marketing, and intimidate competition. Unforeseen was that once the federal law was repealed, the state government would step in. Passalacqua had not fully appreciated that there was now a state agency in charge of issuing alcohol licenses. A certain type of dexterity was needed to navigate the state's bureaucratic maze. Passalacqua had previously succeeded by doing things in his own heavy-handed ways, so he resorted to what he knew: eschewing the delicacies of politics and continuing to push and shove his weight around. The resultant series of entanglements included unending fines, penalties, delays, even a few indictments.

Passalacqua's partners began to turn away from the old model and focused their efforts on consolidating the cannery business. Labor costs became drastically reduced. Cannery workers and orchard pickers remained unorganized as their wages sank even further, and many of their union representatives were stuck behind bars. Passalacqua blamed his plight on the governor, though not for long. Over the summer, it was reported that the governor died from a sudden heart attack while taking a holiday at a bayside property once owned by the Jesuits.

By late August, most of the media attention was on the battle brewing along the San Francisco waterfront and its general strike. For Angelo, this was as good a time as any to settle the matter with Thomas Ripley.

∽

Like any good winemaker, it was a matter of timing. Angelo had planned ahead. He engaged the services of a San Francisco private investigator with the sole assignment of tracking Ripley's daily movements. Payments were anonymous, and the investigator's weekly reports arrived in sealed envelopes delivered to an Excelsior post office box, picked up later by a courier and sent to Angelo. The reports delineated that Ripley worked primarily from his San Francisco office on Montgomery Street, with weekly trips, on Thursdays, to San Jose.

On those Thursdays, his driver would pick up Ripley and his bodyguard from his home in Atherton, on the San Francisco Peninsula, and arrive in the San Jose office by 8 a.m. Those mornings he stayed in his office. Clients would come and go. Most of the time, Ripley did not go out for lunch as food was typically brought to his office. In the afternoons, he occasionally paid calls at city hall and the Hall of Justice. Sometimes, though, he stayed in his office, receiving various calls and visitors. Angelo had no interest in who these clients were. By 6 p.m., Ripley's driver would be waiting outside his office to take Ripley and his bodyguard to the Sainte Claire Club for an evening supper.

At the club, Ripley would invariably sit alone in the same seat at the same table, his back against a wall. The location was both discreet and strategic. He had a view not only of the broad window but of everyone who came in and dined. Ripley's bodyguard often remained at the bar, but sometimes he would leave to smoke outside in the night air, presumably sensing no danger in this benign setting.

While Ripley typically dined alone, occasionally there were patrons who knew him, and he received them briefly. He had an eye for the ladies and often sent a drink, or drinks, to a pretty female who would, depending on the circumstances, accept or refuse the gift. If she was accompanied, her companion might approach Ripley to complain. Though in all such cases the investigator witnessed, the complainer would stop in his tracks, often apologizing, once he recognized who Ripley was.

When his meal was over, usually by 9 p.m., Ripley's driver would return him and the bodyguard to Atherton. On other occasions, before returning home, Ripley desired a taste of "professional dessert," quipped the investigator, at a place tucked away in a judicious location.

❧

Angelo studied the investigator's reports and sketched various scenarios. Then, with the help of Rosalia, he began to instruct his actors. Rehearsals occurred daily based on a script that allowed for numerous variations and inevitable improvisation. A final rehearsal took place in a room at the Torino Hotel, where Angelo booked rooms for several nights.

The premiere was scheduled for a Thursday evening in late August. Precisely at 7:40 p.m., Frank Lagatutta accompanied Victoria to the Sainte Claire Club. He quickly withdrew, and the maître d' escorted her to a table. The first improvisation occurred: The table was not positioned as prearranged. Victoria slipped the maître d' a large bill, and her table was moved to the desired location, in full view of Ripley's favorite perch.

Rosalia had fitted Victoria in a costume that showed her appropriate assets enough to entice but not reveal. Her hair was done up; her earrings shimmered in the overhead lights. Her perfume promised depth and subtle strength: jasmine with a touch of pink grapefruit. Her makeup was perfection. "Full war paint," Rosalia had joked.

Right on time, Ripley walked in and was shown to his usual table. His bodyguard ordered a drink at the bar. Meanwhile, Ripley's driver steered his employer's cherry-red Chrysler Imperial around the block to Letcher's garage. On this night, the driver was greeted by two efficient masked assailants, Oliver and Lagatutta, who forcefully managed the driver to be bound and gagged. He lay on the back seat of the Chrysler, which by then was parked inside the garage with no one the wiser.

Ripley glanced at the menu but soon seemed hungry for something else. To an observer he might have seemed to sniff the air before putting his menu aside in favor of the pleasing view near the window. He motioned for his waiter to bring the young lady a glass of the club's finest sparkling wine. He loved to witness the reactions. Most recipients of the gift would act pleasantly surprised and glance around the room. The waiter would point in Ripley's direction. Ripley would raise his glass, bow slightly, and smile. Some young ladies would become self-conscious, nod and smile nervously. The confident ones he knew were professionals. The woman at the window was neither. She was nonchalant. She did not look around as the others would have but turned directly toward Ripley and smiled, then took her time to drink the full contents of the glass.

Ripley instructed the waiter to pass a note asking whether the lady would join him for supper. She read the note, then whispered to the waiter that she would not, though she might consider dessert. The fish was hooked.

※

Ripley passed his lovely prey another note via the maître d', this time proposing she join him at a private location. Victoria glanced at her watch: 8:45 p.m. She nodded her assent to Ripley's offer. He asked for the respective bills and put them on his account, then asked the maître d' to call for his driver.

Victoria gathered her purse and went to the powder room, where Amelia had been waiting for some time. Victoria emptied the contents of her purse while Amelia passed her a .38 snub-nosed revolver.

"The bodyguard left. I don't know where he is," Victoria whispered before returning to the dining area, where Ripley stood waiting to accompany her out the door.

As requested, the maître d' had placed a call to the garage asking the driver to bring Ripley's car around. Oliver forced the driver at knifepoint to answer the call, in case the maître d' might notice an unfamiliar voice. The original script called for the Chrysler to arrive in front of the club as expected. Lagatutta would be driving Ripley's car with Oliver hunkered down in the back seat. With allowance for extemporization as events unfolded, Victoria would keep Ripley distracted long enough that Oliver could overpower him and force him into his car. And Oliver and Lagatutta would depart with their captive, leaving Victoria and Amelia to quietly walk into the park.

But the problem was Ripley's bodyguard. He remained the wild card in Angelo's carefully constructed street theater. The bodyguard normally accompanied Ripley to the curb, made sure the driver picked Ripley up, and then followed behind in a separate car. The key to the success of the operation would be Amelia's ability to delay the bodyguard's arrival at the curb long enough for the others to get away. She had rehearsed a number of variations.

As the action unfolded, Oliver worried that Ripley might too quickly recognize a different man behind the wheel. He amended the script and forced the driver into his normal spot: this time with a gag balled up in his mouth and a strip of piano wire around his neck. Seated directly behind him, Oliver just needed to yank if the driver failed to cooperate. Lagatutta would be responsible for overpowering Ripley.

Meanwhile, Amelia had gone in search of the bodyguard. She checked the bar. He was not there. Neither was he in the alley alongside the club nor at the service entrance in back. She ran back inside and burst into the men's bathroom. He was relieving himself at the urinal.

Amelia whipped out a short stiletto, sidled up behind the man, pressed the tip of the blade against his hip, and purred, "One move and I'll slice it off."

The bodyguard winced at the audacity of the situation. He continued to pee as he weighed his options. "Just calm down and let me finish."

"Don't move," said Amelia, emphatically. She was sweating, hoping the deed outside with Ripley's abduction had been done.

The stream of piss trickled to an end.

"Do you mind if I have a final shake?"

"One move and your dick comes off."

As she fully expected, the bodyguard quickly swerved toward her. She slashed the blade downward, missing her mark. The man's fist knocked her to the tile floor. She relaxed into the fall as her father had taught her and bet on the bodyguard's instinct to race after Ripley rather than viewing Amelia as a serious threat. It was a correct guess: He sneered at her and started for the door. She sat up and flung her stiletto at his backside, this time hitting her target—the region of his left kidney. He staggered and tried to pull out the dagger and flopped on the bathroom floor. Amelia quickly rolled to her feet and strode past him but slowed to a gentle walk as she maneuvered toward the front door. She immediately stopped. Victoria and Ripley were standing right in front of her, arm in arm, waiting for his driver.

Amelia took a step backward until she saw headlights approach. Ripley's Chrysler stopped at the curb in front of them.

"San Francisco is such an exciting place to visit," Victoria was saying. "I love the—"

Despite the nighttime gloom, Ripley caught sight of his driver; the man was sitting too stiffly. He looked petrified for no obvious reason.

Ripley wrenched his arm away from Victoria and pushed her away. His arm snaked into his jacket as he backed toward the club's entrance. Amelia stepped forward, purposefully colliding with his side, enough to knock him off-balance, and then seized the weapon Ripley held in his jacket.

"Hold it right there," Amelia ordered. She stuck the gun into his chest. Her heart was thumping, but she held the gun steady, finger curled around the trigger.

"Can't we negotiate something, ladies?" Ripley said.

Victoria didn't answer.

Amelia ordered, "Don't move."

Ripley did not move an inch.

Lagatutta quickly got out of the car and hustled Ripley to the back seat next to Oliver. Lagatutta squeezed in next to Ripley. Oliver asked Ripley, "How was your dinner?" Before he could answer, Lagatutta slammed his revolver into Ripley's temple, and Victoria's would-be admirer fell sideways, slouched against Oliver's shoulder. Oliver tugged on the wire and ordered the driver to move.

Victoria and Amelia looked at each other, patted down their dresses, and casually strolled arm in arm across the street and into the park.

The bodyguard stumbled out of the club, bleeding, followed by a very upset maître d'. They were too late. The Chrysler had slipped away into the night. No one noticed the man with the aquiline nose who watched the scene unfold from his car, far enough away to remain unobserved, close enough to intervene if called for. He rolled down his window, smiled, and motioned to the ladies to climb in.

⁘

A man knocked on his hotel door and said a package had arrived. Imagining another report from Washington, Cooper sighed, opened the door, and accepted the parcel. There was no return address. The post office stamp read SAN FRANCISCO. He opened it. No note, just a week-old newspaper: the *San Francisco Examiner*. The front page included numerous stories about the ongoing waterfront battles and an impending general strike. He flipped page after page. Nothing he didn't already know on the national front. Nothing he particularly cared about from the Bay Area. On page 5, an article caught his eye.

A San Francisco businessman named Thomas Ripley was believed to have been abducted outside a prominent establishment in downtown San Jose. A rancher had come upon Ripley's seemingly abandoned car, a Chrysler Imperial, parked along an orchard road north of San Jose. Upon hearing noises, the rancher pried open the trunk and discovered the businessman's driver bound and gagged, though not seriously injured. The rescued man told police that he and his employer had been abducted by mobsters he believed worked for an underworld organization headed by one Paul Passalacqua, also of San Francisco. After interviewing witnesses from the establishment who described seeing Ripley being taken at gunpoint, San Jose Police Chief Charles Blackmun ordered a warrant for the arrest of Paul Passalacqua.

Cooper reread the article, snorted, and then shoved the newspaper into the far reaches of his desk drawer. Standing, he went to the window and gazed out over the horizon. A looming brown dust storm blew across the plains.

Postscript

Although *St. James Park* is fiction, it is rooted in the history of San Jose. The story described in this novel is based on material from numerous newspaper reports, oral histories, journal articles, and books published about the kidnapping of Brooke Hart and the lynching of Harold Thurmond and Jack Holmes.

The lynching occurred around midnight of November 26 to 27, 1933. There still remain questions regarding why the purported kidnappers murdered Hart if ransom was the motivation, whether the kidnappers acted alone, what efforts were taken to coerce the confessions, and who participated in the lynching. The lynching was unique in American political and criminal justice history because of the governor's promise to pardon any of the vigilantes and the willingness by civic and business leaders and law enforcement to allow the extrajudicial killings of Thurmond and Holmes. Also, the district attorney declined to prosecute anyone because he doubted anyone could be found to identify the lynching ringleaders. The county grand jury met the following year, but despite gathering thousands of witnesses, scores of reporters, and hundreds of photographs, they found that no witnesses could identify participants in the lynching, so no charges were filed. The vigilante mob got away with murder.

The lynching also had a chilling effect on union organizing in San Jose. Caroline Decker, a CAIWU leader, stated in an oral interview decades later that when she was returning to union headquarters, she encountered the lynch mob in the park. Fearful of what the mob might do to a "Communist" labor agitator, Decker retreated to safety. Soon thereafter, the CAIWU abandoned their San Jose headquarters. Over the next months, county deputies and vigilantes raided a series of union offices throughout agricultural California. By mid-1934, twenty-four leaders of the CAIWU, including Decker, were arrested for "vagrancy" in Sacramento. The grand jury indicted thirteen of them under the 1919 Criminal Syndicalism Act. Eleven were convicted and sent to prison.

My father attended the University of Santa Clara (now called Santa Clara University) in the 1930s and briefly overlapped with Brooke Hart. The Jesuit-run, all-male school had always considered itself as well regarded, elite, and intimate. Detractors thought of it as a rowdy football school. Its 1933 enrollment was 450 students; everyone must have known each other at least by sight. A local historian, Fr. Gerald McKevitt, described the university at the time as being aloof and protected, a quiet backwater in an agitated sea and obsessed by Communist subversion. When the kidnapping of their fellow graduate occurred, this sparked an intense and visceral reaction. Photographs confirmed the presence of Santa Clara students outside the jail. *The Stanford Daily* laid full responsibility on a "handful of Santa Clara students, roommates and buddies of the murdered Brooke Hart." Thereafter McKevitt described that a pervasive protective silence descended around the entire episode.

My father never mentioned what happened that night in St. James Park. However, decades after he died, I discovered an oral interview conducted by a fellow retired judge. When asked where my father was the night of the lynching, my father confided he had been working in his father's bakery. The lynching occurred around midnight. Baker hours are typically in the early morning. The judge never asked for clarification.

For decades, people did not speak of San Jose's shame. They chose to remain silent.